Harlequin Rich, Rugged Ranchers Collection

Saddle up and get ready for a fantastic ride as these wealthy cowboys set out to wrangle the hearts of the women of their dreams!

Riding the range and herding cattle are only a couple talents these irresistible heroes have. Fiercely protecting their loved ones and stopping at nothing to win the adoration of a good woman are some of the reasons we can't get enough of them.

These ranchers hold honor above all else, believe in the value of a hard day's work and aren't afraid to make the tough decisions. In fact, they have everything under control... except their hearts! And once these men of the West give their love, there's no walking away.

If you enjoy these two classic stories, be sure to look for more books featuring rich, rugged ranchers in Harlequin Desire and Harlequin Superromance.

USA TODAY bestselling author **Barbara Dunlop** has written more than forty novels for Harlequin, including the acclaimed Colorado Cattle Barons series for the Harlequin Desire line. Her sexy, lighthearted stories regularly hit bestseller lists. Barbara is a three-time finalist for the Romance Writers of America's RITA® Award. You can visit her online at barbaradunlop.com. .

Look for more books by Barbara Dunlop in Harlequin Desire—the ultimate destination for powerful, passionate romance! There are six new Harlequin Desire titles available every month. Check one out today!

USA TODAY Bestselling Author

Barbara Dunlop
and
Kimberly Van Meter

A RANCHER'S HOME

⟨H⟩ **HARLEQUIN**® RICH, RUGGED RANCHERS

Recycling programs
for this product may
not exist in your area.

ISBN-13: 978-0-373-60119-6

A Rancher's Home

Copyright © 2015 by Harlequin Books S.A.

The publisher acknowledges the copyright holders
of the individual works as follows:

A Cowboy Comes Home
Copyright © 2012 by Barbara Dunlop

Kids on the Doorstep
Copyright © 2009 by Kimberly Sheetz

Printed in U.S.A.

CONTENTS

A COWBOY COMES HOME
Barbara Dunlop

For Carla Daum and Jane Porter
One Hundred Books Later

One

Dust plumes scattered beneath Caleb Terrell's loafers as he approached the front steps of his former home, looking for the brother who'd despised him for ten long years. A copy of his late father's will was snapped into his Bulgari briefcase, and a million, disturbing questions swirled inside his brain. The Terrell Cattle Company hadn't changed much. The two-story brick house had been meticulously maintained, while the crisp, northern-Colorado mountain air still held the familiar tang of wheatgrass and ponderosa pine.

The soles of his shoes met the smooth wood of the wide, front porch, and for a fleeting moment he wished he'd stopped in Lyndon and changed into blue jeans and boots. But he banished the impulse. He was a businessman now, not a cowboy. And the last thing he wanted to do was feel at home.

His brother, Reed, wouldn't be remotely happy to see

him, but outrageous times called for outrageous measures. Reed would have to deal with it.

Caleb briefly toyed with the idea of bursting in unannounced. He owned the place, after all, and Reed had been dodging his calls for over a week. To be fair, Caleb hadn't tried to contact his fraternal twin brother in ten years. Then again, in all that time, Reed hadn't tried to contact Caleb, either.

But now, their father was dead. Caleb wouldn't have set foot on the Terrell ranch in any other circumstance. He'd probably have been shot if he'd tried. Which made the contents of the will that much more baffling.

He gave three short, sharp knocks.

In the moments of silence that followed, he glanced around the ranch yard, refreshing his memory and bracing himself for the conversation to come.

The main barn had been recently painted a dark green. The square horse corrals were still meticulously maintained, their straight rails gleaming white in the afternoon sunshine. He knew every angle was precisely ninety degrees, and the posts were exactly six feet apart, rail centers at twenty-four-inch intervals.

Beyond the yard, black angus cattle dotted the summer green, hillside meadows between groves of aspen and pine. And the snowy peaks of the Rockies rose up to the misty sky. Caleb blinked against the blinding sun, refocusing closer in.

Half a dozen pickup trucks were backed up in formation in front of the equipment sheds. A freshly washed combine, cultivator and hay truck sat on the far side of the barn, and a few dozen chickens were pecking the ground around the tires. In one of the pens, a black horse whinnied and bucked, tossing its glossy mane as it ran the length of the enclosure before stopping short at the fence, nostrils flaring in annoyance.

Caleb didn't recognize the animal. No surprise there. Though there had been a time when he'd been able to name every one of the fifty-plus horses at Terrell. He inhaled once more, this time catching the sharp scent of manure. His spine stiffened with a latent memory of his father's quick temper. Yeah, most things had stayed the same around here, and he didn't care to revisit any of them.

As soon as he straightened out the mess with the inheritance, he'd climb back into his rented Escalade, head for the Lyndon airport and take the Active Equipment jet back to his corporate headquarters in Chicago.

Sayonara Colorado.

He turned back to the door and knocked again.

This time, there was a sound on the other side. But it was a light, quick step crossing the living-room floor—so, not his brother, Reed.

The door swung full open, and Caleb came face-to-face with a beautiful, brunette woman. She was maybe five feet five, dressed in a cowl-necked, navy T-shirt with four buttons leaving an open V-neck. Her hair was long and glossy, her lips a dark coral pink, skin smooth, brows gently arched and her moss-green eyes clear and assessing.

She looked vaguely familiar. Or maybe that was just wishful thinking. Even in faded blue jeans and scuffed brown boots, she definitely looked like someone Caleb would like to know. His instantaneous attraction was quickly tempered by the thought that she might belong to his brother—a girlfriend, maybe even a wife.

His glance dipped reflexively to her left hand. No ring. But that didn't mean she wasn't Reed's.

"Are you selling…something?" she prompted, glancing from his silk tie to his briefcase. Her melodic, slightly husky voice sent a vibration through the center of Caleb's chest.

It took him a moment to respond. "I'm looking for Reed."

Her delicate brows sloped closer together with curiosity. "Is he expecting you?"

"I called a few days ago," Caleb offered evasively. He hadn't spoken to his brother, only left voice-mail messages, and he wasn't about to discuss his personal business with a stranger.

She crossed her arms over her chest and canted a slim, denim covered hip to one side. "Are you saying Reed invited you here?"

Caleb gave in to curiosity. "Who are you?"

"Who are you?"

There it was again, that feeling that he'd met her somewhere before. "You live here?"

"None of your business."

"Where's Reed?"

She stilled for a split second, her soft, coral mouth pursing into a sexy moue. "Also, none of your business."

He struggled to be annoyed, but he found himself intrigued. "Are you going to tell me anything?"

She shook her head.

"Have we met before?" he asked.

"Is that a line?"

"It's a question."

"It's been my experience that most lines are delivered in the form of a question."

Caleb felt himself crack a reluctant smile, and her green eyes sparkled in return.

He watched her for a few moments, then conceded

defeat, shifting his briefcase from his right hand before holding it out to her. "Caleb Terrell."

Her gorgeous eyes went wide and round. "Caleb?"

Before he could react, she squealed and threw herself into his arms. "You came home!"

His free arm automatically wrapped around her slender waist, returning the hug and holding her lithe body against his own. He inhaled the sweet scent of her hair and found himself desperately hoping she wasn't Reed's girlfriend.

She pulled back and gazed up into his eyes. "You don't remember me?"

He was forced to shake his head, admitting he did not.

She socked the front of his shoulder with the heel of her hand. "It's Mandy."

Caleb felt his jaw go lax. "Mandy Jacobs?"

She nodded, and he pulled her into another hug. Not that they'd been particularly close. She'd been thirteen to his seventeen when he'd left home. He was twenty-seven now. And it felt astonishingly good to hold her in his arms.

He let the hug go on a little too long, then reluctantly let her go.

"You missed the funeral." Her tone was half regretful, half accusing as she backed her way inside the house, gesturing for him to follow.

"I didn't come back for the funeral," he told her soberly as he took a step over the threshold. Reminded of his reason for being here, his mood swung back to determination.

"He was your father," she chided, turning to walk around the corner from the foyer and into the big living room.

Caleb followed, letting his silence speak for itself. Unless Mandy was hopelessly naive, she knew the history of the Terrell family. Wilton Terrell might have been Caleb's father, but he was also the meanest son of a bitch in northwestern Colorado.

Inside the startlingly familiar room, he glanced around, attempting to orient himself. Why was Mandy here, and where was Reed? "So, you and Reed are…"

She shook her head. "He's not here."

"I can see that." It was a big house, two stories, four bedrooms, but if Reed had been around, Mandy's squeal would have brought him running. Now, Caleb found himself impatient to qualify her role. "You live here?"

Her look went blank. "Huh?"

He enunciated his next words. "Do you live here?"

"Are you asking me if I'm sleeping with your brother?"

"I'm asking if you're in a relationship with him, yes." That was the most obvious answer for her presence.

"I'm not." Her left eye twitched. "Either of those things."

"Okay."

Good. Very good. Not that it mattered to Caleb. Nothing about Lyndon Valley or the Terrell ranch mattered to Caleb. This was a temporary glitch on the thoroughfare of his life. Mandy was irrelevant.

Her tone turned tart. "But how very polite of you to inquire about my sex life."

"You're here, and he's not," Caleb reasoned. She'd answered the front door, appeared very much at home. It wasn't such a stretch to think she lived here.

She traced a finger along the beveled edge of a polished cedar side table. "I came up here to check things out." Then a cloud of concern darkened her expression. "I got worried."

"Why were you worried?"

"Because nobody's seen Reed since the funeral five days ago."

Mandy Jacobs had been Reed's close friend for nearly ten years. Before that, she'd felt something close to hero worship for him in high school, ever since the day he'd rescued her when her bikini top flew off as she dove into the Stump Lake swimming hole. The boys in her own grade had howled with laughter, stopping her girlfriends from coming into the water to help her, waiting with wide-eyed anticipation for the numbing cold to force her from the lake.

Just as she was about to give in and cover her dignity as best she could manage, Reed had come along and read the younger boys the riot act. He'd stripped off his boots and waded up to his waist, handing her his own T-shirt. He'd never even peeked while, teeth chattering and toes tingling, she'd struggled her way into the shirt while under water. And then he'd threatened the younger boys with dire consequences if they dared to tease her about it in the future.

When she came home after two years in college in Denver, she and Reed had grown closer still. Over the years, she'd learned about his mother's death, his father's cruelty and the reasons behind his fraternal twin brother, Caleb, leaving the valley.

Reed had no siblings left at home, and Mandy's two brothers did nothing but tease her. Her older sister, Abigail, had been a bookworm, while her younger sister, Katrina, had gone away to boarding school when she was only ten. If Mandy could have chosen a brother, it would have been Reed.

This morning, genuinely worried and determined to

track him down, she'd let herself into the familiar house, listened to his phone messages, hunted her way through his letter mail, even checked his closet before realizing she wouldn't know if some of his clothes were missing or not. She did know his wallet was gone. His watch wasn't lying around and his favorite Stetson wasn't hanging on the peg in the front entry hall.

She had to believe he had left the ranch willingly. The man was built like a mountain. She couldn't imagine anyone forcing him to do anything he didn't want to do.

Still, she was very glad Caleb had shown up when he did. Something definitely wasn't right, and she could use his help to figure out what had happened.

Caleb clunked his briefcase down on the hardwood floor, interrupting her musings as he straightened beside the brown leather couch that sat in front of the picture window.

His gaze pierced hers. "Define *missing?*"

"Reed left the cemetery after the funeral," Mandy explained, casting her memory back again to the events of last week, hunting for little details she might have missed that would give her a clue to what happened. "He drove off in one of the ranch pickup trucks. I assumed he was coming back here."

She focused on the row of pictures along the fireplace mantel, zeroing in on a recent one of Reed at the Lyndon Rodeo. "We all came over to the house afterward for refreshments. I didn't see him, but I didn't think that was particularly odd. He'd just lost his father and, you know, he might have wanted to be alone."

From behind her, Caleb's voice was cool. "Are you trying to tell me Reed was mourning our father?"

She turned back to face him while she framed her answer. She couldn't help contrasting the two brothers. They were about as different as two men could get. They'd both been attractive teenagers who'd grown into very handsome men. But where Reed was rugged and rangy, Caleb was much more urbane and refined.

Reed was nearly six-four, deep-chested, bulky in his arms and legs, and about as strong as an ox. His hair was dark, his eyes darker. While Caleb was closer to six-one, broad shouldered, but with leaner muscles, a chiseled chin and bright blue, intelligent, observant eyes. His hair was a lighter brown, his voice bass instead of baritone.

"Mandy?" Caleb prompted, and there was something about the sound of her name on his lips that made her heart thud an extra beat. Where on earth had that come from?

"I doubt he was mourning your father," she acknowledged.

If anything, Reed and Wilton's relationship had deteriorated after Caleb left. Wilton wasn't capable of anything but criticism, no matter how hard Reed worked. And no matter how much Reed accomplished on the ranch, his father wasn't satisfied and told him so on a regular basis.

Intimidated by the man, Mandy had visited the Terrell house only when Wilton was away. Thankfully, he was away quite often. The very definition of a crotchety old man, he seemed to prefer the company of cattle to humans, and he spent many nights in line shacks on the range.

She'd done everything she could to support Reed. When she was sixteen and Reed was twenty, Wilton had ended a particularly hostile argument by whacking Reed's shoulder with a two-by-four. Mandy had impulsively offered to marry Reed so he could move to the neighboring Jacobs ranch.

But he'd laughed at her and tousled her hair, telling

her he loved her like a sister, not a wife, and he wouldn't turn his back on his father ever again. And by then, he was big enough to defend himself against Wilton.

"He should have left when I did," Caleb broke into her thoughts again, his voice brittle.

"*You* should have stayed," Mandy countered, giving him her unvarnished opinion. If Caleb had been around, it would have been two against one, and Wilton would not have gotten away with so much cruelty.

Caleb's eyes crackled like agates. "And rewarded him for killing my mother, by breaking my back for him day after day?"

"Reed saw it differently." Mandy understood just how differently Reed had viewed the situation. And she admired him for it.

The Terrell Cattle Company had been the merging of both Wilton Terrell's family holdings and those of his young wife, Sasha's. After her death, through thick and thin, Reed had vowed to protect his mother's heritage. He had plans for the ranch, for his future, ways to honor his mother's memory.

Which made his disappearance, particularly now, even more confusing. Where *was* he?

"Reed was a fool," said Caleb.

Mandy found herself taking a step forward, squaring her shoulders, hands curling into fists by her sides, her anger rising in her friend's defense. "I love Reed."

"I thought you said—"

"Like a *brother.*"

"Yeah?" Caleb scoffed, blue eyes glaring right back at her. "Why don't you tell me what that's like?"

His mocking tone was at odds with the trace of hurt that flashed through his eyes, and her anger immediately dissipated.

"Why did you come?" she found herself asking.

Did she dare hope Caleb had reconciliation on his mind? She'd be thrilled to see the two brothers bury the hatchet. She knew that, deep down, Reed missed his brother, and she had to believe Caleb missed Reed.

Suddenly, she remembered one of the letters she'd sorted this morning. Her heart lifted, and her chest hummed with excitement. That had to be the answer. "He *was* expecting you."

"What?"

She pivoted on her heel and headed for the kitchen, bee-lining to the pile of correspondence that hadn't yielded a single clue to Reed's whereabouts.

Caleb's footfalls sounded in the hallway behind her as she entered the bright, butter-yellow kitchen, with its gleaming redwood cabinets and granite countertops.

"Here it is." She extracted a white envelope with Caleb's name scrawled across the front. It hadn't made sense to her at the time, but Reed must have known his brother would be here. Maybe this was the clue she needed.

She strode back across the big, bright kitchen and handed the envelope to Caleb. "Open it," she demanded impatiently.

Caleb frowned. "I didn't tell him I was coming." The messages had been a cryptic "call me, we need to talk." He hadn't doubted for a second Reed would understand.

"Then why did he leave you a letter? It was sitting on the island when I got here this morning." She pointed out the spot with her finger.

Caleb heaved a deep breath, hooking his thumb beneath the end of the flap and tearing open the flimsy paper.

He extracted a single, folded sheet and dropped the

envelope onto the countertop next to the telephone. He unfolded the paper, staring at it for a brief moment.

Then he uttered a sharp, foul cussword.

Mandy startled, not at the word, but at the tone. Unable to control her curiosity, she looked around the paper, her head next to Caleb's shoulder and read Reed's large, bold handwriting. The message said: *Choke on it.*

She blinked and glanced up at Caleb. "I don't understand. What does it mean?"

"It means my brother's temper hasn't changed one bit in the past ten years."

"Do you know where he went?" The cryptic message didn't help Mandy, but maybe Caleb understood.

Caleb growled at the paper. "You stupid, stupid idiot."

"What?" Mandy demanded.

He crumpled the paper into a tight ball, emitting a cold laugh. "He doesn't trust me. He actually thinks I'd screw my own brother."

"Screw him how?" She'd been telling herself Reed was off on his own somewhere, reconciling what had to be conflicting emotions about losing such a difficult father. But now Caleb had her worried.

He stared down at her, blue eyes rock-hard, jaw set in an implacable line. She could almost see the debate going on inside his head.

Finally, he made a decision and spoke. "Wilton Terrell, in his infinite wisdom, has left his entire estate, including the Terrell Cattle Company, to his son…Caleb."

Mandy braced herself on the edge of the island, her breath hitching inside her chest. "He left it to *you?*"

"He left it to me."

A thousand emotions burst through her. This was colossally unfair. It was ridiculously and maliciously, reprehensibly… Reed had given his blood, sweat and tears to this place, and now Caleb was simply going to ride in and take over?

Her voice was breathless with disgust. "How could you?"

"How could *I*—" He gave a snort of derision. "Wilton did it."

"But you're the one who benefited."

"I'm here to give it *back*, Mandy. But thank you for the faith in my character. Your low opinion of me is matched only by my idiot brother's."

"You're going to give it back?" She couldn't keep the skepticism from her tone. Caleb was simply going to walk away from a ranch worth tens of millions of dollars?

"I live in Chicago now. Why in the hell would I want to come back to a place I hated, that holds nothing but bitter memories? And he's my brother. We hate each other, but we don't *hate* each other."

Judging by his affronted expression and the passion in his tone, Caleb truly was going to do the honorable thing. But Reed must have been as skeptical as Mandy. The anger in the note was plain as day, and he'd obviously hightailed it out of there before he had to watch his brother come in and take over.

Fresh worry percolated to life inside her. "We have to find him. We have to explain and bring him home."

"He's not a lost puppy."

"He's your brother."

Caleb seemed singularly unmoved. "What exactly does that mean?"

His brother's house was the last place Caleb wanted to be. He didn't want to eat in this kitchen or sit in that living room, and he definitely had no desire to go upstairs and sleep in his old bedroom.

He'd had enough déjà vu already.

The kitchen might as well have been frozen in time. A spider plant sat in the middle of the island, serving utensils upside down in a white container next to the stove, a bulletin board above the phone, a fruit bowl under the light switch and the coffeemaker beneath the built-in microwave.

He knew the sugar would be on the third shelf of the pantry, the milk in the door of the stainless-steel refrigerator and the coffee beans on the second shelf in the pantry next to the dining room. He'd kill for a cup of coffee, but there was no way he was making himself at home.

Mandy, on the other hand, seemed to feel completely at home. She'd perched herself on one of the high, black-cushioned chairs at the center island, one booted foot propped on the cross piece, one swinging in a small arc as she dialed her phone.

"Are you here often?" He couldn't help asking. He didn't remember anyone ever looking relaxed in this house.

She raised her phone to her ear and gave a small, wry smile. "Only when your father was away. Reed and I used to drink cheap wine and play poker."

"Just the two of you?" Caleb arched a brow. He didn't yet have a handle on the relationship between his brother and Mandy.

She raked her loose hair back from her forehead. "I told you I wasn't sleeping with him." She left a deliberate pause. "When I stayed over, I slept in your bed. Oh, hey, Seth," she said into the phone.

Absurdly rattled by her taunt, Caleb withdrew into the living room to clear his head. This trip was not going even remotely as he'd planned.

It was two hours to the Lyndon airport. He could drive

there and fly back to Chicago tonight. Or he could get a hotel room in Lyndon. Or he could stay here and figure out what on earth to do next.

His gaze strayed to the staircase at the opposite end of the living room. His old bedroom was up there. Where, apparently, Mandy had been sleeping. Of course, she could have been lying about that, simply amusing herself by messing with his head.

Then again, even if she had slept in his bed, why should he care? He didn't. The woman could sleep wherever she wanted.

Her footfalls sounded on the kitchen tiles. Seconds later, she strode through the archway between the kitchen and the living room, tucking her phone into the front pocket of her jeans. "Seth's going to send a couple of hands."

"Send them where?"

She did a double take. "Here, of course."

"Why?"

"To help you out."

"I didn't ask for help." Caleb didn't mean to sound ungrateful, but he didn't need Mandy waltzing in and making decisions for him. He didn't know what happened next, but he knew he'd be the guy calling the shots.

She blinked. "I know. I did it as a favor."

"Next time, please ask permission."

"You want me to ask for permission to do a favor?"

"I want you to ask permission to meddle in my business."

"Meddling? You call lending you two highly qualified hands to take care of your ranch while we look for your brother *meddling?*"

Caleb took in the determined tilt of her chin, the squared shoulders that said she was ready for a scrap and the animated flash in her jewel-bright eyes. He decided it wasn't the right time for a fight.

"Next time," he told her more softly, "please ask first."

"I wouldn't worry about there being a next time."

Fine. No problem. He'd dealt with everything else in his life without help.

He'd find his brother. He'd find him fast and get his life back to normal.

He couldn't help thinking about how his financial lawyer, Danielle Marin, was going to react to him being stuck in Colorado.

Active Equipment was at a critical point in setting up a new division in South America. Danielle was wading her way through Brazil's complicated banking and accounting regulations.

Mandy moved in closer. "What are you going to do now?"

"Find Reed." And drag him home.

"And in the meantime? The ranch? The animals?"

"I'll deal with it."

A mocking lilt came into Mandy's voice. "Sure would be nice if you had a little help."

"Sure would be nice if you minded your own business."

"I'm only doing my duty as a neighbor."

"Are you going for the good-neighbor merit badge?"

She perked up. "There's a badge?"

"Were you always this much of a smart-ass?"

"You don't remember what I was like?"

"You were four grades behind me. I barely noticed you."

"I thought you were hot."

Caleb went still.

"Schoolgirl fantasy," Mandy finished smoothly. "I didn't know your true character back then."

"You don't know my true character now," he retorted.

But her words triggered some kind of hormonal reaction deep inside him. *He* thought *she* was hot, right here, right now, right this very minute. And that was a complication this situation definitely didn't need.

"You married?" he asked her hopefully. "Engaged?"

She wiggled her bare left hand in front of his face.

"Seeing someone?" he pressed, praying for the yes that would make him honor bound to quit thinking of her naked in his arms.

"Why do you want to know?"

"I wondered who I should pity."

Despite the insult, their gazes locked. They flared, and then smoldered. He couldn't seem to tamp down his unspoken desire.

"No," she told him flatly.

"I didn't ask you anything." He didn't want to kiss her. He *wouldn't* want to kiss her.

She tipped her head to a challenging angle, her rich, dark hair flowing like a curtain. "I'm helping you find your brother. Don't get any ideas."

"I didn't ask for your help." What he really wanted was for her to go away and stay away so he could keep him emotions on an even keel.

"You're getting it, anyway, neighbor."

"There isn't actually a badge, you know."

"I want him back, too."

It wasn't that Caleb had an interest in ferrying Reed back to Lyndon Valley. He had an interest in the Terrell ranch no longer being his problem. And there was more than one way to accomplish that.

"I could sell the place," he pointed out.

She stiffened, drawing back in obvious astonishment. "You wouldn't."

"I could."

"I won't let you."

The threat was laughable. "How're you going to stop me?"

She lifted her chin. "I'll appeal to your honor and principles."

"Fresh out," he told her honestly, his desire for her starting a slow burn in his body. There was certainly no honor in lusting after his brother's neighbor.

She shook her head in denial, the tip of her tongue touching her bottom lip. "You're here, aren't you? You came all the way out here to give the ranch back to Reed. You can't undo all those good intentions because you've been slowed down by a day or so."

Caleb hesitated. The faster the better as far as he was concerned. "You think we can find him in a day or so?"

"Sure," she said with breezy conviction. "How hard can it be?"

Caleb wasn't touching that one.

But the flash in her eyes told him she'd heard the double-entendre as clearly as he did. She held up a warning finger. "I told you not to get any ideas."

"You have a vivid imagination."

"And you have a transparent expression. Don't ever play poker."

"Well, not with you."

"So, you admit I'm right?" Her expression held a hint of triumph.

"I can control myself if you can."

"There's nothing for me to control."

"You think I'm hot," he reminded her.

"When I was thirteen and underage."

"You're not underage now."

She pointed to him and then back to herself. "You and me, Caleb."

Sensual anticipation shot through his chest.

But she wasn't finished speaking. "Are going to find your brother, give him back his ranch and then go our respective ways."

Caleb squelched his ridiculous disappointment. What had he expected her to say?

Two

Having escaped to the Terrell's front porch and perched herself on the railing, Mandy tried not to think about the sensual awareness that flared inside her every time Caleb spoke.

And when he'd hugged her.

Hoo boy. She fanned herself with her white Stetson, remembering the tingling sensation that flowed across her skin and the glow that had warmed the pit of her stomach as he'd pressed his body against hers. Though the brothers were twins, she'd never felt anything remotely like that in a hug from Reed.

She heard the sound she'd been waiting for and saw a Jacobs ranch pickup truck careen up the driveway. She stuffed the hat back on her head as the truck caught air on the last pothole before spraying gravel while it spun in the turnaround and rocked to a halt. Two Jacobs ranch hands exited the passenger side, giving her a wave as they headed for the barn, while her brother Travis emerged from the driver's, anchoring his worn hat on his head and striding toward her.

"And?" Travis demanded as he approached, brows going up.

Mandy jabbed her thumb toward the front doorway just as Caleb filled the frame.

At six-two, with long legs, all lanky muscle, Travis easily took the stairs two at a time.

"Came to see for myself," he told Caleb, looking him up and down before offering his hand.

Caleb stepped outside and shook it, while Mandy slid off the rail, her boot heels clunking down on the porch.

"Good to see you, Travis," Caleb offered in a steady voice.

"Figured Seth had to be lying," said Travis, shoulders square, gaze assessing. "But here you are. A little uptight and overgroomed, but at least you didn't go soft on us."

"You were expecting a pot belly and a double chin?"

"And a pasty-white complexion."

"Sorry to disappoint you."

Travis shrugged. "What brought you back?"

Caleb's gaze slid to Mandy.

Travis glanced between them. "What?"

Caleb hesitated, obviously debating whether or not to reveal the information about the will.

"Travis can keep a secret," Mandy offered, moving toward them. Her family would be in a better position to help Caleb if he'd be honest with them.

Travis tipped his chin to a challenging angle, confronting Caleb. "What did you do?"

"Nothing," Caleb stated levelly. "I'm solving a problem, not creating one. But I remember gossip spreading like wildfire around here."

"Welcome home," Mandy put in, struggling to keep the sarcasm from her voice.

Caleb frowned at her. There was nothing salacious in his expression, no inappropriate message in his eyes. Still, the mere fact that he was looking at her sent a flush across her skin.

"Come back to dance on your daddy's grave?" Travis asked Caleb.

"You want a beer?" Caleb offered. Surprisingly, there was no annoyance in his tone at Travis's crass remark.

Mandy took the opportunity to escape from Caleb's proximity again, passing through the doorway and calling over her shoulder. "I'll get them."

She headed straight down the hall to the kitchen at the back of the house, shaking off the buzz of arousal. There was no denying the chemical attraction between her and Caleb, but that didn't mean she had to give in to it. Sure, he was a great-looking guy. He had an undeniably sexy voice, and he could pull of a Saville Row suit.

She had no doubt he'd look equally good in blue jeans and a Western-cut shirt. When they'd hugged, she'd felt his chest, stomach, thighs and arms, so she knew he was rock-solid with muscle. Whatever he'd been doing in Chicago for the past ten years, it wasn't sitting behind a desk.

She checked the wayward track of her brain and extracted three bottles of beer from the refrigerator, heading back down the hall.

When she arrived on the porch, Caleb had obviously brought Travis up to speed on the will. The two men had made themselves comfortable in the painted, wood-slat chairs. Mandy handed out the beers, her fingertips grazing Caleb's as he accepted his. She refused to look in his eyes, but the touch sent an electrical current coursing the length of her arm.

She backed away and perched herself on the wide railing, one leg canted across the rail, the other dangling between the slats.

"Just when you think a guy can't get any nastier," said Travis, twisting off the cap of his beer bottle.

Caleb took a swig of his own beer. "Only Wilton could screw up our lives from the grave."

Mandy had to agree with that. It looked as if Caleb's father had deliberately driven a new wedge between his two sons. The only way to repair the damage was to tell Reed about Caleb's offer to return the ranch.

"How are we going to find him?" she asked.

"We won't," said Travis, "if he doesn't want to be found."

"Probably doesn't," said Caleb. "Which means he's finally come to his senses and left this place in his dust."

"He thinks you're stealing his ranch," Mandy corrected, her voice rising on the accusation.

"Then why didn't he call me and talk about it? I'm listed."

"He probably thought you'd gloat," she guessed.

"Your faith in me is inspiring."

She hadn't meant it as an insult. "I was speculating on what Reed might think. I wasn't saying what I personally thought." She took a swig of the cold, bitter brew. It wasn't her favorite beverage, but sometimes it was the only thing going, so she'd learned to adapt.

"You thought I was going to keep the ranch," Caleb reminded her.

"But I believed you when you said you wouldn't," she countered.

"You want points for that?"

"Or a merit badge." The joke was out before she could stop it.

Caleb gave a half smile. Then he seemed to contemplate her for a long, drawn-out moment. "I should just sell the damn thing."

"Well, that would be quite the windfall, wouldn't it?"

"You think I'd keep the money?"

She stilled, taking in his affronted expression. Oops. She swallowed. "Well..."

Caleb shook his head in obvious disgust, his tone flat. "I'd give the money to Reed, Mandy."

"Reed wants the ranch, not the money," she pointed out, attempting to cover the blunder.

"Then why isn't he here fighting for it?"

"Excellent question," Travis jumped in. "If it was me, I'd fight you tooth and nail. Hell, I'd lie, cheat and steal to get my land back."

"So, where is he?" Caleb's question was directed at Mandy.

"I'm going to find out," she vowed.

Two days later, Mandy was no closer to an answer. Caleb, on the other hand, was moving his alternative plan along at lighting speed, having decided it was most efficient for him to stay on the ranch for now. He had a real-estate broker on retainer, an appraiser marching around the Terrell ranch and a photographer compiling digital shots for the broker's website. He'd told her that if they didn't find Reed in the next few days, the ranch was going on the market.

Trying to keep her activities logical and rational, despite the ticking clock, Mandy had gone from checking Reed's web-browser history for hotel sites, to trying his cell phone one more time, to calling the hospitals within a three-hundred-mile radius, just in case.

At noon, tired, frustrated and hungry, she wandered

into the Terrell kitchen. She found a chicken breast in the freezer, cheese in the refrigerator along with half a jar of salsa, and some tomatoes, peppers and onions in the crisper.

Assuming Caleb and the appraiser would be hungry when they finished their work, she put the chicken breast in the microwave and set it to defrost. She found a thick skillet, flour, shortening and a rolling pin, and started mixing up a batch of homemade tortilla shells.

When Caleb walked in half an hour later, she was chopping her way through a ripe tomato on the island's counter, the chicken frying on the stove.

She glanced up to see Caleb alone. "Where's the appraiser?" she asked.

"On his way back to Lyndon."

"He wasn't hungry?"

Caleb snagged a chunk of tomato and popped it into his mouth. "He didn't know there was anything on offer."

"You didn't offer to feed him?" It was more than two-and-a-half hours back to Lyndon.

"I didn't think it was worth the risk."

She gave him a perplexed look.

"I don't cook," he clarified.

"Don't be ridiculous." She turned her back on him to flip the last of the tortillas frying in the pan. "Everybody cooks."

"Not me."

She threw the vegetables in with the chicken. "How is that possible? You said you lived alone. Please, don't tell me you have servants."

"I don't have servants. Does anybody have servants in this day and age? I live in a high-rise apartment in downtown Chicago. I'm surrounded by excellent restaurants."

"You eat out every night?" She couldn't imagine it.

"I do a lot of business over dinner," he told her easily. "But most of the restaurants in the area also offer takeout."

"It's hard to believe you survive on takeout." She turned back, returning to chopping the tomato on the island. How could he be so fit eating pizza, burgers and chicken?

"There's takeout. And then there's takeout." He spread his arms and rested the heels of his hands against the lip of the granite countertop, cornerwise from where she worked. "Andre's, around the corner from my apartment, will send up filet mignon, baby potatoes in a sweet dill sauce and primavera lettuce salad with papaya dressing."

Suddenly, her soft-taco recipe seemed lame. She paused. "You must make a lot of money to afford meals like that."

He was silent for a long moment, and she quickly realized her observation had been rude. It was none of her business how much money he made.

"I do okay," he finally allowed.

"Tell me something about your job." She tried to graciously shift the subject.

She also realized she was curious. What had happened to the seventeen-year-old cowboy who landed in Chicago with nothing more than a high school education. It couldn't have been easy for him.

"The company's called Active Equipment." He reached out and snagged another chunk of tomato.

She threatened him with her chopping knife.

But he only laughed. "We sell heavy equipment to construction companies, exploration and resource companies, even ranchers."

"So, like a car dealership?"

"Not a dealership. It's a multinational corporation.

We manufacture the equipment before we sell it." With lightning speed, he chose another piece of tomato from the juicy pile and popped it into his mouth, sucking the liquid from the tip of his finger.

"There's not going to be any left for the tacos," she warned.

"I'll risk it."

"So, what do you do at this corporation?"

Caleb swallowed. "I run it."

"What part of it?"

"All of it."

Her hand stilled. "You run an entire corporation?" He'd risen all the way to the top at age twenty-seven? That seemed impossible.

"Yes."

"I don't understand."

He coughed out a laugh. "I'm the president and chief executive officer."

"They gave you *that* many promotions?"

"Not exactly. They let me run things, because they have no choice. I own it."

She set down the knife. She couldn't believe it. "You *own* Active Equipment?"

He nodded.

"How?"

He shrugged. "Hard work, intelligence and a few big financial risks along the way."

"But—"

"You should stop being so surprised that I'm not a loser."

He paused, but she didn't know how to respond to that.

"Though it's true that I can't cook," he allowed with a crooked smile. "I guess I concentrated on the things I was good at and muddled my way through the rest."

"With filet mignon and baby potatoes. Poor you." She kept her tone flippant, but inside she acknowledged he was right. She should stop being so surprised at his accomplishments.

"It wasn't always that way," he told her, tone going more serious. "In the beginning, it was cheap food, a crappy basement suite and two jobs."

Then he straightened his spine, squaring his shoulders. "But I was never coming back here. I'd have starved to death before I'd have come back to Wilton with my tail between my legs."

She found her heart going out to the teenager he'd been back then. "Was it that bad? Were you in danger of starving?"

His posture relaxed again. "No real danger. I was young and healthy. Hard work was good for me. And not even the most demanding bosses could hold a candle to Wilton Terrell."

She retrieved the knife and scraped the tomato chunks from the wooden cutting board into a glass bowl. "So now, you're a self-made man."

"Impressed?"

Mandy wasn't sure how to answer that. Money wasn't everything. "Are you happy?"

"Delirious."

"You have friends? A social life? A girlfriend?" She turned away, crossing the short space to the stove, removing the tortilla shell, setting it on the stack and switching off the burner. She didn't want him to see her expression when he started talking about his girlfriend.

"No girlfriend," he said from behind.

"Why not?" she asked without turning.

"No time, I guess. Never met the right girl."

"You should." She turned back. "Make the time. Meet a nice girl."

His expression went thoughtful, and he regarded her with obvious curiosity. "What about you? Why no boyfriend?"

"Because I'm stuck in the wilds of Colorado ranch country. How am I going to meet a man?"

"Go to Denver. Buy yourself a pretty dress."

She couldn't help glancing down at her simple T-shirt and faded blue jeans with a twinge of self-consciousness. "You don't like my clothes?"

"They're fine for right now, but we're not dancing in a club."

"I've never danced in a real club." A barn, sure, and at the Weasel in Lyndon, but never in a real club.

"Seriously?"

She rolled her eyes at his tone of surprise. "Where would I dance in a club?"

He moved around the island, blue eyes alight with merriment. "If we were in Chicago, I'd dress you up and show you a good time."

"Pretty self-confident, aren't you?" But her pulse had jumped at the thought of dancing with Caleb.

He reached out, lifted one of her hands and twirled her in a spin, pulling her against his body to dance her in the two-step across the kitchen. She reflexively followed his smooth lead.

"Clearly, you've been practicing the Chicago nightlife," she noted.

"Picture mood lighting and a crowd," he whispered in her ear.

"And maybe a band?" she asked, the warmth of his body seeping into her skin, forcing her lungs to work harder to drag in the thickening air.

"You like country?" he asked. "Blues? Jazz? There are some phenomenal jazz clubs in Chicago."

"I'm a country girl," she responded brightly, desperate to mask her growing arousal.

"You'd like jazz," he said with conviction.

The timer pinged for the simmering chicken, and they both halted. Their gazes met, and their breaths mingled.

She could see exactly what he was thinking. "No," she whispered huskily, even though she was definitely feeling it, too. They were not going to let this attraction go over the edge to a kiss.

"Yes," he responded, his fingertips flexing against the small of her back. "But not right now."

Caleb had known it was only a matter of time before Maureen Jacobs, Mandy's mother, extended him some Lyndon Valley hospitality. He wasn't really in a mood for socializing, but he couldn't insult her by saying no to her dinner invitation. So, he'd shut the ranch office computer down early, sighing his disappointment that the listing hadn't come up on the broker's web site yet. Then he drove the rental car over the gravel roads to the Jacobs ranch.

There, he returned friendly hugs, feeling surprisingly at home as he settled in, watching Mandy's efficient movements from the far reaches of the living room in the Jacobs family home. The Jacobses always had the biggest house, the biggest spread and the biggest family in the valley. Caleb couldn't count the number of times he had been here for dinner as a child and a teenager. He, Reed and Travis had all been good friends growing up.

He'd never watched Mandy like this. She had always blended in with her two sisters, little kids in pigtails and scuffed jeans, and was beneath his notice. Now, she was all he could focus on as she flitted from the big, open-concept kitchen to the dining area, chatting with her mother and sister, refilling glasses of iced tea, checking on dishes in the oven and on the stove, while making sure the finishing touches were perfect on the big, rectangular table.

Caleb couldn't imagine the logistics of dinner for seven people every single night. Tonight, one of Mandy's two sisters was here, along with her two brothers, Travis and Seth, who was the oldest. And her parents, Hugo and Maureen, who looked quite a bit older than Caleb had expected, particularly Hugo, who seemed pale and slightly unsteady on his feet.

"I see the way you're looking at my sister," Travis said in an undertone as he took the armchair opposite Caleb in the corner of the living room.

"I was thinking she suits it here," Caleb responded, only half lying. He was thinking a whole lot of other things that were better left unsaid.

"She does," Travis agreed, "but that wasn't what I meant."

"She's a very beautiful woman," Caleb acknowledged. He wasn't going to lie, but he certainly wasn't going to admit the extent of his attraction to Mandy, either.

"Yes, she is." Travis set his glass of iced tea on the small table between them and relaxed back into the over-stuffed chair.

Caleb tracked Mandy's progress from the stovetop to the counter, where her mother was busy with a salad, watching as the two of them laughed at something Mandy said. He didn't want to reinforce Travis's suspicions, but his curiosity got the better of him "Did she and Reed ever…?"

Travis shook his head. "It was pretty hard to get close

to your brother. He was one bottled up, angry man after you lit out without him."

Caleb felt himself bristle at the implication. He hadn't deserted Reed. He'd begged his brother to come with him. "It wasn't my leaving that did the bottling."

"Didn't help," said Travis.

Caleb hit the man with a warning glare.

"I'm saying he lost his mother, then he lost you, and he was left to cope with your father's temper and crazy expectations all on his own."

Caleb cleared his dry throat with a sip of his own iced tea. "He should have come with me. Left Wilton here to rot."

"You understand why he didn't, don't you?"

"No." Caleb would never understand why Reed had refused to leave.

"Because of your mother."

"I know what he said." But it had never made sense to Caleb.

Their mother was gone. And the legacy of the ranch land didn't mean squat to Caleb. There was nothing but bad memories here for them both. Their father had worked their mother to death on that land.

The sound of female laughter wafted from the kitchen again. Caleb couldn't help but contrast the loud, chaotic scene in this big, family house to his own penthouse apartment with its ultramodern furniture, crisp, cool angles of glass and metal, its silence and order. Everything was always in its place, or at least everything was sitting exactly where he'd last left it.

Maureen passed her husband, Hugo, giving him a quick stroke across the back of the neck. He responded with a secretive smile and a quick squeeze of her hand.

Here was another thing that wasn't in Caleb's frame

of reference, relaxed and loving parents. He couldn't remember his mother ever voluntarily touching his father. And his father had certainly never looked at his wife, Sasha, with affection.

Travis shifted his position in the armchair. "Reed thought you were afraid to stay and fight."

Caleb straightened. "Afraid?"

Travis shrugged, indicating he was only the messenger.

"I hated my old man," Caleb clarified. "But I was never afraid of him."

That was a lie, of course. As a child, Caleb had been terrified of his father. Wilton was exacting and demanding, and quick with a strap or the back of his hand. But by the time Caleb was seventeen, he had a good two inches on his father, and he'd have fought back if Wilton had tried anything. Reed was even bigger than Caleb, and Wilton was no physical threat to Reed by then.

"Where do you think Reed went?" Travis asked.

"I couldn't begin to guess," Caleb responded, thinking Reed's decisions were finally his own. He honestly hoped his brother was happy away from here.

He'd thought a lot about it over the past two days. Reed was perfectly entitled to live his life any way he saw fit. As was Caleb, and Caleb had become more and more convinced that selling the ranch was the right thing to do.

Reed could do whatever he wanted with the money. And, in the short term, Caleb was in no position to hang around Lyndon Valley and run things. And he sure couldn't continue to depend on the Jacobses to help him out.

He supposed he could hire a professional ranch manager. But, then what? It wasn't as if he was ever coming back again. And Reed had made his choice by leaving. If

Reed had any interest in keeping the ranch, all it would
have taken was for him to jot down a contact number in
his cryptic note. Caleb would have called, and they could
have worked this whole thing out.

Mandy swished across the room, a huge bowl of
mashed potatoes in her oven-mitt-covered hands. She'd
changed from her usual blue jeans to a pair of gray
slacks and a sleeveless, moss-green sweater. It clung to
her curves and brought out the color of her eyes. The
slacks molded to her rear end, while her rich, chestnut-
colored hair flowed like a curtain around her smooth,
bare shoulders.

"I see the way you're looking at my sister," Travis
repeated.

Caleb glanced guiltily away.

"You hurt her," Travis added, "and we're going to
have a problem."

"I have nothing but respect for Mandy," Caleb lied.
While he certainly had respect for Mandy, he was also
developing a very powerful lust for her.

"This isn't Chicago," Travis warned.

"I'm aware that I'm not in Chicago." Chicago had
never been remotely like this.

"We're ready," Maureen announced in a singsong
voice.

Mandy sent Caleb a broad smile and motioned him
over to the big table. Then she seemed to catch Travis's
dark expression, and her eyes narrowed in obvious confusion.

"She's a beautiful, intelligent, strong-minded woman,"
Caleb said to Travis in an undertone. "You should worry
about her hurting me."

Travis rose to his feet. "I don't care so much about

you. And I'm not likely to take her out behind the barn
and knock any sense into her."

Caleb stood to his full height. "Does she know you
try to intimidate guys like this?"

The question sent a brief flash of concern across Travis's expression. Caleb tried to imagine Mandy's reaction to Travis's brotherly protectiveness.

It was all Caleb could do not to laugh. "Stalemate."

"I'll still take you out behind the barn."

"I'm not going to hurt Mandy," Caleb promised.

Not that he wouldn't let Mandy make up her own mind
about him. She was a grown woman, and if she offered a
kiss, he was taking a kiss. If she offered more, well, okay,
he didn't imagine he'd be around long enough for that
to happen. So there was no sense in borrowing trouble.

He deliberately took a chair across the table from
Mandy instead of sitting next to her. Travis grunted his
approval.

As dishes were passed around and plates filled up,
the family's conversation became free-flowing and bois-
terous.

"If there's a competing interest lurking out there,"
Mandy's sister Abigail was saying, "I can't find it. But
it's important that as many ranchers as possible show up
at the first meeting."

"We need a united front," Hugo put in, helping himself to a slice of roast beef before passing the platter to
Travis. "It's suspicious to me that they're calling the review five years early."

"The legislation allows for a water use review anytime after thirty years and before thirty-five," Abigail
responded. "Technically, they're not early."

Seth, the eldest brother, stepped in as he reached for a
homemade bun. "When was the last time the state gov-

ernment did anything at the *earliest* possible date? Dad's right, there's something they're not telling us."

"I've put in an access to information request," said Abigail. "Maybe that'll solve the mystery."

"That won't get you anything," Hugo grumbled. "The bureaucrats will just stonewall."

"You should catch Caleb up," Mandy suggested.

"This is important to you, too," said Travis, and Caleb waited for him to elaborate.

"Any decrease in the flexibility of our water licenses, will devalue the range land."

"Devalue the range land?" Seth interjected. "Who cares about the land value? It'll impact our grazing density. There are operations up and down the valley that are marginal as it is. The Stevensons, for example. They don't have river access anywhere on their land. A couple of tributaries, but they depend on their wells."

"Seth," Maureen put in, her voice stern. "Did anyone ask you to bring your soapbox to the dinner table?"

Seth's lips thinned for a moment. But then he glanced down at his plate. "Sorry, Mom."

Maureen's face transformed into a friendly smile. "Now, Caleb. How long do you expect to be in Lyndon?"

Caleb swallowed a mouthful of potatoes smothered in the best gravy he'd ever eaten. "A few days. Maybe a week."

"We're sorry you missed the funeral, dear." Maureen's tone was even, but he detected a rebuke. One look at Mandy's expression told him he'd detected correctly.

"I was tied up with work," he said.

"Did you know Caleb owns his own company in Chicago?" Mandy asked.

Caleb appreciated the change in topic, and silently thanked Mandy. The Jacob family would learn soon enough that he was planning to sell the Terrell ranch. Just like everyone would soon learn about Wilton's will. But he was in no hurry to field the inevitable questions.

"Active Equipment," he told them. "Heavy machinery. We're making inroads into Asia and Canada, and we hope to succeed in the South American market soon."

"That's lovely, dear," said Maureen, her quick gaze going from plate to plate, obviously checking to see if anyone was ready for seconds.

"Active Equipment?" asked Hugo, tone sharp and vaguely accusing. "*The* Active Equipment, loaders and backhoes?"

"Yes," Caleb confirmed.

"So, you can get me a discount?"

Maureen scowled at her husband. Travis laughed, and Mandy's eyes danced with amusement.

"Absolutely," Caleb answered, unable to look away from Mandy. Her green eyes sparkled like emeralds under the chandelier, and he didn't think he'd ever seen a more kissable set of lips. "Just let me know what you need."

"Seth and I will come up with a list," said Hugo.

"Happy to help out," said Caleb.

Mandy's lashes swept briefly down over her eyes, and the tip of her tongue moistened her lower lip. He didn't dare glance Travis's way.

Three

Mandy couldn't help but stare at the tall, elegant, brunette woman standing on the porch of the Terrell ranch house. She wore a chic, textured, taupe jacket, with black piping along the neck, lapels and faux pockets. It had a matching, straight skirt, and the ensemble was layered over a black, lace camisole. Her black, leather pumps were high heeled, closed toed with an open weave along the outsides.

Her earrings were large—a woven, copper geometric pattern that dangled beneath short, stylishly cut hair. Her makeup was subtle, coral lips, soft thick lashes, sculpted brows and dusky shadow that set off her dark, hazel eyes. She held a black, rhinestone purse tucked under one arm, and a leather briefcase in the opposite hand.

How she'd made it to the porch dust-free was beyond Mandy.

"Can I help you with something?" Mandy belatedly asked.

"I'm looking for Caleb Terrell." The woman's voice was crisp and businesslike.

"I'm afraid he's not here at the moment."

The woman's lips compressed in obvious impatience.

"Was he expecting you?" Mandy asked, confused and curious in equal measure.

"*I* was expecting *him.* Two days ago in Chicago." The woman clearly had a close enough relationship with Caleb that she had expectations, and she was free to express frustration if he didn't meet them.

A girlfriend? A lover? He'd said he had none, but evidence to the contrary was standing right here in front of Mandy.

"Would you like to come in?" she offered, remembering her manners, telling herself Caleb's personal life was none of her business. "He should be back anytime."

Sure, he'd made a couple of flirtatious allusions in their conversations. But they were harmless. He hadn't even kissed her. She certainly hadn't taken any of it seriously.

The woman smiled, transforming her face, and she held out a slim, perfectly manicured hand. "Forgive me. I'm Danielle Marin."

Mandy hesitated only a brief second before holding out her own, blunt-nailed, tanned and slightly callused hand.

She couldn't help but wish she was wearing something other than a plain, blue cotton blouse and faded jeans. There was some eyelet detail on the collar, and at least she didn't have manure on her boots. Then again, she'd been sweating in the barn all morning, and her casual ponytail was certainly the worse for wear.

"Mandy Jacobs," she introduced herself. "I'm, uh. I've been helping out on the ranch."

"I'm sure Caleb appreciates that." Danielle waved a hand in the air as she stepped into the house. "I have to say, this whole situation borders on the ridiculous."

Mandy closed the door behind them. She couldn't disagree. "Once we find Reed, things will smooth out."

"Any progress on that?" Danielle asked, setting her purse on the side table in the entryway and parking her briefcase beneath. "Caleb told me you were spearheading the effort."

Mandy didn't know what to say to that. She didn't want to share details with a stranger, but she couldn't very well ask about Danielle's relationship with Caleb without being rude.

Danielle strolled her way into the great room, gazing at the high ceiling and the banks of windows overlooking the river. "I assume you've already checked his usual hotels."

Mandy followed. "Reed never traveled much. But I have checked hotels, hospitals and with the police as far away as Fort Collins."

"Car-rental agencies?"

"He took a ranch truck."

Danielle nodded. "Have you tried checking his credit-card activity?"

Mandy tried to figure out if Danielle was joking. Judging by her expression, she was serious.

"I wouldn't know how to do that," Mandy said slowly. Was she even allowed to do that? It sounded like it might be illegal.

"It's not a service we could provide, but I do have some contacts..." Danielle let the offer hang.

Mandy didn't know what to say. Was Danielle suggesting she could help Mandy break the law?

The front door opened, and a pair of boots sounded in the entryway. Mandy took a couple of steps back and crooked her head to confirm it was Caleb. Thank goodness.

He gazed quizzically at her expression as he strode down the short hall. Then, at the living-room entrance, he halted in his tracks. "Danielle?"

"Yes," Danielle answered shortly as she moved in on him.

"What on earth are you doing in Colorado?"

"What on earth are *you* still doing in Colorado?"

"I told you it was going to take a few days."

"That was a few days ago."

"*Two* days ago."

"Do you want this to work or not?"

Mandy scooted toward the kitchen, determined to get away from the private conversation. One thing was sure, if Caleb kept flirting with other women, his relationship with Danielle was definitely not going to work out.

"We have to be in Sao Paulo by the sixteenth," Danielle's voice carried to the kitchen. "We've made a commitment. There's no cancellation insurance on this kind of deal, Caleb."

"Have I done something to make you think I'm stupid?" Caleb asked.

Mandy wasn't proud of it, but her feet came to a halt the moment she was around the corner in the kitchen, intense curiosity keeping her tuned to what was happening in the living room.

"You mean, other than moving to Colorado?" Danielle asked.

"I haven't moved to Colorado."

There was a moment of silence, and Mandy found herself straining to hear.

"You have to come back, Caleb."

"I can't leave yet."

"You said you were going to sell."

"I am going to sell."

Mandy was forced to bite back a protest. For years, she'd fantasized about the two brothers reconciling, and they were so close right now. Whatever hard feelings were between them, she was confident they loved each other. And they were the only family each of them had.

"You can look at offers just as easily from Chicago," said Danielle.

"And who runs the ranch until then?"

"What about that Mandy woman?"

"She's doing me a favor just by being here." There was another pause. "Mandy?" Caleb called. "Where did you go?"

"Kitchen," she responded, quickly busying herself at the counter. "You two want coffee?"

"You don't need to make us coffee," Caleb called back.

"It's no problem."

She heard him approach.

Then his footfalls crossed the kitchen, his voice lowering as he arrived behind her. "You *don't* need to make us coffee."

She didn't turn around. "You and your girlfriend should sit down and—"

"My *girlfriend?*"

"Talk this out," Mandy finished. "But, can I say, I really hope you'll give it some time before you sell, Caleb, because I know Reed—"

Caleb wrapped a big hand around her upper arm and turned her to face him. "She's not my girlfriend."

"Oh." Then what was she doing here? Why were they making plans for a vacation in Brazil?

"She's my financial lawyer."

"Sure." Whatever. It didn't mean they weren't romantically involved.

He lowered his voice further. "And why did your mind immediately go to a romance?"

"Because she's gorgeous," Mandy offered, counting on her finger. "Because she's here. Because she just told you if you didn't come back to Chicago, things weren't going to work out between you."

Caleb's voice lowered to a hiss. "And what exactly do you think I've been doing with you?"

She was slow to answer, because she really wasn't sure what the heck he'd been doing with her. "A harmless flirtation. I assumed you didn't mean it the way—"

"I did."

"I'd love some coffee," came Danielle's sultry voice from the kitchen doorway.

"Coming up." Mandy quickly turned away from Caleb.

"She thinks you and I are dating," he said to Danielle in a clear voice.

Danielle's response was a melodic laugh. "Like I'd get you to sit still long enough for a date."

"See?" Caleb finished before backing off.

"I'm setting up a corporation for him in Brazil," Danielle explained. "Do you by any chance have an internet connection? A scanner?"

"In the office," Caleb answered. "Up the stairs, first door on the right."

When Mandy turned around, two stoneware mugs of coffee in her hand, Danielle was gone.

Caleb was standing in front of the table in the breakfast nook. "I'm not dating her."

"Got that." Mandy took a determined step forward, ignoring the undercurrents from their rather intimate conversation. "Brazil?"

"It's a huge, emerging market."

She set the two mugs down on the table. "Are you, like, a billionaire?"

"I've never stopped to do the math."

"But you might be." No wonder he could give up the ranch without a second thought. He wasn't quite the philanthropist he made himself out to be.

"The net worth of a corporation is irrelevant. All the money's tied up in the business. Even if you did want to know the value, you'd spend months wading your way through payables, receivables, inventory, assets and debts to find an answer. And by the time you found it, the answer would have changed."

"But you don't need the money from the ranch," was really Mandy's point.

Caleb drew a sigh. "I'm giving the money to Reed because he earned it." Caleb's hand tightened around the back of one of the chairs. "Boy, did he earn it."

"Then don't sell the ranch."

"I can't stay here and run it."

Mandy tried to stay detached, but her passion came through in the pleading note of her voice. "Reed doesn't want the money. He wants the ranch."

"Then, where is he?"

"He's sulking."

Caleb gave a cold laugh. "At least you've got that right. He's off somewhere, licking his wounds, mired in the certain and self-righteous anger that I'm about to cheat him out of his inheritance. Nice."

"Reed doesn't trust easily."

"You think?"

"And you've been gone a long time."

"When I left, I *begged* him to come with me."

"Well, he didn't. And you have a choice here. You can make things better or you can make them worse."

"No. Reed had a choice here." Caleb's voice was implacable. "He could have stayed."

"He'll be back."

Caleb shook his head. "I don't think so. And he'll be better off with the money, anyway. He can go wherever he wants, do whatever he wants. He'll be free of this place forever."

"If he wanted to be free," she offered reasonably, "he'd have left with you in the first place."

Caleb's eyes narrowed. "Why do you want him back here so badly?"

Mandy wasn't sure how to answer the question. What she wanted was for Caleb and Reed to reconcile. She wanted the ranch to stay in the Terrell family for Reed's children, for Sasha's grandchildren. Reed had sacrificed ten years to protect his heritage. Caleb had no business pulling it out from under him.

Caleb watched the last of the dozen pieces of paper disappear into the ranch house office fax machine. The machine emitted a series of beeps and buzzes that indicated the pages were successfully reaching the Lyndon real-estate office.

"You did it, didn't you?" Mandy's accusing voice came from the office doorway. It was full dark, and the ranch yard lights outside the window mingled with the glow of the desk lamp and the stream of illumination from the upstairs hallway. Danielle had retired to the guest room half an hour ago. Caleb thought Mandy had already left.

"The Terrell Cattle Company is officially for sale,"

he replied, swiping the pages from the cache tray and straightening them into a neat pile.

"You're making a mistake," said Mandy.

"It's my mistake to make."

She moved into the room. "Did you ever stop to wonder why he did it?"

"Reed or Wilton?"

"Your father."

Caleb nodded. "I did. For about thirty-six hours straight. I called Reed half a dozen times after I left my lawyer's office that day. I thought he might have some answers. But he didn't call back. And eventually his voice-mail box was full and I knew it was hopeless."

"Danielle's office?"

"Different lawyer."

"Oh."

Caleb set down the papers and turned to prop himself against the lip of the desk. "I guessed maybe Reed and the old man had a fight, and leaving me the ranch was Wilton's revenge."

"They had about a thousand fights."

Caleb gave a cold chuckle. "Wilton fought with me, too. A guy couldn't do anything right when it came to my old man. If you piled the manure to the right, he wanted it to the left. You used the plastic manure fork, you should have used the metal one. You started brushing from the front of the horse, you should have started from the back—" He stopped himself. Just talking about it made his stomach churn. How the hell Reed had put up with it for ten extra years was beyond Caleb. The guy deserved a medal.

"My theory," said Mandy, moving farther into the dimly lit room, "is that once you were gone, he forgot you were such a failure." An ironic smile took the sting out of her words.

"While Reed was still here to keep screwing up over and over again?"

"Got a better theory?"

"He found my corporation thanks to Google and decided I was worth a damn?" Even as he said the words, Caleb knew it was impossible. He'd spent the better part of his adult life warning himself not to look for his father's approval. There was nothing down that road but bitter disappointment.

Mandy perched herself on the inset, cushioned window seat. She was silhouetted now by the lights from the yard. "You have to know you are worth a damn."

"You're too kind."

"Reed's worth a damn, too."

"No argument from me."

She tucked her feet up onto the wide, bench seat, and he noticed she was wearing whimsical sky-blue-and-pale-pink, mottled socks. It surprised him. Made her seem softer somehow, more vulnerable.

"I don't understand why you're in such a rush to sell," she said.

"That's because you live in the Lyndon Valley and not in Chicago."

"Rash decisions are compulsory in Chicago?"

He moved across the room and took the opposite end of the bench, angling his body toward her and bracing his back against the wall, deciding there was no reason not to give her an explanation. "I've had two weeks to think about it."

"Reed had ten years."

"In many ways, so did I."

Mandy shifted her position, smoothing her loose hair

back from her face. His gaze hungrily followed her motion.

"Did you ever wish you'd stayed?"

He hesitated at the unsettling question, not sure how to answer. Back then, he'd second-guessed himself for months, even years, over leaving Reed. But it all came down to Wilton. "He killed my mother," Caleb said softly. "I couldn't reward him for that."

"She died of pneumonia."

"Because it was left untreated. Because she was terrified of telling him she was sick. Because he would have berated and belittled her for her weakness. Terrells are not weak."

"I never thought you were."

"I'm not," he spat, before he realized it wasn't Mandy he was angry with.

She tossed back her hair. "Reed wasn't weak. Yet, he stayed."

"He squared it in his head somehow."

Reed claimed he wanted to protect his mother's heritage, since half the ranch had belonged to her family. Which, looking back, was obviously the reason Wilton had married her. The man was incapable of love.

"She was twenty years younger than him," Caleb remembered. "Did you know that?"

"I knew she was younger. I didn't know by how much. I remember thinking she was beautiful." Mandy's voice became introspective. "I remember wishing I could be that beautiful."

Caleb couldn't hold back his opinion. "You are that beautiful."

Mandy laughed. "No, I'm not." She held out her hands. "Calluses. I have calluses. Danielle has a perfect French manicure, and I have calluses." She peered at her small hands. "I think there might even be dirt under my fingernails."

"Danielle has never had to clean tack."

"No kidding."

"I mean, she lives a completely different life than you do."

Mandy's face twisted into a grimace. "She goes to parties and I shovel manure?"

"Her world is all about image. Yours is all about practicality."

"I'm just a sturdy little workhorse, aren't I?"

"Are you wallowing in self-pity, Mandy Jacobs?"

She went silent, her glare speaking for her.

Caleb moved inches closer, fighting a grin of amusement. "Are you by any chance jealous of Danielle?"

Mandy tossed back her hair in defiance. "Jealous of a stunningly beautiful, elegant, intelligent, successful lawyer, who's flying off to Rio—"

"Sao Paulo," Caleb corrected, enjoying the flash of emotion that appeared deep within Mandy's green eyes.

"They're both in Brazil."

"It's a big country. One's a beach resort, the other's full of skyscrapers, banks and boardrooms." He fought the urge to reach out and touch her. "But I'd take you to Rio if that's where you wanted to go."

She cocked her head sideways. "You'd take me to Rio?"

"I would." He dared stroke an index finger across the back of her hand. "We'd dress up, and go dancing at a real club and have blender drinks on the beach. You could even get a manicure if you'd like."

"Are you flirting with me?"

He met her gaze full on. "Absolutely."

"You have women like Danielle in your life, and yet you're flirting with me?"

"I am."

"Why?"

Caleb debated for a moment before answering. But then he reminded himself he was in Colorado. People were forthright around here. And he owed Mandy no less than she was giving him.

"Because you're real," he told her. "You're not some plastic package, constructed to appeal to a man's anthropological triggers. When you laugh, it's because you're happy. When you argue, it's because you have a point to make. And when your eyes smolder, it's because you're attracted to me, not because you've spent days and weeks practicing the exact, right look to make a man think you're interested in him."

"I'm not interested in you."

"But you are." He smoothed a stray lock of her hair and tucked it behind one ear. "That's what's so amazing about you. Your body language doesn't lie."

"And if my body language slaps you across the face?"

"I hope it'll be because I've done something to deserve it." Because, then the slap would be worth it.

"You're impossible." But her voice had gone bedroom husky. Her pupils were dilated, and her dark pink lips were softened, slightly parted.

"It's not me you're fighting," he told her.

She didn't answer. Her breathing grew deeper while a pink flush stained her cheeks.

He moved the last couple of inches. Then he dared to bracket her face with his hands. Her skin was smooth, warm and soft against his palms. His pulse jumped, desire igniting a buzz deep in his belly.

He bent his head forward, his lips parting in anticipation of her taste. He hadn't even kissed her yet, and desire was turning his bloodstream into a tsunami.

She sucked in a quick breath, her jade-green eyes fluttering closed.

Caleb could tell stop signals from go signals, and this was definitely a go. Her head tilted sideways, as she leaned into his palm. He crossed the final inches, her sweet breath puffing against his face in the split second before his lips touched hers.

Desire exploded in his chest. He'd meant it to be a gentle kiss, but raw passion pushed him forward.

He'd known it would be good, guessed she would taste like ambrosia, but nothing had prepared him for the rush of raw lust that made his arms wrap around her and his entire body harden to steel.

He opened his mouth, deepening the kiss. She whimpered in surrender, giving him access, her small tongue parrying with his, while his broad palm stroked its way from her waist to her hip, to the curve at the side of her breast.

He shifted his body, pulling her into his lap, never breaking the kiss as her soft, pert behind settled against him. He raked the satin of her hair out of the way, his fingertips convulsing against her scalp. Her small hands clung to his shoulders, hanging on tight, while her rounded breasts pressed erotically against his chest.

He wanted to rip off her clothes, push her back on the seat, or down on the floor, and ravage her body until neither of them could see straight. He knew he couldn't do that, knew he was losing control, knew he had to drag them back to reality before their passion got completely out of control.

But then her hot hands slid the length of his chest, and

he put sanity on hold. She freed the buttons of his cotton shirt, her palms searing into his bare skin.

His hand closed over her breast, feeling its weight through the fabric of her shirt and the lace of her bra. He kissed her harder, deeper, settling her more firmly on the heat of his need. Her kisses trailed to his chest, over his pecs, across one flat nipple, and he groaned in reaction.

"We can't," he whispered harshly, even as he buried his face in her fragrant hair and prayed she'd keep going.

She stilled, her breath cooling a damp spot on his bare skin.

They were both silent for a long moment, while Caleb tried unsuccessfully to bring his emotions under control.

"I'm sorry," she whispered, lips grazing his skin.

"Are you kidding me?" he breathed. He forced himself to draw back, tipping up her chin and gazing into her passion-clouded eyes. "I have never—"

The cell phone in her jeans pocket buzzed, startling them both.

"—ever," he continued, trying to hold her gaze, reluctant to let the moment go.

The cell phone buzzed again.

"Fortuitous?" she asked, seeming to regain her equilibrium.

"Not the word I would have used." He sighed.

She shifted off his lap, slipping her hand into her jeans pocket to retrieve the cell phone.

"Abigail," she announced while she pressed the talk button. "Hey, Abby."

Caleb couldn't believe she could sound so normal. He sure wasn't that capable of turning on a dime like that. Desire was still pulsing its way through his extremities. It was going to be long minutes before he would be able to do anything more than breathe.

"When?" Mandy asked into the phone, her voice going guttural.

Her gaze locked on to Caleb's, fear shooting through her irises. "I don't—"

She swayed on her feet, and he instantly leaped to his, holding her steady.

"Where?" she asked hoarsely, bracing herself by grasping his arm. "Yes. Of course." She nodded reflexively. "Yes."

She was silent for another moment, her hand squeezing his arm in a vice grip. "Right now," she told her sister. "I'll be there. Bye." Her tone was whispered as she lowered the phone.

"What?" Caleb prompted, his stomach clenching hard. Something had obviously gone terribly wrong.

"My dad," she managed, blinking back twin pools of gathering tears. "They think it was a stroke."

"Is he…" Caleb couldn't finish the sentence.

"The medical airlift is on its way."

"How bad?"

"Numbness, speech problems, confusion." She broke away from Caleb's hold. "I have to get home."

"I'll drive you."

"No, I can—"

"I'll *drive* you." There wasn't a chance in hell he was letting her speed down the dark, dirt ranch road all alone.

Four

All the lights were blazing when Mandy and Caleb drove up to the ranch house. Caleb's rented SUV had barely come to a halt when she flung open her door, feet barely touching the dirt driveway as she sprinted across the porch. She rushed through the entry hall to the big living room.

There, she saw Seth first, his strong face pinched in concern where he sat on the sofa, holding her mother's hand. Her sister Abby was furiously hitting keys on the computer, while Travis paced in the middle of the room, obviously ready for action and obviously frustrated because there was nothing he could do to help.

"Mom." Mandy rushed forward, sliding down beside her mother and wrapping an arm around her slim shoulders. Her mother's face was pale, eyes red-rimmed and hollow looking.

"The helicopter left about five minutes ago," said Seth.

"They said there wasn't room for Mom." Travis sounded angry.

Mandy heard Caleb enter the house and cross the foyer behind her, but she didn't turn. She felt guilty for being attracted to him, guilty for kissing him, guilty as sin for getting lost in his embrace while her father fell ill and collapsed.

"I'm trying to find her a ticket out of Lyndon for the morning," Abigail put in.

"They're taking him straight to Denver," said Travis. "There's a specialist there, a whole team with the latest technology for early stroke intervention."

"That sounds good," Mandy said to her mother, rubbing Maureen's shoulder with her palm.

"Damn it. The connection is bogged down again," said Abigail.

Caleb stepped fully into the room. "My corporate jet's on the tarmac in Lyndon."

Everyone turned to stare at him.

Seth came to his feet. "How many of us can you take?"

"As many as need to go." He captured Mandy's gaze for a long second.

"I'll stay here," Travis put in, drawing everyone's attention. He glanced at his siblings. "I'm probably the least help there, but I'm the most help here."

Seth nodded his agreement with the suggestion.

Responding to Seth's concurrence, Caleb pulled out his cell phone. "I'll have the pilots meet us at the airport. Mandy, why don't you put together an overnight bag for your mother?"

Abby swiveled back to the computer. "I'm booking a hotel for us in Denver."

"See if there's an Emerald Chateau near the hospital," said Caleb as he pressed the buttons on his phone.

"We have a corporate account. Call them and use my name." He put his cell phone to his ear and turned toward the foyer.

Mandy squeezed her mother's cool hand. "Did you hear that, Mom?"

Maureen gave a small nod of acknowledgment.

"Good." Mandy struggled to keep her voice even. Breaking down right now wouldn't help anyone, least of all her mother. "I'm going to pack you a few things. You just sit tight."

"He couldn't speak." Maureen's voice was paper dry, her hand squeezing Mandy's. "He tried, but his words were all muddled. Syllables sometimes, then nonsense."

Mandy swallowed the lump in her throat. "I think that's really common with a stroke. And it's sounds like they've got a great team in Denver. He'll get the best care." Her gaze met her brother Seth's and he motioned with his head for her to go pack.

She nodded in response, gently releasing her mother's hand. The sooner they got to Denver, the better.

As she headed for the staircase, she passed Caleb in the foyer, where he was talking on the phone to his pilot. "Two hours, tops," he said. "Right. We'll be there."

She stopped and turned back, reaching out to lay the flat of her hand on his chest, mouthing the words "Thank you."

He placed his hand over hers and gave one quick squeeze then pointed her toward the staircase.

Mandy had never been on a private plane. The flight to Denver was, thankfully, quick and smooth. The Active Equipment jet had room for eight passengers, and Caleb had arranged for a car to take them directly from the airport to the hospital. There, Mandy's mother was the only person allowed to see her father, and the nurse would let her into his room for only a few minutes.

The doctors were medicating him and monitoring him closely to watch for additional strokes. They told the family they needed to keep him calm. The initial prognosis was for a slow, potentially limited recovery. There was no way to tell how much of his speech and mobility he would regain. A doctor told them the first few days were critical.

Although Abby had booked regular rooms at the Denver Emerald Chateau, a word from Caleb to the front-desk clerk had Mandy, Abby and her mother in a luxurious, two-bedroom suite. Caleb and Seth had taken an identical suite at the opposite end of the twentieth-floor hallway.

It was nearly three in the morning before Mandy's mother finally got to bed. Thankfully, she fell asleep almost immediately, and Mandy joined Abby, Seth and Caleb in the suite's living room.

Abigail was handing Seth her cell phone. "Your brother wants to talk to you."

"Thanks, tons." Seth scowled as he accepted the phone.

The only vacant seat was on a small couch next to Caleb, and Mandy sat down. She felt his gaze on her profile, swore she could feel his energy through her pores, but she didn't turn.

"Must we do this *now?*" Seth was asking into the phone.

Mandy gave her sister a quizzical look.

"Seth was talking about dropping out of the Lyndon mayoralty race," Abby explained. "Travis disagrees."

Mandy disagreed, as well, strenuously. Her oldest brother had been planning this political move for over two years. "It'll be weeks before he even needs to campaign."

Abigail huffed as she crossed her arms over her chest. "That's what I told him. And that's what Travis's telling him."

Mandy shook her head. "Dad won't want him to drop out."

Their father had been totally supportive of Seth's decision to run for mayor. The ranching community was slowly being pushed out of the economic framework of the district as tourism operations and small businesses moved in and began to lobby for their own interests.

"Who's going to run the place?" Seth demanded into the phone. "You?"

He listened for a moment, then gave a cold laugh. "Don't make promises you can't keep."

Caleb leaned toward Mandy. "This is a terrible time for them to have this conversation. They have absolutely no perspective at all."

She knew he was right and nodded her agreement. They were all exhausted and their emotions were raw.

Caleb rose to his feet. He moved in front of Seth and motioned for him to hand over the phone. Seth scowled at him, but Caleb persisted. When Seth finally complied, Caleb put the phone to his ear.

"Travis? It's Caleb. You need to go to bed. So does Seth and so do your sisters."

There was a pause.

"In the morning. No. You listen. I don't care who started it. I'm the only one here who's not operating on grief and fear, and I'm telling you to shut it down."

Caleb paused again. "Yes. I will." His gaze slid to Mandy for a brief second. "Of course not."

Abigail rose from her chair to lean over and give Mandy

a quick hug. "I'm beat," she whispered in Mandy's ear. "Mind if I use the bathroom first?"

"Go ahead." Mandy squeezed her sister tight, grateful to have her siblings close to her tonight.

"We're going to have to call Katrina in the morning." Abigail referred to their youngest sister who lived in New York City.

"It's almost morning there now," said Mandy.

"When we get up is soon enough. I'm sure it'll be early."

"Yeah," Mandy agreed on a sigh. It was going to be a long day tomorrow.

Abigail made her way to the second bedroom and its en suite bathroom.

Caleb put the cell phone on the coffee table.

Seth rose. "I'm ordering a single malt from room service," he told Caleb. "You want one?"

"Yeah," said Caleb. "I'm right behind you."

Mandy came to her feet to give her oldest brother a big hug.

"You okay?" he whispered gruffly in her ear, ruffling her hair.

"I'll let you know in the morning." Mandy dreaded having him leave the suite, having her sister fall asleep, leaving her alone with her thoughts and fears. She wasn't going to sleep. Her family had just turned on a dime. She had no idea what would come next.

Seth shut the door behind him, and Caleb turned to her. "You're not okay."

"I'm not okay," she agreed, her body turning into one big ache.

He stepped closer. "Anything I can do to help?"

"You already have." She drew a shuddering breath,

trying to put the night's events in some sort of order.
"You have a jet?"

"Active Equipment has a jet."

"But you own Active Equipment."

"True enough."

"Thank you for bringing us all here. I know my mom
was terrified…" She swallowed, her throat going raw all
over again. "I was so afraid he'd die before—"

Caleb drew her into his strong arms, cradling her
against his body. "Of course you were. But he didn't.
And you're here now. And there may very well be good
news in the morning."

Mandy found herself lying her cheek against Caleb's
chest, taking comfort in the steady thud of his heartbeat
and the deep, soothing rumble of his voice.

He leaned in and kissed her gently on the temple,
bringing all her earlier feelings rushing back. She felt
off balance, out of sync, like she was floating in space
without a lifeline.

"Caleb," she stuttered. "What we—"

"Shh. Not now. Nothing matters right now."

She closed her eyes. "Are you always this nice?"

"I'm hardly ever this nice." He paused. "You need to
sleep now."

"I know." She wished she could lie down right there,
right then and stay safe in Caleb's arms for the rest of the
night. Deep down inside, she knew she was being foolish. She was emotional and vulnerable, and he seemed
strong and safe. It was that simple.

These feelings would probably go away by morning,
but right now, they were powerfully strong.

The next morning did bring positive news. Caleb was
surprised, along with everyone else, by Hugo's rapid

progress. Hugo recognized all the family members. They were each allowed to visit him, and he was able to say Maureen's name, along with several other rudimentary words, enough to get his general meaning across. His meaning, Caleb noted, was that Seth should continue to plan his campaign for the mayoralty race, Abigail should stay in Denver with Maureen, while Mandy should go home and run the ranch with Travis.

Caleb had to admire the tough old man. Less than twenty-four hours after the stroke, Hugo was regaining movement in his right arm, and he also had some movement in his right foot and ankle. The doctors were very pleased with his progress and feeling optimistic about his eventual recovery, although they cautioned it would take weeks, possibly months.

Seth decided to stay in Denver for some political meetings, so Caleb and Mandy returned alone on the Active Equipment jet. Once in Lyndon, they exited down the airplane staircase and onto the tarmac outside a small maintenance building at the private area of the apron. It was late afternoon, and thick clouds were gathering as the sun made its descent and the air cooled down.

Caleb switched on his cell phone, and Mandy did the same. Hers immediately rang, and they picked up their pace to get away from the sound of the airplane engines.

She plugged one ear and called "hello" just as Caleb's phone rang. They made it around the end of the building, blocking the noise.

Caleb answered his phone with one hand, unlocking and swinging open the chain-link gate with the other. There were few cars in the parking area.

"It's Travis," came the voice at the other end.

"Just touched down in Lyndon," Caleb offered. "Did you talk to your mother?"

"Just got off with her," said Travis. "Dad's progress is still good. The doctors are amazed."

"Good to hear." With his free hand, Caleb hit the unlock button on his key fob and opened the passenger door first. Mandy was focused on her own conversation as she absently accepted his offer and climbed inside.

"About Danielle," Travis continued.

"Were you able to reach her?" Caleb had tried Danielle's cell this morning and got her voice mail. Odds were good that she'd headed back to Chicago and was on an airplane. Still, he'd asked Travis to retry the call and check the ranch just in case. He'd rushed off so fast last night, he'd barely had time to explain. Danielle wasn't the most patient woman in the world.

"I drove up to your place," Travis confirmed.

"So, she's on her way back to Chicago?"

"Not exactly."

"She's not?" Caleb swung into the driver's seat and slid the key into the ignition.

"You know that hairpin turn where you come out at Joe Mountain?"

"What?"

"Where the rear wheels always break loose?"

Uh-oh. Caleb didn't like where this was going. "Is Danielle all right?"

"She's fine. Now."

"Give me the bad news."

Travis confirmed Caleb's fears. "She couldn't recover from the slide, missed the turn. Got stuck at the edge of the pond. She wasn't hurt, but evidently, there's no cell service at that particular spot."

Caleb groaned and thudded his head on the steering wheel. Mandy spared him a glance of confusion.

"How long was she stuck?" he asked Travis.

"A few hours. I have to give the girl points for moxie. She spotted the Eldridge barn and decided they might be able to help her."

"That barn's seventy years old. And it's half a mile from the road."

"Hard to judge, I guess. Miss Danielle may want to have her distance vision checked. She climbed through the barbed-wire fence and started hiking."

Caleb groaned again.

"Didn't go well," Travis confirmed. "Apparently you owe her for a designer blazer that got torn. Oh, also the shoes that weren't made for hiking."

"Did she make it to the barn?"

"Barely. By the time she realized it was a derelict, a herd of cattle had cut her off from her car. I guess a bull made some threatening moves, and she ended up climbing into the loft. It's dusty up there and, apparently, there are quite a few spiders."

Caleb shouldn't laugh. He really shouldn't. "I'm in a lot of trouble, aren't I?"

"Hell, yeah. You and me both."

"Why you? I assume you rescued her."

"By the time I got there, she'd been trapped for a few hours."

"Do I by any chance need a new lawyer?"

"She was pretty desperate for a restroom."

Caleb rewhacked his head. Anything less than marble fixtures was considered slumming it for Danielle.

"I told her to go behind the barn," said Travis with an obviously suppressed chuckle.

"Are you laughing?"

"You also owe her for a pair of designer undies. There were nettles."

"Could you just shoot me?"

Mandy had finished her call, twisted her body in the passenger seat and was now staring unabashedly at Caleb.

Caleb met her curious gaze.

"We had to tow her car back with a tractor," said Travis. "Scooter says it needs parts. Hey, can you stop by the auto-parts store while you're in Lyndon?"

"Sure," Caleb agreed fatalistically.

"We'll text you a list."

Caleb braced himself. "She doing okay?"

"She's been in the upstairs bathroom for two hours. I don't know what women do in there, but hopefully it'll improve her disposition."

"Hopefully," Caleb agreed, but he wasn't holding his breath. "Thanks, Travis."

"No need to thank me. That was the best entertainment I've had all month."

"Don't tell her that."

"Already did. See you, Caleb."

Caleb signed off, pocketing his phone.

"Were you talking to Abigail?" he asked Mandy.

She nodded. "The news on Dad just gets better and better. I'm *so* relieved."

"Good to hear," Caleb agreed.

"You were talking to Travis?" she asked him in return, raising her brows in a prompt.

"Danielle had some car trouble."

"She's still in Colorado?" Mandy was obviously surprised by the news. "I got the impression she was going to be on the first flight out."

"They're sending us a list of parts for the car." Caleb turned the ignition key and started the Escalade.

"Is she okay?"

"She's fine. Travis helped her out. But she's frustrated to be stuck in Lyndon."

His phone rang again, but he didn't recognize the number. He flipped it open. "Caleb Terrell."

"Mr. Terrell? It's Frank Cummings here, Mountain Real Estate. I have some good news for you."

"Hello, Frank."

"We have an interested buyer."

"This soon?" Caleb was surprised. It had been less than twenty-four hours since he'd listed the ranch.

"The gentleman has been watching for opportunities in the area, and he'll be in Lyndon tonight. I'm meeting him for dinner. I was wondering if we might touch base with you by phone in a couple of hours? If all goes well, we'll want to arrange a viewing."

"I'm in Lyndon."

"Right now?"

"Right now."

"Then you should join us for dinner." Frank sounded excited at the prospect.

"Sure." Why not? If it was a serious buyer, Caleb would like to look him in the eye and make his pitch. "I'm with someone," he told Frank, his glance going to Mandy.

"Up to you, but feel free to bring them along."

"Where and when?"

"Riverfront Grill at six."

"We'll be there." He ended the call.

Mandy arched a brow. "We'll be where?"

He pocketed his phone and pulled the shifter into Reverse. "Is there any chance I can trust you?"

Mandy buckled up. "To do what?"

"To behave yourself—"

She sputtered an unintelligible protest.

"Frank Cummings has a buyer," he finished.

She froze, jaw dropping. "For the ranch?"

He reversed the SUV out of the parking spot, tires slipping to a stop on the gravel scattered on top of the pavement. Then he shifted into Drive. "Only thing I'm selling."

"But… You… That's too fast!"

"I don't think there are any speed regulations."

"Who's the buyer? What does he want? Is he going to keep it as a working ranch?"

Caleb shot her a look of annoyance. "You can't ask him questions like that. It's none of our business."

She clenched her jaw.

"I mean it, Mandy. If you come to dinner, you have to behave yourself."

"You make me sound like a child."

"You're about as emotional as one."

"Can you blame me? Really, Caleb. Can you blame me for trying to protect your land and your family—"

"It's not yours to protect."

"—from someone so determined to make such a stupid mistake?"

"You're referring to me?"

"If the shoe fits."

He glanced sternly at her one more time. "You want to come to this dinner, or not? I'm serious, Mandy. I don't want to dump you off on the side of the road, but I'm not taking a lit stick of dynamite into a business meeting."

She seemed to have to think about it for a moment.

He waited.

"I won't ask him his plans for the ranch," she finally promised, folding her hands primly on her lap, staring straight ahead and looking for all the world like a mischievous young girl.

He squelched an urge to waggle his finger at her. "You

are to say nothing but cheerful, positive things about Terrell Ranch and the Lyndon Valley."

She turned to him, tone dripping with sarcasm. "I *love* the Lyndon Valley."

"And if you could do that little pouty thing with your mouth, make the guy think he'll have a sexy, farmer's daughter living next door—"

Mandy socked Caleb soundly in the shoulder. "Watch your mouth."

"I'd rather watch yours."

"And you're worried about *my* behavior?"

He cracked a grin. "I'll be good if you will."

And then he found himself second-guessing the wisdom of that particular promise. Honestly, it might be worth letting her blow the sale if it meant they could flirt instead.

Five

At a window table at the Riverfront Grill, Mandy plucked the cherry from the top of her hot-fudge sundae. She considered it consolation food, since Caleb's sales meeting was going so well. Frank Cummings had come prepared with everything from surveyors' drawings to photographs and climate charts. Nathan Brooks, a fifty-something man from Colorado Springs, was enthusiastic and obviously interested in the ranch.

She licked the whipped cream from the cherry and popped the fruit into her mouth, catching Caleb's gaze as she chewed contemplatively and swallowed.

"I'm sorry?" Caleb turned his attention back to Nathan. "Can you repeat the question?"

"The upkeep of the house?"

"Has been regular, thorough maintenance, from paint and fixtures to plumbing and electrical."

Mandy selected one of the dessert spoons. The waiter

had provided four and set them in the middle of the table. She assumed it was to make her feel less self-conscious about being the only person at the table to order dessert. Not that she cared. It was only a chocolate sundae. Caleb was about to sell his birthright.

She scooped up a mound of whipped cream.

"The house is on a separate well?" asked Nathan.

"A well for the house. One for the outbuildings, and a third for the staff quarters."

"Those cabins are all less than five years old," Frank put in. "They're a great draw for couples or families who are interested in working at the ranch."

"What about irrigation?" asked Nathan.

"Two-hundred acres are irrigated and seeded to hay," Caleb answered.

"Four-hundred," Mandy put in.

Everyone looked her way.

"They doubled it," she explained, seeing no reason to leave the man with a misconception.

"Thanks," said Caleb.

She waved her spoon in acknowledgment, then dug into the ice cream and warm fudge.

"There are water rights on the river." Frank produced a sheaf of papers. "Spelled out in the agreement with the state."

Mandy swallowed her smooth, cool mouthful. "You might want to tell him about the review."

Both Caleb's and Frank's eyes went wide. Nathan turned to look at her. "Review?"

"The water rights are up for review." She dug her spoon in again, going for a big glob of the thick, cooling fudge. "It's a provision under the regulations. The first stakeholders meeting is this weekend. Here. In Lyndon. You must have seen the notices."

"Well," Frank put in heartily, "I don't think it's so much a review of existing—"

Nathan's eyes narrowed across the table at Frank. "You knew about this?"

Mandy stopped midbite, taking in the men's expressions. Nathan looked angry. Frank looked like a deer in the headlights. While Caleb was glaring at her in obvious frustration.

Okay, can of worms, she'd own up to that. But surely they hadn't expected to keep the review a secret. The man deserved to know what he was getting into.

Nathan pushed back his chair and threw his napkin down on the table. "Thank you for your time, gentlemen. Ms. Jacobs."

Frank quickly hopped up. "It's not what you might think. If you'd like, I can email a link to the Colorado information site."

Nathan headed for the exit, with Frank hustling along behind.

Mandy finished the bite of fudge sauce.

"You did that on purpose," Caleb accused, as he waved a waiter over to the table.

"I did not." She brandished her spoon. "But I hope you're not going to sit there and defend a plan to keep Nathan Brooks in the dark about the water review."

"No one's officially served notice to the property owners."

"You *were* going to keep him in the dark," Mandy accused. She couldn't believe it. She never would have expected it of Caleb.

"And *you* were going to behave yourself at this meeting," he countered.

The waiter stopped beside their table.

"Glen Klavitt, on the rocks. A double," said Caleb.

"I can't believe you would intentionally keep a buyer in the dark."

"Hey, I'm not his nursemaid."

"But you know the water rights are under review."

"I also know it's a routine review. And we're talking about preliminary discussions to determine if there should even be an official review."

"You've been doing your homework." Despite her disappointment in his principles, Mandy had to admire that.

"Which is what Nathan Brooks ought to have done. And what he likely would have done, *after* he'd seen the ranch and maybe fallen in love with it. And at that point, he would have been far more interested in making a compromise and listening to reason."

Okay. Mandy had to admit, when you looked at it like that, Caleb wasn't completely amoral.

"You don't lead with your flaws, Mandy."

The waiter set Caleb's drink down on the table.

Caleb nodded his thanks. "Marketing 101."

"I never studied marketing," she told him, scooping up another bite of ice cream, feeling a little like celebrating now. The sale was dead. She had some more time to find Reed.

"Did you study manipulation?" Caleb asked.

"They didn't have it as an elective at Metro State."

"Too bad. You're a natural."

"Do you really think I did that on purpose?" She hadn't meant to scare Nathan off. Then again, her heart wasn't exactly on the side of selling, either.

"I think you were very effective."

She made a show of shaking her head. "You must have studied paranoia."

He took a swig of the scotch. "Are you trying to tell me, you had no idea telling him about the review might scare him off? None at all? It never occurred to you? Not for one second?"

Okay, so as the words were coming out of her mouth, particularly when she saw Caleb's expression, of course it had occurred to her. But it didn't seem prudent to admit that now. "I was simply providing information." She stuck to her original story.

"Serves me right," said Caleb, polishing off the drink. "I never should have brought you along."

Mandy battled a twinge of guilt, setting down her dessert spoon, deciding she'd had enough of the sweet concoction.

Frank returned to the table. "I'm afraid we lost him. Permanently." Then his affable expression hardened as he focused on Mandy. "And you. I trust you learned a valuable lesson—"

"Leave her out of it," Caleb immediately put in, tone dark.

"But—" Frank began. Then he took in Caleb's expression and cut himself off.

"Win some, you lose some." Caleb tossed his credit card on the table. "Thank you for your time, Frank."

"I…" Frank snapped his mouth shut. "Right. I'll be in touch."

Caleb nodded a dismissal, and Frank deliberately straightened his suit jacket, tugged at the sleeves and headed for the exit.

"You didn't need to defend me," Mandy felt compelled to point out. Caleb standing up for her made her feel even guiltier than she had a few moments ago.

The waiter came by and smoothly accepted Caleb's credit card.

"It's none of his business what you do or do not say." Caleb swirled the ice cubes in his glass. "But it is my business. And it's my responsibility to make sure you're never in a position to do anything like that again."

The intensity of his expression made a shiver run through her. "That sounded like a threat."

He tapped his fingertips against the white tablecloth. "I don't threaten. It's a waste of time. I just deliver."

"In this instance—" she couldn't seem to stop herself from asking "—what exactly are you going to deliver?"

While she waited on his answer, he helped himself to one of the extra dessert spoons and took a scoop of the sundae. "You, Mandy Jacobs, are off the list."

Okay, that didn't sound too dire. "There's a list?"

He took his time savoring the mouthful of ice cream. "The list of people who are invited to my meetings with perspective buyers."

She took his lead and retrieved her own dessert spoon. "I thought I added value to the conversation. I was the one who knew about the four-hundred acres."

"I'll give you that," he allowed, scooping into a swirl of whipped cream. "You were doing great, right up until you blew the entire deal."

"There's another way of looking at this, you know."

"And, how is that?"

"A second chance."

"Didn't you hear Frank? That buyer is gone for good."

She concentrated on mining a vein of the gooey fudge. "I didn't mean a second chance with the buyer. I meant, a chance to make the right decision."

"The right decision?"

"To change your mind about selling the ranch."

He rolled each of his shirtsleeves two folds up his forearms. "I can't wait to see how you try to sell this."

She licked her spoon, gathering her thoughts. "I don't think you can discount the possibility that this was fate."

"You telling Nathan Brooks he might not be able to water his cattle was fate?"

"Exactly."

"Please tell me that's not the end of your argument."

"First," she counted, "Nathan asks for a meeting with Frank. Second, you and I happen to be in Lyndon. Third, I happen to be free for dinner. And fourth, the subject of the water rights came up in conversation. Those are either four separate coincidences, or it's fate."

Caleb waggled his spoon. "Wow. You really had to reach for it, but that was a pretty good spin."

"Thank you." She took a bite.

"I'm not changing my mind."

"I'm only asking for a few more days, maybe a couple of weeks."

"I don't have a couple of weeks."

"Sure, you do. You've put this false sense of urgency on a situation that doesn't—"

"The Brazilian government is the one with the sense of urgency."

"I'll look after the ranch," she offered. "I can do it. You know I can. And then it'll be waiting when Reed—"

"Reed made his choice. And you have your own ranch to run."

"Travis's there to run—"

But Caleb was shaking his head. "Your family needs you, Mandy. And I'm not chasing after Reed like some preschool nanny. I've made my decision."

She set down her spoon, struggling to hold her temper, and struggling to stay calm. "Your decision is wrong."

He set aside his own spoon. "You might not like it, but it is the right thing to do. And there's nothing to be gained by prolonging it."

"Caleb—"

"No. I've listened. I've considered your perspective—"

"You're joking, right?"

The man hadn't considered anything. He was being closed-minded and reactionary. And he was going to destroy what was left of his family.

But Caleb's jaw went hard. "I've considered your perspective, Mandy. And I disagree. And that's that."

Now her temper was taking a firm hold. "And that's the end of the discussion?"

"That's the end of the discussion."

"I see." Mandy rose to her feet, and Caleb instantly followed suit.

She drew a sharp breath, looking him square in the eyes. "Then, thank you for dinner. I can find my own way back to the ranch."

"Is this your version of a temper tantrum?"

Mandy clamped her jaw tight.

"It's dark outside, Mandy. And it's starting to rain."

She didn't respond. She was an intelligent, capable, functioning adult. She didn't need a man to escort her home on a rainy night.

Before he could say anything else, she turned on her heel and headed for the exit. At the very least, there were buses. She'd hop on a bus, and Travis or one of the hands could meet her at the end of the ranch road. They wouldn't mind.

"I'm getting us cottages at the Rose Inn," Caleb's deep voice came from behind her. "We'll drive back to the ranch tomorrow."

"Go away." He might be a sexy, intelligent, compelling man, but he was a stubborn jerk, and she didn't want anything more to do with him.

* * *

Mandy was still scowling when Caleb swung back into the driver's seat and handed her the key to cottage number six. He slammed the door shut behind him. The rain was now pounding down on the roof, and the wind was lashing the trees around them. Caleb's clothes and hair were soaked from the sprint to the small office building and back again.

"I'm in seven," he offered amicably. "We're down at the end of the river road." He pulled ahead, carefully maneuvering the SUV through the muddy ruts and around the deepest of the puddles.

"Thank you," she offered stiffly, eyes straight ahead.

"We should probably try to get away early in the morning," he continued, while the bright headlights bounced against the dripping, undulating aspen branches.

Mandy gripped the armrest and braced her feet against the floor.

"The restaurant opens at seven. That good for you?"

"I'll be ready," she said.

"Great." He supposed he'd have to be content with her agreeing to drive with him at all. Cordiality was probably still a fair way down the road.

The dark outline of a two-story cottage came into view. His headlights picked up the signs for numbers six and seven on the post out front. There were porches on both stories and a long staircase running between them.

"You're on top," he told Mandy as he brought the vehicle as close to the building as possible.

She reached for the car door handle.

"Hang on," he cautioned, opening his own door.

He quickly rounded the hood as she opened her door. His boots sank into the mud, and a river of water flowed over them.

"Hold still," he told her, putting a hand out to stop her progress. He reached into the vehicle to lift her from the seat.

"Back off," she warned him, holding up a finger.

"Don't be ridiculous." Undeterred, he slid an arm around the small of her back. "There's no sense in both of us ruining our shoes."

"I've waded through mud before."

"Bully for you." He wove his other arm beneath her jean-covered knees. "Hang on."

"This is ridiculous," she muttered, but her arms went around his neck, anchoring her to him.

He straightened and shoved the door shut with his knee. Then he ducked his head over hers and mounted the stairs.

"Key?" he asked, setting her down as they made it to the narrow shelter in front of the cottage door.

"Right here." With dripping hands, she inserted the key into the lock.

Caleb turned the door handle, yawing the door wide into the dark room. He felt for the light switch on the inside wall, finding it, flipping it, bringing two lamps to life on either side of the king-size bed.

The room was peak-ceilinged and airy, with a cream-colored love seat and two padded armchairs at the far end. The living room grouping bracketed a sliding-glass door that opened to a small balcony. The bed was covered in an English country floral quilt, with six plump pillows and a gauzy canopy. Candles and knickknacks lined the mantel above a false fireplace. And a small kitchenette next to the bathroom door completed the suite.

"They said the heater was tricky," Caleb explained to Mandy, crouching down next to the propane unit, squinting at the faded writing on the knobs.

"I'm not cold," she told him.

He pressed the red button, turning the black knob to pilot. "If you do get cold, you can adjust it up like this." He turned to find her still standing next to the open door. "Will you come and look?"

"I'm sure it's not that complicated."

"You're behaving like a two-year-old."

"Because I won't roll over and play dead? I have to wonder what kind of people you employ, Caleb. Do you have a string of yes-men who follow you around all day, never questioning your infinite wisdom?"

"No," he answered simply, deciding he liked it better when she was giving him the silent treatment. "Do you want to know how to work the heater or not?"

"Not."

He shrugged and rose to his feet, dusting off his hands. "Suit yourself."

Refusing to cater to her temper any longer, he crossed the room, bid her good-night and firmly closed the door behind him, trotting swiftly down the staircase to open his own cottage.

His suite was slightly larger than Mandy's, but with the same English country look, deep mattress, plump pillows and floral curtains. He adjusted his own heater, slipped off his wet leather boots and stripped his way out of his soaking clothes.

The cottage provided a health kit with a toothbrush, toothpaste, comb, shaving razor and cream, along with a few other necessities, including scented body wash, which he set aside in favor of the plain bar of soap.

Half an hour later, Caleb felt refreshed. He'd opened the minibar to find a light beer, chose a magazine from the selection on the coffee table and stretched out under the quilt in his boxers.

He entered the password into his phone and chose the email icon. He scrolled through the messages, finding one from Danielle labeled *stranded*. With an anticipatory grin, he clicked it open, scanning his way through a series of complaints, threats and colorful swearwords.

He responded, telling her he'd be back to the ranch tomorrow morning with a box full of auto parts and a fat, bonus check. He didn't let on that Travis had told him the whole story. He might as well let Danielle keep some of her dignity.

He dealt with the most pressing issues on his phone, then switched to the sports magazine, finding an article on his favorite basketball team. He read it and then checked the NASCAR stats. A crack of thunder rumbled in the distance, and the wind picked up outside. Sudden waves of rain battered the windowpanes, while the lights flickered, putting the room in darkness for a split second.

A few power flickers later, Caleb felt himself dozing off, and he set the magazine aside.

The next thing he knew, he was jolted awake by a deafening crash. The room was in pitch darkness, and the storm howled on outside. He rocketed out of bed, rushing to the window, guessing at the direction of the sound.

A flash of lightning revealed the Escalade was intact. But a large tree had fallen across the dirt road, crushing the low fence in front of the cottage, its topmost branches resting against the front wall. Perfect. They were going to need a chain saw before they could go anywhere in the morning.

He let the curtain drop, and as he did, a loud, long crack reverberated through the building. Before he could react, a roar shattered the air and the building jolted, wood groaning and splintering in the night.

Caleb was out the door in a shot, taking the stairs

three at a time, terrified that the tree had come through the roof and Mandy had been hurt. He flung open her door. It was either unlocked or he'd broken it down. He wasn't sure which. But his entire body shuddered in relief at the sight of her standing next to the sofa, peering out the glass doors, lightning illuminating the room like a strobe light.

"It was a tree," she told him, turning in her bra and panties. "Sheared the balcony railing right off."

He strode across the room. "Are you okay?"

She nodded. "I'm fine. Wow. That's some storm going on out there." Lightning strikes were coming one after the other, thunder following almost instantaneously.

"I don't think you're safe up here." He found himself putting a protective arm around her shoulders. His gaze went reflexively to her sky-blue bra and silky underwear. It was completely inappropriate to stare, but he couldn't help himself.

"I'm fine," she argued. "How many trees can possibly—"

Another tree cracked and crashed in the woods nearby.

She blinked at him. "This must be the storm of the century."

"Put your clothes on," he told her. There was no way he was leaving her up here.

She glanced down at her body, seeming to suddenly remember what she was wearing. She quickly folded her arms across her breasts.

"I'm not looking," he lied. "Now, let's get downstairs." He wanted a sturdy story between them and any falling debris.

Mandy crossed the room and struggled into her jeans, slipping her arms into her shirtsleeves.

Caleb tried mightily not to watch, but he couldn't stop himself from taking a few surreptitious glances.

"Should we call the office?" she asked.

"I think they've long since closed. And I'm pretty sure they know the property's getting wind damage. Nobody should go out in this."

"I guess staying here is the safest," she agreed, tucking her messy hair behind her ears as she bent to put on her boots.

She turned then, and she seemed to realize for the first time that he was nearly naked.

"I rushed up here," he defended. "I thought you might be hurt."

Her mouth tightened into a smirk. "You're a knight in shining…boxers?"

He crossed to the door and pulled it open. "You can't embarrass me."

She moved toward him. "Not modest?"

"Not at all. You can see me naked any old time you want."

"Pass," she tossed over her shoulder, striding out into the rain.

He shut the door tight, double-checking it before he followed her downstairs. Rain splattered against his hair, wind chilling his wet skin, while the lightning and thunder continued to crack through the black sky.

In his own suite, he lit a couple of the decorative candles, dried off with a towel and switched his wet boxers for his damp jeans. Going commando under his jeans wasn't the most comfortable feeling in the world, but his options were limited.

She stood in the middle of the room, hands on her hips. "I suppose you'll want the bed."

He flipped back the comforter and stretched out. The

love seat would barely fit a ten-year-old. "You're welcome to share," he told her.

"I don't think that's a good idea."

"As opposed to one of us staying awake all night? It's a big bed, Mandy."

"Can I trust you?"

He rolled his eyes. "Trust me to do what? Not to attack you while you sleep?" He leaned over and pulled back the opposite edge of the covers. "Give me a break, Mandy."

The thunder rumbled as she took a single, hesitant step forward, looking decidedly uncertain. Not that he blamed her. Despite his bold words, it was going to be a challenge to keep his hands to himself.

"Can I trust *you?*" he countered, hoping to keep things light.

"Ha. I'm still mad at you."

"Doesn't mean I'm not hot," he goaded.

In response, she marched defiantly to the bed. "You're not that hot."

"I'm sorry to hear that."

She stuck her nose in the air, turned her back and plunked down on the edge of the bed, tugging off her boots and dropping them to the wooden floor. Her socks followed. Then her hand went to the snap of her jeans, and he heard the zipper pull down, and she shimmied out of them.

Okay, he was a gentleman, and he was proud of his self-control. But, good grief. Was the woman insane?

Six

An insistent, intermittent buzzing dragged Mandy from the depths of a deep sleep. She was comfortable, toasty warm, and she sincerely hoped it wasn't time to get up yet.

As consciousness returned, she felt Caleb shift against her. She knew she should recoil in shock at having cuddled up to him while she slept. But his big body felt so good against her own, that she decided to pretend she was asleep for a few more seconds.

The buzzing stopped, and his deep, husky voice penetrated the darkness. "Yeah?"

He didn't pull away, either, and she let herself sink into the forbidden sensations. She'd kept her blouse on, while he was wearing his blue jeans, so there was no danger of intimate skin contact. Still, her belly was snuggled up to his hip, her breast against his arm and her calf against his.

"Anybody hurt?" His voice sounded stronger, and her

brain engaged more thoroughly on his words. "Good. So, how bad is it?"

She heard the rustle as he swiped a hand across his forehead, into his hairline, and she could picture him blinking his eyes open in the darkness.

"Tell her to call Orson Mallek. He can source the parts worldwide." Caleb shifted, his arm grazing her nipple, and it was all she could do not to gasp in reaction. "A week will cripple us," he said. "Tell them forty-eight hours max."

Arousal invaded her system, hijacking reason. The urge to wrap herself around Caleb and give in to her desires, to hell with the consequences, was quickly gaining traction in her brain.

"Colorado," he said into the phone.

She felt him shift, and knew he was squinting at her in the dim light, probably wondering if she was awake or asleep. It was getting to the point of unreasonable that she could have slept through the conversation.

It was time to put up or shut up.

Grabbing a final scarp of sanity, she drew away, shifting onto her back, putting some space between them.

"Call me when you know something. Thanks."

"Something wrong?" she asked sleepily, hoping against hope he'd buy that she'd only just woken up.

"A breakdown in the chassis plant."

"Is it serious?"

"Depends on how long it takes to repair." He moved to his side, propping on an elbow, facing her in the predawn glow. "We can go a couple of days before we have to start cutting back shifts. After a week, we're looking at temporary layoffs. I hate to have to do that."

She found herself curious. "How many people work for your company?"

"In that plant, a few hundred."

"Overall?"

"I don't know. Thousands, anyway."

"You have thousands of people working for you?" It defied Mandy's imagination.

"Not directly." He chuckled.

"Nobody works for me."

"And you don't work for anyone else, either. It's a whole lot simpler that way."

"Technically, I work for my dad. Though," she allowed, "that's definitely going to change for a while."

"Who'll take over the ranch?" Caleb asked, laying his head back down on the pillow. "Is Seth the heir apparent?"

Mandy thought about it. "It's hard to say. Especially with his mayor campaign coming up. Travis's the most hands-on of us all, but he's more of a day to day, roll up his sleeves guy. Seth definitely takes the strategic view, but he's not out on the range very often these days. Abigail's the organized one. She knows pretty much everything about everything."

"And you?" Caleb asked. "What's your strength?"

"I don't know. Diplomacy, maybe."

He chuckled. "You have got to be kidding me."

"Hey," she protested. "People like me. I broker compromises all the time."

"Not for me, you didn't."

"Jury's still out on that one. I predict that someday you'll be thanking me for my role last night."

"I wouldn't hold your breath."

"My point is—" she fought the urge to engage further in a debate with him about selling the ranch "—we all have different strengths."

"What about your other sister, the little one?"

"Katrina?"

"I haven't seen her yet."

Mandy resettled herself, bending one knee, which brushed up against Caleb's thigh. She let it rest there, pretending she didn't realize she was touching him. "That's right. You left before it happened."

"What happened?" There was concern in his voice.

"Nothing bad," Mandy hastily put in. "Katrina attended a fine arts boarding school in New York City. She's still in New York. A principle dancer with Liberty Ballet Company."

"Seriously?"

"I'm serious. She loves it. Then again, she always did hate the ranch."

His tone turned contemplative. "So, Lyndon Valley produced more than one city dweller."

"You two would probably have a lot in common." Mandy kept her voice flip, careful not to betray her disquiet at the thought of Caleb and Katrina. She wasn't jealous of her baby sister. She'd never cared about being glamorous before, and she wasn't about to start now.

"What about you?" Caleb asked. "Do you like the ranch, living and working so closely with your family?"

"Absolutely." Mandy couldn't imagine any other life. She loved the quiet, the simplicity, the slower pace and the wide-open spaces.

"What about when you get married?"

"Nobody's asked me yet."

"You plan to raise your children on the ranch?"

"I do." She nodded with conviction. "Kids need fresh air, hard work, a sense of responsibility and purpose."

Caleb was silent for a long moment.

"What about you?" Mandy asked. "You plan to raise your children in a high-rise apartment?"

He stretched onto his back, lacing his fingers behind his head. "That's a very long way off."

"But you do plan to have children one day."

"I don't know." He sighed. "I didn't have much of a role model for a father."

"You're nothing like he was."

"I'm nothing like your father, either." He turned to look at her. "He's a fantastic family man. I'm better at business, focused, driven and narcissistic."

"You cared that you might have to lay people off just now," she pointed out. "That isn't narcissistic behavior. It is empathetic, compassionate behavior."

He turned toward her again, his thigh coming fully up against hers, his midnight-blue gaze capturing hers in the gathering dawn. "You comfortable behind those rose-colored glasses?"

"You cared, Caleb."

"I'm not the devil incarnate. But that doesn't mean I should be raising children."

"What *do* you want to do? With your future?"

"I've been thinking in two- or three-month increments for an awful long time now."

"Okay," she allowed. "Where do you want to be in three months?"

His gaze softened on hers, and he reached out to smooth back a lock of her hair. "I can tell you where I want to be in five minutes."

Her chest hitched, and her lungs tightened around an indrawn breath. His finger traced down the curve of her cheek, along her neck, to trace the vee of her blouse. Her pulse jumped and prickly heat formed on her skin.

"You took off your jeans," he told her in a husky voice. "Why did you take off your jeans?"

"They're uncomfortable to sleep in."

"I thought it was to make me crazy."

She shook her head. "You kept your pants on, I figured we were safe enough."

His mouth curved in a small smile. "Since you cuddle in your sleep?"

"I never knew I did that." She felt as though she could fall forever into the depths of his sexy eyes. "I've never slept with a man before."

"No way."

"I was in a girls dorm in college."

His hand dropped away, and his expression turned guarded. "You're not…"

"A virgin?" She couldn't help but laugh at the guilt on his face. "Didn't I just tell you I went to college?"

"You scare me, Mandy."

She sobered, unfamiliar feelings bubbling to life inside her. She might not be a virgin, but her experience was with swaggering eighteen- and nineteen-year-olds. They were about as different from Caleb as a person could get.

"You scare me, too," she told him on a whisper.

"Scaring you is the last thing I want to do."

She nodded, and he slowly leaned in to kiss her.

His lips were firm but soft, confident as they slanted across hers. They parted, hot and delicious. And he pressed her back into the pillow, one arm snaking around the small of her back, pulling her up against him.

A surge of desire swelled inside her. Her back instinctively arched, and she parted her own lips, opening to his tongue, savoring the intense flavor of his passion. Her arms went around his neck, anchoring her, while her breasts rubbed against his chest. Her nipples went hard, tight, intensely sensitive.

He groaned, sliding his hand down her hip, over her silky panties, down her bare thigh. His kisses wandered along the crook of her neck, circling her ear, separating her blouse to kiss his way to the tip of her shoulder.

She pressed her lips against his neck, drawing his skin into the heat of her mouth, tasting salt and dried rainwater. His hand convulsed on her bottom, voice going hoarse. "You're killing me, Mandy."

"Is that good?" It felt good from her side. Very, very good.

He kissed her shoulder, kissed her neck, kissed her mouth, dragging her pelvis tight against his. "You need to tell me yes or no."

She opened her mouth to say yes.

But he pulled back, and his sober expression stopped her.

"I…" She suddenly hesitated. This wasn't college. This was far more complicated than college.

"We step over this cliff," he warned her in an undertone, "we can't come back again."

She struggled to interpret his words. "Are you saying no?" she asked in a small voice.

When he didn't answer, her stomach clenched tight. Was she being swept along on this tidal wave alone? How humiliating. She stiffened.

When he finally answered, his voice was controlled and compassionate. "I'm saying you're not the kind of woman I usually date. You need to think about this."

She pulled back farther, feeling as if she'd been doused in cold water. She hardened her tone. "Excellent suggestion."

Without giving him a chance to say anything more, she flounced out of the bed and snagged her jeans from the floor. "In fact, now that you mention it, breakfast is probably a much better idea."

She strode her way toward the bathroom, hoping

against hope the light was too dim for him to get a good view of her scantily clad rear end.

Feet apart, wearing the brand-new pair of steel-toed boots he'd purchased at the Lyndon shopping mall, Caleb chainsawed his way through the third fallen tree on Bainbridge Avenue. The physical work felt good, and tearing trees apart gave him an outlet for his sexual frustration.

Lyndon was a mess this morning. Mandy hadn't been far off when she'd guessed last night was the storm of the century. The wind, rain—and even hail in some places—had taken down trees, damaged buildings and sent several people to the hospital. Fortunately, no one had serious injuries.

Mandy was on the clearing crew a few hundred yards down the road. Hands protected by leather gloves, with about a dozen other people, she was hauling branches and sections of tree trunk to waiting pickup trucks. Though Caleb's gaze strayed to her over and over again, he told himself that this morning had been for the best. If she wasn't ready, she wasn't ready. And he wasn't going to push her into something she'd regret.

In other parts of town, Caleb knew many other crews were working, while construction experts, carpenters and engineers assessed the damage to buildings and other town infrastructure.

His phone buzzed in his breast pocket, and he shut down the chain saw, setting it on the ground by his feet. He stripped off his leather gloves, releasing the pocket button and fumbling his way into the deep pocket to address the persistent buzzing.

"Terrell here," he barked shortly.

"Caleb? It's Seth."

"Oh, hey, Seth." Caleb swiped back his sweaty hair. "Everything all right with your dad?"

"Better and better. They're going to start some physical and speech therapies in a few days."

"That's great news."

"Agreed. Listen, have you seen any of the storm coverage? It's all about how bad Lyndon got hit last night."

"We're in the thick of it," Caleb replied, glancing around once more at the destruction. "Mandy and I are still in town."

Seth's tone turned worried. "Is she okay?"

"She's a hundred percent. We're helping out with the cleanup."

"Good. That's a relief. Listen, the cleanup is what I wanted to talk to you about. As the president of Active Equipment, is there a possibility of you making a donation to the town? Maybe a couple of loaders."

"Absolutely," Caleb responded, wondering why he hadn't thought of it himself. "Let me see which dealers are closest, and how quickly they can respond."

"That would be terrific."

"Hey, no problem. They can use all the help they can get here."

"And...uh...Caleb?"

"Yeah?"

"Would you be comfortable with me making the public announcement? I don't want to steal your PR or anything."

Caleb got it. "But it wouldn't hurt your mayoralty campaign any to be the front man on this?"

"Exactly."

"Hey, go for it," said Caleb. "It was your idea. You deserve the credit."

"Thanks." Seth's tone was heartfelt.

"Happy to help out. Are you coming into town?"

"I'm going to try. But it may take a while. The airport's closed."

"Wow." Caleb was surprised to learn about the airport. "I'm working on Bainbridge. This thing must have hit the entire town."

"Get to a television when you can. They've got aerials."

"I'm on the business end of a chain saw for the moment. And I think power's out all over the place."

"Mandy's okay?" Seth confirmed.

"She's a trouper," said Caleb, his gaze going to where she struggled with a section of tree trunk that had to be thirty-six inches across. To his astonishment, she smiled while she worked, obviously making a joke to the man beside her.

"That, she is," Seth agreed. "I'll be there as soon as I can."

"Roger, that." Caleb signed off.

After making a few calls to Active Equipment headquarters and giving them Seth's contact information, Caleb resettled his gloves and yanked on the pull cord for the chain saw. The action restarted the engine, and he braced his foot on the big log in front of him, ripping his way through the next section of the downed cedar tree.

Working methodically, he made it to the end of the tree, sheering off branches and bucking the trunk into manageable sections. Then he glanced up to see Travis approaching, thirty feet away.

Caleb shut it down again, wiping his forehead. "Where'd you come from?"

Travis glanced around. "Whoa. This is unbelievable."

"Tell me about it. You should have heard them coming down last night. You here to help?"

"I am now." He tugged a pair of work gloves out of the back pocket of his jeans. "My original plan was to bring Danielle in to the airport."

Caleb glanced around but didn't see Danielle among the workers. "Airport's closed."

"We know that now. But she was getting pretty antsy this morning."

"Where is she?"

"I dropped her off at the coffee bar. She wasn't exactly dressed for brush clearing."

Caleb cracked a smile. "I think it would be dangerous to let her loose out here."

"She might break a nail?"

"She might get somebody killed."

Travis raked a hand through his short hair. "Yeah, she's definitely better with a computer than with power tools. She's making calls to see what her options are for getting back to Chicago."

"She can take my jet," Caleb offered, seeing an opportunity to make amends for some of the unfortunate complications of her trip to Colorado.

Caleb retrieved his phone and dialed Danielle's cell. He made the offer of the jet and asked her to touch base with Seth to make sure the heavy-equipment donation went quickly and smoothly. Then he signed off.

"That'll give her something productive to do," he told Travis.

Travis glanced around. "Where do you need me?"

"See the tall kid in the blue T-shirt?"

"At the black pickup?"

"He's keeping the chain saws fueled and sharp. Grab one, and you can start at the other end of that tree." Caleb pointed as he moved on. "If we can open up this next hundred yards, we'll have a corridor to the highway."

"Will do," said Travis. "By the way, it was nice of you to let Seth organize that equipment donation."

"His idea," said Caleb, flipping the switch and setting up to restart the chain saw. "Besides, Lyndon will be lucky to have him as mayor."

Mandy hopped up onto the tailgate of a pickup truck to take a break from the heavy hauling work. She was tired and sweating, and her shoulders were getting sore.

Somebody put a cup of coffee in her hand. She offered her thanks and took a grateful sip. She normally took cream and sugar, but she wasn't about to complain. It was nearly two in the afternoon, and she'd been hauling brush steadily since breakfast.

Her animosity toward Caleb had been forgotten when the sun came up and they saw what the storm had done. In fact, it seemed frivolous now to have even been thinking about lovemaking this morning.

"You eaten anything?" Danielle's voice startled Mandy, and she glanced up to see the perfectly pressed woman picking her way across the debris-strewn road to the pickup truck.

"What are you doing here?" Mandy couldn't help exclaiming.

Danielle was wearing slacks today, but they looked like expensive, dove-gray linen, and they were topped with a jewel-encrusted mauve sweater and paired with pewter-colored calfskin boots. Her makeup was perfect, and not a single hair was out of place.

"Travis brought me into town."

"Travis's here?" Mandy glanced around, but didn't catch a glimpse of her brother.

"I was hoping to catch a flight to Chicago. But the airport's closed."

As Danielle arrived at the truck, Mandy looked for a blanket or a stray piece of clothing to throw on the tailgate to protect the woman's expensive slacks. She spotted a quilted shirt, grabbed it and shook it out, laying it inside up on the tailgate and motioning to it.

"Thank you," said Danielle, awkwardly hopping up and settling herself. She snapped open her designer handbag and extracted a deli sandwich, handing it to Mandy.

"You're a saint." Mandy sighed, accepting the offer.

"You're amazing," Danielle returned. "How on earth can you work this hard?"

"Practice." Mandy took a big bite of the thick sandwich.

"Well." Danielle smoothed her slacks, setting her handbag down in her lap. She gave a delicate, self-deprecating laugh. "I've been dialing my fingers to the bone."

Mandy smiled at the joke. "Nobody expects you to do manual labor. Any more than they'd expect me to compose a legal brief."

"That's very kind of you to say."

"Don't even worry about it. Thanks for the sandwich."

They sat in silence for a moment, the sound of chain saws, truck engines and shouts surrounding them. Bainbridge Street was a hive of activity.

"I've been working with your brother Seth."

Mandy swallowed. "On what?"

"Caleb's having him coordinate a donation from Active Equipment to the town of Lyndon, loaders, backhoes, etc. He'll be on Channel Ten to make the announcement in a few minutes."

Mandy's tone went thoughtful. "Really?" Her gaze went to where Caleb was bucking up trees. "I assume it's a political stunt?"

"Move," said Danielle. "A political move. And a smart one. Everybody wins."

"I suppose they do." Though it seemed a little slick to Mandy, she couldn't say she saw any serious flaws.

"Speaking of everybody wins..." Danielle looked straight at Mandy. "I have an idea."

"For Seth's campaign?" Mandy hoped it didn't involve her. She was planning to stay firmly on the ranch and out of sight throughout the mayor race.

"For finding Reed."

Mandy swallowed, her attention perking up. "I'm listening."

"I don't know how long it normally takes to sell a thirty-million-dollar ranch. But, I'm assuming it's a while." She brushed some imaginary lint from the front of her slacks. "So, I've been thinking, and I've come to the conclusion that my best interests may be the same as your best interests."

Her gaze drifted to Caleb. "He's having a little too much fun out here. I need him back on the job, and the shortest route to that end would appear to be finding Reed."

"You think he's having fun?" Mandy couldn't help interjecting. "He hates it here. He can't wait to leave."

"So he says."

"He doesn't want to be in Colorado," Mandy insisted. And he sure didn't want to be in the Lyndon Valley, on his own ranch, surrounded by painful memories.

Danielle smiled patiently, and a wealth of wisdom seemed to simmer in her hazel eyes. "I'm not going to take that chance." Then she became all business. "Here's what we're going to do. You're going to give me your cell phone, and I'm going to dial a number, and you're going to talk to a man named Enrico. Tell him everything you know about Reed's disappearance."

Mandy hesitated. She couldn't help remembering Danielle's suggestion that they track Reed's credit-card use. She wanted to find him, but this felt a little too off the beaten path for her. "Is Enrico a code name?"

Danielle's laughter tinkled. "His name is Enrico Rossi. He's a private investigator."

"Would I be breaking the law?"

"You? No?"

Mandy felt her eyes go wide, and her blood pressure slipped up a notch. "But Enrico will?"

Danielle cocked her head. "I haven't the first clue what Enrico might or might not do. But he will find Reed."

Mandy was tempted. Frightened, but tempted. "Will I go to jail for this?"

"None of his clients have so far."

Mandy tried to figure out if Danielle was joking. "You're scary, you know that?"

"I'm practical." Danielle waved a dismissive hand. "There's an off chance he'll hack a password or two, but he's not going to steal anything, and he's certainly not going to harm anyone. And, since you won't be paying him, there's absolutely no legal trail that leads back to you."

"I won't be paying him?" This was sounding stranger and stranger all the time.

"He owes me a favor."

Mandy felt her shoulder slump. "Good grief."

"It's nothing clandestine or mysterious. I was his defense attorney. Pro bono. When I was first out of law school."

"So, he's a criminal." A criminal who could find Reed and stop Caleb from making a colossal mistake that would reverberate for generations. Where was the moral balance on that?

"He had a misspent youth."

"What did he do?" Mandy was absolutely not getting caught up with thieves and murderers, not even to find Reed.

"He was a big bad street kid, who got into a fight with another big bad street kid, who it turned out, was trying to recruit Enrico's little brother into a gang. Enrico won. He was charged with assault. I got him off."

That didn't sound so bad. In fact, it sounded kind of noble. "What happened to his brother?"

"He just won a scholarship to UIC. He wants to go into law."

"So, Enrico's a good guy?"

"Enrico's a great guy. Eat your sandwich, and we'll make the call."

It turned out that Enrico didn't sound remotely like a tough, streetwise criminal. He was articulate and seemed intelligent, and he said he was confident he would find Reed. When Mandy saw Caleb and Travis approaching the pickup truck, she quickly finished the call and disconnected.

"Thanks," she whispered to Danielle as the two men approached.

"You look unexpectedly cheerful," Travis said to Danielle.

While Caleb focused on Mandy. "You holding up okay?"

"I'm feeling optimistic," Danielle responded, sending a brief glance to Mandy.

"I'm just fine," Mandy answered Caleb. She drew a breath, both nervous and excited after her call with Enrico.

"Pretty hard work," Caleb observed.

"Piece of cake," Mandy responded with a shrug. She was tired, and she'd definitely be sore in the morning, but she still had a good few hours left in her.

Danielle retrieved two more sandwiches from her purse and passed them to the men. Both smiled and voiced their thanks, digging right in.

"Any news from the outside world?" Caleb asked Danielle between bites.

"Seth should have made the announcement on air by now. Equipment will be on a flatbed truck coming out of Northridge this afternoon. They're hoping to have the airport up and running by tomorrow. And I was able to book a couple of rooms at the Sunburst Hotel." She looked to Travis. "I guessed you might want to stay over?"

"You guessed right," he responded, glancing around at the destruction. "They'll need me another day at least."

"Mandy and I can keep our cottages at the Rose," Caleb put in. "Apparently, they're structurally sound. Though they can't guarantee we'll have electricity. But they did offer us a discount."

"I'll take the cottage at the Rose," Travis put in. "Mandy can stay at the Sunburst with Danielle. She'll be more comfortable there."

Caleb's jaw tightened, and his eyes narrowed in what was obvious annoyance at Travis's unilateral decree.

"Sure," Mandy quickly agreed. She didn't care where she slept. It wasn't as if she and Caleb had plans for a clandestine meeting.

She might have been swept off her feet in his bed this morning. But she'd had plenty of time to reframe her mind-set. Caleb had been right to suggest some sober second thought on the matter. Making love with him would have been a colossal mistake. One she had no intention of making.

Seven

All the way back from Lyndon, Caleb told himself he
had done the right thing by giving Mandy the option to
change her mind. It was the honorable thing to do, and he
didn't regret it for one minute. Though he'd desired her
beyond reason, he couldn't ignore the fact that she wasn't
worldly, she was a family friend, and compared to the
women he normally dated, she was quite innocent—in
a fresh, compelling way that even now had him wishing
he could have thrown caution to the wind.

Damn it.

He had to get her out of his head.

He pushed the door to the Terrell ranch house open,
forcing himself to walk into the quiet gloom. Without
Mandy or Danielle here, the place seemed to echo around
him. He dropped the small duffel bag he'd bought in
Lyndon onto the floor of the hall, flipped on a light and
made his way into the living room.

Ghosts of his memories hovered in every room, in every knickknack, in every piece of furniture. He'd liked it in Lyndon. It had been a long time since he'd worked that hard physically, longer still since he'd had that sense of community and accomplishment.

He wondered what was going on at the Jacobses' place. He pictured Mandy, imagined her voice, her laughter, her jokes and the convoluted rationale for her contrary opinions. He missed her arguments most of all.

The vision disappeared, and the silence of the house closed in around him. A small, family portrait propped up on the mantel, seemed to mock his presence.

He moved closer, squinting at it.

The picture had been taken when Caleb and Reed were about fifteen. His father had dressed them up, gathered them together in the living room and insisted on wide, happy-looking smiles. Seeing it now, all Caleb could remember was that his father had screamed at Reed earlier that day, pushing him to the ground and demanding he resand an entire section of fence because of some perceived flaw.

He lifted the photo. If he looked closely, he could see that Reed's hands had been bleeding. Closer still, and he could see his and Reed's brittle eyes. His mother had the haunted look that Caleb remembered so vividly. Though he'd pushed the memories away after he'd left, the fear that he hadn't known the half of his mother's anguish rushed back now.

If he'd known back then what he knew now, he might have taken a shotgun to his father. He should have taken a shotgun to his father. He'd have spent the rest of his life in jail, but his mother would have lived, and his brother would have been spared ten years of hell.

He glared at his father's expression, the false smile,

the ham fists, the mouth that had spewed abuse, sending fear into the hearts of everyone around him.

Caleb's hand tightened on the frame.

Before the impulse turned into a conscious thought, he reflexively smashed the picture into the stone hearth. Glass shattered in all directions, the wooden frame splintered into three pieces, mangling the photo. He gripped the mantel with both hands, closing his eyes, concentrating on obliterating the memories.

"And you really think selling the place will bring you closure?" Mandy's voice was soft but implacable from the entryway.

Caleb straightened and squared his shoulders. "I didn't hear you come in."

"No kidding."

"I need a shower." He turned on his heel, heading for the staircase, stripping off his shirt as he crossed the room. He wasn't fit company right now. And he wasn't going to let himself take his temper out on Mandy. What he needed was to scald some of his anger away.

Hopefully, when he finished, she'd have the sense to be gone.

He hit the top of the stairs, and pivoted around the corner, tossing his shirt to the ground and reaching for the snap of his jeans. He passed his brother's room; a shiver ran up his spine. His feet came to a halt, and he stood still for a long moment, gritting his teeth, his fists clenched, a sharp pain pounding through the center of his forehead. He swallowed hard, then kept walking, slamming the bathroom door behind him.

He twisted the taps full on and finished stripping off his grimy clothes. Then he wrestled the shower curtain out of the way and stepped into the deep tub. Under the pulsing spray, he scrubbed his body, shampooed his hair, then he stood there, staring at the familiar tile pattern until the water finally turned cold.

He turned the taps to Off, and the nozzle dripped to a stop while he valiantly tried to stuff his memories back into their box. He was beginning to realize he never should have come here.

There was a tentative rap on the bathroom door. "Caleb? You okay?"

He flung the curtain aside in frustration. "Go home, Mandy."

There was silence on the other side.

"I mean it," he shouted. The gentleman in him was exhausted, and he didn't have the fight left to keep his hands off her. She needed to get far away.

"Right," came a short, angry response. It was followed by a few footfalls and then silence.

Thank goodness.

He methodically toweled off, then rubbed a circle in the steam of the mirror. Once again, he borrowed his brother's shaving gear, telling himself that getting cleaned up, eating a decent meal and getting a good night's sleep would give him some perspective. The memories were from ten years ago, not from yesterday. It would be easier to get rid of them this time.

Finished shaving, he wiped his face and tossed the towel into the hamper in the corner of the bathroom. Naked, he turned and opened the door, and found Mandy sitting cross-legged on the floor across the hall.

He barked out a pithy swearword, while she quickly turned her head, squeezing her eyes shut.

"What the hell are you doing?" he demanded.

"I didn't want to leave," she squeaked, coming to her feet, face turned to the side, eyes still squeezed shut. "You seemed really upset downstairs."

"And you couldn't have foreseen *this?*" He wrapped a towel tightly around his waist, stuffing in the loose end.

"At our house, we don't… I mean, there are six of us living there."

"Well, there's nobody else living here." There was no need for him to cover up to cross the hall.

"Sorry."

Her contrite voice took the fight right out of him. It wasn't her fault. What the hell was the matter with him, anyway?

"Don't worry about it." Truth be told, he was more sorry about giving her an eyeful than he was about being seen naked. He couldn't care less about that.

"I'm the one who's sorry," he offered.

She opened one eye and cautiously peeked back at him.

He propped his bare shoulder against the doorjamb and folded his arms over his chest. "What are you doing here, Mandy?"

"We haven't had a chance to talk. You know, alone. Since…"

"Since you turned me down that morning in Lyndon?" It had been the topmost thing on his mind, too.

Her brows went up. "You mean, since *you* turned *me* down."

That sure as hell wasn't the way he remembered it. "You were the one who said you preferred breakfast."

"You were the one who said I should think about it."

"So?"

Her voice rose. "So, who tells a girl who's kissing him back to *think about it?*"

"Someone who's a gentleman and not a frat boy."

"I thought you'd changed your mind."

"I thought you'd changed yours."

She took a step toward him. "So, what you meant was…"

He straightened away from the doorjamb and met her in the middle of the hall, letting his desire for her pulse free once more. "What I meant was that you needed to be sure."

"I'm definitely not sure," she admitted.

"That's what I thought." He swallowed his disappointment, and he told himself he had no right to be annoyed.

In the silence that followed, she lifted her index finger and pushed it tentatively toward his bare chest. Before she could touch him, he snagged her wrist and held it fast. His gaze bore into hers. "I'm not going to let you do this to me again." He was a man, not a saint. And she'd have to practice her little seduction games somewhere else.

She took a step in, brushing up against him, her eyes going smoky, her lips slightly parted in an invitation that was clear as day. "So, your answer is no?"

He gave his head a little shake. "Maybe you'd better make sure I understand the question."

She tossed her thick, chestnut-colored hair, tipping her chin to gaze up at him, pressing closer still, and he braced himself to hold them both steady.

"The question, Caleb Terrell, is do you want to make love with me?"

Before he could form a conscious thought, his lips swooped down on hers, kissing her deeply, drinking in her sweet, fresh taste. He bracketed her face with his hands, backing her against the hallway wall, letting his fingertips explore the satin of her skin, the softness of her hair. He kissed her a second time, and a third and a fourth, desperately wishing the moment could last forever.

When he finally forced himself to stop, all but shaking

with the effort, he breathed deeply and drew back a few inches, gazing into her eyes. With the pad of his thumb, he smoothed her flushed cheek, drinking in her extraordinary beauty. When he spoke, his voice had dropped to a husky whisper. "The answer, Mandy Jacobs, is yes."

She smiled. "I couldn't stop thinking about you." Her arms twined around his neck. He hugged her close, lifting her from the floor, kissing her deeply, crossing the short distance to his bedroom.

Moonlight filtered through the window, while a glow of light cascaded in from the hallway. Caleb set her gently on her feet. She was wearing a plain, hunter-green T-shirt and soft, faded jeans. She'd discarded her boots, and her sock feet made her seem shorter than normal.

He pulled up from the hem of her T-shirt, slowly peeling it away from her body, popping it over her head to reveal a lacy, mauve bra.

"I love your underwear," he breathed.

She smiled, and her eyes glowed moss-green in the soft light.

He flicked open the snap of her jeans. "I want to see more of it." He slipped his hand beneath her waistband, leaning in for a gentle kiss, stroking his thumbs along the smooth softness of her skin. Her abdomen was flat, waist indented, hips gently rounded.

One palm strayed to the mound of her breast, cupping it through her bra, feeling the distinctive pebble beneath the wispy fabric.

She gasped in response, thrusting forward, and he circled the sensitive spot with his fingertip.

He tasted her neck, kissed his way along her shoulder, sliding her bra strap out of the way.

Her palms pressed against his bare chest, smoothing

their way down to his belly, as he used his free hand to push down her zipper.

"You're overdressed." He tugged down her jeans, slipping them off along with her socks, tossing them all to the floor. Then he stared at her for a long minute, unable to drag his gaze from her perfection.

"You're making me self-conscious," she complained.

He reached out, grazing his knuckles over her navel. "Do you have any idea how gorgeous you are?"

"I'm a sturdy little workhorse."

He grinned. "Not hardly." He slipped his hand beneath the low waist of her panties. "You're a sexy, sculpted fantasy come to life."

She met his gaze, and he could see her skepticism.

"That's not a line, Mandy." He toyed with the other bra strap, pushing it off her shoulder, staring at the picture she made, not quite believing it could be real.

With anticipation killing him, he drew her back into his arms, kissing her hot mouth, probing with his tongue, bending her backward. He tugged off the towel, then moved his hands to her bottom, pressing her close, feeling the silk of her panties against his bare skin.

Her hands went to his hairline at the back of his neck, her fingers burrowing their way upward. She kissed him back, deeply and thoroughly, small purrs forming deep in her throat.

He flicked the clasp of her bra, discarding it with the rest of her clothes, covering her bare breast with his palm, groaning at the intense sensation of her spiked nipple and the softness that molded to his fingertip.

"Tell me you have condoms," she breathed.

"Oh, yeah." There was no way he was stopping this time.

Her small fingers stroked the length of his chest, over

his belly, across his thighs, closer and closer, until he hissed in a breath. "You are definitely killing me now."

He hooked his thumb in her panties, stripping them down, getting them off at least one ankle before he reveled in her nakedness pressed against his. His mouth zeroed in on her breasts, feasting on one and then the other.

She whispered his name, her hands convulsing against his hair. He lifted her, pressed her back onto the bed and stretched out beside her. He kissed and caressed the length of her body. She dampened his neck, his shoulder, his chest, kissing her way down his abdomen, until he stopped her, pressing her onto her back, moving over her, letting his weight move between her spread legs.

He took a second with the condom.

Their gazes locked, hers a clouded jade, his barely able to focus.

He brushed his thumb across her lower lip, dipping it inside the hot cavern of her mouth. She suckled, swirling her tongue across the sensitive pad.

He kissed her hard, and she arched her back, twisting her hands into the quilt.

"I'm sure," she gasped, and he arched forward.

The second he was inside her, a roaring need took over his brain. Desire pulsed to every point of his body. His hands roamed her breasts, his lips moved from her mouth, to her shoulder, tasting everything in between.

She was all motion beneath him, her breaths coming in small gasps, her body arching to meet his rhythm, her arms rigid, head tipped back and her eyes closed shut.

He lost track of time, sensation after sensation building within him. He held on as long as he could. But when she cried out his name, and her small body convulsed, he followed her over the edge, oblivion washing over him in waves.

The roaring in his ears slowly subsided. Though his muscles were spent, he braced his elbows, worried that his weight might crush her. But he didn't want to move, didn't want to withdraw, didn't want real life crowding in on paradise.

When worry for her comfort trumped his longing, he moved off. But he bent one knee, laying his leg across her thighs, and he wrapped his arms around her, pulling her into the cradle of his body, resting a palm across her warm, smooth belly to keep the connection intact. "You're amazing," he whispered huskily in her ear.

"You're not so bad yourself."

"Glad to hear it." He kissed her lobe, thinking he could happily start all over again.

They breathed in sync for a few minutes, and even as reality returned, a strange sense of calm stole over him.

It was odd. This was still his childhood bedroom, still the family ranch. Three oil paintings of quarter horses hung on his wall. The scents of the fields wafted in the window. And the sounds of the animals punctuated the night.

But for some reason it felt softer, the edges didn't seem so sharp.

"What?" she asked, twisting her head to look at him in the half light.

"I didn't say anything."

"You sighed like the world was coming to an end."

"It's not."

"Are you upset?"

"No."

She moved to a sitting position, her expression pensive. "Regrets?"

"No." He vigorously shook his head, pulling her back

down, wrapping an arm tightly around her. "Absolutely none."

She seemed to relax, and her fingertips brushed across his chest, while her warm breath puffed on his neck. He burrowed against her thick hair and inhaled the clean, citrus scent.

"It's funny," he ventured. For some reason, he wanted to put the feeling into words. Unusual for him, but he plunged on. "This is the closest I've ever come to being content in this room."

"That's good." She twisted her neck to look up at him. "Do you think maybe we banished some demons?"

"Maybe," he allowed.

"I feel very powerful," she joked.

"Then again—" he kept it light "—it could be that you are the most fun I've had in this house since my mom made chocolate mint fudge on our eighth birthday."

She grinned. Then she sobered and drew back, eyeing him quizzically. "Wait a minute. Did I beat the fudge, or was it the other way around?"

"Not a fair comparison. Apples to oranges."

She socked him in the shoulder. "Man, did you ever miss that opportunity."

"Ouch. Sorry."

"You better be. Chocolate mint fudge. Like it could hold a candle to me."

"It could when I was eight."

"You're not making this better, Caleb."

He chuckled low.

"You know," she began, coming up on her knees, "we may be on to something here."

He reached for her, not wanting this space between them. "Oh, I think we are. And I think we should do it again."

She batted at his hand. "I meant, changing your perception of the ranch. Not just your bedroom. And not just with sex. But the whole thing."

Something cold settled into Caleb's stomach. Was she really going to turn this into a sell-the-ranch, don't-sell-the-ranch thing?

"I know exactly how we could do it," she rattled on, voice decisive.

"Mandy, don't—"

"You need to talk to Reed, *really* talk to Reed."

"How the hell did Reed get into this conversation?" Annoyance put an edge to Caleb's voice.

She stopped. She blinked.

He tried but didn't quite keep the edge out of his tone. "Last time I checked, it was just you and me in this bed."

"But… He's your brother."

"That means something completely different to you than it does to me."

Caleb knew his anger stemmed from disappointment. But what had he expected? He and Mandy were still the same people. They still had divergent goals. Nothing had fundamentally changed because they'd sweated naked in each other's arms.

She shook her head in response to his statement, her rich hair flowing with the motion. "No, it doesn't. This land, your family, Reed. They're all part of your history and your heritage. You couldn't erase them by running away when you were seventeen, and you can't erase them by selling out now."

His annoyance was growing to full-out anger. "I did *not* run away."

"Semantics." She waved a dismissive hand. "Why did you smash the picture?"

Caleb set his jaw but didn't answer. He'd smashed the

picture because he couldn't stand to see his father's smug face staring out at him one minute longer.

"Why did you smash the picture?" she repeated.

"Drop it, Mandy."

Her tone turned softer. "If you didn't care anymore, you wouldn't have smashed the picture." She gave a heartfelt sigh. "Staying away for ten years didn't fix it, did it?"

"This is none of your business," he told her firmly. It was temporary, a blip on his radar. A few days—a few weeks, max—and he'd be back to his regular life in Chicago. The ranch would cease to exist for him. And that's the way he wanted it.

"Do you think you've been repressing your true feelings?"

Suddenly, Caleb simply felt tired. He didn't want to fight with her. Mandy was the sole bright spot in all this madness.

He reached for her, urging her back down into his arms, genuinely trying to see things from her perspective.

"If it makes you happy," he told her. "Yes, I've been repressing my feelings. My childhood sucked. Reed made a stupid choice from which our relationship will probably never recover. And, I'm sorry to have to be so blunt. But there's nothing you can do to help. I know you disagree, but I'm making the right choice."

"It's—"

He pressed his index finger across her warm, swollen mouth. "For me, Mandy. It's the right choice for me."

Her green eyes turned soft and sympathetic.

He forced out a smile. "But you've made it better for right now." He couldn't resist, so he kissed her mouth one more time. "You've made things much better for right now."

Desire surging, he wrapped an arm around her waist and pulled her close. She was instantly kissing him back, her soft, sinuous body wrapping itself around him one more time.

He made love to her slowly, gently, savoring every second of the peace she offered.

Afterward, they lay still and silent for a long time.

It was Mandy who finally broke it.

"I need to go home," she whispered.

His eyes came open. "Why?" He didn't want her to leave. He didn't want her to move an inch, at least until morning.

But she twisted her neck to look at him. "It's coming up on eleven."

"You have a curfew?"

"Travis looked pretty suspicious when I left."

"So?"

Travis's interference was definitely not welcome in this. Whatever was between Caleb and Mandy was none of her brother's business.

"So, if I come home after midnight, he's going to put two and two together."

"And?"

"And, he'll be upset."

Caleb propped himself on one elbow. "Are you telling me this was a clandestine fling?" Even as he said the words, he asked himself to come up with an alternative. What were they going to do? Date until he left for Chicago? Own up to her brothers that they'd slept together?

"I think that's the best way to handle it, don't you?"

"You're an adult," he reasoned out loud. "Your private life is none of your brother's business."

Mandy laughed. "You going to tell him that?"

Caleb was willing, if that's what Mandy wanted him to do.

"I could tell him," she mused with a nod. "But then there'd be a fight."

"I'm not afraid of Travis." Caleb had no intention of lying about his relationship with Mandy.

"I meant with me, not you. And, with everything else going on, I really don't have the energy to fight Travis."

"I don't like this," said Caleb. He wanted her to stay right where she was. He wanted to hold her in his arms all night long, maybe even beyond that.

She cocked her head, defying his mood by giving him a saucy grin. "A few minutes ago, you seemed to like it just fine."

"I don't want to go sneaking around behind your family's back."

She patted his chest. "For now, let's just keep it quiet. Who knows what happens next between us. Maybe nothing."

Caleb was hoping for a lot more than nothing.

"If you go ahead with your plan to sell, you know you could be gone in a matter of days," she reasoned. There was no inflection to her tone, impossible to tell if she'd miss Caleb or not.

Then she gave a wry half smile. "You want to start world war three over something this insignificant?"

Insignificant?

"Because, believe me, Caleb, Travis is as overprotective as they come." She glanced at her watch. "I go home now, he can wonder, but he won't know. And if he doesn't know, he can't go off the deep end."

Caleb ran his fingers through her messy hair. "This is a stupid plan."

"But it's my plan." This time, there was a distinct edge

to her voice. "Some decisions you get to make, Caleb. This one is mine."

He stared at the determination in her green eyes.

"Okay," he finally agreed. He'd keep the secret. Lady's choice. And he didn't kiss and tell.

The lights were on, and Travis was still up when Mandy came through the front door of the Jacobses' ranch house. He appeared in the kitchen doorway, a screwdriver in one hand, a rag in the other.

He stared at her for a long, silent minute as she tugged off her boots and tucked her loose hair behind her ears.

He took two steps forward. "Tell me you didn't."

"Didn't what?" She steeled herself for a moment then met his gaze full-on.

"Mandy." He smacked the screwdriver and rag on top of the dining-room table. "He'll break your heart."

"I have no idea what you're talking about." She had her suspicions, but she didn't know for sure, so it wasn't a lie.

"What do I always tell you?" He came forward at an angle, giving her the impression he was circling in.

"You're going to have to be a little more specific."

"We're not like you, Mandy. We're guys. We'll say anything, do anything—"

"Caleb's not like that."

Travis scoffed out a cold laugh. "What did he tell you?"

"He didn't tell me anything. And I don't know what you're talking about." She stomped to the sofa and flopped down, picking up this month's *Equestrian* magazine and opening it in front of her. "And I really don't want to have this conversation with you."

Travis moved to the armchair across from her. "He's from Chicago, Mandy. He's not staying."

"Don't you think I know that?" Mandy didn't expect Caleb to stay. Her wildest wish was that he'd hang around long enough to meet up with Reed. Beyond that, she had absolutely no illusions.

"The women he goes out with," Travis continued. "They know the score. They expect the lies. They know they're lies."

"Caleb has not lied to me."

"Then how'd he get you into bed."

Mandy determinedly flipped her way through the pages of the magazine. "None of this is any of your damn business."

"I love you, Mandy."

"Shut up."

"He doesn't."

She glanced over the top of the magazine. "What a ridiculous thing to say. Of course he doesn't love me. Why would he love me?"

"Then why won't you believe I have your best interest at heart?"

"I'm not a child, Travis. I like Caleb. Caleb likes me. Despite your cynicism, that's all there is to it. I'm not about to get hurt. And that's all you need to know."

"Then, why were you up there tonight?"

"He needs help," Mandy answered honestly.

"And you're going to be his Florence Nightingale?"

"He needs to see Reed. The two of them need to talk, really talk. You don't know what they went through as children." She breathed deeply, absolutely sincere in her argument.

Travis sat back, his posture relaxing. "I have a pretty good idea what they went through. I knew them both quite well."

Mandy dropped the magazine and sat forward. "Then

help me find Reed. Caleb is determined to sell the ranch out from under him. He almost did it while we were in Lyndon. If I hadn't spoken up about the water rights, we might already have new neighbors. Reed needs the ranch, and Caleb needs Reed."

"You spoke up about the water rights review?"

"Yes."

"To Caleb's potential buyer?"

She paused. "It came up in conversation."

"And you think Caleb still likes you?" Travis asked on a note of astonishment.

"He understood."

"Mandy, the world isn't the happy fun place you seem to picture. People aren't sweet and kind and friendly, looking to do each other favors 24/7."

"Will you stop?"

"Reed and Caleb are grown men," Travis warned her darkly. "Neither of them is going to thank you for interfering."

Well, at least Danielle was on her side. She'd definitely thank Mandy for interfering.

"What if it was you?" Mandy asked. "What if you and Seth were estranged? Would you not want someone to facilitate your reunion? If you were about to lose the ranch, would you not want someone to help you out?"

Travis moved from the armchair and angled himself next to Mandy on the sofa. "Those two men have a very dark past. They're not going to recognize what you're doing as helpful. They're going to hate you for interfering."

"Reed would never hate me." And she had to believe Caleb wouldn't, either. Oh, she was under no illusion that he was falling for her in a romantic sense. But he had been a gentleman, more than a gentleman.

"Reed's been hurt pretty bad."

"Yes, he has," Mandy agreed. She paused, looking directly at the brother she'd loved all her life. "And he's our friend. Do you really want me to turn my back on him?"

Travis mouthed a swearword, rocking back on the sofa. "You shouldn't be sleeping with Caleb, Mandy."

"I am not going to—"

"Stop talking right now," Travis barked. "Before you have to lie to me. If you fall for him, it's going to be a disaster." He paused, his mouth turning into a thin line. "Then again, if you're sleeping with him, it's already too late."

Mandy felt her throat close up with emotion. She couldn't think about her feelings for Caleb, not right now, not when so much was at stake. "I have to find Reed."

Travis hesitated, then he reached out and rubbed her shoulder. "Okay, little sister. Okay. I'll help you find Reed."

"You will?" she managed.

"I will."

"Good." She nodded, feeling stronger already. "Great. Danielle gave me a name—"

Travis recoiled. "Danielle?"

"Yes. She wants Reed to come back, so that Caleb will go back to Chicago. There's some Brazilian deal with a ticking clock." Mandy waved a dismissive hand. "Anyway. She put me in touch with a private investigator. And he's going to find Reed for us. All we have to do is keep Caleb from selling the ranch until then."

Eight

Caleb gazed up and down the wide hallway of the main Terrell barn, overwhelmed by the magnitude of the job in front of him. He'd had his secretary calling moving and storage companies this morning, but they all said they needed an estimate of the volume to be moved and stored. So Caleb had to figure out what to keep and store, and what to sell with the ranch.

He couldn't see the point of keeping the saddles and tack. Those things they'd sell as is. They'd also sell the horses and livestock. Same with the equipment and the vehicles. Whoever bought the ranch would likely have a use for much of the equipment, and Caleb was inclined to give them a good deal if it meant streamlining the sale.

The office—now, that was a different story. His boots thumped against the wooden floor as he crossed the aisle to stare in the open door of the office. It held two desks, five file cabinets and a credenza that stretched under the

window. Some of the paperwork would stay, but a lot of it
would be personal and business records that would have
to be kept for the family. Well, for Reed. And that meant
sorting through everything.

Caleb let his shoulders slump, turning his back on that
particular job and making his way farther into the barn.
About twenty horses were stabled inside. He made a mental note to make sure the hands were exercising each of
them every day. He'd spoken briefly to their half dozen
full-time hands, the cook and with the two men who were
up from the Jacobses' place.

Everything was at least under temporary control.

A horse whinnied in one of the stalls, drawing Caleb's attention. He took a step closer, squinting into the
dim stall.

"Neesha?" he asked, recognizing the Appaloosa mare.
"Is that really you?"

She bobbed her head, seeming to answer his question.

A beauty, she was chestnut in the front, with just a hint
of a white blaze. Her hindquarters were mottled white
above a long, sleek tail.

She lifted her head over the stall, and he scratched
her nose, rubbing her ears. She'd been a two-year-old
when he left, one of the prettiest foals ever born on the
ranch. He glanced into tack room, realizing her saddle
and bridle would be easy to find using his father's ultra-
organized system. He also realized he'd love to take her
out for a ride.

Someone entered through the main door, heavy steps,
long strides, booted feet, likely one of the hands.

"Caleb?" came Travis's flat voice.

Caleb's hands dropped to the top rail, fingers tensing
around the rough board. He was under no illusion that
Mandy could keep up a lie to her brother. So, if Travis

had pressed her last night, he was likely here looking to take Caleb out behind the barn.

Caleb braced himself and turned.

Travis came to a halt, but when he spoke, there was no malice in his voice. "I guess it's been a while since you saw Neesha."

"It's been a while," Caleb agreed, watching Travis carefully. A sucker punch was no less than he deserved.

"You up to something?" asked Travis.

Caleb had no idea how to answer that question.

"Hear from any new buyers?" Travis tried again.

"Nothing so far." Caleb allowed himself to relax ever so slightly. Perhaps Mandy was more devious than he'd given her credit for.

"I'm trying to get an estimate for moving and storage." His gaze was drawn past the big double door, toward the ranch house. He couldn't begin to imagine how big a job it would be sorting through the possessions in the house. In addition to the rooms, there was the attic, the basement. He'd like to think he was emotionally ready to tackle it, but a thread of uncertainty had lodged itself in his brain.

Travis nodded. "A lot of years' worth of stuff in there."

"It's a bitch of a situation," said Caleb.

"That it is," Travis agreed. "We've got to ride the north meadow fence today. You up for it?"

"With you?"

"With me."

For a brief second, Caleb wondered if Travis was luring him away from the homestead in order to do him harm. But he quickly dismissed the suspicion. If Travis wanted to take his head off, he'd have tried by now. From everything Caleb knew and had learned, the man was tough as nails, but he wasn't devious.

"Sure," Caleb agreed. The house could wait. It wasn't as though it was going anywhere.

"I'll take Rambler," said Travis.

The two men tacked up the horses and exited into the cool morning sunshine. The meadow grass was lush green, yellow-and-purple wildflowers poking up between leaves and blades, insects buzzing from plant to plant, while several of the horses in the paddock whinnied their displeasure at being left behind.

They went north along the river trail, bringing back Caleb's memories of his childhood, and especially his teenage years. He, Reed and Travis had spent hours and hours on horseback out in the pastures and rangeland. They'd had a special clearing by the river, where they'd hung a rope swing. There, they'd swam in the frigid water, drank beer they'd bribed the hands to bootleg for them, bragged about making out with the girls at school and contemplated their futures. Funny, that none of them ever planned to leave the valley.

"I did a search on Active Equipment," Travis offered, bringing Rambler to walk alongside Neesha. "You've been busy."

"Had nothing better to do," Caleb responded levelly, though he was proud of his business achievements.

Travis chuckled. "I bet you fly around the world in that jet, going to parties with continental beauties, while your minions bring in the millions."

"That's pretty much all there is to it." Caleb pulled his hat down and bent his head as they passed beneath some low-hanging branches. He was surprise by how natural it felt to be in the saddle.

"Gotta get me a job like that."

Caleb turned to look at Travis. "Are you thinking of leaving Lyndon Valley?"

"Nah, not really. Though I wouldn't mind tagging along on one of your trips sometime, maybe Paris or Rome. I hear the women are gorgeous."

"Open invitation. Though, I have to warn you, it's mostly boardrooms and old men who like to pontificate about their social connections and their financial coups."

"You're bursting my bubble."

"Sorry."

They were silent while the horses made their way down a steep drop to a widening in the river. There, they waded hock-deep to pick up the trail at the other side, where they climbed to the flat.

"You remember the swing?" asked Travis.

"I remember," Caleb acknowledged. If they turned north and followed the opposite riverbank, instead of veering across the meadow, they'd be there in about ten minutes.

"You remember when Reed dislocated his shoulder?"

Caleb found himself smiling. It was the year they were fifteen. Reed's arm had snagged on the rope, yanking his shoulder out of the socket as he plummeted toward the deep spot in the river. He'd shrieked in pain as he splashed in, but he'd been able to swim one-armed through the frigid water back to shore.

Fresh off a first-aid course in high school, Caleb and Travis managed to pop the shoulder back into place.

"He never did tell my dad," Caleb put in.

Caleb had helped his brother out with his chores as best he could for the next few weeks, but Reed had pretty much gritted his teeth and gutted it out.

"I thought it was funny at the time," said Travis. "But five years ago, I dislocated my own shoulder. Codeine was my best friend for about three days. Your brother is one tough bugger."

Caleb knew Reed was tough. Reed had been taller and stronger than Caleb for most of their lives. He'd uncomplainingly taken on the hardest jobs. When Caleb had become exhausted and wanted to quit, risking their father's anger, Reed was the one who'd urged him on, one more hay bale, one more board, one more wheelbarrow load. He would not quit until he'd finished an entire job.

"And he never backed down from a fight," said Travis.

Caleb stilled. He let his mind explore some more of the past, remembering the day he'd walked away from the ranch. For the first time, it occurred to him that Reed probably saw leaving as backing down, and staying behind as a way of holding his ground against their father. He'd wanted Caleb to stay, begged him to stay, asked Caleb to stand toe to toe with him when it came to Wilton.

"And he hasn't changed," Travis continued. "It's a little harder to make him mad now, but once you do, stand back."

Caleb knew he'd made Reed angry. Back then he'd done it by walking away. Now he'd done it all over again by inheriting the ranch. It didn't matter that he was right. It didn't matter that Reed was misguided. The damage was done.

An image of his brother's mulish, teenage expression flashed into Caleb's brain. His throat suddenly felt raw. He knew a line had been drawn in the dust. He also knew he was never going to see his brother again.

He pressed his heels into the mare and leaned forward in the saddle, urging her from a walk to a trot to a gallop. He heard Travis's shout of surprise, and then Rambler's hooves pounded behind them.

The world flashed past, Neesha's long strides eating up the ground, her body strong beneath him, her lungs expanding, breaths blowing out. He settled into the rhythm, breathing deep, fighting to clear his mind of memories.

But the memories wouldn't stop. He saw Reed when they were seven, wrestling on their beds when they were supposed to be asleep, their father's shouts from the living room, the two of them diving under their covers, and lying stock-still while they waited to hear Wilton's footsteps on the stairs.

He saw them chasing down an injured calf when they were thirteen, waving their arms, yelling until they were hoarse, corralling it where they could look at the gash on its shoulder. Reed had held it still, while Caleb applied antibiotic ointment and crudely stitched the wound.

Unfortunately, their efforts had only served to make their father angry. He told them they'd wasted far too much time and effort on a single calf and made them work an extra two hours before allowing them to come in for a cold dinner.

But there were also good times, when Wilton had been out on the range, sometimes for days at a time. When their mother would relax and smile, and they'd play board games, watch silly sitcoms and eat hamburgers on the living-room sofa. Reed had been there for the good times and the bad. They'd struggled through homework together, commiserated with each other over unfair punishments, drank illicit beer, raced horses and teased each other mercilessly at every opportunity.

Travis shouted from behind him, and Caleb saw they were coming up on the fence-line. He pulled back on the reins, slowing the mare to a walk, forcing deep breaths into his tight lungs.

"You going for a record?" Travis laughed as he caught up. Both horses were breathing hard, sweat foaming out on their haunches.

"Haven't done that in years," Caleb managed without looking in Travis's direction.

"It's like riding a bike."

"Tell that to my ass." Caleb adjusted his position.

Travis laughed at him. "And we're going all the way around Miles Butte."

"That'll take all day." And half the night. "We'll be lucky to get home by midnight."

"You got something you have to do?" Travis watched Caleb a little too carefully, waiting for his answer.

Yes, Caleb had something he wanted to do. He wanted to see Mandy again.

But, apparently, Travis wasn't about to let that happen.

Mandy hadn't seen Caleb in two days. She'd read in one of Abigail's women's magazines that if a man wasn't into you, there was little you could do to attract him. But if a man *was* into you, he was like a heat-seeking missile, and nothing would slow him down.

Caleb definitely wasn't a heat-seeking missile. And it had occurred to her more than once over the past two days that he might have got what he wanted from her and now moved on. Maybe Travis was right, and that was the way they did it in Chicago.

Even this morning, they were taking two vehicles from the ranch to Lyndon for the first water rights review meeting. Seth, Abby and Mandy ended up in the SUV, while Travis and Caleb drove the pickup truck. It wasn't clear who had orchestrated the seating arrangements, but surely any self-respecting heat-seeking missile could have managed to get into a vehicle with her.

Mandy tried not to focus on Caleb as they turned off the highway onto Bainbridge. There was plenty to be optimistic about between her father's continuing progress at the rehab clinic in Denver and Seth getting more and more excited about the upcoming campaign. He and Abigail had been discussing and debating political issues all the way from the ranch to Lyndon. And, with Seth and their father pretty much out of the picture, Travis seemed to be relishing his new role as de facto ranch manager.

Not that Mandy was jealous.

Though, now that she thought about it, everyone in her family seemed to be moving into some kind of new phase in their lives. Except for her. Other than supporting Travis at home, finding Reed and getting the Terrell family back on track, what was next for her?

"Mandy?" Abby interrupted her thoughts from the front passenger seat.

"Hmm?"

"Can you check my briefcase back there? I want to make sure I brought all five copies of the information package."

Mandy reached for the briefcase where it was sitting on the SUV floor, pulling it by the handle to lay it flat on the seat beside her. She snapped the clasps and pulled it open.

"The green books?" she asked, thumbing her way through the rather professional-looking coil-bound, plastic-covered volumes."

"Those are the ones."

Mandy counted through the stack to five. "They're all here."

"Thanks," Abby sang. Then she turned her attention to Seth. "I've got us all at the Sunburst. You're sharing with Travis, and I'm with Mandy. I put Caleb on his own. I figured, you know, the big, bad, Chicago executive might not be used to sharing a bathroom."

Seth laughed, but Mandy couldn't help remembering

that Caleb had shared a bathroom with her at the Rose Inn. He'd seemed perfectly fine with that. Then again, they'd been trapped in a storm. It could be considered an emergency situation. But he'd worked like a dog for the next three days. And he hadn't complained in the slightest about the accommodation, the food or the hard work. He didn't strike her as somebody who required creature comforts.

She opened her mouth to defend him, but then changed her mind. She really shouldn't be thinking so much about Caleb. She should be thinking about Reed, and how to find him, and how soon she could reasonably touch base with Enrico Rossi and check the status of his investigation. Or maybe she could call Danielle directly. Perhaps she'd heard something from Enrico.

Seth pulled into the parking lot at the side of the Sunburst Hotel. Travis's pickup truck was already parked, and he and Caleb were getting out. Mandy watched Caleb's rolling, economical movements as he pulled a small duffel bag from the box of the pickup truck. His gaze zeroed in on the SUV, finding hers as he strode across the parking lot toward them.

She quickly looked away and concentrated on climbing out the back door. He swung open the back hatch and began loading his arms with their luggage. Travis followed suit. Seth grabbed the last bag, and beeped the SUV lock button. Mandy was left with nothing but her shoulder bag to carry into the lobby.

Caleb fell into step beside her.

"How're you doing?" he rumbled.

"Just fine," she told him primly, concentrating her focus on the short set of concrete steps that led into the glass entrance.

A set of double glass doors slid silently open in front of

them, welcoming them into the gleaming high-ceilinged, marble-floored, floral-decorated lobby. Pillars formed a big circle around a patterned tile floor, while the service desks formed an outer ring in front of the walls.

"I've got a copy of the confirmation," Abby announced, slipping a sheaf of papers from a side pocket in her bag.

"Let me get the check-in." Seth strode up to a uniformed woman at the registration desk.

Caleb lengthened his strides after Seth, leaving Mandy behind. He caught up and put his credit card on the counter. Seth immediately shoved the card back toward Caleb. The two men had a brief debate, and it looked like Seth was the one to back off.

Mandy positioned herself beside a pillar, out of the route of direct walking traffic, next to Abigail and the luggage.

A few minutes later, Caleb returned to them.

"Ladies." He nodded. "I assume these are your bags?" He scooped up their suitcases.

"Those are ours," Abigail confirmed.

"Then, right this way. You're on the tenth floor. As am I, and Caleb and Seth are on seven."

"One second," said Abigail, finding a glass-topped table to set down her briefcase.

She opened it, pulled out two of the green packages and took a few steps across the lobby to hand them to Travis. "Lunch is at the Red Lion next door. The meeting starts at one o'clock. We have dinner reservations at the Riverfront Grill. And then I thought we'd go to the Weasel." She did a little shimmy as she mentioned the name of the most popular dancing bar in Lyndon. "It's Friday night, so they'll have a band."

Travis took the books from her hands, giving her a mock salute. "Works for me. See you guys in a few."

Caleb headed for the elevator, and Mandy fell into step behind him.

On the tenth floor, they exited, finding their room five doors down. Abby inserted the key card, holding the door open for Caleb with the bags. Mandy brought up the rear.

"This looks nice," Caleb noted politely, setting the bags on the padded benches at the foot of each of the queen-size beds. The room had a small sitting area near a bay window with a view of the town. The two beds looked thick and comfortable, and the bathroom appeared clean, modern and spacious.

"I'll see you both at lunch," he finished, heading for the door.

He opened it, got halfway out and then stopped, turning back. "Mandy? You have a minute? I've got something I want to ask you about, but it's buried in the bottom of my bag." He gestured into the hallway. "You mind?"

Surprised and confused, and worried it might have something to do with the sale of the ranch, Mandy nodded. "Uh, sure. No problem." She moved after him, telling herself it couldn't be a sale. Not this fast. Not without any warning.

"Great." He flashed a smile at Abigail. "Thanks."

Outside in the hallway, they moved three doors farther down. Caleb inserted his own key card, opening the door to a larger room with a king-size bed and a massive lounge area beside a pretty bay window.

They entered the room. He dropped his bag on the floor. The spring-loaded door swung shut and, before she knew what was happening, Mandy was up against the back of the closed door. Caleb's hands had her pinned by her wrists, and he was kissing her hard and deep.

She was too stunned to move. "What the—"

"I've been going crazy," he groaned between avid kisses. "You're making me crazy. I thought we'd never get here. I thought we'd never get checked in. I thought we'd never get a second alone."

Mandy recovered her wits enough to kiss him back. So, not the sale of the ranch. And okay, this was definitely a heat-seeking missile.

She relaxed into the passion of his kisses.

His lips moved to her neck, pulling aside her shirt. A rush of desire tightened her stomach, tingling her skin. Her eyes fluttered closed and her head tipped back, coming to rest against the hard plane of the door as her toes curled inside her boots.

"I don't understand," she managed to mutter, clinging to his arms to balance herself. "You've ignored me for two days. I didn't hear a word."

"That was Travis. He used every trick in the book to keep me away from you." Caleb pulled back. "What did you tell him, by the way?"

"I didn't… Well, I mean, I didn't *tell* him. But he knows."

"Yeah, he knows," Caleb agreed. "But can we talk about your brother later? I figured we've got about three minutes before they come looking for us."

She blinked at him in astonishment. "You don't mean?"

"Oh, man. I *wish*. But, no. I was only planning to kiss you some more."

The regional water rights review meeting was shorter than Mandy had anticipated. The state representative introduced the process and told participants how they could provide written comments in advance of the next meet-

ing. Having five people attend from the Jacobs and Terrell families, along with dozens of other ranchers from
the Lyndon Valley area served its purpose in showing
the organizers the level of interest from the valley and
from the ranching community.

There were also a number of people representing non-
ranching interests. That had been one of Seth and Abigail's concerns, that ranchers might be pushed out as the
area tried to attract newer industries.

Caleb asked questions, and Mandy was impressed with
both his understanding of the process and his ability to
zero in on the significant details. If she found Reed, and
if he returned to the ranch, she hoped Caleb would stay
involved until the end of the review. Even if he had to
do it from Chicago.

As the meeting broke up, and the group made their
way toward the doors of the town hall, Abigail linked
an arm with Mandy. "Did you bring along a dress for
tonight?"

"A what?"

"A dress. You know, that thing that replaces pants on
formal occasions."

Mandy gave her sister a look of incredulity. "No, I
didn't bring a dress." Why on earth would she bring a
dress? This was a community meeting. In Lyndon.

"Well, we've got a couple of hours before dinner. Let's
go to the mall and be girls for a while."

Mandy glanced over her shoulder at Caleb. She'd been
hoping to steal a few more minutes alone with him before
they all convened for dinner. "I'm not sure—"

"Come on. It'll be fun." Abigail raised her voice.
"Wouldn't you guys like to escort two gorgeous women
out on the town tonight?"

Travis stepped up. "Why? You know some?"

She elbowed him. "Mandy and I are going for a make-over."

"Great idea," said Travis, voice hearty. "You two ladies take your time. Have fun."

Mandy shot Caleb a helpless look.

He came back with a shrug that clearly stated "see what I mean?"

"Fine," Mandy capitulated, mustering up some enthusiasm, even as she wondered whether Travis had co-opted her sister to the cause of keeping her and Caleb apart.

"I haven't been in Blooms for ages," said Abigail, towing Mandy toward the SUV. She called back over her shoulder. "You guys okay to walk back to the hotel?"

Seth waved them off. "We'll see you at the restaurant."

Abigail hit the unlock button for the vehicle, and its lights flashed twice. "They can go find a cigar bar or something."

"Did Travis put you up to this?" Mandy asked across the roof of the vehicle.

Abigail gave her a blank look. "What do you mean? Why would Travis care what we do?"

Mandy peered closely at her sister. Abigail wasn't the greatest liar in the world. And she always had been much more interested in hair, makeup and fashion than Mandy. Maybe this was some kind of a bizarre coincidence.

"So, you just want to go shopping?"

"No," said Abigail. "I want to go shopping, hit the hair salon and get our makeup and nails done. I'd also suggest a facial, but I don't think we have that kind of time."

"Fine." Mandy threw up her hands in defeat. "Let's go be girls."

Abigail grinned and hopped into the driver's seat.

They drove the five miles to Springroad Mall, parked next to the main entrance, stopped to make sure the salon could fit them in later in the afternoon, then made their way through the main atrium to Blooms, the town's biggest high-end ladies' wear store. It occurred to Mandy that the last thing she'd purchased here was a prom dress.

"Something with a kick," said Abby, leading the way past office wear and lingerie. "I want a little lift in my skirt when I'm dancing."

"What happened to you in Denver?" Mandy couldn't help asking.

"I realized life was short," Abigail responded without hesitation. "I should be out there having fun and meeting people. So should you." She stopped in front of a rack of dresses.

"I'm really interested in the campaign," Abigail continued. "But I'll admit, at first, I wasn't crazy about the idea of spending so much time in Lyndon and Denver. But now I'm really looking forward to it. I'm going to stretch my wings."

Suddenly, Mandy become worried. "You're not planning to leave the ranch, are you?" They'd already lost one sister to the bright lights of a big city.

"Of course not. Not permanently, anyway. But I do want to test other waters. And this seems like a good time to do it." She held up an emerald-green dress. "What do you think? Does the color go with my hair?"

Abigail's hair was shoulder length and auburn. Colors could be challenging for her, but the green was perfect.

"Absolutely," Mandy replied.

A salesclerk arrived, offering to start a dressing room for each of them. She took Abigail's choice of the green dress, and they moved on to the next rack.

Abigail quickly selected another. "You should go for red," she exclaimed, holding up a short, V-necked, cinnamon-red dress. It had black accents and a multilayered skirt that would swirl when she danced.

"Oh, sure," Mandy drawled sarcastically. "That looks just like me."

"That's the point. 'You' are blue jeans and torn T-shirts. We need to find something that is completely not you."

"My T-shirts aren't torn," Mandy protested. Okay, maybe one or two of them were, but she wore those only when she was mucking out stalls or painting a fence.

Abigail waved the dress at the salesclerk, who promptly took it from her arms and whisked it off to the dressing room.

Abigail's next choice was basic black. She considered one with a sequined bodice, but discarded it. Mandy had to agree. They were going to the Weasel. It was a perfectly respectable cowboy bar, but it wasn't a nightclub.

They ended up with four dresses each. Mandy considered they were all too formal, but her sister seemed to be having such a good time, she didn't want to be the wet blanket.

In her dressing room, she put off the red dress to the very last. She tried a strapless, straight-skirted design in royal blue, but they all agreed the neckline didn't work. Then a basic black cocktail dress, which was too close to one of the few she already owned. Then she tried a patterned, empire-waist, knee-length concoction, with cap sleeves and a hemline ruffle. It made her look about twelve. Abigail actually laughed when she walked out to model it.

Abigail had already decided to go with the green, so she was waiting in her regular clothes when Mandy exited the dressing room in the red dress.

Her grin was a mile wide. "It's stunning," she pronounced.

The salesclerk nodded her agreement. "I wish I had legs like that," she commented, looking Mandy up and down. "It fits you perfectly."

Mandy glanced to her legs. She didn't see anything particularly interesting about them. They held her up, helped her balance on a horse and could walk or jog for miles when necessary. That's all that counted.

"You probably want to shave them before we go out."

"Thanks tons, sis."

"But I've never seen you look so beautiful," Abigail declared. "You absolutely *have* to get it."

"I don't know when I'll ever wear it again." Mandy glanced at the price tag. It was about three times as much as she'd ever spent on a dress before.

"Well, you'll wear it tonight," said Abigail.

"And after that?"

"After that, who knows. You're about to become the sister of the Mayor of Lyndon."

The salesclerk gave Abigail a curious look.

"Our brother Seth Jacobs is running for mayor this fall," Abigail put in smoothly. "Make sure you vote."

"There'll be the swearing-in dance," the clerk offered to Mandy. "And that's always formal."

"We're only going to the Weasel tonight," Mandy noted, considering different angles in the mirror.

Okay, so the dress did look pretty darn good. It accentuated her waist. It would twirl enticingly while she danced. And it showed just enough cleavage to be exotic without being tacky. She wouldn't mind Caleb seeing her in this.

Behind her, in the mirror, the salesclerk waved a dismissive hand. "You can wear anything to the Weasel.

Lots of the younger girls dress up to go there, especially on a Friday night."

"There you go," said Abigail. She glanced at her watch. "You'd better made a decision quick because we have to get to the Cut and Curl."

Mandy drew a breath. Okay. The red dress it was. Her lips curled into an involuntary smile. "You talked me into it."

Nine

If Mandy was trying to drive Caleb stark raving mad, she was certainly going about it the right way. Her hair was up. Her heels were high. And the professionally applied makeup had turned her face from beautiful to stunning.

Her sassy red dress was enough to give a man a coronary.

When they walked into the Weasel, he hadn't even bothered asking her to dance, simply swirled her out onto the crowded dance floor and wrapped her tightly in his arms, before anybody else could get their hands on her. Since then, he'd been shooting warning glares at any guy who dared look twice.

Abigail was also quick to attract her share of partners. Caleb and Seth parked it at the bar, ordering up a round of beers.

Once he recovered the power of speech, Caleb put his lips close to Mandy's ear, keeping the volume of his voice just above the music of the country band. "You look gorgeous."

"You like?" she asked.

"I love."

She grinned at him, showing straight, white teeth, while her eyes flashed emerald. "Abby made me buy it."

"Abigail's my new favorite person."

"She'll be thrilled to hear it."

He spun Mandy around, then smoothly pulled her back against his body. "You should do this more often."

"Dance with you?"

"Well, yeah. That, too. But I meant dress up."

She arched a brow. "Something wrong with my blue jeans?"

"Don't be so sensitive. I prefer silk to denim on my dates. Deal with it."

"Well, I prefer blue jeans to suit jackets."

Caleb frowned at her. Then he made a show of glancing around the crowd. "Any casually dressed guy in particular catch your eye? I could dance you over and let him cut in."

"Sure," she teased right back. "What about the guy in the yellow hat?"

Caleb shook his head. "Looks a little too old for the likes of you."

"The one with the red boots?"

"Too short."

"Well..." She continued to scan the room before returning her attention to him. "Okay, what about you?"

"I'm wearing a suit. And I'm already dancing with you."

"A girl, Caleb. Pick out a girl. Who looks good to you?"

He kept his eyes fixed firmly on her. "I'm dancing with her."

"That's a cop-out."

"It's the truth. If there are any other girls in this room, I didn't notice."

"Smooth talker," she told him, but their gazes locked and held.

"What are you doing later?" he rumbled.

"I'm rooming with my sister."

"This is ridiculous," he griped, frustrated by the barriers that kept flying up in their way. "I feel like we're in high school."

"You think if it wasn't for Abigail, I'd be jumping into bed with you?"

Her question surprised and embarrassed him. Was he being presumptuous? Had he been that far wrong in reading her signals? Had he imagined her response to his lovemaking?

Sure, they'd argued afterward, but then they'd made love again. And she'd been all he could think of ever since, despite the fact Travis had kept him away from the ranch and out of cell range for two long days.

Did Mandy feel differently?

"I'm sorry," he began, feeling like a heel. "I didn't mean—"

"That's the problem, Caleb." Her look was frank. "I don't know what you mean. I just spent two days wondering what you mean."

"What I mean is that I like you, Mandy," he answered her as honestly as he could. "I like you a lot. I think you're beautiful and exciting and real. And I can't seem to get enough of you. I want to spend every minute in your company." His voice rose in frustration. "And I want to ditch all of your siblings so they'll stop getting in my way."

She broke into a smile. "That was a good answer."

"Thank you," he grumbled.

"But it's okay if you just think I'm sexy."

"I think you're that, too."

Her expression sobered. "When I didn't hear from you, I thought maybe once was enough."

"Twice," he corrected.

"Twice is enough?"

"No! I meant we did it twice already." He gathered her closer, adding some intimacy to the conversation by putting his mouth closer to her ear. "Twice is definitely not enough."

"You want to pick a number?" There was a thread of laughter in her tone. "That'll keep me from guessing where this is going and when it's going to end."

"Fifty," he told her.

"Ambitious."

"Always."

The band ended the song with a pounding drum solo, and the lead singer announced they were taking a break.

Abigail appeared next to them, commandeering Mandy for the ladies' room, and Caleb wound his way toward the bar.

He ordered a beer.

Travis stepped up. "Make it two."

"Find someone to dance with?" asked Caleb.

"Not a problem. I went to high school with half the people here."

"I recognize a few faces." Caleb glanced around the room, seeing at least a dozen people he'd known as a teenager.

The bartender set two bottles of beer on the bar, and Caleb handed him a twenty. He and Travis turned to face the crowd, Caleb scanning for Mandy.

"I see the way you're looking at my sister." Travis took a long swig of his beer.

Again? Caleb *really* didn't want to have this conversation. "Every man in the room is looking at your sister."

"Every man in the room isn't dancing with her."

"Only because I won't let them."

Travis opened his mouth to respond.

But Caleb interrupted him, squaring his shoulders as he angled to face Travis. He was getting this over with here and now. "You've got to back off, man. She's a grown woman."

The piped-in music throbbed through the speakers, and a few dancers took the floor again.

"You don't have a sister."

Caleb crossed his arms over his chest. "I don't. But that doesn't change anything."

"It would change your attitude."

"Let's assume my attitude is not going to change in the next five minutes."

Travis took another pull on his bottled beer. "Yeah, I know."

"She's a smart woman, Travis. She's realistic and self-confident, and I'm not pressuring her to do anything."

"I'm backing off," said Travis.

The statement surprised Caleb, leaving him at a loss for words. Thanking Travis didn't seem remotely appropriate. So, he took a drink instead.

Seth appeared from the crowd. "What's going on?"

Caleb shot Travis a sidelong glance, wondering what he was going to say to his brother.

"Not much," Travis responded with a shrug.

Seth signaled for a beer and parked himself next to Caleb, facing the room along with them. "I think we're going to have to keep an eye on our sisters tonight."

Travis coughed out a laugh. "You think?"

"I never think of them as particularly beautiful," Seth continued. "But they clean up pretty good."

It was Caleb's turn to laugh. "Your sisters are drop-dead gorgeous, Seth."

"I know," said Seth in some amazement. He scooped a handful of peanuts from the bowl on the bar. "I'm picturing them on the campaign trail."

"What trail?" Travis challenged. "You're running for mayor, not governor."

"There'll still be photo ops. What do you think? One on each arm?"

"You'll look like Hugh Hefner."

"Hmm," Seth mused. "Guess I'd better rethink that."

At the far side of the room, Mandy reappeared with Abigail.

Men immediately took notice, sending interested gazes and shifting themselves in the women's direction, some of them obviously setting up to make a move. Caleb abandoned his beer and pushed away from the bar, setting a direct course for Mandy. Seth and Travis could look out for Abigail. But Caleb wasn't letting Mandy out of his sight.

Back in the hotel room, Mandy stripped off her high shoes. Abigail followed suit, stretching her bare feet out on an ottoman in their compact sitting area.

"My feet are definitely not in shape for strappy sandals," Abigail complained.

"I hear you." Mandy flopped down on the opposite armchair, stretching out her own sore feet, sharing the ottoman. She liked to think she was pretty tough, but she'd definitely been defeated by a dance floor. By midnight, even a few more minutes in Caleb's arms hadn't been enough of an incentive to add an extra blister.

"Felt a little like Cinderella, though, didn't it?" asked Abigail.

"Tomorrow, we go back to cleaning the fireplace."

"Well, horse stalls," said Abigail. "At least, that's your fate. I've been getting away with a lot of office work lately."

"I hate the office work."

"Lucky for me."

Mandy plucked at the silky layers of her dress. "Do you think the campaign is going to keep you in Lyndon a lot?"

Abigail shrugged. "More than usual, for sure. Why?"

"It's been awfully quiet at home."

Abigail grinned at her. "You missed me?"

"I did," Mandy admitted. "With Mom and Dad staying at the rehab center, and you and Seth in Denver and Lyndon, and Travis always out on the range, it'll just be me at lunch and probably just me at dinner."

"I think Travis likes his new role," said Abby. "With no Dad and no Seth, he's going to have a lot more responsibility."

Mandy had to agree. Travis seemed very happy. Once again, she got the feeling she was the only one left behind.

"Are you suffering from empty-nest syndrome?" Abigail asked, compassion in her dark, hazel eyes.

"Maybe I am," Mandy realized. "Weird. I never thought about how much my life depended on the rest of the family being there. It's like nobody needs me anymore."

"The ranch can't run without you and Travis."

"Without Travis, maybe. But you're the one who does

the paperwork. The foreman knows what to do day to day. The hands know what to do. I'm... Okay, this is depressing. I think the Terrells need me more than my own family."

Abigail's eyes narrowed. "The Terrells?"

"Getting Reed back." Mandy was surprised Abigail didn't immediately understand. "Caleb's off on this crazy 'sell the ranch' tangent, and Reed's lying low. And somebody has to knock some sense into the both of them."

Abby moved her feet to the floor and sat forward in her chair. "They're grown men, Mandy."

"That doesn't mean they have a brain between them."

"That doesn't make it your responsibility."

Mandy shook her head. Her sister wasn't getting this. How had nobody else noticed? "The universe is out of balance, Abby. It has been for ten years. I love Reed."

"We all love Reed."

"There you go. I can't abandon him at a time like this, can I? He's my third brother."

Abby's face winkled in consternation. "Do you think there's any chance." She paused, watching Mandy carefully. "Any chance at all that—I mean, right now—you're somehow substituting Reed for your own family."

"I'm not—"

Abigail held up a hand. "Hear me out. We're all busy. And you're feeling adrift. And along comes this very juicy family problem that you think you might be able to solve."

"A *juicy problem?* You think I'm getting some kind of emotional satisfaction out of Caleb Terrell threatening to sell his family's ranch?"

"I think you're like a moth to a flame. Someone's hurt? There's Mandy. Someone's upset? There's Mandy. Two people in a dispute? There's Mandy."

"You say that like it's a bad thing."

"It's not a bad thing. It's a great thing. And it's an important role, *in your own family.* But when you start franchising out, it's a problem."

"This is Reed Terrell, not some stranger I picked up on the street."

Abigail chuckled at that. "All I'm saying is don't get too invested in Reed and Caleb Terrell. This may not be a problem you can solve."

Mandy's hand clamped down on the padded arms of the chair. In her mind, failure was not an option. "I have to solve it."

"And, if you can't?"

Mandy wasn't going to think about that right now. Reed gone from the Valley forever? Someone other than the Terrells living down the road? And Caleb gone, with no reason to ever return.

She hated to admit it, even to herself, but she'd started hoping he'd reconnect with Lyndon Valley, maybe come back once in a while. He did have his own jet. And then, they could...could...

Okay. Shelving that thought for now.

Abigail was watching her expectantly. "And if you can't?" she repeated.

"If I can't get them to reconcile," Mandy responded breezily, "then, that's that. Reed will move and life will go on."

There was a long pause. "Why don't I believe you?"

"Because you're naturally suspicious. You have that in common with Travis."

"Ha. I'm naturally fun and exciting." Abigail was obviously willing to let the argument go. "Did you see all the guys who asked me to dance down there?"

Mandy smiled at her sister's exuberance, forcing herself to relax again. "Green is definitely your color."

"I'm wearing it more often. Five of them asked for my number."

"Did you give it out?"

"Nah. I'm not particularly interested in cowboys. What about you?"

"Nobody asked for my number."

Abigail's dark eyes glowed with interest. "I think Caleb's already got your number."

Mandy felt her cheeks heat.

Abigail sat up straight, staring intently. "So, I'm not crazy. You are into him."

"He's a good guy," Mandy offered carefully.

"You just told me that he's trying to sell the ranch, and you're trying to stop him. That doesn't sound like a good guy."

Mandy's cheeks grew hotter still. "Okay," she allowed. "Aside from that particular character flaw, he's a good guy."

Caleb was misguided, that was all. She was confident he'd eventually see the light. Assuming she could keep him from selling the ranch between now and then.

"He's definitely hunky," said Abigail.

Mandy nodded. There was no point in pretending she was blind. "Sexy as they come."

"So?" Abigail waggled her brows. "Did he kiss you?"

Mandy hesitated, wondering how much, if anything, she dared share with her sister.

"He *did,*" Abigail cried in triumph. "When? Where? I want the details."

A few beats went by in silence.

"Are you *sure* you want the details?" Mandy asked, a warning tone in her voice.

"Yeah."

Mandy screwed up her courage. "Everywhere."

Abigail blinked in confusion. "What do you mean?"

"I mean, he kissed me *everywhere*."

Abigail's eyes went round. "We're not talking geography, are we?"

Mandy shook her head, a secretive grin growing on her face.

"When?"

"Two days ago."

"At the ranch?"

"His ranch."

"You didn't?"

"We did."

Abby plunked back in her chair, her expression a study in shock.

"Then I didn't hear from him afterward." Mandy found the words rushing out of her. "And I thought, okay, that's it, he's from the big city, and it was a one-night stand, and I can handle it. But then we got here—"

"And he made that stupid excuse to take you down to his room."

"Yes."

"And?"

"And it was like no time had gone by. He grabbed me, kissed me, talked about going crazy for not seeing me." For Mandy, it had been both gratifying and confusing. Her emotions had done a complete one-eighty in the space of about ten seconds.

"So, why didn't he call you?"

"Out on the range. Out of cell service. Apparently Travis was keeping him busy, and he didn't have a chance to see me. He said he tried."

"And while you were dancing tonight?" asked Abigail. "Did he proposition you again?"

Mandy nodded. That appeared to be the thing about a heat-seeking missile. They didn't leave you guessing.

Abigail's brows went up. "And you're sitting here with me, because…?"

The answer to that was pretty obvious. "Because two of my brothers and my sister are in the same hotel, and I don't want to upset anyone."

"You think *I'll* be upset because you spend the night with Caleb?"

"I think you'll be… I don't know." Mandy tried to put it into words. "Disappointed?"

"You're twenty-three years old. Besides, you already did it once. You think my delicate sensibilities can't stand being five rooms away while you have a sex life?"

"And there's Travis."

"What's Travis got to do with this?"

"He warned Caleb to keep his hands off me."

Abigail sputtered out a laugh. "Grow up, Travis. It's none of his damn business."

"I know that. And you know that. And believe me, that's Caleb's opinion. But I don't want to upset Travis."

Abigail sat forward again. "Mandy, honey, this family's emotional health is not your responsibility. I'm not suggesting you sleep with Caleb or you don't sleep with Caleb. What I am suggesting, is that you make up your own mind. You're allowed to do that."

It wasn't as simple as Abigail made it out to be. In families, people had a responsibility to the group, they couldn't just selfishly think of themselves alone.

"You think that when I date a guy, I'm worrying about your opinion?" Abigail asked.

"Well, I'd never—"

"I don't. And neither does Travis when he's dating a woman. And you shouldn't, either. Now." Abigail brought her palms firmly down on her lap. "If the rest of us weren't here, what would *you* do?"

Mandy pondered her sister's question. If she had it to decide all on her own, remembering their lovemaking from last time, thinking about his words and her feelings on the dance floor, taking into account that Caleb was here only temporarily?

Mandy bit down on her lower lip.

Abigail waited.

"I'd already be down the hall in his room," she admitted. "I'd be with Caleb."

Abigail's grin was a mile wide.

Three minutes later, standing barefoot outside Caleb's hotel-room door, Mandy was forced to tamp down a swell of butterflies battering her stomach. She was pretty sure he'd be glad to see her, but there was no way to be positive. Other than to knock on his door.

Right.

She brushed her palms against the skirt of her red dress, took a deep breath, glanced both ways down the corridor and knocked.

After only a few seconds, Caleb opened the door. His expression registering surprise, but the surprise was followed quickly by a broad smile that lit the depths of his blue eyes.

He reached for her hand, tugging her quickly inside the room.

"Hey, Mandy," he whispered gruffly.

As the door swung shut behind her, his lips came down on hers in a long, tender kiss.

He pulled back, grin still firmly in place as he smoothed back her hair. "You're here."

She couldn't hold back her answering smile. "I am."

"Can you stay?"

She nodded, and he drew her into a warm, enveloping hug, wrapping his body possessively around her.

For some reason, she suddenly felt trapped. "Uh, Caleb?"

"Hmm?" he asked between kisses.

"I know you probably want to jump straight into bed."

He immediately pulled back again, his hands gently, loosely cupping her bare shoulders. "Hey, no."

There was genuine regret in his eyes. "I'm sorry about what I said earlier. That was presumptuous and disrespectful. You being here, in my room, doesn't mean anything you don't want it to mean." His words sped up. "Seriously, Mandy. No pressure."

Her heart squeezed with tenderness. "I'm not saying we shouldn't go to bed at all. I just thought, maybe first—"

"You want a glass of wine?" He took her hand and led her to the big sitting area at the far end of the huge, rectangular room. A big, bay window overlooked the river and the moon hung high above the mountains. It was a clear night, with layers of stars twinkling deep into space.

"Wine sounds good." She perched on one end of the couch.

"We can talk," he said as he moved to the wet bar, stopping to turn on some soft music, before returning with two glasses of red wine. "Merlot okay? I can order something else if you'd like."

She accepted the glass. "This'll be fine."

He sat down at the opposite end of the couch, leaving a wide space between them.

She leaned back, and their gazes locked for a long, breath-robbing minute. The air seemed to sizzle, and her skin broke out in goose bumps while her heart sped up, throbbing deep in her chest.

"Tell me about Chicago," she managed, hoping to keep from throwing herself at him for at least five minutes.

"What do you want to know?"

"Where do you live?" She took a sip of the robust, deep-flavored wine. It danced on her tongue, then warmed her extremities as she swallowed. Or maybe it was Caleb's presence that warmed her extremities. It was impossible to tell for sure.

"I have an apartment. It's downtown. On top of a thirty-five-story building."

"So, it's a penthouse?" That shouldn't have surprised her. But she found it was hard for her to get used to Caleb's level of wealth. Though the fact that he owned a jet plane should have made it clear.

"I guess you could call it that," he answered easily. "I bought it because it's close to our head office. The plants are all in industrial parks in the outskirts of the city, but it makes sense to have the head office downtown."

"You don't have to apologize to me for having a downtown office."

He chuckled. "When I'm talking to you, it feels a little extravagant. Truth is, most of our international clients stay downtown, so it's for convenience as much as anything else. I'm not trying to impress anyone."

"I wouldn't think you'd have to try." She imagined people would be impressed without Caleb having to lift a finger in that direction.

He gave a mock salute with his wine glass. "Was that sarcasm?"

"Truthfully, it wasn't. Though I am struggling to picture you with a list of international clients."

"That's why I'm forced to wear a suit. It helps them take me more seriously."

She smiled at his joke and drank some more wine, feeling much more relaxed than when she first walked in.

"We've had inroads into Canada and Mexico for quite some time," Caleb elaborated. "Our first expansion of a plant outside of the Chicago area was Seattle. With the port there, we had access to the Pacific Rim. It turned out to be a really good move. So, now, we have buyers from Japan, Korea, Hong Kong, as far away as Australia. That's when we bought the jet. We started doing trade shows over there. In many Asian cultures, status is very important. So that meant I had to go, as president of the company. Otherwise, we couldn't get the right people in the room for meetings." He paused. "Do you have any idea how long it takes to fly from Chicago to Hong Kong?"

"I haven't a clue."

"Long time."

"Is that why there's a bathroom in the jet?"

"And why the seats turn into flat beds."

"Not to brag," she put in saucily, "but I went as far as Denver this year."

"You're lucky. If I could do all my work in Chicago, I'd never travel at all."

Mandy didn't like the idea of Caleb not traveling. The only way she'd ever see him in the future is if he traveled to Colorado. "The jet seemed pretty comfortable," she noted.

"So, you see my point."

"Your point being, why fly commercial when you can take your own Gulf Stream?"

"Okay, now that was definitely sarcastic."

"It was," she admitted with a grin.

He sobered. "It's funny. What looks like luxury and unbelievable convenience that ninety-nine percent of the population can't access, is really just me trying to survive." He set down his wineglass and shifted closer to her. "I don't know if I'm saying this right. But money and success aren't what you expect. The responsibility never goes away. You worry everyday. Literally thousands of people depend on your decisions, and you never know who's your friend, who's using you and who's out to get you. The risks are high. The stakes are high. And you go weeks on end without an opportunity to catch your breath, never mind relax."

Mandy thought she did understand. "Are you relaxed now?" she asked.

He nodded. "Amazingly, at this moment, yes."

"That's good."

"It's you."

It was her turn to toast him, keeping it light. "Happy to help out."

He tapped his fingers against his knee. "You know, I believe you're serious about that. It's one of the things I like best about you."

"I'm relaxing?" She wasn't sure whether to take that as a compliment or not. Relaxing could also be boring. And she couldn't possibly be anywhere near as exciting as the women he usually dated.

Dated. She paused. Was this a date?

"You're not thinking about what I can do for you," said Caleb. "You're sitting over there, looking off-the-charts gorgeous, enjoying a rather pedestrian wine, without a single complaint."

She glanced at her glass. "Should I be complaining? Do I have poor taste in wine?"

"I'm definitely not saying this right. You care about how I feel, about what you can do for me. Do you know how rare that is?"

"Do I really have bad taste in wine?"

Caleb laughed, picked up his glass, toasted her and drank the remainder. "It tastes perfectly fine to me." He stared softly at her for a long moment. "But I know you know what I mean."

She fought an impish grin, going with the impulse to keep joking. "I figure it's a toss-up between you saying I'm boring and you saying I'm unsophisticated."

He deliberately set down his empty glass. Moved so he was right next to her and lifted her glass from her fingers. "You, Mandy, are anything but boring."

"But I am unsophisticated."

He opened his mouth, but she kept talking before he could say something that was complimentary but patently untrue. "I'm a ranch girl, Caleb. I've barely left the state. I haven't even seen my own sister at Liberty in New York."

Caleb blinked in obvious surprise. "You haven't seen Katrina dance?"

"Oh, I've seen her dance a few times, during the last years she was at college." Mandy thought back to the experiences. "She is incredible. But I haven't been to New York since she joined Liberty. I haven't seen her perform at the Emperor's Theatre as a principle dancer."

"You need to do that," he said decisively.

"I do. And maybe I should take in a wine-tasting class while I'm in the city. Clearly, my palate needs some work."

"Your palate is perfect." He kissed her. "Better than perfect." He kissed her again.

She responded immediately, arms going around his neck, hugging him close, returning the kiss with fervor, reveling in the feel of his strong body pressing itself up against hers.

"I'm taking you to New York," he whispered against her lips.

"Now?"

"Not now." His warm hand covered her knee, sliding up her bare thigh, beneath the red dress. "Right now, I'm hoping to take you someplace else entirely."

She smiled against his mouth. "I can hardly wait."

He drew back to look at her. "But after this, Mandy. Whatever happens with…" He seemed to search for words. "Whatever happens with all the stuff that's around us… Afterwards, I am taking you to New York. We're going to watch your sister perform, drink ridiculously expensive wine and stay in a hotel suite overlooking Central Park."

"Is that before or after you take me to Rio for a manicure?"

"Your choice."

His fingertips found the silk of her panties, and she groaned his name.

"Oh, Mandy," he breathed, kissing her deeply, lifting her into his arms.

He stood, striding toward the king-size bed, flicking the lights off as he passed each switch.

He set her on her feet next to the bed, threw back the covers, then gently urged her down, following her, stretching out, his gaze holding hers the entire time.

He gently stroked her cheek with the backs of his fingers, smoothed her hair, ran his fingertips along her collarbone, pushing down the straps of her dress. "I am so very glad you're here."

She kissed his mouth, ran her tongue over the seam of his lips, then opened wide and kissed him deeply and endlessly. "There's nowhere else I want to be."

He took it slow, gently and tenderly lingering over every inch of her skin with his kisses and caresses. Mandy had never felt so cherished. And when they were naked, and fused together, she curled her body around him, holding him tight, gasping as his slow deliberate strokes took her higher and higher.

Reality disappeared, and she clung almost desperately to lovemaking that went on and on. When she finally cried his name, they collapsed into each others arms. She was certain she'd ended up in Heaven.

Her heartbeat was deep and heavy. Her lungs worked overtime. And she inhaled Caleb's musky scent, clinging tightly to him, fighting sleep and willing the rest of the world away for just as long as possible.

Ten

The next day, Caleb couldn't seem to bring himself to let go of Mandy. He held her hand, occasionally pulled her sideways against him. She'd put up with it for a short time, but then she kept freeing herself, obviously not comfortable with the intimacy around her family. Caleb didn't care who saw them, as they wandered through the grounds of the Lyndon Regional Rodeo. It was opening day, and everyone agreed it was worth staying to watch.

The rodeo had always been a fun, lighthearted, family affair, and Caleb was astonished to see how much it had grown since he'd last attended. He'd ridden bucking broncs that year. He was seventeen and too young to realize he was mortal.

He hadn't finished in the money. But Reed had won the trophy for steer wrestling. Cocky, reckless and in high spirits, they'd spent his five-hundred-dollar prize on beer and flashy new boots for both of them. Now, Caleb found himself wondering if those boots, barely worn, were still stored in his bedroom closet, and what Reed had done with his pair.

He and Mandy made their way through the midway, toward the main arena. The announcer was pumping up the crowd for the first event. Children ran from ride to ride, shrieking with excitement, sticky cotton candy in their hands and balloon hats on their heads.

One young boy cried as his helium balloon floated away. Seth was quick to snag a wandering vendor and replace the balloon. They boy's mother was grateful, and Seth was sure to introduce himself by his full name.

"Hopefully, another vote," Abigail said to Mandy and Caleb in an undertone.

"He's very good at schmoozing," Caleb agreed. He had to admit, he admired Seth's easy manner with the crowds. He seemed to know everybody, and they seemed to respect him. Those he didn't know, he quickly met.

"Are we here for the rodeo or a campaign stop?" Mandy asked her sister. Abigail just laughed in response.

Caleb was dressed in blue jeans, boots and a white Western-style dress shirt. But it was all new, and he felt like a dandy, more than a little out of place among the working cowboys. He wondered how many people assumed he was a tourist. Certainly, all the competitors would peg him right off. He wished there was time to scuff up the boots and fade his jeans.

"Hey, Mandy," a woman called from behind them.

Mandy turned and so did Caleb, and her hand came loose from his.

The woman looked to be about thirty years old. She wore a pair of tight jeans, a battered Stetson hat and a wide, tooled leather belt. She was a bit thick around the middle, her hair was nondescript brown, and her red checked shirt was open to reveal a navy T-shirt beneath. She clearly belonged here at the rodeo.

"You riding today?" she asked Mandy.

Caleb looked at Mandy with curiosity. She competed in rodeo events?

"Not today," Mandy answered. "We just happened to be in town and thought we'd take it in."

"Heard about your dad," the woman continued, her expression switching to one of sympathy. "I was real sorry about that."

"Thank you," Mandy acknowledged. "We appreciate it. But he's doing very well, making more progress every day."

"Good to hear. Good to hear." Then the woman stuck out her hand to Caleb. "Lori Richland."

"Used to be Lori Parker," Mandy put in.

Caleb recognized the name. Lori had been a year behind him in high school. He didn't remember very much about her.

He accepted her hand. "Caleb Terrell."

"Woo hoo," she sang. "Wait till I tell Harvey I got a look at you." She gave Caleb's hand a playful tug, looking him up and down. "We heard you were back in town. Sorry to hear about your dad, too."

"Thank you," Caleb said simply.

Lori turned her attention to Mandy. "I've got Star Dock over at the stables if you want to enter the barrels."

"I hadn't planned—"

"Go for it," Lori insisted. "He loves competing." She looked back at Caleb. "The crowds and the applause does something for that horse."

"Hey, Abby," Lori called over Mandy's shoulder. "Steer undecorating?"

Abby approached them. "Yeah? If you've got a horse here, I'm game."

"Pincher's been doing really well lately. And tell your brothers to check with Clancy over at the pens. We need some good local competitors in team, steer roping."

Caleb had a sudden flashback to him and Reed practicing roping out on the range. They'd had plans to someday compete together, but Reed's big body made him a natural for steer wrestling, while Caleb had liked the adrenalin rush of the bucking horses.

Lori looked directly at Caleb. "What about you? What are you going to enter?"

Caleb held up his palms in mock surrender. "Not today."

He was not getting anywhere near anything that bucked. And he was completely out of practice for all of the events.

Mandy leaned over to Lori and spoke in a mock whisper. "He's been away in the big city. Riding a desk for a few years."

Lori checked him out up and down. "Doesn't look too soft."

"Why does everybody keep being surprised about that?" Caleb asked Mandy.

"Because it's true." She patted his shoulder consolingly. "You don't look too bad for a city slicker."

"You're too kind," he drawled.

"You should take it as a compliment," said Mandy.

"Maybe we'll throw you in the greased pig chase," Lori teased Caleb.

"Pass," said Caleb. "But you go right ahead and have a good time with that."

Lori tipped her head back and gave a throaty laugh.

"Barrels start in about an hour," she said to Mandy.

"Better check the schedule for the rest." With a wave, she strode away into the crowd.

"You're going to compete?" Caleb asked.

"Sure," said Mandy. "I could win a thousand dollars."

"Don't want to pass up a chance like that." He found his gaze drifting to Travis and Seth. Abigail had obviously given them the news about the chance to enter the rodeo, and they now had their heads together talking strategy.

For a sharp second, Caleb missed Reed so badly, it brought a pain to the centre of his chest.

Then Mandy slipped her hand into his. She leaned in, and her tone went sultry. "You want to be my stable hand?"

He tugged her tight against his side. "I'll be anything you want me to be."

She grinned. "I'm holding you to that."

He kept her hand in his as they headed for the horse pens in the competitors area around back of the arena.

There, she quickly got down to business, signing up, paying the entry fee and checking out the horse and tack Lori had offered her.

When she was ready to go, Caleb crossed to the competitors grandstand, where he could get a better view. He caught sight of the other Jacobs siblings in the distance, getting ready for their own events, and he had to struggle not to feel like the odd man out.

But once the barrel-racing event started, he got caught up with the cheering, coming to his feet when Mandy galloped into the arena. She made a very respectable run. Halfway through the competition, and she was in second place.

She joined him sitting in the stands for the last few competitors, leaning up against him as they laughed and cheered. She managed to hang on to third place until the last competitor knocked her to fourth, just out of the money.

Caleb gave her a conciliatory hug, telling her he was sorry.

But she shrugged philosophically. "Easy come, easy go."

"I'll spring for a corn dog if it'll make you feel better," he offered.

She turned up her nose. "What corn dog? I'm holding out for Rio."

He pretended to ponder for a moment. "I suppose I could do both."

"Truly?" She blinked ingenuously up at him.

"Yes," he told her sincerely. He realized in that moment he'd give her anything she wanted.

"You're a gentleman, Caleb Terrell," she cooed, threading her arm through his.

"And, dust notwithstanding—" he pretended to wipe a smudge off her cheek "—you, Mandy Jacobs, are a lady."

Her face was scrubbed clean of makeup today, and her hair was pulled back in a simple ponytail, but in the sunshine she looked just as beautiful as she had last night. He had trouble tearing his gaze away from her.

Her attention went to the ring. She cheered and gave a shrill whistle as the barrel-race winners received their awards in the middle of the arena.

"You just whistled." He laughed.

"Bet the girls back in Chicago don't do that."

"They don't eat corn dogs, either."

"Poor things. They don't know what they're missing."

The team roping had started. Caleb couldn't help but admire the talent of the cowboys and the rapt attention of well-bred horses. A few of the steers escaped, but most were swiftly roped and released by the cowboys.

"Here we go." Mandy leaned forward as her brothers lined up in the box. The steer was released, and the men sprang to action, horses' hooves thundering, ropes spinning around their heads. Travis took the head, turned the spotted steer, and Seth quickly followed up with the heels.

The horses stilled, and the flag waved. Their time was five point three seconds, causing Mandy to shout and punch a fist in the air. The time had put them in first place. They released their ropes and tipped their hats to the crowd, acknowledging the cheers.

They shook hands as they rode out of the arena, and Seth playfully knocked off Travis's hat. One of the clowns retrieved it for him, and the two disappeared from sight around the end of the fence.

Caleb felt another hitch in his chest. His reaction was silly. Even if he did meet his brother after all these years, it wasn't as if they'd be doing any team roping. Caleb was way too far out of practice. Besides, he was too old to come off a horse.

"Are you hungry?" Mandy asked.

"You don't seriously want a corn dog."

"I was thinking a funnel cake. Sprinkled with sugar, please."

"How on earth do you stay so slim?" Most of the women he knew in Chicago survived on leaf lettuce and bok choy.

"Exercise and clean living," she answered.

"So, you're serious?"

"I never joke about funnel cake."

Caleb shook his head in amazement, coming to his feet. "One funnel cake, coming up. You going to eat the whole thing, or will you share?"

"With you, I guess I could share."

He gave her a wink and made his way down the worn wooden benches, meeting Travis and Seth at the bottom.

"Nice." He nodded, shaking each of their hands in congratulations. He checked the board to find them still on top with six competitors left. "Looks like you might finish in the money."

"Seven-hundred and fifty bucks," Travis confirmed with a sharp nod. "That'll pay for the trip."

"I'm going on a funnel-cake run. Anyone interested?"

"Gads, no," said Seth. "I don't know how Mandy eats those things."

"She's got a sweet tooth," said Travis. His level gaze stayed on Caleb for a couple of beats.

Caleb raised his brows. If Travis had something to say, he might as well spit it out.

Seth glanced between the two men.

"You heard anything from Reed?" Travis asked, surprising Caleb.

The question triggered emotions that were close to the surface today, and it took him a second to recover. He shook his head. "Not a word."

"He still takes first in the steer wrestling every year," said Travis.

Caleb nodded his acknowledgment but didn't answer.

But Travis wasn't finished yet. "Mandy thinks you should talk to him before you sell the ranch."

The announcer's voice became more animated over the loudspeaker as the next team of ropers left the box, stirring up a cloud of dust.

"Mandy thinks a lot of things," said Caleb.

"I'm not sure she's wrong on this."

"Well, I can't talk to him if he's not here." Caleb made to leave.

"You can hold off on the sale," said Travis.

"You're selling?" asked Seth, an obvious note of incredulity in his voice. "Why on earth would you do that?"

"Yes," Caleb answered shortly, pivoting in the dust and starting to walk away.

"Whoa." Seth caught up to him, but Travis, at least, had the good grace to stay behind. "What gives?"

"What gives is that I'm not explaining myself to you and Travis in the middle of a rodeo crowd."

"Fair enough." Seth nodded easily, keeping pace. "But what about Reed? He get a say in this?"

"Reed left town, no forwarding address, no phone number."

"But how can you sell it without him?" Seth paused. "You know, I honestly thought he'd inherit the whole thing."

Caleb altered his course to angle toward the concession stands. "Well, he didn't. I did."

"Not the whole thing."

"Yes, the whole thing."

"But—"

"Haven't a clue," Caleb preempted the obvious question.

Seth's tone turned thoughtful. "And that's why Reed disappeared."

"I would think so." They came to the lineup and joined the end.

"Are you getting a funnel cake?" Caleb asked Seth.

"Just keeping you company."

"Not necessary."

But Seth didn't leave. After a few minutes of silence, he spoke up again. "Do you need the money?"

Caleb laughed darkly at that suggestion. "The money's Reed's. It's going to sit in a bank account until he shows his face."

"And the rush is?"

"Has it occurred to you that this is none of your business?"

"Absolutely."

"Then, go away."

"Has it occurred to you that I'm your friend?"

Caleb couldn't form an answer to that one. He liked and respected Seth, but he was beginning to feel as if he was surrounded by kind, well-meaning meddlers, pushing him in a direction he didn't want to go.

"Seriously, Caleb. This is a huge decision."

"It's already listed."

"Unlist it."

"I don't want it," Caleb barked. "I don't need it. And Reed's better off without it." He glared at Seth, while the festival swirled around them, midway rides jangling, children shrieking and the rodeo announcements blaring in the distance.

After a long minute, Seth gave a curt nod of acquiescence. And Caleb turned to the teenager in the paper hat and placed his order.

Eleven

The trip to Lyndon and the rodeo day over and done with, Mandy and the local vet were working their way through a list of minor injuries and ailments in the ranch's horses. Midafternoon, they were inside the barn looking at a quarter-horse colt who'd been limping on and off for about a week. The colt's left fetlock felt warm, and Mandy was worried about infection.

"Mandy?" a whispered voice questioned from behind them, the person obviously being careful not to spook the colt.

Mandy smoothly rose from the colt's leg and turned to find Robby, one of the young hands, waiting.

"There's someone on the office phone for you," he told her quietly. "Danielle something? She's pretty insistent."

"I'll take it," Mandy agreed, optimism rising within her. "Can you give Dr. Peters a hand while I'm gone, Robby?" She dusted her hands off on her jeans and moved from the stall to the main barn aisle.

The young man set aside his manure fork and took Mandy's place in the stall.

Anticipation tightened Mandy's stomach as she paced her way quickly to the small office that sat just inside the main door of the barn.

She closed the door behind her for privacy and picked up the phone. "Danielle?"

"Mandy?"

"It's me." Mandy forced herself to sit down on the leather chair with wheels, telling herself to stay calm. "You have news?"

"I do. Enrico found Reed."

Mandy's spirit soured. "Yes!" They'd found him. They'd finally found him. "Thank you."

"Right now, he's staying at a hotel in Helena."

"Really?" That information surprised Mandy. "Reed is in Montana?" She'd assumed he was at least still in Colorado.

"The Bearberry Inn. He's been there a couple of days, but there's no way of knowing how long he'll stay."

"Don't worry. I'm leaving right away." Mandy hopped up from the chair, cataloging exactly what she'd have to do to get to the airport, get to Helena and find Reed. When she did, she was cornering him and demanding to know what the heck he thought he was doing.

Okay, maybe she wouldn't demand. Maybe she'd just ask him. But, first, maybe she'd just hug him. After the past few weeks like he'd had, the man was going to need a hug.

"Call me when you get there," said Danielle. "And please, please convince him to come home. Whatever it takes."

"I will," Mandy promised.

"If we can wrap this up by Wednesday, my life gets a whole lot easier."

"Uh, okay." Two days. "I'll do my best." Mandy signed off.

As she headed across the yard, toward the house, she remembered the Brazilian deadline was looming. That was obviously the rush. Danielle was going to do everything in her power to get Caleb to Sao Paulo in time to deal with the banking regulators.

That meant there was every chance he'd be gone before Mandy got back. As soon as Reed agreed to return, she'd have to call Danielle. Danielle would obviously call Caleb, and Caleb would have no reason to stay in Colorado, especially if his business depended on him getting to Brazil.

That meant the two brothers might not even see each other. They might not get a chance to talk. And once the crisis was over, things could easily go back to the status quo, Reed here, Caleb there, still estranged from each other.

Mandy trotted up the stairs, across the porch and into the ranch house foyer. Maybe keeping Danielle's search a secret from Caleb had been the wrong idea. Taking Caleb with her to Helena made much more sense. If he'd come, he'd have to talk to Reed. That would break the ice. And he'd still have time to make it to Brazil. And, afterward, maybe he'd come back.

She pulled off her boots in the front foyer and headed for the second floor, intending to have a quick shower and pack an overnight case.

She warmed to her modified plan. Reed was sure to be happy with Caleb's honor and generosity. The two brothers could talk in Helena, resolve things and then…

Well, the plan got a little fuzzy after that, but at least it was a start.

She stripped of her shirt, peeled off her jeans, discarded her underwear and stepped into a hot shower.

She hadn't talked to Caleb since they'd returned from Lyndon last night after the rodeo. Seth and Travis had finished in second place, and after a celebratory beer and a round of burgers, she and Caleb had driven back together.

He'd been unusually quiet on the drive, but had kissed her good-night, and he'd told her he was going to miss her overnight. Nothing wrong with that. Everything was fine between them. She could safely broach the subject of Reed.

Perhaps she could do it between kisses. That would be manipulating the situation. But it was for a good cause.

Then again, that was probably a bad idea. She'd go with a straight-up outline of the facts. Caleb liked facts, and the facts were on her side in this.

She dressed, blow-dried her hair, put on a touch of makeup, a pair of clean jeans, a striped T-shirt and a navy blazer. Then she tossed a few clothes into the overnight bag, left a note to her brothers, saying she'd call them when she got to Helena, and jumped into a pickup truck.

The ride to the Terrell ranch took its usual twenty minutes, but it felt much longer. She pulled up to the house, took a very deep, bracing breath and set out to reason with Caleb.

When she knocked, he called out a huffed "come in."

"Caleb?" she called back as the door opened. She could hear scraping sounds coming from the living room.

She followed the noise, rounding the corner from the foyer to find him surrounded by cardboard packing boxes, a tape dispenser in his hand, as he sealed one of them up.

"What are you doing?" Her tone came out sharper than she'd intended.

"Packing." He voiced the obvious.

"But, why?" What had happened? Had she missed something? Had he already sold the ranch?

"Mostly, because it's not going to pack itself," he answered.

"But I thought—"

"Can you hand me another box?"

Mandy was too stunned to move. She felt sick to her stomach.

"Did you sell?" she managed on a harsh whisper.

"Not yet."

She put out a hand to brace herself against the back of the sofa, all but staggering in relief. There was still time.

"A box?" he asked again.

"Sure." She picked up a flattened box from a pile beside her feet and handed it over. She met his gaze. "And, if we find Reed?"

His jaw tensed. "Seriously, Mandy. I'm not having that conversation all over again."

She swallowed against her dry throat. "But, if we did find him. Like, right away. Would you be willing—"

He smacked the box on the coffee table in the middle of the room, startling her. The thread of anger in his voice was crystal clear. "What is *with* you people? This isn't a Jacobs family decision. It's my decision."

His tone set her back. "But—"

"No." He jabbed his finger in her direction. "No, Mandy. I am packing. I am selling. I am going to Brazil and then back to Chicago. And I'm not changing my mind. You won't change it. Seth won't change it. And neither will Travis."

So much for gentle. So much for reasonable. "You're a stubborn fool."

"You're not the first one to notice."

She came around the end of the pile of boxes, staring straight into his eyes, lowering her voice. "You step over this cliff, Caleb, and we can't come back."

He went still for a very long moment, staring levelly back. "We, as in you and me?"

"As in your brother, your family, your heritage."

"I can live with that." It was obvious he was serious, completely serious. There was no way she'd get him to Helena.

Though she told herself it was a much less significant matter, she couldn't seem to stop herself from asking. "What about me and you?"

His expression didn't change. He leaned in and gave her a fleeting kiss. It wasn't exactly a cold kiss, but it didn't invite anything further. "Me and you are still going to Rio."

She tried not to let his words hurt her, but they did. So her voice was laced with sarcasm when she answered. "Is that an 'I'll call you sometime, babe'?"

"That's not what I said."

She bit her tongue. He was right. He'd been up front and honest all along the way. All he'd ever offered was Rio and New York City. If it wasn't enough for her, she should have spoken up a long time ago.

She knew she couldn't change Caleb. But she could still help Reed. Pretending everything was fine, she stretched up and kissed Caleb on the cheek. "Rio sounds good. I gotta go. The vet's working with the horses today, and he's, well, they'll need me down there."

"Sure," Caleb agreed, flipping the box over to reinforce the bottom with a strip of tape. "See you later."

"Later," she echoed, turning to leave.

Caleb worked for about an hour, reassuring himself he was doing exactly the right thing. He couldn't stay here. He growing frighteningly attached to Mandy, and it got worse every day.

But every time he turned around in this house, there was another picture, another memento, another annoying memory trigger, like the woodsy scent of the throw blanket his mother had knit for the back of the sofa.

It had taken a long time for Chicago to feel like home, and he wasn't about to lose that. Not for the sake of his family's land, and not to be near Mandy for a few more days.

Mandy. He blew out a breath. He hadn't wanted to fight with her. But she had to understand. There was no hope that he'd erase his childhood, nor would he ever come to terms with it. The best he could hope for was to leave it far, far behind. So he didn't have to think about it every day of his life.

Still, he shouldn't have taken it out on her.

She was entitled to her opinion. And she held that particular opinion only because she was a compassionate, generous, caring person. She couldn't stand to see anyone hurt or upset, and that included Reed. And what did she get from Caleb for her trouble? Anger and the cold shoulder.

He needed to apologize.

Silently acknowledging he'd been a jerk, he deserted the packing job and headed for his SUV. He rammed it into Drive and peeled out.

Down the ranch roadway, he took the corners fast, his back tires breaking loose on the gravel ranch road. Then he sped along the main valley road to the arched gateway to the Jacobses' ranch. It was five minutes up the driveway, and then he was pulling up front of the house.

He knocked once, then let himself in to find Travis and Seth at the table, digging into steaks.

He glanced around. "Is Mandy upstairs?"

Seth shook his head. "You didn't talk to her before she left?"

"Left?"

Mandy sure hadn't said anything to Caleb about leaving.

"For Helena," said Travis. "I thought you must have gone with her, taken your jet."

Caleb walked farther into the room, his hands going to his hips. "She didn't say anything to me."

Seth glanced at his watch. "She said she'd call us when she landed at the airport. You hungry?"

No, Caleb wasn't hungry.

Mandy was gone. She'd left after their fight. What did that mean? Was she going to pull the same stunt as Reed and disappear when things didn't go her way?

What the hell was the matter with her?

He struggled to keep the anger from his voice. "Did she say where she was going in Helena?"

"Nope," said Travis, obviously unconcerned. Sure, *now* he didn't worry about his sister.

"Do you have any business interests there, suppliers?" Caleb pressed.

"Nothing," said Seth.

"She did have a college friend who was from there," Travis offered. "I don't know her name or anything."

"But it was a woman?"

Seth gave him a confused look.

Travis scoffed out an amused laugh.

Caleb headed for the door. "If you hear anything, send me a text."

"Will do," said Travis.

"Where you going?" Seth called out behind him.

"Helena," Caleb answered. "Let me know if you hear from Mandy."

"What on earth is going—" Seth's voice abruptly disappeared as Caleb shut the front door.

Caleb stomped his way back to the SUV. It seemed impossible that Mandy had a sudden desire to visit an old friend. Unless the old friend was in trouble. But, if that was the case, she should have told him. He could have lent her his jet to get to Helena.

Unless it was Mandy going to see her old friend for solace. Could she be that angry with him? She'd said yes to Rio. That was a good sign, right?

He started the vehicle and pulled it into gear, wheeling through the roundabout and back out the driveway. He reached for his phone and dialed her cell with his thumb.

He got voice mail, and didn't really care to leave a message.

By the time he hit the main road, his confusion had turned to anger. No matter what her reason for leaving, the least she could have done was call him, or send him a text if she was too mad for a civil conversation. She'd let her brothers know where she was headed. Well, at least the rudimentary details. A motel name would have been nice.

Coming up on the highway, he dialed the pilot. It would be late before he got to Lyndon, but the airport was equipped for after-dark takeoffs, and they could land in Helena on instruments.

* * *

Having managed to get a flight from Lyndon to Denver last night, then a flight into Helena this morning, Mandy had camped out in the restaurant of the Bearberry Inn for over two hours. It was three in the afternoon, but there was still no sign of Reed.

The front desk had refused to give out his room number, and she didn't want to call him, for fear he'd refuse to see her. She'd chosen a table in a back corner where she could watch both the restaurant and the front desk across the lobby without being easily seen.

She figured her last hope was to get him to come back to Lyndon Valley right away. If she did it quickly, there was a chance Caleb would still be there. If not, she was certain he'd finish packing and leave for Sao Paulo, sale or no sale. But if she could make it in time, Caleb, the stubborn fool, would be forced to have a conversation with his brother.

Just as Mandy was ordering her third cup of coffee, her patience was rewarded. She caught a glimpse of Reed's profile, his tall, sturdy frame, striding across the lobby toward the bank of elevators. Quickly canceling her order, she tossed some money on the table and jumped up, grabbing her shoulder bag and slinging it over her blazer.

She trotted out of the restaurant, determined to catch him. A few feet away, she called out his name.

He turned and stared at her in obvious shock.

"Mandy?" He glanced around the expansive lobby. "What on earth are you doing here?"

"I'm looking for you." She immediately hugged him, and he hugged her back. But her joy at finding him turned almost instantly to frustration. Drawing back, she socked him in the shoulder. "What is the matter with you?"

"Me? I'm not the one who appeared out of nowhere."

"Do you have any idea how worried I've been?"

A couple of guests gave them curious glances as they walked past, causing Reed to take Mandy's arm and lead her toward a glass door that led to the hotel courtyard.

"Why would you worry?" he asked. "What are you doing in Helena? How on earth did you know I was here?"

They made it outside to the relative privacy of an interior courtyard with a table-dotted patio, a manicured, green lawn, towering trees and colorful, raised brick gardens.

"I didn't know if you'd been kidnapped, shanghaied, injured, arrested or mugged."

"Kidnapped? You've got to be kidding me. Like somebody's going to hold me for ransom."

"You know what I mean."

"I'm fine. Nobody's going to mug me, Mandy. At night, on the darkened streets? *I'm* the guy people are afraid of."

"I can't believe you didn't call me."

"I can't believe you were worried."

"Why didn't you at least send me a text?"

"Because I didn't want anyone to know where I was."

She jabbed her thumb against her chest, voice going up. "*I'm* not anyone."

"You'd have told your brothers."

"I would not."

He gave her a look of disbelief.

Okay, maybe she would have, if they'd asked. She wasn't the world's best liar.

He glanced around the courtyard. "Do you want to sit down?"

"Sure," she agreed, taking a deep breath. She'd found him. Whatever else happened, at least she'd found him.

He guided her to one of the small tables, pulling out

her chair before taking the seat across from her. "You shouldn't have come."

Okay. Now was the time to tread carefully. She had to make Reed want to come back to the ranch and be willing to speak to Caleb. Otherwise, she'd never get him to budge.

She struggled with where to start.

"Mandy?" he prompted.

"Why Helena?" she asked, giving him a smile, intending to ease her way in, telling herself to relax and act as though everything was normal.

"Besides the fishing? It's good ranch country, Mandy. I've had a job offer here."

"Of course you've had a job offer. You could probably have a thousand job offers if you wanted them."

He allowed himself a smile. "You're such an optimist."

"I am," she agreed. "And I have faith in you. You're an amazing person, Reed, a phenomenal person—"

"You know, don't you?"

She played dumb. "Know what?"

"About the will." He waited.

"Fine," she conceded. "I know about the will."

"How?"

She straightened in her chair, leaning over the round metal-framed, glass-topped table. "Can I start by saying I understand that you're upset."

"You can if you want. But that doesn't tell me anything. And it only puts off whatever it is you're dancing around here."

"It was a mistake to leave, Reed."

He scoffed out a laugh.

"You don't understand what's going—"

"How do you know about the will?"

"I want you to come back."

"You do, do you?"

"I do."

"You don't know what you're asking."

She reached across the table for his big hand. "I know exactly what I'm asking. If you'll just—"

"How did you find out about the will, Mandy?"

She closed her eyes for a brief second. "Fine. Caleb told me."

Reed gave a snort of derision, pulling his hand back. "Didn't take him long."

"Didn't take me long at all," came another deep, masculine voice.

Mandy's heart all but stopped.

She turned her head. "Caleb," she breathed.

"Was this stunt part of some grand plan?" he asked her, not even acknowledging his brother.

Reed came to his feet.

"I found Reed," she stated the unnecessary. "That's what I wanted to tell you—"

"You hoped I'd follow you?" Caleb demanded.

She was confused by his statement. "Follow—"

He gave a cold laugh. "Of course you knew I'd follow you. How could I not follow you?"

"What?" she couldn't help asking, giving a small shake of her head. If she'd wanted him to follow her, she'd have told him where she was going.

"That's what this was all about, all along." His blue gaze crackled into hers. "You realized you couldn't get me to talk to him by being honest."

What? No. Wait a minute.

Reed stepped forward. "Nobody invited you to join us."

Mandy whirled her gaze. "Reed, no. Let him explain."

Caleb sized up his brother. "What the hell is the matter with you?"

Reed's voice was stone cold. "Somebody stole my ranch."

"You didn't stay to defend it."

"Right. Like I'm going to hang around under those circumstances."

"You hung in there with Wilton."

Reed clenched his jaw down tight, and the edges of his mouth turned white. "Shut up."

"I don't think I will."

Mandy was starting to panic. She stepped between the two angry men. "Reed. Listen to me. He's giving it back. Caleb's giving you back the ranch."

"I'm selling the ranch," Caleb countered.

She ignored him and continued talking to Reed, her words spilling out fast. "That's how I found out about the will. Caleb came to Colorado to give it back to you."

"It doesn't matter," said Reed.

"How can it not matter?" she practically wailed.

"I don't want it," he spat.

"That's ridiculous," said Mandy. Her gaze took in both of them. "Come on, you two, quit being such—"

"You heard him," said Caleb.

She rounded on Caleb. "Of *course* he wants it back."

"Are you reading his mind?"

"I'm using logic and reason." Her expression of frustration took in both of them. "Something that seems to be in ridiculously short supply in this conversation."

Caleb angled his body toward Mandy, arms still by his sides, hands curled into fists. "You heard him. He said no."

"He'll change his mind."

"No, he won't." Caleb's gaze flicked to Reed. "He's as stubborn as a mule."

"At least I don't cut and run," Reed returned.

Caleb glared at his brother. "Back off."

"That's your specialty," said Reed. "And it's exactly what you're doing right now."

"I'm getting rid of an albatross that's been around our necks our entire lives."

"Around your neck?" Reed countered, squaring his shoulders, voice getting louder. "*Your* neck."

Caleb ignored the outburst. "I'll send you a check."

"Don't bother."

Mandy's stomach had turned to churning concrete. "Please, don't fight."

"Quit it," Caleb told her.

"Don't you yell at Mandy." Reed inched closer to his brother, shoulders squared, eyes hard as flints.

For a horrible moment, she thought they might come to blows.

"I'm not yelling at Mandy." When Caleb glanced back down at her, his expression had softened. "I'm not angry with you, Mandy. I swear I'm not. But you have your answer. He doesn't want the ranch."

"He does," she put in weakly.

"Are you ready to go home now?" Caleb asked.

Mandy shook her head. "I'm not going home. I just got here. Reed and I haven't even had a chance to—"

Caleb's voice went dark again, suspicion clouding his eyes. "To what?"

For a second, she thought she must have misunderstood. But his expression was transparent as usual. He actually thought there was something between her and Reed.

Mandy threw up her hands. "You can't possibly think that."

After all they'd been through? Could Caleb honestly think that? He'd asked her three times, and she'd told him over and over that they were just friends.

"So, you're staying here with him?" Caleb pressed.

She mustered her courage. Fine. If he wanted to think that, let him think that. "Yes, I am. I'm staying here with Reed."

Caleb's voice went quiet. "Is that what this was all about?"

She didn't understand the question.

"All along? Your plan was to make me like you, worm your way in until I can't—"

"Are you *kidding me?*" she all but shouted.

Did he seriously think she'd sleep with him to get him to stay? To not sell the ranch? Had he gone stark, raving mad?

He stared at her for a long minute. "Then, prove it. Prove you were being honest about your feelings all along."

What was he asking?

"Him or me, Mandy. What's it going to be?"

She froze.

Caleb couldn't ask this of her. She wasn't leaving Reed. If she did, Reed would disappear, and this time they wouldn't find him.

"So, it's him." Caleb's voice was completely devoid of emotion.

She hated his expression, hated his tone, hated that he was putting her in this impossible position. Under these circumstances, there was only one answer.

"Yes," she ground out. "It's him."

Caleb was silent, the breeze wafting, birds chirping

in the trees, faint traffic noise from the other side of the building.

Finally, he gave her a curt nod, turned abruptly and stomped back into the hotel lobby.

She and Reed said nothing, simply staring at each other.

"I didn't mean for it to go this way," Mandy offered in a small voice, trying desperately not to picture Caleb getting in a cab or maybe a rental car in front of the hotel, making his way back to the airport, flying to Lyndon, packing up the ranch, maybe meeting with another buyer and never seeing her again.

Reed sat back down at the table, his expression implacable. "Did you honestly think putting yourself in the middle would help?"

Her chest tightened, and her throat started to close. "I…" She was at a loss for words. She'd thought it would help. She'd hoped it would help.

"Mandy, all you did was give us something more to fight about." Reed's words pierced her heart.

"I didn't mean…" She'd thought it would work. She'd honestly thought once they saw each other, they'd realize they were still brothers, that they still loved each other, and they'd reconcile.

But now she was in the middle, and Caleb was furious with her. He thought there was actually a chance that she was romantically interested in Reed. And he was gone. Likely gone for good.

Her voice began to shake. "I was only trying to help."

Reed nodded, and his fingers drummed on the glass top of the table. "I know. You can't help being you."

She drew back in confusion.

His expression eased. "We should get you a cape and

a mask, Mandy. Swooping in, solving the problems of the world."

"I'm not…" But then Abigail's words came back to haunt her. Was this what she'd tried to warn Mandy about? *Was* Mandy substituting Reed for her own family? *Had* she become way too invested in Reed and Caleb's relationship?

Had she made a colossal mistake that was going to hurt them all?

Reed's dark eyes watched her closely while she struggled to bring her emotions back under control.

"Mandy?" he asked softly, a sad, ghost of a smile growing on his face. "How long have you been in love with Caleb?"

Mandy's stomach dove into a freefall. *"What?"* she rasped. "I didn't… I'm not… It isn't…" She could feel her face heat to flaming.

Reed cocked his head and waited.

She couldn't explain.

She wouldn't explain.

She didn't have to explain.

"I only slept with him," she blurted out.

Reed's lips formed a silent whistle. "And you just forced him to walk away and leave you with me? Oh, Mandy."

"I'm not in love with him," she managed. Falling in love with Caleb would be the most foolish move in the world. "It was a fling, a lark. It was nothing."

Reed reached across the table and took her hand in his. It was big, strong, callused. "You shouldn't have come here."

"I know that now," she admitted. She should have listened to her big sister. She should have minded her own business. Maybe if she had, Reed and Caleb would have found their way back without her.

"Go to the airport," Reed advised. "Go to Caleb right now."

But Mandy vigorously shook her head.

It was far too late for her to go to Caleb. And it wasn't what Reed thought. Caleb never offered her anything more than a plan for a fling in Rio. And even that was over now. She was pushing Caleb right out of her heart. Forever.

Twelve

Caleb's jet took off from the Sao Paulo airport, heading northwest into clear skies. The past two days had been an exercise in frustration, but with Danielle's help, he'd defeated the Brazilian banking system's red tape, and they were ready to start shipping raw materials next week.

They had a plant manager in place who spoke very good English. Their accounting and computer systems were set up, and they'd approved the hiring of three foremen who were now looking for local skilled trade workers.

"I'm going to set up a meeting with Sales and Accounting for Friday," said Danielle, punching a message into her PDA. "We have to watch the gross sales ceiling for the first six months, and I want everybody to understand the parameters."

"I'm not sure about Friday," said Caleb. He had to give

final instructions to the moving company. The sooner the better as far as he was concerned.

"Why not?"

"I need to go to Colorado."

She whirled her head in his direction. "Wait a minute. *What?*"

"The outstanding water rights issue is playing havoc with property values, but I told the broker to take any deal. I want this done."

"But, your brother."

"What about my brother?"

"We found him. He's back. Sign the damn thing over to him and forget about it."

Caleb wasn't sure he'd heard right. "What do you mean *we* found him?"

Danielle straightened, her tone completely unapologetic. "Mandy wasn't going to get anywhere on her own, so I had Enrico make a few calls."

"Enrico found Reed?"

"Yes."

"And you didn't think you should run this by me?"

"I didn't charge you anything. Besides, you were off in la la land, reconnecting with your roots and ignoring your own best interests."

Caleb coughed and shifted in his airplane seat. "Okay, setting aside for a second that you went behind my back, Reed doesn't want the ranch. He turned it down."

"So? Put it in his name, anyway. I can have something drafted by the time we land in Chicago."

"I'm selling it," Caleb stated flatly, his frustration growing by the second.

"That's a ridiculous waste of your time. We need you in your office, with your head in the game, not out on the range, chasing—"

"Since when is my life managed by consensus?"

"Since you stopped managing it for yourself."

"I take a couple of weeks, a couple of weeks to visit my hometown."

"Since when could you care less about your hometown?"

Caleb didn't care about his hometown. Okay, maybe he did. A little. It was fun hanging out with Travis again. And Seth was a great guy. And Mandy. He sucked in a breath. Mandy was going to be impossible to forget.

He'd tried to tell himself she'd lied about her feelings for him. But then he'd been forced to admit, she was. He'd been an absolute ass to accuse her of sleeping with him to get him to give Reed back the ranch. She'd never do that.

He'd even tossed the idea of seeing her again back and forth in his brain about a thousand times. Assuming that she'd be willing.

"Is it Mandy?" Danielle asked, startling him from his thoughts.

"Mandy what?"

"Are you going back to see Mandy?"

Caleb pressed his head hard against the high-backed seat. He had no idea how to answer that question. Mandy and the ranch were two completely different issues, but somehow they'd gotten all tangled up into one.

"If you've got a thing for her, you might as well go get it over with."

Caleb didn't have a thing for Mandy. Okay, well, he definitely had a thing for her. But the way Danielle put it, it sounded so crass. "How is this any of your business?"

"It's not. But we have this lawyer-client confidentiality thing going on, so I feel like I can be honest."

"Go be honest with someone else."

"Caleb." Her voice took on a tone of exaggerated pa-

tience, and she folded her hands in her lap. "We agreed
that the solution was to give your brother back the ranch.
I've handed it to you on a silver platter. You need to take
it."

"I'm selling it," he repeated. He held the trump card,
because there was nothing she could do to change his
mind.

"Why?"

"Because he doesn't want it, and he's better off without it."

"So, you're doing this for him."

"Right."

"Yet, you haven't spoken to him in ten years."

"I spoke to him the other day." And it had been a sur-
real experience.

The person he'd fought with in Helena had been Reed,
only not Reed. The new Reed was a twenty-seven-year-
old man, broader and stronger than he'd been as a teenager, self-confident, self-assured. Part of Caleb had
wanted to sit down and talk things over with him. And
part of Caleb had wanted to throw Mandy over his shoulder and carry her away.

Mandy had said they were just friends. Yet, she stayed
behind with Reed.

No, Caleb wasn't going to go there. Mandy told him
she wasn't romantically involved with Reed, and he was
going to believe her. The remaining question was whether
she was interested in being romantically involved with
Caleb.

Three days ago, he might have said maybe. Today,
he'd definitely say no. But what if he went back? What
if he treated her properly this time? Was there a chance
of something between them?

He'd regretted walking away from her the second his

feet hit the pavement in Helena. And he'd regretted it every minute since.

"I'm going to Colorado," he told Danielle with determination.

She shook her head and leaned back in her seat. "I can't save you from yourself, Caleb."

Sitting at his office desk, hitting send on a final email before he headed to the Chicago airport, Caleb heard someone enter through the open door.

He didn't look up. "Tell the driver I'll be ten more minutes."

"You have a driver?" came a deep, male voice.

Caleb turned sharply, swiveling his high-backed, leather chair to face the doorway.

Reed's large frame nearly filled the entrance. His boots added an inch to his six-foot-three-inch frame, and his midnight-black, Western-cut shirt stretched across his broad shoulders. In the office, he looked even more imposing than he had outside the hotel.

Caleb instantly came to his feet.

Reed didn't look angry, exactly. But he didn't look happy, either.

"What are you doing in Chicago?" was the only thing Caleb could think to say. He couldn't help but wonder if Mandy was with him.

"Wanted to talk to you," said Reed, taking a few paces into the office.

"Okay," Caleb offered warily. He'd been feeling off-kilter since he last saw Mandy, and his emotions continued to do crazy things to his logic. He really wasn't in the mood for a fight.

Reed stepped up to the desk. "Don't sell the ranch."

Caleb's jaw went lax.

"It's mine," said Reed.

Caleb didn't disagree with that. Morally and ethically, the ranch belonged to Reed.

"And I want it," Reed finished.

"You want it?" Something akin to joy came to life inside Caleb. Which was silly. The ranch wasn't good for Reed.

"Yes."

"Just like that." Caleb snapped his fingers.

Reed's dark eyes went hard. "No. Not just like that. Just like ten years of sweat and blood and hell."

"I was going to give you the money."

"I don't want the money. I want the land. My land. Our mother's land."

Caleb's heart gave an involuntary squeeze inside his chest.

"Did you forget her great-grandmother was born at Rock Creek?" asked Reed, voice crackling hard. "In that tiny falling-down house next to the waterfall?"

Of course Caleb hadn't forgotten. His mother had told them that story a hundred times.

"And her grandfather, her father. They're all buried on the hill, Caleb. You going to sell off our ancestors' bones?"

"You going to live with the memory of *him?*" Caleb blurted out.

"You going to let him defeat us?" Reed squared his shoulders. "He was who he was, Caleb."

"He killed her."

"I know. Do you think I don't know? And I can't bring her back." Reed's voice was shaking with emotion. "But do you know what I can do? What I'm going to do?"

Caleb was too stunned by the stark pain on his brother's face to even attempt an answer.

"I'm going to have her grandchildren. I'm going to find a nice girl, who loves Lyndon Valley, and I'm going to give her babies, and my first daughter will be named Sasha, and she will be loved, and she will be happy, and I will never, ever, *ever* let anyone hurt her."

Caleb's chest nearly caved in, while his heart stood still.

"Are you going to stand in my way?" Reed demanded, bringing his fist down on the desktop.

"No," Caleb managed through a dry throat.

"Good." Reed abruptly sat down and leaned back, crossing one boot over the opposite knee.

Caleb slumped in his chair. "Why didn't you say all that in the first place?"

"I've said it now."

"You're going to find a nice girl?" Caleb couldn't help but ask.

Reed nodded. "I am. A ranch girl. Someone like Mandy."

Caleb's spine went stiff, and his hands curled into fists.

Reed chuckled, obviously observing the involuntary reaction. "But not Mandy. Mandy's yours."

"No, she's not."

"Yeah. She is." Reed's tone was gruff, his eyes watchful. "Unless you're going to cut and run on her, too."

"I've never—"

"She's in love with you, Caleb. Not that you deserve her."

Reed had it all wrong.

"No, she's not. She's…" Caleb wasn't sure how to describe it. "Well, ticked off at me for one thing."

"Because you were such a jerk in Helena?"

"So were you."

Reed shrugged. "She'll forgive me in the blink of an eye, once I tell her I'm moving back."

"I'll sign it over to you today," Caleb offered. Now that the decision was made, he felt as if a weight had been lifted from his shoulders.

"What about Mandy?"

"That's between me and Mandy."

Caleb's brain was going off in about a million directions. Was it possible that she loved him? Had she told Reed she loved him? What business did she have loving him? She was a Lyndon Valley woman, and he was a Chicago man. How was that going to work?

"You slept with her, right?"

"None of your damn business."

"Do you think a woman like Mandy would sleep with just anyone?"

Of course Caleb didn't think she'd do that. And he couldn't help remembering how it felt to have her sleeping in his arms, the taste of her lips, the satin of her skin. And he wanted to feel it all again, so very, very badly.

"I thought you were going to take my head off in Helena." Reed chuckled low. "She had no idea what she did, by the way, telling you she was staying with me."

Caleb remembered that moment, when she had a choice and she hadn't picked him. He never wanted to feel that gut-wrenching anguish again. Mandy belonged with him. Not with Reed and not with any other man. Him, and him alone.

"You should go talk to her," Reed suggested.

"I *was* going to talk to her. Good grief, can I make at least one decision on my own?"

"Apparently not a good one. When were you going?"

Caleb pasted Reed with a mulish glare. "The jet's warming up on the tarmac."

"You have a jet?"

"Yes."

"Bring a ring."

Caleb drew back. "Excuse me?"

"You better bring a ring. You've been a jerk, and you need to apologize so she'll forgive you. And that whole thing's going to go a whole lot smoother with you on one knee."

"You haven't spoken to me in ten years, and you come back and the first thing you do is tell me who I should marry?"

"Second thing, technically," said Reed.

"Where do you get your nerve?"

"I'm bigger than you. I'm stronger than you. And it's not me who wants you to propose."

Caleb scoffed out a laugh at that. "It's not?"

"No. It's you."

Caleb stared at Reed, suddenly seeing past everything to the brother that he'd loved, still loved. Because, despite everything that had happened between them, it was still the same Reed. And he was still smart and, in this case, he was also right.

Caleb grinned. "You want to catch a ride back to Lyndon?"

Mandy had sworn to herself she wouldn't wallow in self-pity. She wouldn't pine away for Caleb, and she wouldn't let herself get involved any further in the brothers' conflict. She was going cold turkey.

Abigail was right. It was none of Mandy's business. They were grown men, and she had to let it go and let them work it out for themselves. Or not.

When it came down to it, Travis was right, too. Getting involved with Caleb had brought her nothing but heartache. What had she been thinking? That she could spend days and nights with a smart, compelling, exciting, successful man, and her heart wouldn't become involved.

She ran a curry comb over Ryder's haunch, dragging the dust out of the gelding's coat.

It was ironic, really. She'd spent the better part of her life giving advice out to people. She could be quite obnoxiously meddlesome at times. But she was always so certain she was right. She harped on people to take her advice, since she usually had some distance from the problem and a better perspective than the person who was in the thick of it. Yet, when people who loved her gave her perfectly reasonable, logical, realistic advice, she blew them off and did it her own way.

It served her right.

And she was now exactly where she deserved to be, losing Reed as her dear friend and neighbor and desperately missing Caleb. Reed had been right. She loved Caleb. She was madly, desperately in love with a man who'd never again give her the time of day.

If she closed her eyes, she could still feel his arms around her.

"Mandy?" his voice was so real, it startled her.

Her eyes flew open, and she blinked in complete astonishment. "Caleb?"

How could he be standing in her barn?

But he was.

She blinked again.

He *was*.

"Hello, Mandy." His tone was gentle. He was wearing a pair of worn blue jeans and a soft flannel shirt, looking completely at home as he slowly walked toward her.

She gripped the top rail of the stall with her leather-gloved hand. "What are you doing here?" she managed.

A slow smile grew on his face as he drew closer under the bright, hanging fluorescent lights. "You want to go to Rio?"

She watched his expression closely. "Is that a joke?"

"I'm completely serious."

"No. I am not going to Rio with you." She meant what she said. She was completely done with the Terrells.

He came to a halt a few feet away from her. "You said you would."

"That was before."

"Before what?"

Before her plan to fix everything had crashed and burned around her ears. Before she'd learned the truth about herself. Before she'd fallen in love with him and opened herself up to a world of hurt.

"Before we fought," she said instead.

"We didn't fight."

She shot him with a look of disbelief.

"Okay," he agreed. "We fought. And I'm sorry. I know you were just trying to help."

She shook her head, rubbing her palms across her cheeks and into her hair, trying to erase the memories. "I meddle. I know I meddle. And *I'm* the one who's sorry."

"I forgive you. Now, come to Rio."

"No."

"Come to Rio and marry me."

"N— *What?*"

"I thought…" He moved slowly closer, carefully, as if he was afraid to spook her. "I thought we could fly to Rio, get a manicure, have a blender drink and you could marry me."

There was a roaring inside her brain while she tried to make sense of his words. "Caleb, what are you try-ing to—"

He reached out and took her hands. "I'm trying to say that I love you, Mandy. And I like it when you meddle. I especially like it when you meddle with me."

Her heart paused, then thudded forcefully back to life, singing through her chest.

He loved her? He *loved* her?

Exhilaration burst through her.

She let out an involuntary squeal and launched herself into his arms. He hugged her tight, lifting her off the ground and spinning her around.

"Why? How?" she couldn't help but ask, voice muffled in the crook of his neck. She didn't expect this, didn't deserve this.

"I don't know why, but how? Mostly I just think about how beautiful you are, how sexy you are, how smart and caring and funny." He drew back and kissed her mouth. His lips were warm, soft, delicious and tender.

When he finally drew back and lowered her to her feet, she gazed up into his eyes. "I love you, too, Caleb. So very much."

"So, you'll come to Rio?"

"You know my family won't let you marry me in Rio."

"They can come along. I have a pretty big plane."

"We have to wait until my dad gets better."

"Of course we do," he agreed, kissing her all over again.

He captured both of her hands in his. His blue eyes danced under the lights. "You by any chance interested in a ring?" he asked.

She swallowed, unable to find her voice.

He tapped his shirt pocket, and she made out a telltale square bulge.

Joy flooded her. "You brought a ring to this engagement?"

"I did. A diamond."

Her lips broke into a grin. "Let's see it."

He reached into his pocket and extracted a small, white leather box. "It was Reed's idea."

"You talked to Reed?"

"He's inside with your brothers."

"Reed is *here?*" She couldn't believe it.

"Any chance we can focus on the ring right now?" Caleb popped open the spring-loaded top.

A beautiful, square-cut diamond solitaire in yellow gold was nestled against deep purple velvet. The sight took her breath away.

He leaned in and spoke in a husky whisper. "Do I know how to do a proposal or what?"

"That's one gorgeous ring."

"You like it?"

"I love it."

"Because we can exchange it if you want."

"Are you kidding? What else could I possibly want in a ring?"

Using his blunt fingers, he extracted it from the box.

She held out her left hand, and he smoothly pushed it onto her ring finger. It fit. She held her hand at arm's length, flexing her wrist and watching the sparkle.

"This should shut Travis up," she mused.

"Yes." Caleb kissed her finger with the ring. "Because that was my secret plan. I figured, you know, if you'd marry me, it would be a bonus. But what I was really looking to do was get your brother off my back."

"We're really going to do this? You and me? Us?" Both her brain and her emotions were operating on overload. Caleb had come back to Lyndon Valley. He loved her. They were staying together. It defied imagination.

"Just as soon as you'll let me."

Uncertainty suddenly overtook her. "But, what then? Where do we go? Where do we live? My family's here. You're there."

"Well, Reed will be back living at his ranch."

She froze. "Seriously?"

Caleb nodded.

"He's coming home?"

"He's already home."

She hugged Caleb tight, and his arms went fully around her. "Part time here," he said. "Part time in Chicago. We made it work for two weeks. I'm sure we can make it work for the rest of our lives."

Mandy sighed and burrowed herself in his chest. "For the rest of our lives."

Once again, Caleb couldn't seem to bring himself to let go of Mandy.

Back inside the ranch house, her brothers, Abigail and Reed all gathered around them, admiring her ring, hugging and kissing and laughing their congratulations. When they eventually gave way, Abigail went to the kitchen to find a bottle of champagne.

Caleb lowered himself into a leather armchair, and drew Mandy down into his lap, settling her against his shoulder, holding her hand and toying with the engagement ring on her finger.

His brother shot him a knowing grin, and Caleb smiled back, marveling at how the years had melted away. On the airplane and later in the car, he and Reed had talked. They'd talked about their years as children and teenagers, what had happened to each of them after Caleb had left for Chicago and Reed's plans for the future.

Seth retrieved six champagne glasses from the china cabinet, setting them out on the dining-room table. "So,

Caleb. Are you moving back here, or are you taking our sister away?"

"Both," said Caleb, casting a long glance at Mandy's profile. "We'll have to play it by ear to start. I'm hoping Reed won't mind if we stay at his place while we're in the valley."

"Welcome anytime," said Reed.

"Seriously?" Mandy asked in obvious surprise. "You're going to stay at your ranch?"

"Seriously," Caleb told her. "A very wise woman once told me I needed to change my perception of it."

He leaned in close to her ear. "I figure we'll need to make love in every room in the house."

She whispered back. "Not when Reed's around."

"What are you two whispering about?" asked Abigail as she appeared with a bottle of champagne.

"I'm sure you don't want to know," Travis sang, lifting the bottle from his sister's hands and peeling off the foil.

"I've been thinking," Caleb said to Reed, framing up an idea in his mind. "It's not really fair for Mandy and I to set up a permanent place in your house."

Reed frowned at him. "Why not?"

"I think we should be partners."

His brother shrugged. "Keep half of it if you want. But you're on the hook for the years we have a loss."

Caleb shook his head. "The ranch is yours. Danielle's already drafted up the papers. But I'll buy half of it back from you."

Reed scoffed out a laugh. "Right."

The champagne cork popped, and Abby laughed as the foam poured over Travis's hand.

"It's been recently appraised," Caleb noted. "So there'll be no trouble establishing a price."

Reed stared levelly across at him. "You think you're going to give me fifteen million dollars?"

"Fourteen five, actually. I hear the water rights are screwing with land values."

Abigail and Travis began handing around the full glasses.

"I'd take the offer," Seth told Reed.

"Don't be ridiculous," Reed countered.

"I'd play hardball if I was you," said Abigail. "Where's he going to find another ranch with such terrific neighbors?"

"Play hardball," Mandy agreed with her sister. She bopped the side of her head against Caleb's chest. "Give him the fifteen."

Then she sat up straighter and accepted a glass of champagne from her sister.

Travis handed one to Reed.

Reed brandished his own glass like a weapon. "I'm not taking any money for the ranch. And that's final."

"Mandy," Caleb intoned.

"Yes?" she answered, twisting her head to look at him.

"Please meddle."

She grinned, leaned in and gave him a very satisfying kiss on the lips. "Whatever you say, darling."

Caleb crooked his head to one side to paste Reed with a challenging look. "She's my secret weapon."

Seth raised his glass. "Congratulations, Caleb. You are the luckiest man in the world."

"Agreed," Caleb breathed.

Reed spoke up. "To the Jacobs and the Terrells. A new family."

"Here, here," everyone agreed, clinking glasses all around, then taking a drink.

"To my beautiful bride," Caleb whispered, gently touching his glass to Mandy's.

Her green eyes glowed with obvious joy. "Do you really want me to convince Reed to take the money?"

"Absolutely. Go get him, tiger."

* * * * *

KIDS ON THE DOORSTEP
Kimberly Van Meter

To the mothers of the world: raising children is the most important job we as adults will ever have, as they are our legacy and our future.

To my sister, Kristen, who wears the badge of motherhood with pride and inspires people to love without reservation, without judgment, without fear. She is a mama bear and a wonder to watch in action!

One

John Murphy had just stoked the fire and returned to his well-worn leather chair with his newspaper in hand when an urgent knock at the front door had him twisting in surprise.

It was nearly ten o'clock at night and the rain was quickly turning to sleet. This storm was supposed to hit the California Sierra Nevadas pretty hard by dumping a load of snow in the high country and plenty of it even in the foothills, so anyone with any kind of sense knew better than to be out and about. A bad feeling settled in his gut. There was no one he could imagine who would venture into this storm without good reason.

"John? It's me, Gladys."

The sound of his neighbor's voice, thin and reedy, alarmed him. It was too late for house calls of an ordinary nature and Gladys—after going through surgery a few days prior—should've been in bed resting.

He opened the door and Gladys offered him a weak and somewhat pained smile as she and three little girls were ushered in from the biting cold.

"What the hell is going on?" he asked yet immediately guided Gladys to his leather chair. "What in the Sam Hill are you doing out in this storm in your condition? You just had surgery, woman. Are you trying to kill yourself?"

"Don't yell at her. It's not her fault," piped up the middle girl whose short stack of wild hair was matted to her head. The poor kid looked like a drowned pixie. She rubbed at her pert nose but stared John down with attitude. "Daddy didn't stay long enough to listen that she was sick."

John ran his hand through his hair. "And you are? And who's your daddy?"

"We're the Dollings and I'm Taylor," the little tyke proclaimed, ignoring the nervous jostling from her older sister to be quiet. "Who are you?" she asked without hesitation.

"John Murphy," he grunted in answer. "And your daddy?"

Gladys broke in with a grimace. "This is Alexis, Taylor and the little one is Chloe. Oh, John, it's the most deplorable situation and I didn't know what to do. Look at them, the poor chickpeas, they're practically frozen to the bone and wearing nothing more than rags. I could throttle that irresponsible boy for this!"

"Throttle who?" John was growing more perplexed by the moment, but Gladys was obviously distressed enough without his blustering adding to it so he tried for patience. "Tell me what's going on here."

Gladys compressed her lips to a fine line. "My sister's grandson, Jason, God rest her soul that she never saw how badly he turned out, just showed up on my doorstep with the girls, saying he couldn't handle it anymore and he needed me to keep them for a while until he got back on his feet. More likely so that he can be footloose and fancy-free, is what I think but before I could talk some sense into him, he was gone." Her gaze softened as she took in the children's forlorn appearance but when she turned to him again, her expression was full of worry and embarrassment. "I didn't know what to do. I don't want to take them to the authorities. They are my family, even if only distantly."

The littlest, she couldn't be more than three he wagered, sneezed and he realized they were still standing there soaked. He went to the hall closet and returned with three blankets. Giving one to each girl, he told them to warm up by the fire while he tried making sense of things with Gladys.

"Start from the beginning," he instructed in a low voice so as not to scare the kids. "Where is their father and when is he coming back? Or how about their mother for that matter? They have to have a mother somewhere."

"Daddy said Mommy left us," Taylor answered before Gladys could. John turned toward Taylor and she continued, bundled in the blanket, despite several attempts by her older sister to shush her. She glowered at her sister. "Well, that's what he said."

"It's no one's business," the older one said, adding in a low tone, "Especially no stranger."

John looked to Gladys. "He split? No number, nothing?"

"Nothing. He barely took time enough to push the girls out of the car with their bag and then was off again. I tried to stop him but he was too fast for me." That last part came out accompanied by a trembling lip and John knew Gladys was ashamed of her weakened state. Under normal circumstances the older woman was like a hurricane but the last year had been rough on her and her age was starting to slow her down. He patted her knee in some semblance of comfort but he was certainly caught in a bad spot. It was clear Gladys was loath to involve the authorities but she wasn't in any shape to care for the kids herself.

John eyed the older girl. "Alexis, right? I take it you're the oldest?" She nodded warily. "How old are you?" he asked.

Alexis raised her chin. "I'm nine, almost ten. Taylor is five and Chloe is three."

So incredibly young. Essentially abandoned. John was at a loss of what to do. The closest he'd ever come to babies or children were his nephews and they only visited on holidays. Frankly, he was about as equipped to deal with these kids as a dog was to teach a cat how to fetch. But he knew he couldn't very well toss them out on their ears. Gladys had come to him for help even though the old girl was a little addled if she thought he was her best option. The girls stared up at him, waiting, and he realized he couldn't just stand there scratching his head.

"You need to get out of those wet clothes. If you don't already have pneumonia, you will by tomorrow," he grumbled, wondering what he could possibly find to fit three little girls. "And then, I think we ought to call Sheriff Casey, she'll know what to do for you guys."

"We're girls," Taylor corrected him.

"Sorry. My mistake. You *girls,*" he said, moving to the phone.

Gladys stopped him with a hand on his arm, beseeching him silently as she said, "I know it's what we *should* do but no one says we have to do it this very second.

Let's wait to make that call. Maybe Jason will be back tomorrow and everything will work itself out on its own. No sense in dragging in outsiders if we don't have to."

"You sure?" he asked, torn between wanting to make that call and wanting to reassure Gladys that everything was going to be fine. She nodded and his shoulders tensed even though he let out a gusty sigh. He turned to the girls. "Looks like you're going to bunk here tonight until we get things figured out. Alexis, I need you to help your sisters get settled in. The little one looks about ready to fall over, she's so tired. You been driving all night with your daddy?"

"Yeah."

"I thought so. Your great-aunt Gladys is real tired. She's not feeling good right now. What say we look at this problem with fresh eyes in the morning?"

"I guess." Her arm went around the baby protectively. "Where are we gonna sleep?" she asked after giving the entire room a quick once-over as if assessing the space herself. "That couch over there is big enough, I s'pose."

"There's no need for you girls to curl up on the couch. You can sleep in the guest bedroom. There's a bed big enough for the three of you. All right?"

"I seepy, Lexie." The little one's mouth stretched in a yawn so big it nearly knocked her over, then an awful, wet-sounding cough followed that John had a feeling needed antibiotics to clear up.

"She sick?" He gestured at the little one and Alexis picked up her baby sister as if to shield her, although as thin as all the girls were it just made the whole scene more pathetic and worrisome. "That cough doesn't sound good."

"It's just a cough. She'll be fine," Alexis said, but there was something in those blue eyes that told him she was more worried than she wanted to let on and it made him wonder how long that baby girl had been making those wet, gurgling sounds in her chest. His gut reaction told him she needed a doctor. And he was rarely wrong when his instincts started to clang like cowbells. But he didn't think it warranted a trip to the emergency so there wasn't much he could do about it until morning. He shot Gladys a meaningful look and she gave an imperceptible nod telling him she knew where his thoughts were going and agreed.

"Time to hit the hay," he said.

Gladys smiled her gratitude and sank a little farther into his chair as if it were swallowing her up and he shook his head at the circumstances. He'd always had a soft spot for lost critters and rehabilitating abused horses was part of his livelihood, but he never figured his tender side might catch him three lost little girls. "All right, Gladys, you ought to be in bed, too. You can take the other guest bedroom."

"Are you sure?" she asked, but her expression filled with ill-disguised relief. "I don't mean to be making trouble."

He helped her out of the chair. "Who are you kidding, old woman. You're nothing but trouble."

His comment elicited a weak chuckle as she allowed him to walk her down the hall and into the cold bedroom. He got her settled with a few extra blankets and as he turned to leave so she could change and climb into bed, her voice stopped him at the door frame. "Thank you, Johnny. I know this isn't your idea of a fun time. Tomorrow, we'll get out of your hair. I'll figure something out. It's not your problem and I'm sorry for dumping it in your lap. I…panicked a little. I know I shouldn't have but, oh, what a mess."

He nodded but otherwise remained silent. Gladys was the closest thing he had to a mother. If she had a problem, it was his problem, too. "See you in the morning, Gladys," he said and shut the door.

Returning to the living room where the girls remained, color returning to their cheeks as the fire warmed their frozen little bodies, Alexis ventured forward, surprising him with her question.

"Mister…" Alexis said hesitantly. "Before we go to bed do you got anything we could eat? Bread or something?"

"Let me guess…no dinner?"

Alexis gave a short shake of her head but didn't elaborate. A curse danced behind his teeth as he picked up clearly what she hadn't said. Probably missed more than a few meals here and there judging by the sharp points of their shoulders. Neglect was a form of abuse, too. He'd saved more animals from the brink of starvation than he cared to count but seeing the evidence of neglect in children made his stomach clench with disgust. This was why he kept himself apart from nearly everyone except for the handful of family he had. On the whole, most people disappointed and annoyed him. In this case, he went way past annoyed and straight into pissed off.

"Follow me," he instructed, his voice gruffer than he intended and he winced inwardly as he saw the baby flinch, her rail-thin arms clutching at her sister's neck. *Ah hell…*he cursed himself for scaring her. These kids were traumatized to varying degrees but he could see the baby was particularly jumpy. He needed to treat them as he would a traumatized horse. Voice calm yet firm. Trying again, he said, "Let's see what we can rustle up."

He walked to the kitchen and flipped the light as he

went. Reaching into the fridge he pulled out the beans and rice that he'd made earlier in the day.

Alexis had set the baby down to come and peer into the pots as he put them on the stove to reheat. "What's this?" she asked, her eyes wary.

"Beans and rice. All I got on such short notice. Take it or leave it."

Chloe scrambled to the table and climbed into the chair despite the fact that it was way too big for her small frame. The thick oak chair nearly swallowed the toddler but she didn't seem to care as she eyed the pots with blatant desire. "I like beans," she said.

Taylor joined her sister. "Me, too."

John looked to Alexis but she was too busy checking out her surroundings. When she took her tentative spot at the table, he surmised that beans and rice were okay with her.

He grabbed three bowls, heaped a mound of rice and then dumped a ladleful of beans on top and handed the girls their dinner.

They shoveled the food into their mouths without reservation and as one bite cleared the spoon, they were digging in for the next. He wanted to ask when they'd eaten last but a part of him didn't want to know. It would just intensify the burn that was already stoking his temper.

He decided to keep them talking in the hopes that the food would distract them into divulging some details about their situation. "So, where you girls from?"

"Arizona," Taylor answered, scooping the last of her beans onto her spoon with her fingers. She looked to him with her empty bowl, her small tongue snaking out to lick her lips. "Is there more?"

Alexis looked up from her bowl. "Don't be a little piglet."

Taylor shot Alexis a scowl. "I'm no piglet. But I'm still hungry."

John smiled and took Taylor's bowl. "There's plenty more where that came from. I made extra this time around."

He handed Taylor her refilled bowl and focused on Alexis who seemed intent on her supper yet John got the sense that she was covertly taking everything in.

"What's your mom's name?" he asked.

Alexis ignored John's question and, noticing that Chloe had stopped eating, pushed her bowl away. "We're tired. Can we go to bed now?"

"Chloe's not finished with her supper," he said.

Alexis squared her jaw but remained silent. He wondered what was going through her head.

Sighing, he decided this battle wasn't worth fighting. He wasn't going to get any answers tonight. He was looking into the face of a child who knew something about keeping secrets. He hated to think of what the kid was hiding from. "All right, no more questions. Bedtime."

The ranch house was plenty big enough for three small, uninvited guests and an elderly companion but the house rarely had so many people milling around, not since he and Evan were kids and their mom had once rented the extra rooms out to help make ends meet.

He gave them each one of his T-shirts to sleep in and after they'd changed in the adjoining bathroom, they ran to the bed.

Alexis helped Chloe up and Taylor climbed up by herself.

"You need anything else?" he asked gruffly.

"Mister—"

"John," he corrected Chloe.

"Mr. John, do you have a mommy here?"

"A mommy?"

Alexis clarified. "She means do you have a wife?"

He shook his head. "No. Just me and the horses."

Taylor, who had already snuggled into the pillows, sat up with a gap-toothed grin. "Horses?"

"That's right. This is a horse ranch. I've got about ten stabled right now. Why? You like horses?"

Taylor nodded. "Can I see them tomorrow?"

He didn't want to make promises. The first order of tomorrow would be to call the authorities. "We'll see."

Clicking off the light, he closed the door but not before catching a glimpse of Alexis's face turned to the window, an incredibly sad expression on her young profile.

He suspected that little girl felt responsible for her sisters but there was only so much a child could do. It wasn't right. But it happens. That was something he knew well. He just hated seeing it because it dredged up a litany of feelings he'd buried a long time ago. Something about that little girl's expression poked and prodded at the tender spot in his heart in the same way an animal did that everyone else would rather give up on than save.

And to be honest, he didn't know how he felt about that but he suspected his quiet life was about to get noisy.

Chloe coughed, the sound worrying him. No matter what else happened tomorrow, at the very least he was taking that baby to the doctor.

Renee Dolling drove slowly down the dirt driveway, glancing once again at the address she'd scratched on a piece of paper before leaving Arizona, and prayed that Jason's great-aunt hadn't moved in the ten-plus years since she'd last seen the old woman. From what she remembered, Gladys Stemming was a mouthy one although harmless. But then, Renee had only met her once and who knew what she was like now.

She'd come here as a last-ditch effort. She'd been to all the usual places Jason used to frequent in their neck of the woods in Arizona and had come up empty. Far as Renee knew, Gladys was Jason's only living relative so it served to reason, he might've taken the kids there before he split. If they weren't here…

Think positive. You've gotten this far, don't give up now.

She went to the door and knocked, the absolute stillness of the countryside unnerving her. She knocked again, harder than the first time but the sound just echoed into the inky dark. She glanced around, noted the absence of a vehicle as well as any other sign of civilization and fought the wave of despair. She didn't even know if this was where Gladys still lived. *Okay. Focus. Look for some kind of sign that she does,* Renee instructed herself so she didn't dissolve into a puddle of frustrated tears. Walking across the short porch, she peered into a window and saw the lumps of furniture but nothing that might tell her who lived there.

She rubbed her arms briskly. She'd forgotten how cold it got here. Stomping her feet to keep the circulation moving, she caught the shadowed outline of the mailbox at the end of the driveway. Climbing into the car, she drove to the edge of the road and pulled open the mailbox to feel inside.

Bingo.

Pulling a stack of mail, she glanced at the address and nearly went weak with relief. Gladys Stemming. She still lived here. But even as she thumbed through the hefty stack her elation was short-lived. Apparently, it'd been at least a week since the mail was picked up, which could mean the old woman hadn't been home for a while. Replacing the mail, she chewed her bottom lip. She'd have to come back tomorrow, maybe go into town and ask around. Somebody was bound to know where the old woman was and perhaps, if Gladys had them, her children.

Putting the car into drive, she looked down at the bedraggled and ugly stuffed rabbit that had belonged to Taylor. Renee had found it, abandoned, at their old house after she'd gotten out of rehab. That was four months ago. She'd been searching for him and the girls ever since. Renee didn't much care where Jason went—heaven help him if she managed to get her hands around his neck for this latest stunt—but she needed her girls.

Tears pricked her eyes again but she sniffed them back. She was close. She could feel it.

A fresh flood of anger followed. Damn you, Jason. *Where the hell have you taken my kids?*

Renee reluctantly drove away, refusing to believe that her children were far, that Jason had taken them to a place where she'd never find them. She tried to ignore the guilt that rose to slap her in the face whenever she let herself remember that she was the first one to walk out on their children.

It wasn't her proudest moment but hitting rock bottom usually isn't. Admitting to herself she was an alcoholic trapped in a loveless marriage was a tough pill to swallow, and even as she was committed to sobriety the price had been pretty steep.

Ten long years of missteps and mistakes with Jason, a man who had less depth than a cartoon character. It was enough to make her want to hide in shame over every bad decision she and Jason had put their girls through but she'd vowed things would be different once she got out of rehab.

Only to find them gone. Renee imagined Jason made the decision to take off shortly after she told him she wanted a divorce. He'd known this was the best way to hurt her. And damn, he knew her well.

Every day without her girls felt like knives in her heart.

Two

The following morning just as he always did, John rose at 5:30 a.m. to start the day and for a split second, as he set the coffee to percolating and stoked the coals in the fireplace to a fresh blaze with kindling and a small piece of seasoned oak, he almost forgot that he wasn't alone. But when a person had been a bachelor as long as John there were some things that didn't slip your notice. Such as the prickling feeling at the back of your neck when you know someone is behind you, staring. He turned and found Taylor standing in the archway, scratching her leg with her toe, her eyes fixed on him.

"Go back to bed. It's too early."

"You're up," she pointed out as she scrubbed at her pixie nose with her palm, her gaze wide and expectant.

"I'm a grown-up. You're still a kid—" *practically still in diapers* "—and kids need their rest. Don't you want to grow up big and strong?"

She thought about it for a second before nodding but then said, "But I can't rest if I'm not sleepy. Can *you*, Mr. John?"

Not really. He didn't much see the point in lounging in bed if he wasn't tired, either. But if he didn't send her back to bed with her sisters, he'd have to find something to entertain her with and he didn't have a clue as to how to entertain a five-year-old little girl. He eyed her speculatively. "You hungry?"

She nodded eagerly. "Are we having more of them beans?" she chirped as she followed him into the kitchen. "They were real good. You're a good cooker, Mr. John."

"I don't know about that, and stop calling me Mr. John. Just John, okay?"

"Okay," Taylor agreed easily, plopping into the chair she'd taken last night. "What's for breakfast, then?"

"Oatmeal." He caught her expression falter and he added quickly, "Or eggs. Take your pick."

"Eggs, please. I like them all mixed up. Do you like them that way? Chloe doesn't like eggs so maybe she could have the oatmeal. But me and Lexie like eggs a lot. Chloe didn't like the way Daddy made his eggs, she said they tasted funny. I didn't think so but sometimes he made her a special kind. Maybe she didn't like just his special eggs because when Lexie made eggs she ate 'em right up. Do you make them special, Mr. John?"

The dizzying speed of the child's twisting and nearly nonsensical dialogue almost had John staring in confusion as he tried to decipher even a quarter of what she'd said but something in that monologue had struck a chord of alarm. "Special eggs, Taylor?"

"Yeah, sometimes he made Chloe her own eggs but—" Taylor's little face scrunched in distaste "—they always made her tummy hurt afterward. Maybe Daddy wasn't a very good cooker."

"Maybe not," John murmured, though he was starting to feel a little sick to his stomach himself. "How come your Daddy always made Chloe her own special eggs?"

Taylor shrugged. "I dunno. But Daddy yells at Chloe a lot."

"Why's that?"

"He just does." Taylor's expression dimmed with sadness and John felt something in his chest pull. Her voice dropped to a scared whisper. "She gets lots of spankings."

Chloe was hardly more than a baby. No one should be raising a hand to her little body.

John stiffened at the anger pouring through his veins at what he was hearing and moved to the fridge to grab the eggs. He'd heard enough and by the time he filled the sheriff's ear with what he'd learned, there was no way in hell those kids were going back to that son of a bitch. He offered a smile to the little tyke even though he was itching to put his fist through the wall, and went through the motions of cooking up a batch of mixed-up eggs that weren't *special* in any way.

Gladys didn't look very good, John thought as he brought her a cup of coffee.

"You sure you don't want to go see that doc of yours?" he asked.

She waved away his concern. "I'm fine. Just a little winded is all from the excitement last night. I just don't know what to do about those poor babies. I don't even know if they've been in school or what kind of lives they've been living. I'm just beside myself."

"What about the mother? Do you know where she might be? Maybe I could place a few calls."

Gladys made a look of distaste. "Oh, don't waste your time with that one. I only met her once but she never made much of an impression. A little snooty and stand-offish if you ask me and we never really hit it off. Not that I was close with Jason, mind you, but at least he was family. I've known him since he was a boy. Never had much of a character. Nothing like you and Evan. If you boys had been anything like Jason your mama would've lost the ranch the moment the tax man had started calling. No…I knew from the time he was a young man he wasn't going to amount to much but I'd hoped I was wrong. There's no satisfaction in being right in this instance."

"So you think the mother just took off or something like Jason did?"

Gladys sighed. "I don't know but what kind of mother would leave her babies behind? I can only imagine," she said, her voice catching as the ghost of an old pain re-appeared.

John agreed privately but allowed the quiet to dull the edge of Gladys's long-ago loss. Even after all this time Gladys felt the agony of her stillborn son. He supposed that was a hurt that never truly healed. Not even with decades of time as a balm.

"So what do we do?"

Gladys looked at him sharply then sighed. "We? Oh, Johnny, this isn't your problem. I'll figure something out."

"Don't be ridiculous," he said. "You're in no shape to be tending to three little kids. And frankly, I don't care what you say, I think you need to see your doctor. That surgery might've taken more out of you than you realize."

Gladys was silent for a moment and John had a feeling she was wrestling with her pride, which was no small thing. She wasn't accustomed to being dependent on someone else and it was probably killing her. But it was a temporary thing and she realized this, too, and finally nodded in agreement.

"You might be right," she conceded with a sigh. "And I've been thinking about what you said about contacting the authorities. Maybe that's the best thing to do. I don't think Jason or Renee were doing a great job with these girls. Chloe is most definitely going to need an antibiotic for that cough and something tells me she's been sick for a while. The poor baby has no color to speak of. They ought to have to work to get them back. Maybe it'll teach them a lesson in being parents."

"So you're saying you're okay with me calling the sheriff?"

"Yes, on one condition…the children stay together. They need each other."

"I'll make the call," he said, moving to grab the phone. "And then I'm taking Chloe to the doctor."

Renee pulled to a stop and took a cursory glance around the ranch that bordered Gladys's property. She'd waited two agonizing days, but by 11 a.m. the third day Renee figured she ought to start poking around. If Gladys had gone on vacation, she might've left instructions with a neighbor to watch the house for her. Either way, Renee might get some kind of information that might be useful in finding Jason and the kids.

She was nearly to the door when a deep voice startled her.

"Didn't you see the sign?"

Her heart jackhammering in her chest, she stammered a bit as she turned, her gaze catching the sign he was talking about. Trespassers Will Be Shot. No Exceptions. She swallowed and got straight to the point. "I'm sorry…I'm looking for Gladys Stemming but she doesn't seem to be home and I wondered…"

"What do you want with Gladys?"

She frowned at his tone. "I'm Renee Dolling. Uh, well, she's my aunt, by marriage, and I—" Why was she explaining herself to this man? Renee straightened. "Has she gone on a trip? If so, do you know when she'll be back?"

"Dolling?" He repeated, a sudden shrewd light entering the hard stare coming at her from beneath a dusty and worn baseball cap. Little ducktails of dirty blond hair too long to be fashionable stuck out from under the hat as if to clearly state he had no time for such niceties as regular haircuts. And his sun-darkened face had a boyish charm that was completely at odds with the stern expression pinching his mouth as he said again, "Did you say your name was Dolling?"

"Yes…do I know you?"

"Name's John Murphy and, no, we've never met, but you've sure got some explaining to do."

"Excuse me?"

"Three days ago your husband dumped your kids with a sixty-seven-year-old woman and took off without so much as a 'see you later' and she'd just had surgery for a triple bypass, but you wouldn't know that now, would you, because you dumped your kids before he did."

"He's not my husband," she muttered yet felt heat blooming in her cheeks at his words. *At least he wouldn't be in a few months.* The divorce wasn't quite final in the eyes of the courts but as far as she was concerned Jason could take a long walk off a short pier after the hell he'd put her through. *Selfish bastard.* Wait a minute… "Did you just say my husband dropped the girls off with Gladys?"

"I did."

A relieved smile broke through her annoyance at being interrogated and she exhaled loudly. "Oh, thank God. Where is she? I've been looking for the girls for months and I've been worried sick."

Her relief was short-lived as the man continued to openly assess her, as if he were weighing something heavy in his mind, and unease fluttered in her stomach. "Is there a problem?" she asked stiffly.

"I'd say so."

"Which is?"

"You don't have custody any longer."

Renee's knees nearly snapped out from under her as she sucked in a pained gasp. "What?"

"Yesterday afternoon your girls were placed in the protective custody of their aunt Gladys as a temporary measure until things can be sorted out. No mother, no father...Gladys was their closest relative. Simple as that."

"Well, I'm back so that won't be necessary, now will it?"

"Doesn't work that way. Courts are involved. Convince *them* you've decided to be a mom again and then we'll see. But, can't say that will be easy. Seems the courts around here don't take lightly to parents abandoning their kids."

She bristled at the thinly veiled disgust behind his seemingly mild statement and allowed the building anger to hold the panic at bay.

He didn't have the right to judge her. No one did. "Not that it's any of your business but my reasons for leaving my children with *their father* are my own. I didn't know he was going to do what he did. Just point me in the direction of my children and we'll get out of your life."

"I already told you I can't do that." He shifted lazily

against the fence he was leaning against, the slow action belying the fierce set of his jaw.

"What?"

"You heard me. The girls are in Gladys's custody. If you want your kids, you're going to have to talk to the court."

"This is ridiculous," Renee said, her voice hitting a shrill note. "What the hell is going on here? Are you telling me that you're keeping my girls from me? You're *stealing* my children?" Her voice rose to a hysterical pitch on that last question while her heart beat so hard it felt as if it might burst right out of her chest. This wasn't happening. This had to be a bad dream. A horrific, horrible dream. Total strangers didn't just get to keep other people's kids. It just didn't happen.

"No. The way I see it, three little girls were abandoned by their no-account parents and the law stepped in to protect them. If that's not the way you see it, then you need to prove otherwise to the judge. Until then, get off my property."

Three

John watched as the blonde marched over to her car. She shot him one last burning look filled with animosity but he didn't care. Something Taylor had said was still sticking in his mind in a terrible way. Was it possible that their father had put something bad into the baby's eggs? And if so, did the mom know about it? He watched as the woman, Renee, climbed into her car and slammed the door. No doubt she was wishing his head were caught between the door and the chassis. She sat in her car glaring at him, clearly debating her next move.

The front door opened and Gladys appeared with the children flocked around her, each bundled in an odd assortment of secondhand clothes that looked old enough to earn a spot in a museum somewhere, and John knew that any chance of a peaceful resolution was over.

"Lexie?" The woman had jumped from the car and was now running toward the girls until John blocked her path with a warning that she didn't heed. "Get out of my way," she said in a low growl. "Those are my girls and you're not going to stop me from at least seeing them!"

John turned to Gladys, who was watching the scene with alarm, and instructed the older woman to go back inside with the kids.

"Those are my kids! You can't keep me from them. I have a right to see them. Let me go or you and I will have major problems that go way beyond your manners and rude disposition. Do you hear me?"

"I hear you just fine. Now you listen to me. I don't know you from Adam but I do know you're not going anywhere near those girls until we get things sorted out. They've been through plenty without you traipsing into their lives acting like you're here to pick up lost luggage after a long plane ride."

She paled and her bottom lip actually trembled slightly but John wasn't swayed. Where had she been when her girls were going without food? When Chloe got sick and had no one to take her to the doctor? Those little girls needed someone to champion them and right now, he was it.

"You don't know anything about my life."

"About that you're right and, woman, I don't care to know. *You* walked out on your kids. Their *daddy* walked out on them. I didn't ask for this but it landed in my lap just the same and I'll be damned if I'm going to let those girls go to the first ditzy broad who comes my way saying she wants her babies back." She gasped and he gave her arm a little shove as he released her. "Now, the best thing you can do right this minute is to get off my property before I have you arrested for trespassing."

Tears welled in her eyes but she didn't let them fall. Rubbing at her arm where he'd kept a firm grip, she sent him a scathing look and promised to return with the authorities.

"You can't just keep someone's kids like you would a stray puppy! They're mine and you can't—"

"Yack, yack, yack. You do what you feel is necessary. Until then, get lost."

Renee drove like a crazy woman straight to the Sheriff's Department in Emmett's Mill, part of her sobbing with elation that she'd finally found her girls and the other part railing at the asshole who had the audacity to keep them from her as if he had the right.

Coming to an abrupt stop in front of the police station, she pushed open the double doors and stalked inside. She approached the reception desk and banged on the little bell for service when the woman behind the desk was slow to open the sliding protective glass window.

"I need to talk to an officer right away," she said to the dispatcher-receptionist, ignoring the woman's look of annoyance. "A man is keeping my children from me and I need an officer to go out there and get them."

"Excuse me? Come again? You say someone's holding your kids?"

"Yes. A man named John Murphy—"

"That name sounds awful familiar...does he own the Murphy ranch out on the outskirts of town?"

"Yeah, I guess it was a ranch of some kind." She vaguely remembered seeing a few horses and a dog. Renee let out a short breath as incredulity warred with extreme frustration at the woman's failure to grasp that a serious crime was being committed. She seemed more interested in playing the Name Game, and Renee tried again. "Yeah, it was a ranch but I hardly think that's relevant when I'm trying to tell you that this John Murphy has *kidnapped* my children. He has my kids and I want them right now. Can I speak with a deputy please?"

"Don't get huffy." The woman's mouth pinched, causing little lines to crease her lips in a most unflattering way. "All the available deputies are out on a call. But if you leave a name and number—"

Renee slapped her hand down on the counter, making the woman jump and her hand flutter to her chest in alarm but Renee was past caring about making waves. She wanted her kids. "I will not. A crime is being committed and I want a goddamn officer. Do you hear me?"

The woman's deep-set eyes narrowed and Renee knew she'd just crossed over to the place of No Return and she was pretty sure that place was also nicknamed Up Shit Creek Without a Paddle because moments later, those deputies that were previously unavailable came pouring out and Renee found herself in handcuffs.

"What are you doing?" Renee shrieked as the deputy led her to a small single cell in the rear of the building. "I come here for help and you're arresting me?"

"Nancy pressed the panic button, which means you must've done something to cause her to panic. This is for everyone's safety until we figure out what's going on."

A woman officer entered the room. "I got this, Fred. You can go ahead and take that coffee break you were wanting earlier." She waited for Deputy Do-Right Fred to leave and then she introduced herself. "I'm Sheriff Casey. Seems you're making friends wherever you go. I got a call from John Murphy about a half hour before you showed up and started abusing my staff. Want to tell me what's going on?"

Renee's cheeks warmed at the cloaked rebuke and took a minute to calm herself before she answered. "My ex-husband, Jason Dolling, took off with our kids and

I've been trying to find them for the past four months. I remembered that Jason had a great-aunt in the area and so I came looking for my girls here and found them at the neighbor's house!"

"Are you sure they're your kids?"

Renee stared at the woman. "Are you kidding me? Of course I know for sure. They're *my* kids. That's not something you forget."

"According to John, you walked out on them. That true?"

"I left them with their father for personal reasons," Renee said, fuming. "I don't see how that's relevant."

"I'm the one asking the questions. Why'd you leave them?"

"I told you. It was personal."

"Yeah…it usually is." The woman regarded her shrewdly and Renee felt her jaw tense. She got the distinct impression this small-town sheriff was judging her and there was nothing Renee hated more than to be put on display just so someone else could offer their opinion. The sheriff sighed. "Well, we've got ourselves a situation."

"Yes, I agree. Some hillbilly horse rancher has my children and I require your assistance to retrieve them," Renee said.

"That's not exactly how I see it," the sheriff admitted with a shake of her head.

"Oh? Is there any other way to see things? Perhaps you'd like to swab my cheek for DNA to make sure I'm their mother."

The sarcasm in her voice did little to soften the sheriff toward her but Renee was losing patience with this whole ridiculous routine. And to think she'd thought the hardest part of this mess would've been to find Jason and the girls, not pick them up. Noting the narrowed stare and gathering frown on the sheriff's face, she tried again. "Listen, I'm tired and I just want to get my girls. It seems there's been a misunderstanding but no harm done. So if you'll just provide a police escort, we'll be out of your hair before you know it and everything can go back to the way things were before me and my girls ever stepped foot in this godfor—" she checked that part of her sentence "—uh, town."

The sheriff smiled but Renee felt the chill before the woman started talking. "You never answered my question." At Renee's blank stare, the sheriff asked again, "Why'd you leave your kids behind with a man who, by the sounds of it, wasn't fit to water a dog much less care for three babies?"

No one hated the truth of that answer more than her, but if she lied it would only make her look worse so Renee grit her teeth and admitted her greatest shame to a total stranger. "Because I was in rehab."

"Rehab."

In that one word, Renee heard a wealth of condemnation and she wanted to scream. She'd get no help from the sheriff. Fine. *On to Plan B.* Inside she was shaking with frustration but she kept her expression calm, knowing if she had any chance of getting her girls she had to first get the hell out of this jail cell.

The sheriff sighed. "Okay, here's the deal. John told me Gladys Stemming has temporary guardianship for the time being so until you get in front of the judge and have that amended, the order stands and I can't let you charge out there and take the kids. But seeing as you haven't actually committed a crime I can't keep you here so, if I let you out of this cell, you're going to promise me that you're not going to rattle any more cages with your screeching and hollering. That's not how things are done around here, you hearing me?"

Renee swallowed and nodded though it killed her to agree to those terms, especially when her first instinct was to drive straight back to that ranch and take the girls and run. Fortunately, good sense prevailed and she rationalized that once she got in court—in front of someone normal instead of these small-town hillbilly types who made up the rules as they went along—she knew she'd get her girls back and they could leave this nightmare behind.

"I hear you. Loud and clear," Renee answered. "I'm sorry for freaking out your receptionist. I was upset. I haven't seen my girls in months and contrary to what you may think about me, I've been desperately searching for them since Jason took off," she added, with a dose of humility that wasn't entirely fake for she really hadn't meant to frighten anyone.

"Um-hmm. Well, just see that you keep your nose clean until you can get to court. I don't want to have to lock you up again."

That makes two of us.

John sat across the table from Alexis and Taylor while Chloe helped Gladys bake cookies in the kitchen.

"Was that your mama?" he asked the girls. Both were wearing solemn expressions, though there was a hint of anger in Alexis's. He sighed. "If that woman was your mama, she's going to come back and if the courts decide she's fit, you're going to have to go with her. Don't you want to see your mama?"

Taylor looked uncertain but as she slanted a quick glance at her older sister, who had remained stoic, she chose to keep her answer locked up tight. Though her silence didn't last long.

"I want to stay with you, Mr. John," Taylor blurted. "I like it here. It's warm and you're a good cooker and I don't mind sharing a bed with my sisters because it's soft and I don't get woken up by bugs running across my toes. Please don't make us leave, Mr. John."

That last part—delivered with a child's earnestness—hit him square in the chest. He didn't want to give the kid false promises but he couldn't imagine breaking her heart like everyone else in her short life had done. "There are rules when it comes to kids," he started, hating that it wasn't as simple as Taylor saw it. "If your mama isn't fit then you have to go to a court appointed something-or-another. This is a temporary thing that we got going on right now." Tears sprang to Taylor's eyes and Alexis pulled her closer. Ah hell… rules were meant to be broken, weren't they? "Listen, I'll see what I can do but if you stay here, there are rules here, too. Chores, helping out. I run a working horse ranch and I don't have time to be chasing after three little girls who aren't prone to listening." He gave Alexis a short look. "Am I clear?"

Taylor nodded. "Can I help with the horses?"

John exhaled loudly, feeling as if he'd just agreed to take on the world for three little strangers. "We'll see. In the meantime, why don't you go help Mrs. Stemming with those cookies. I need to talk with your sister."

He watched as Taylor hopped from her chair and skipped to help Gladys, a bright smile wreathing her small face as Gladys handed her a bowl with cookie dough and told her to start rolling it into little balls for the oven. He'd told Gladys she shouldn't be up and about so much but the old gal wanted to feel useful and wouldn't be deterred. He figured for now it was all right but he was going to get her to see the doctor soon.

Once Taylor was suitably occupied he gestured for Alexis to follow him into the living room, which was a far enough distance from the kitchen to allow them some privacy.

She took a seat opposite him, perched on the edge of the cowhide sofa as if poised to bolt if the need arose. Everything about Alexis, from her rigid posture to her sharp, alert and wary gaze, told him that this girl had lost her childhood somewhere along the way of her life. He could relate somewhat. He'd often felt like Evan's father rather than just his older brother after their mom died. The weight of that responsibility had a tendency to suck the fun right out of growing up. He eyed her intently. This kid didn't know what it was like to be coddled and so he'd talk to her straight.

"You mad at your mama? It's okay if you are. She did a bad thing, leaving you like she did. But it seems maybe she has changed a bit since you saw her last. She seemed real upset, don't you think? Maybe you could sit down and chat with her for a bit, get a feel for what she's saying."

Alexis softened imperceptibly. "What do you mean?"

"Well, I know you still have feelings for your mama and that's okay, too. We can be mad at the people we love. But if you don't talk with her about your feelings, they'll just fester up inside of you and make you sick. It's like having an invisible infection inside your heart and it never gets better unless you treat it."

Alexis gave a stiff nod but remained quiet.

"I need to ask you something about Chloe." At the mention of her baby sister, her demeanor became protective. Her little fists curled and he doubted she even realized it.

"What about Chloe?"

"Was your daddy mean to her?"

"Daddy was mean to all of us."

"Yeah, I get that. He sure as hell ain't up for Father of the Year but I mean did he pick on Chloe more than the rest of you?" At first Alexis seemed reluctant to answer, her small mouth compressed as if trying to hold back what wanted to fall out, so he waited. His patience was rewarded when Alexis started talking in a barely audible whisper.

"Yes," she said, tears glittering in her eyes. "It got really bad when our mom left."

"Do you know why?" he asked gently and Alexis shook her head. Drawing a deep breath, he asked the question that had been bothering him the most. "Do you think your daddy was trying to make Chloe sick?"

Alexis bit the side of her cheek and her face paled as she struggled to hold back the tears that welled in her eyes.

"It's okay, you can tell me. I know you did your best to keep your sisters safe. Tell me what your daddy was doing to Chloe."

Alexis gulped and when she spoke again her voice shook. "Special eggs. He made her eat eggs that he made special and they always made her sick. The last time, right before we left Arizona, I watched him as he made Chloe's breakfast. He put something in it from under the kitchen sink and I know that's not where we keep the salt and pepper. We only keep cleaning supplies down there. So I didn't let her eat them."

"How'd you do that?"

"When he wasn't looking I switched our plates. I knew he hadn't put anything in me and Taylor's eggs and then I told him I didn't feel good. I threw my eggs away. He didn't care about me, but he made sure Chloe ate every bit on her plate before he'd let her get down from the table. I think my daddy—" She stopped on a painful sob and John felt her struggle as if it were his own. Alexis had confirmed his worst fear. The girls' father had been trying to poison his youngest daughter.

He caught Alexis's red-rimmed stare and made her a solemn promise. "You're never going back to that man. And if your mom isn't up to snuff...you aren't going back to her, either. That okay with you?"

Her answer was slow in coming but he suspected it came straight from her heart as she nodded and said, "Fine by me."

Good. First things first... "I'm friends with Sheriff Casey. You need to tell her everything you just told me."

"Are you sure we're not going to go back to Daddy?" she asked, her eyes scared.

"Not if I have anything to say about it."

"Daddy was real mean to Chloe," she said. "I'm afraid of what he'll do if we go back. He told Chloe if she didn't stop peeing her panties he'd put her outside like a dog because she smelled like one. He left her out there for hours in the rain. I went out and got her after he went to bed. It took all night to warm her up but the cough she has now...it's from that night. Sometimes she coughs so hard, she can't breathe."

"I know, honey, that's why I took her to the doc. She's got some medicine and we're taking care of that nasty cough so you don't need to worry anymore," he said, careful to keep his voice neutral and calm when inside he was to the boiling point. He couldn't imagine little Chloe locked outside, shivering in the rain, crying for her sisters and huddled against the door while her father sat in relative comfort inside the house. God help him if John got his hands on that man. But for now, he needed to lift the weight from this little girl's shoulders. "All right. Here's the deal. Sheriff Casey is a good person. There's no way you're going back to your daddy after you tell her what you told me. But you have to be honest with her so she can help. Okay?"

Alexis nodded and wiped at the remaining tears glistening on her downy cheek. "Why did she leave us with him?" she asked quietly, more to herself than to John. Suddenly, she looked at him as if expecting an answer though he didn't have one. "Maybe if she'd taken us with her...Chloe wouldn't have been hurt." She rose and glanced away, seeming much older than she really was. When she spoke again, her voice was cold. "I hate her. No one can make me love her again. Not you. Not anybody. I'll hate her forever and it doesn't matter if she's changed."

As John watched her stalk from the room to join her sisters, he didn't doubt a single emotion flowing from that little girl's strong heart. In a way he felt bad for the storm that was heading in the direction of Renee Dolling. That woman would have to dig deep to find the loving daughter she'd left behind. And, given what the girls had been through, Renee might find her way to China much easier than the way to her daughter's closed-off heart.

He didn't envy her. Not one bit.

Four

"Court ruling stands. Temporary guardianship will remain with Gladys Stemming until family court has had a chance to review the case further." The rap of the gavel brought Renee out of her stunned stupor. What had just happened?

She shot from her seat. "Excuse me? What the hell just happened?"

The Honorable Judge Lawrence Prescott II gave her a sharp look just as the bailiff started to move forward to deter her from approaching the bench. "You'll watch your language in my courtroom, miss," he said with a soft drawl that betrayed southern roots somewhere in his lineage. He gestured for her to take her seat and once she reluctantly returned to her chair, he said to his court reporter, who in Renee's opinion looked a lot like the receptionist at the sheriff's department, "Please repeat the judgment for Mrs. Dolling, Nancy."

Renee stared, unable to believe what she was witnessing, as indeed dour-faced sheriff's receptionist Nancy pulled the tape from the machine and repeated in a clipped voice the judgment that had just been rendered.

Schooling her voice into something less screeching and more reasonable, she tried a different tactic. "I heard the judgment. What I don't understand is how the court can appoint a virtual stranger as guardian for my children when I am their mother. They should be with me. Surely, you can understand that?"

Judge Prescott gave her a wintry glare and Renee felt her hopes of putting this nightmare behind her anytime soon freezing to the point of death. "What I understand is that you're a fickle woman prone to bad decisions when it comes to your children. That's what I know about *you*. What I know about Gladys Stemming is that she's solid and dependable." The judge glanced at John Murphy sitting opposite to Renee. "And since Mr. Murphy has offered the use of the ranch while she recuperates from her surgery, it is the court's determination that the children have a safe and stable environment while this whole situation is sorted out. In addition to that, the children themselves have expressed a desire to stay with their aunt...not you."

Renee sucked in a sharp breath at the rejection and blinked back tears. "Sir, if you gave me a chance to talk with my girls I would explain the circumstances and I'd get them to understand. In time, they might even forgive me for making a terrible mistake but if you keep them from me how can I hope to make everything right again? I love my girls and if I had the chance to do things over, I'd do it all much differently."

"Be that as it may, you didn't do things differently and your children suffered. Particularly your youngest."

What did he mean by that? Renee frowned. "Chloe? I don't understand how she suffered the most…"

Judge Prescott peered over his glasses at Sheriff Casey and continued, "Your youngest daughter is suffering from bronchial pneumonia due to horrific abuse at the hands of your ex-husband. The doctor she was taken to discovered old bruises and a hairline fracture in her left arm that had been left to heal on its own."

Renee felt sick. "I wasn't aware…"

"Yes, well, the court isn't interested in your excuses, Mrs. Dolling. The fact remains that you left your children in the hands of a dangerous and abusive man. It is the court's belief that only through the vigilant actions of your other children that Chloe is still alive."

Renee caught the stare of John Murphy—the man who was essentially getting her children—and she expected to see the same condemnation she was getting from the rest of the room, but she saw a flicker of something close to sympathy that took her by surprise. She looked away abruptly. She didn't want his pity—or anyone else's. Not that it was coming her way in waves at the moment but the scraps of her pride demanded she hold her head high. "How long is this temporary arrangement in effect?" she asked.

"As long as I deem necessary."

She took a risk as she said, "Forgive me, Your Honor, but I think it would be more appropriate for my children to go to a state-approved foster home rather than that of some man you happen to know from school. How do I know that this John Murphy isn't some kind of pervert?"

Nancy the court reporter-sheriff's receptionist gasped and her eyes widened before she returned her attention to her typing. Yep. Nancy's reaction pretty much clinched

Renee's sinking suspicion she just made things worse, but Renee wasn't going down without a fight.

"I've had just about enough of your mouth," the judge warned. Renee caught Sheriff Casey shaking her head as if Renee was just about the dumbest person on the planet to question the judge in such a manner, but Renee felt desperation setting in and, well, desperate people do dumb things. The judge shuffled his papers from the case and handed them to the court secretary for filing. "Get a job. Get a place to stay and then, when you get your ducks in a row, we'll talk about modification. In spite of your infernal mouth, I get the sense that you didn't know what a monster you'd left your kids with but that doesn't erase what happened to those girls. They need stability. They need someone they can trust. And they trust John and Gladys. I could order them into foster care but that would likely traumatize them more as I'd have to break them up because the system's full. They'd probably even go to separate counties. You want that?"

She couldn't imagine separating the girls. "No," she answered in a small voice.

"Then stop your complaining about how unfair things are *for you* and start focusing on getting your life back together so that your girls would rather be with you than a stranger."

That hurt. Renee swallowed the sharp retort that flew to mind as her defenses went up, because she knew as whacked out and nuts as this whole court drama was, there was a certain kindness directed at her children. If the girls wanted to be with John Murphy for the time being, she'd go along with it. But as soon as she won their trust back, they were packing it out of this place—fast.

* * *

Gladys met John at the door, her expression anxious. He allayed her fears quickly. "Court ruling stands but their mother, Renee, gets monitored visitation for the time being."

"Oh, thank goodness. Those poor babies have been tied up in knots since you left this morning. Alexis takes it the hardest. That poor lamb. I can only imagine what she's been through trying to protect her sisters from that man. It boggles my mind why their mother left those babies in Jason's care."

"In court she mentioned something about being in rehab when Jason split," John said, chewing the side of his cheek as he mulled over the information himself. What kind of rehab she didn't elaborate but drugs of any sort were bad news by his estimation. "But Judge Prescott didn't seem to care much for her excuse. I don't think he much cared for her, not that she helped matters at all. Her mouth sure does overload her ass a lot."

Gladys nodded. "I'm sure. I remember she had quite the smart mouth when I met her all those years ago. I'm just glad Larry was sitting on the bench today instead of a temporary judge that they sometimes bring in from the city to help with the backlog. Someone else less conservative might've given those babies back," she said with a shudder. "Makes me sick to think of it."

He agreed. Judge Prescott was an old-school kind of guy. If the law still allowed a hanging tree, he'd be the kind to supply the rope. "Where are the girls?" he asked, looking around.

She gestured toward the living room, where the faint sound of the television could be heard. He frowned. "I don't think they should be watching so much TV. Rots your brain from what I hear."

Gladys shooed him. "Stop being such a bear. Those babies could use a little pampering. Besides, now that we've gotten the court stuff out of the way we can start getting the older girls enrolled in school. They're going to need some routine and stability after what they've been through and school will keep their minds busy. I've already placed a few calls. It's going to be a couple days before we can track down Alexis's transcripts but until then they're going to need some clothes. They can't go to school in those rags."

He'd already been thinking about that, seeing as the clothes they showed up in weren't fit to line a dog's bed. "Maybe I could pick up a few pairs of jeans at the hardware store," he speculated, which earned him a scowl from Gladys.

"Hardware store? You can't put Rustlers on a bunch of girls. What's wrong with you? They need pretty things, not work boots and coveralls. Leave it to me. I'm handy on the computer and Macy's delivers anywhere in the United States."

John fished his wallet out from his back pocket and pulled his credit card free from the plastic holder. He handed it to Gladys. "Buy them whatever they need," he said. "I don't care how much it costs."

"John...that's too generous," Gladys protested softly but her eyes shone with love. She tucked the card into her apron pocket and gave his cheek a pat. "You're a good man, Johnny. Now, go on and do something useful. Don't you have horses to tend to?"

He did and Gladys giving him the go-ahead should've been a relief but he felt oddly compelled to check on the girls himself. He supposed that was only natural given the extreme circumstances but it still knocked him silly at odd moments that he was even in this situation. Him. The bachelor. With a house full of kids that he barely knew.

And despite his stern instruction not to, his thoughts kept pulling him in the direction of Renee. She ought to be the last person he was thinking about—just the fact that he was gave him serious pause—but he'd be a liar if he didn't admit where his thoughts kept wandering. She truly looked stricken when the judge told her of Chloe's injuries. Either she was a really good actress or she felt sick inside at the knowledge that her ex-husband had abused her baby. But the question that nagged at John was, why only Chloe? It seemed Jason Dolling had singled out that poor kid—not that he was going to win any parenting awards—but the other girls seemed to have been spared the brunt of his anger. Little Chloe didn't fare the same. A shudder of discomfort shook him as he realized just how close Chloe may have come to leaving this world if it hadn't been for her sisters, mostly Alexis, looking out for her. The doc found traces of arsenic lingering in Chloe's system from the repeated doses slipped into her "special eggs." Doc said she should be fine now but a few more doses and it could've been fatal. Peeking around the corner, he spied the three towheaded girls snuggled up to one another, watching television, and he knew there would be hell to pay if anyone—including their dingbat mother—tried to hurt them again.

He didn't understand his own vehemence but he knew enough not to question it. What was true, was true, and the protective feelings curling around his heart were solid even if he didn't understand where they were coming from.

A few days later, Renee returned to the ranch that was her children's temporary home and realized her palms were sweating. She could still see Alexis's frozen expression, caught between her previous happiness and shock, and knew she was the cause of her daughter's unpleasant reaction.

She knew better than to expect her daughters to run to her with open arms—least of all Alexis—but the open rejection hurt a lot more than she imagined it would. Today was the first of their scheduled visitations and Renee was going to make the most of her time with her girls. She didn't chase them all over California and back again to give up now. She'd help them to understand why she left and why she would never leave them again. Renee fingered the small badge pinned in a discreet corner on the lapel of her jacket and prayed for strength before exiting the car and walking toward the house.

But before she reached the front door, that infernal rancher, John, once again intercepted her and she wanted to throw something heavy his way. She didn't even try to hide her scowl as she said, "It's my court-appointed visitation day. Check your paperwork."

"I know what day it is. I just want a few words first."

She tensed. "Why?"

"I want to make sure you don't try to pressure the girls into doing something they don't want to do."

"Excuse me?"

"I know you don't think much of this arrangement. It's pretty much written all over your face, much the same as it was in the courtroom, that you think this is a bunch of bullshit, but at this point you're in no place to judge. I don't care about you or your feelings. All I care about is that those little girls aren't hurt again by either of their parents. And let me give you a fair warning right now… if that ex-husband of yours even comes near these kids, I won't hesitate to shoot him just for the sheer fun of it.

So, if you and him are still cozy, make sure you give him that message. I'm not one to kid about things this important. You hearing me, Mrs. Dolling?"

Her first instinct was to slap him across his scruffy face for the insult he so casually tossed her way. Hadn't he heard her when she said Jason *stole* their kids and she'd been chasing after them ever since? The very thought of being friendly much less *cozy* with Jason made her physically ill. But the very fact that this man who was no blood relation to her children was championing them in a way that their own father had not kept her hot words and temper in check—though the action was not without great effort on her part.

"I hear you just fine. I'm not deaf," she said, meeting his steady gaze without flinching. She imagined that when this man stared people down he won most of the time. He was the kind of man who gave no quarter but expected none, either, yet somehow her girls had found the one soft spot in his heart and he wasn't letting go. Her stomach gave a discomforting tingle and she slammed the door shut on wherever her thoughts were going. "Are you finished? I've waited months to see my kids. Despite your scintillating conversation skills, I didn't come to see you."

"Fair enough. I just wanted to make sure we're clear. They're inside. Mrs. Stemming will monitor your visit. Don't give her any grief, either. She's taken to the girls and I won't have you upsetting her."

What a wonderful opinion he had of her. "As long as she doesn't give me any grief, I won't feel the need to dish it out."

And with that she started walking straight up the steps to the house. She didn't wait for his approval or his invitation and gave the front door a solid knock. Her bravado did wonders for the appearance that she wasn't scared to death of her own children but did little to stop her hands from shaking or her knees from weakening. She glanced over her shoulder and saw John watching her intently, his eyes never leaving her. She suppressed a shudder at that strong stare and knocked again. This time, the door opened and an older woman with a full head of white hair stood between her and her girls.

Renee tried putting on a cheerful face. No sense in making enemies purposefully, her own aunt used to say. "Hello…Aunt Gladys," she said, trying for some sense of familiarity, hoping that it might soften any lingering hard feelings. "It's been a long time. I'm Renee."

"I know who you are." Gladys's expression was pinched and disapproving as she moved aside. "Come in. They're waiting for you."

Mean old bat. Wiping her slick palms across the seat of her pants she followed the older woman into the expansive ranch house and despite the foreign surroundings could sense that this house was warm and inviting with its lived-in look and strong masculine accents. She rounded the corner and there sat her girls, their little faces pulled into solemn masks filled with anxiety and trepidation, and her heart broke from a heavy combination of joy and deep agony.

Chloe sat on Alexis's lap while Taylor sat beside her older sister. The three couldn't have looked more miserable yet stuck to each other as if glued.

Coming forward, wanting desperately to wrap them all in her arms and never let go, she stopped short when she saw Alexis tighten her arms around Chloe protectively. Pain arced through Renee but she didn't want to push the girls too fast. Taking Alexis's lead, she moved to the chair closest to them and took a seat.

"How about some cookies and tea?" Mrs. Stemming

broke in with a modicum of manners though there was no warmth directed at Renee in those bright, alert eyes. Renee was tempted to tell her to stick her cookies where the sun didn't shine but she held her tongue in the interest of playing nice. When Gladys spoke again, Renee was glad she'd remained quiet. "Taylor and I made a fresh batch of gingersnaps this morning and they're mighty good," she said, sending a genuine smile to Taylor who returned it tentatively.

Although mildly allergic to ginger Renee smiled and nodded. If suffering through hives was the price she had to pay to win her daughters' love back, she'd eat an entire batch of gingersnaps and risk anaphylactic shock for the privilege. "I'd love some."

But Alexis wasn't going to let her off that easy. "She hates gingersnaps," Alexis said, her mouth forming a hard line.

"I don't hate them, Lexie," Renee gently corrected. "I'm slightly allergic but I'd love to try Taylor's cookies."

"Whatever."

Renee drew back at the flippant sarcasm in Alexis's voice and her hopes for a happy reunion sank to the bottom of her heart. Gladys looked to Renee for direction and she gave her a weak smile. "I'd still love to try the cookies."

"Are you sure?" Gladys asked, uncertainty etched into her expression, no doubt from the fear that Renee might fall over dead from a simple cookie.

"It'll be fine," Renee assured her. "Promise."

Gladys left the room and Renee sought a safe subject to fill the empty air. "Tell me what you've been doing lately. I want to hear all about your adventures. I've missed out on so much. I have a lot to catch up on. Taylor, sweetheart, why don't you start?"

But before Taylor could open her mouth, Alexis started talking. The anger in her young voice fairly vibrated her body as she spoke.

"What do you wanna know?"

Renee faltered, not quite sure how to talk to this angry stranger. "Anything, honey. I want to hear about everything," she said, her gaze darting to Taylor, hoping for some help from her little chatterbox, but she received none. Taylor remained quiet and wide-eyed, waiting for a cue from her sister on how to act. "Taylor?" she prompted but Alexis shut her down before she could say a word.

"You really wanna know or are you just trying to play like you care?" Alexis said, her gaze hot.

Renee drew back, stung. "Of course I want to know. And I *do* care."

Alexis smirked, the expression on her young face entirely too mature for her actual age of nine and a half. "Okay. Daddy's been trying to kill Chloe by giving her rat poison. He put her outside in the rain when she peed the bed and he used to hit her with his belt until he broke her bones. Do you wanna see the bruises?" Renee could only stare in shock. Alexis shrugged. "You asked. Oh, and I'm a year behind in school because Daddy moved us around too much. And Taylor gets nightmares. Are we done catching up?"

Without waiting for Renee's answer—not that she could've mustered one—Alexis rose with Chloe still in her arms and stalked from the room, calling for Taylor to follow. Alexis whirled before exiting, her blue eyes blazing. "And stop calling me Lexie. I *hate* that name and I never want to hear it again."

Tears sprang to Renee's eyes and she didn't care that the old bat was watching as she let her head sink into her hands. She was a fool to think that Lexie—no, Alexis—

would ever forgive her. And rightly so. Who was she to even ask for forgiveness when her children had suffered so much?

"She's a smart girl," she heard the old woman say, then crunch into a cookie, presumably the gingersnaps she'd offered earlier. "She's not one to eat up bullshit, if you know what I mean."

She did. Lifting her head, she eyed the woman. "You're no expert on my daughter after spending a few days with her. I'd appreciate if you kept your opinions to yourself," Renee said, standing stiffly.

Gladys shrugged. "Doesn't seem like you're much of an expert, either, and you've been around her for at least some of those nine years she's been on this planet, so I'd watch where you're slinging that attitude of yours," Gladys said before finishing the rest of her cookie.

"I know my daughter," Renee retorted, her cheeks heating but her heart ached privately. What Alexis said… Renee would never have guessed that Jason would have been capable of hurting Chloe. Never even imagined, though she should've figured with his more recent drug history. He'd become unpredictable. She struggled to keep her voice calm. "She's smart. She'll come around."

"Maybe." The older woman nodded, then bit into another cookie. "If she thinks you deserve a second chance."

"She will. I'm her mother."

"Don't get your dander up. I'm just saying she's a smart girl and if you don't blow it by cutting out on them again, she'll likely loosen up. Kids are more forgiving than adults."

"Thanks." The word was difficult against her lips but she sensed this woman was not her enemy even if she wasn't her friend. She blew out a breath and rolled her shoulders to release the tension building behind her blades. "How are they doing?"

"Good as to be expected I guess. You might want to talk with John, though. He's got all the details you're probably looking for. I just bake and keep them occupied when John has to tend to the horses."

Renee smiled softly, thinking of how Taylor must love being around the horses. "Does Taylor get to see the horses?"

"Oh, yes, that one is hard to keep out of the stables. John lets her help him feed them in the morning, though I suspect when he gets them enrolled in school, she's going to put up a fuss when she can't hang around the barn all day."

Alarm spiked through Renee. "School? He's enrolling them in school? Here?"

Gladys looked nonplussed. "Well, of course, here. Where else? They have to go to school. It's the law. It's bad enough that riffraff of a father dragged them from one place to another with no thought as to how they'd get an education, but the judge was adamant that they get enrolled right away. The only reason they're not enrolled yet is because of some hiccup with Alexis's transcripts."

She supposed that made sense but enrolling them in school suggested permanence and she didn't want the girls to think they were staying any longer than the court order required. And the fact that the judge wanted them enrolled didn't bode well for a quick resolution in Renee's estimation. "Where is the school here?"

"Well, the high school kids get bused to Emmett's Mill or Coldwater but there's an elementary school just down the road a bit that the local country kids go to. That's where they'll go."

"Is it a good school?"

Gladys smiled proudly. "One of the best. It's not big on fancy things like new computers but the teachers are warmhearted and the classes are small. The girls will fit in right away. Don't you worry."

"My girls are strong. They'd fit in anywhere," she bluffed, only hoping that was true. The truth was, as Gladys had already pointed out, she didn't know her girls at all.

But, as her gaze drifted out the front window to the arena where John was working with a horse, she aimed to rectify that no matter what—or who—stood in her way.

Five

John crossed his arms across his chest and stared. "You want me to what?"

Renee lifted her chin. "Hire me."

"For what and why?"

"Well, you need someone to help with the girls and by the looks of your house, someone to help out with general upkeep. I figure the best way to stay close to my girls and get to know them again is to be around them as much as possible and I can't do that if I live and work twenty miles away. Plus, there's really not much to choose from as far as jobs go. You live in the sticks of the sticks." Renee paused to take a breath and he realized more was coming. "And, I was thinking that perhaps you could let me stay here in that guesthouse you have behind the main house. I'd be out of your way and it would take care of two of the requirements the judge set forth in the judgment."

"Why would I want you moving into my house? Have you forgotten I don't much like you? And just what the hell are you insinuating about my house?" Was she saying he was a slob? He shot her a dirty look. "You sure have a funny way of asking for a favor, you know that?"

She returned his glare but the way she chewed her bottom lip told him she realized she might've been a little harsh. "I didn't mean to insult you. All I'm saying is your house is clean enough for a bachelor but a woman's touch is needed around here." She gestured to the drapes at the front window. "When was the last time those things were aired out? Or how about the floor? This old hardwood needs to be waxed every now and again. I figure you don't have the time to be doing stuff like that."

He glanced at the floor. Looked fine to him. So it didn't shine like it used to when his mama was alive but it was still in good shape. And whoever heard of airing out drapes? How dirty could they be? They just hang there. "How do you know so much about cleaning house?" he asked.

She bristled at his open speculation but answered even though he suspected she would've rather told him to shove it and mind his own business. "My mother was a bit of a stickler when it came to keeping a clean home. She was known to fire the staff for not adhering to her standard," she muttered.

Staff? His ears pricked at the small tidbit of information but his interest didn't compel him to inquire further. The woman was becoming a bit of a mystery that only gave him a headache when he tried to figure her out.

He read nothing but honesty as she said, "I just want to do what's best for the girls, and contrary to what you or that nutty judge may think my girls need their mother."

He could argue they needed their mother to protect

them when their father was being a monster but he figured there was no sense in poking at a beehive when you knew full well nothing but pissed off bees were going to fly out. But that didn't mean he wanted her moving in. "I don't want you moving in and I don't need your services," he maintained stubbornly.

She squared her jaw, not willing to give up. "Gladys seems nice enough but you can't really expect an old lady to keep up with three little girls. She can't even lift Chloe and that's who she'd be around when the older girls are in school. What if there was an emergency and you weren't around? Gladys tells me that you work outside a lot. What if she had a heart attack or something?"

"Gladys is fine," he growled. But he knew he couldn't expect Gladys to keep up with the girls and he did worry when he had to be outside for any length of time, which given his trade was hard to get around. Still, having Renee here…at the ranch? It smacked of trouble. "The court might not approve of you being around the girls without supervision."

"I'm not a danger to my own children," she said quietly and John couldn't help but soften a bit toward her. "I just want to get to know them again. This is the easiest and most helpful way for both of us. I need a job and a place to stay. You and Gladys need help with the girls. It's a win-win for us both. And, once the girls and I patch up our relationship, we can all get out of your hair. That's what you want, right?"

"I want what's in the girls' best interests and I don't know if that includes letting them leave with you anytime soon," he snapped, knowing full well he hated the idea of letting the girls leave with this nut but as much as she taxed his patience, she'd made valid points in her favor. "Let me think about it," he said with no small amount of

ire in his tone. "I have to talk with the girls first. I don't
want to upset them more than I have to. Their first day
of school is tomorrow and neither of the older kids is too
happy about it."

"Alexis used to love school," Renee murmured, her
expression sad. She looked up hopefully. "Maybe I could
go with you when you take them."

He slanted his gaze at her, her blue eyes so much like
her oldest daughter's that he suspected when Alexis grew
up she'd be the spitting image of her mama. If that were
the case he'd have to beat the boys off with a stick—that
is if the girls were still around here by that time, which
wasn't likely. Shifting in annoyance at his thoughts, he
grunted an answer.

She blinked at him. "What? I'm sorry…was that a
yes or a no?"

"I said fine. Do what you want. Just don't upset the
girls."

"What time?"

"I'm supposed to have the girls at the school at seven-
thirty." He chewed the inside of his cheek, wondering if
he was doing the right thing. Alexis was pretty angry
with her mom and he didn't want to put her through more
than she'd already experienced but Renee had a point.
She needed to spend more time around them if they were
going to repair their relationship. But a part of him could
give a fig about Renee getting her kids to love her again.
She was the one who screwed up and walked away. Why
should she get a second chance at messing with their
hearts? But even as the angry thoughts scrolled through
his head, he shot a look at Renee and caught the very
real fear in her eyes that her girls might never forgive
her, and he realized she was probably beating herself up
more than he ever could.

Unsure of how he really felt and not particularly interested in digging to find out, he grunted something else in the way of goodbye and headed out to the stables. Working with horses was something he knew and understood. He'd just stick with that.

Renee watched as John stalked off and seeing as she wasn't entirely sure if he'd just told her to get off his property or go ahead and enjoy an iced tea, she decided to seek out the girls before she returned to town. He hadn't agreed to her offer but he hadn't expressly turned her down, either. Renee chose to think optimistically. Perhaps she could get Gladys on her side. Going to the house, she hesitated at the front door, wondering if she should knock or just go in. Deciding it was best to proceed with caution, she gave the door a soft knock and waited.

She could hear the laughter of her girls, at least Taylor, and Renee smiled. Taylor was always her most exuberant child. A tomboy with a wild nest of blond hair that was stick straight and likely to be standing on end each morning. Renee used to fight with her, trying to get a brush through that mess. Tears sprang to her eyes as the memory of being with her girls every day—before she made the decision to leave—made her stiffen against the bittersweet moment. She was different now and she'd never be the woman she was then. Her fingers strayed to the badge on her jacket and as the pads grazed the hard metal, she sought strength from within and from God. She had just enough time to suck a deep breath of cleansing air before the door opened and Taylor stood there.

"Hi, sweetheart," Renee said, fighting the urge to sweep the little girl into her arms. "Can I come in and visit for a bit?"

"I have to ask Grammy Stemmy," Taylor said solemnly

before running from the door. Renee stepped over the threshold and could hear Taylor yelling in the kitchen. "Renee is here. Can she come in and visit?"

Fresh pain spiked through Renee as her child referred to her by name as if she were a stranger. No doubt Alexis had a hand in that. The girls would do whatever their older sister told them and right now Alexis was more than willing to sever any tie to their mother. But Renee was tougher than that and she was *still* their mother, no matter what they called her.

"I suppose," Gladys said warily, wiping her hands on a dish towel. "We were just about to have some hot cider and cherry turnovers. Would you like to share some with us?"

"Sounds wonderful. Thank you."

Renee followed Gladys around to the kitchen and took a seat at the expansive oak table, noting that the two little girls clambered into seats right beside her but Alexis was nowhere to be seen. Disappointed that her eldest daughter was purposefully avoiding her, she focused on the joy at having her little girls flocked around her. As she accepted a small plate with a pastry from Gladys, she started casual conversation.

"Are you excited about starting school, Taylor?"

Taylor's expression dissolved into a mutinous scowl even as she chewed on her turnover. "I hate school."

"How do you know that, sweetheart? You've never been to school yet. Besides, it's only kindergarten. I bet you'll have a wonderful time and make lots of new friends."

"I don't want friends. I want to work with the horses and Mr. John."

"Well, I'm sure Mr. John loves your help with the

horses but he wouldn't want you to miss out on school. He knows how important it is."

"Yeah, I guess. Daddy never made us go to school. He said school never did him any good so why should he make us go?"

Renee burned inside at Jason's stupid statement and wondered how in the hell she ever considered him the love of her life. Struggling with her answer, she smiled and said in the nicest way she could muster, "Uh, sometimes Daddy didn't know what he was talking about. School is very important and I think you're going to love it."

"Why?" Taylor's bell-like voice tinkled softly as she suddenly looked intrigued. "Do they have horses at school?"

"Not that I'm aware but they have libraries with lots of books that they will let you check out for free and then you can read all about horses."

Taylor seemed to consider this but suddenly her face screwed into a frown. "I don't know how to read," she said.

"All the more reason to go to school. Your teacher will teach you how to read and then you can read anything you like. But in the meantime, before you learn to read, they have what's called picture books and I'll bet there are picture books devoted completely to horses. Would you like to see pictures of pretty horses?"

"There's no prettier horse than Mr. John's Cisco. He's very pretty but you can't get too close to him because he's been spooked by a bad person."

"Spooked?" Renee asked.

"Yeah, Mr. John works with horses that are sad or mean 'cuz someone wasn't nice to them. And Cisco is my favorite."

Renee was mildly impressed in spite of herself. She had to admit she had a soft spot for abused animals, as well. "What does Cisco look like?"

Taylor flung her arms as wide as they would go. "He's bigger than this and real tall. Mr. John said he's seventeen hands but I don't know what that means. I think it means he's like a giant 'cuz he is."

"He sounds very big," Renee agreed, returning to the subject of school. "So, you think you might be willing to check out school then, if we can find some horse picture books?"

Taylor nodded. "Maybe I'll go just to check out this library thing. But I'm not making promises that I'll like school."

"Absolutely. No promises." Renee smiled and suddenly remembered something. Opening her purse, she pulled out Mr. BunBun. The moment Taylor saw what was in Renee's hand, her eyes widened and she clasped her hands tightly as her voice hit a high-pitched squeal of delight that felt like heaven against Renee's ears despite its ear-drum shattering quality.

"Mr. BunBun!" Taylor hugged the bedraggled stuffed animal to her small chest and nearly squeezed the stuffing out of it in her excitement. "How'd you find him?"

"When I was looking for you girls I found the house you were living in with your dad and Mr. BunBun was all by himself. I knew you would miss him so I grabbed him before leaving."

"Thank you so much!" Taylor said and impulsively kissed Renee's cheek.

Chloe, watching her sister, copied the gesture and Renee received a sloppy kiss from her youngest daughter. Unable to help herself, Renee scooped both girls into a tight embrace, her heart cracking from the unparalleled joy cascading through her body. The girls giggled and Renee smiled through her tears. The moment was nearly perfect. She only wished Alexis were there in the cuddle. Seconds later, Renee's unspoken wish was granted—albeit not in the way she'd been hoping.

"What are you doing?" Alexis's imperious tone cut through the happy moment as easily as a hot knife through butter and the girls scattered.

Taylor held up her rabbit. "Renee brought me Mr. Bun-Bun," she said, though her chastised tone scraped on Renee's nerves. Alexis shouldn't make her sisters feel bad for showing affection to their mother. Taylor moved farther away from Renee and Chloe followed.

Renee caught Gladys's watchful stare as the scene unfolded. Standing, Renee met her daughter's hot gaze and knew the moment was now or never to remind her daughter that she was still their mother. "Alexis Janelle Dolling, you will not speak to your sisters that way," Renee said, knowing she was likely digging the hole even deeper between the two of them but she couldn't stand by and watch as Alexis bullied the girls. "We were having a lovely moment until you came in and started glaring at the girls for even being near me. That will stop right now."

"You can't tell me what to do." Alexis sneered, but her eyes welled with moisture. "And you're not our mother anymore. You stopped being our mother the day you walked out on us."

"I made a terrible mistake. I admit that. I will gladly spend the rest of my life making up for it but that doesn't mean that you can talk to me or your sisters so disrespectfully."

"We don't want to hear your excuses," Alexis said. "And Taylor left behind that dumb stuffed animal for a reason. It's trash. Isn't it, Taylor?" She looked pointedly at Taylor until Taylor's bottom lip trembled as she struggled to let her precious bunny go a second time. Renee was shocked at the level of Alexis's anger that she'd be willing to sacrifice Taylor's feelings for her own spite.

Renee stopped Taylor from dropping the bunny to the table, and ignoring Alexis for a moment, tucked a wayward strand of white-blond hair behind Taylor's ear as she said softly, "Sweetheart, you don't have to give up Mr. BunBun. He's your special bunny and only you can decide when it's time to let him go. Okay?"

Taylor nodded slowly and clutched the bunny tightly. Looking to Alexis she said, "He's not trash!" and ran from the room.

Sensing the tension, Chloe started to cry and out of instinct Renee scooped the toddler into her arms. Alexis reacted violently, running to Renee and trying to jerk Chloe out of her arms. Renee twisted so that Chloe wasn't accidentally hurt in the process and suddenly John was there, plucking Alexis up as if she weighed nothing and placing her firmly away from Renee.

Renee realized as she soothed Chloe that John must've been watching the scene from the hallway.

"Alexis," he said, commanding her daughter's attention as angry tears streamed down her face. "Never attack your mother like that. That's not okay in this house. You could've hurt someone, especially your sister. Do you understand?"

She nodded jerkily but Renee caught a nasty look just the same.

"Can you apologize?" he asked and she shook her head. As if understanding, he patted her on the shoulder and said, "All right then, go on to your room and think about what you're so riled up about and maybe we can talk about it later."

"I don't want her here," Alexis said in a low tone. "Please make her leave."

At that Renee felt a section of her heart splinter and fall to pieces. Her daughter hated her and that would probably never change. Tears blinded her as she pressed a kiss to Chloe's head and handed her to John. "I'll see you tomorrow morning," she said, then added to Alexis, "I'm not leaving you girls ever again. That's a promise. You can be mad for as long as you want but that's not going to change the fact that I love you, Alexis. And deep down, you love me, too."

Six

John resisted the urge to follow Renee out but his eyes tracked her progress as she drove out of the driveway.

He caught Gladys's watchful stare and he couldn't help the scowl that followed. "Don't start thinking there's more to this than there is. There's no rule that says I can't feel bad for the woman for the mess she's created. I'm human, too."

"Oh, stop your blathering. I never said anything. But no matter what you say I think it was right decent of you to come to her rescue when Alexis flew at her like that. I think her heart just about broke when Alexis reacted that way."

"Yeah. I saw that. Think I should talk to Alexis?"

Gladys considered it for a moment and then shook her head. "No. I'd let her work through it on her own. She's got a deep well full of misery to deal with and we don't need to heap more on her plate. Besides, I think you got your point across pretty good. If she doesn't show up for dinner maybe you ought to check in on her but until then, let's just give her some space."

John heaved a private sigh of relief. He didn't know how to console an angry little girl but he hated to see her so upset.

"She has a long road ahead of her with that child," Gladys commented as she packaged the remaining turnovers. "I don't envy her."

"That makes two of us," he agreed. "You think she can change?"

Gladys shrugged. "Time will tell but I'm not holding my breath at the moment. She's got to adjust that attitude of hers or else she's just going to spin her wheels with Alexis."

John glanced away, voicing his private thoughts on the subject. "There's no excuse for leaving your family behind."

"You're right about that and I know you know what that's all about. Did you ever forgive your father for leaving?"

"No."

Gladys chuckled. "Didn't think so. Like I said, that woman's got a rough row to hoe but in the meantime, we'll be there to catch the girls before they fall this time around."

He shifted, hating how he'd somehow, unwittingly, wandered into emotional territory. Gladys was a tricky one. Always had been. Probably why she and his mom had been such tight friends. They were peas in a pod. She prodded at him and he emitted a low groan as her point went straight home. "I'd be a liar if I said I've never said or done anything I regret," he admitted in a tight voice. "But I don't understand how a mother could leave her babies. Gladys, I don't think I'll *ever* understand and if *I* can't understand how is that little girl going to?"

"No one is asking you to figure things out for her. She's a smart kid. She'll do that on her own. But," Gladys sighed as if hating to agree with Renee on anything, and then said, "in the meantime, she needs to be around her mother."

"Renee suggested I hire her for help around the house with the girls. Said you were too old."

Gladys chuckled. "That woman's got spunk, I'll give her that. But as much as I hate to admit it, these old bones are feeling the years piling up behind them," she admitted grudgingly. "I could use a hand around here. Chloe is a handful even though she's sweeter than freshly churned butter and I think she would love to have her mama around. She doesn't remember her very well and she harbors the least amount of piss and vinegar. I think it would be smart for Renee to start rebuilding with Chloe first. I'll be here to smooth out the rough spots but she's right. I am a bit long in the tooth to be chasing after a toddler while the other girls are in school."

John heaved a heavy sigh and nodded. "I guess I could fix up the guesthouse. Although I hate the idea of harboring that woman on my property," he added with a glower. "Frankly, if it weren't something the girls probably need to get over this mess, I'd tell her to pound sand. I don't give a shit about her feelings in this."

"What about the court stuff?"

"Oh, Sheriff Casey isn't going to make a stink over anything as long as those girls are safe and happy. Besides, the order doesn't say anything about Renee keeping her distance or anything. I suppose as long as everyone is happy, no one needs to be the wiser."

"So it's settled, then? Renee is moving in?" Gladys's

mouth firmed, no more happy about it than John but willing to see it through for the girls' sake just like him.

"I suppose she is." He walked from the kitchen, his pace brisk, but not even his quickened step could keep him from the realization that he was about to invite more complications into his life and if the warning tingle in his gut was any indication, he might've just changed his life forever.

Renee walked with Taylor's hand firmly in her own as Alexis practically jogged three steps ahead with John and Chloe somewhere in between.

"I don't want you walking me to class," Alexis declared, looking pointedly at Renee before continuing with strong purposeful steps toward the entrance.

Renee looked down at Taylor. "How about you?"

"You can walk me to class if you want to, I suppose," Taylor answered. "You can show me where these picture books are that you were talking about."

"Deal."

The school was an old brick building with a bell at the top, a remnant of when the school was first built in the late 1800s, and it looked right out of an episode of *Little House on the Prairie.*

"Do you think that bell still works?" Taylor asked.

"I don't know but we can ask your teacher," Renee said, smiling.

She glanced up at John and wondered if this was where he went to school. He seemed to know his way around well enough as they went straight to the front office and a few people even nodded in surprise at seeing him there.

"Old school chums?" Renee surmised once she'd caught up to him.

"I guess you could say that," John answered, but didn't

elaborate further. Talk about a man of little words. If he strung together more than two sentences in a row she'd fall over in shock. Grumbling to herself, she kept the rest of her annoyed thoughts silent as the principal greeted them.

"John Murphy? I haven't seen you in a while but I do know you don't have kids. Who do I have the pleasure of meeting?"

Before John could answer, Renee piped in, saying, "They're mine. We're just staying with John at the ranch for now. Renee Dolling, pleased to meet you, Mr...."

"Curtis Meany," he answered with a broad smile, coming forward to envelope her hand in a firm handshake. "Don't let the name fool you, I'm really a softie at heart. If I'm not careful these students run all over me. Are you from around here? I don't recall the name."

"No, we're new." Renee smiled and left it at that. She didn't want to go into details and ruin this nice man's impression of her. It was hard enough dealing with John much less another judgmental local. "My girls, Alexis and Taylor, are starting classes today."

"Yes, here are their teachers' names and classroom numbers. If you have any questions or concerns, my door is always open. Good to see you again, John."

"Curt." John inclined his head and then gesturing for the paper in Renee's hand, said, "Let's get this show on the road. I have a horse coming in an hour."

"You can go if you like," Renee offered and was mildly surprised when he frowned in response. "If you're in a hurry..."

"I didn't say that."

"You implied."

He started to say something but then thought better of it and snapped his mouth shut. "Perhaps I did."

Renee smiled down at Taylor. "Let's go find your teacher, shall we?"

She didn't wait for John nor did she try to convince Alexis to let her walk her to class, as well. She knew her daughter well enough to know any attempt at this point would be rudely rebuffed. She'd have to let Alexis come to her. She fought back a well of fear when she considered the very real possibility that that day might never come and instead focused on the happy start she was being granted with her middle daughter.

John watched as Renee led Taylor to her new classroom. To look at them one would never guess their circumstances. Renee looked every part the doting mother, her eyes fairly shone with love and adoration that John was almost apt to believe, if not for the reminder of Renee's defection standing beside him wearing a fierce scowl.

"She seems to be trying," John noted, almost to himself but it was really directed toward Alexis. She took the bait quite readily.

Alexis snorted. "My mom used to want to be an actress. You shouldn't believe a word she says. She's a good liar." And then she adjusted her pack and stomped in the direction of her new classroom.

An actress? It shocked him but then again…it didn't. She was sure pretty enough to fill a big screen. That blond-hair-blue-eye combination was a killer. Not to mention those curves… John shifted on the balls of his feet wondering where his mind was going and who gave it permission to wander like that.

Renee returned a short time later, a warm glow suffusing her expression that was nearly contagious.

"She settled in all right?" he asked.

"Yeah. I think she's going to have fun. Taylor has an adventurous spirit. She's game for anything that can hook her interest. But then you've probably already figured that out about her."

He had. It was one of Taylor's more endearing qualities. "She's got a sharp mind. I think school will be a good challenge for her."

Renee nodded and they walked out the front doors. The children quickly dispersed as they ran to their individual classes when the bell rang. Once at their vehicles, John climbed into his truck and then stopped to call out to Renee.

"Yeah?" she asked, her brow furrowing subtly as she regarded him warily.

"If you're still interested in the job, I suppose it's available."

"You're saying that you're willing to hire me to help out with my kids?" There was a sparkle in her eyes that he couldn't help but catch and it made him bite back what he might've said to her clever comment. She didn't give him a chance to rescind the offer and quickly jumped. "Sounds perfect. When can I move in?"

John startled at the gooseflesh that rioted up and down his arm. He swallowed. *Moving in.* It created a wealth of imagery that made his heartbeat thud painfully. Scowling, he said, "Since you're in an all-fired hurry, I suppose Friday is fine."

"Friday?" Her expression fell. "But it's only Monday. I was hoping—"

"I know what you were hoping but the guesthouse won't be ready for anyone until then. It's the soonest I can accommodate you into my schedule. It should go without saying that I still have a job to do and it doesn't include making room for yet another Dolling. You get me? Take it or leave it."

He winced privately at how surly he sounded. Damn, if he didn't sound like a cantankerous old fart but she rubbed him the wrong way in the *worst* way. She had no business looking the way she did and coming around as if she was pretending to care when John knew full well she hadn't cared when it mattered to those little girls. Right? *Ah, great. Talking to yourself now,* he mentally chastised himself. John's lips pressed against one another and he figured that was the smartest thing he could do at this point—keep his damn mouth shut.

"Friday, 8 a.m. sharp. Don't be late." He slammed the truck door, eager to get the hell away from her and his confused thoughts.

Seven

Renee returned to the hotel, her mind buzzing and her heart full of hope for the future. Taylor was the key to breaching the wall Alexis had built around them. She didn't blame Alexis for her attitude even if it hurt. Of all the kids, Alexis remembered many details that were lost to Taylor and unknown to Chloe. Renee rubbed her palm across her stinging eyes and fought back the bad memories that always threatened to surface when she wasn't being vigilant enough.

The fights. The screaming. And the alcohol. Always a lot of that around the Dolling house. It became her way of coping with a failed life and living with a man she didn't love any longer. She'd had such big dreams as a kid. But Jason Dolling had been persuasive and her hormones had been listening. She couldn't regret everything that happened during their life together. Her girls were the shining example that even when everything else was going to shit, there was always something to be grateful for.

She wished she could take every bad memory from her daughter's mind but that wasn't an option. All she could do was be there and promise their lives would be different. And that was something she could do without reservation.

Getting sober hadn't been the easiest thing in the world but she'd had really solid motivation. She never tried to compare her journey to that of others because they're never the same or even comparable. Renee had definitely come to appreciate that old saying, Never judge a man until you've walked a mile in his shoes, because when she'd made the decision to get sober at first it was natural to assume others had it easier or harder, take your pick, but she'd learned quickly not to judge. She'd seen lawyers and doctors sitting side by side with drug addicts and no one had it easy.

She'd been no different—and no worse.

But to explain to a child the reasons why her mother left…were there words in the English language that would ever convey the reason in a way a child would understand? Renee didn't know but she desperately wanted to find out. Alexis was her soldier, her first born. She'd bonded to that girl from the moment she came screaming into the world, her lusty squall a balm to Renee's young heart, the calm in the storm that surrounded her and Jason.

Taylor was the let's-try-and-save-the-marriage baby. And by the time Chloe arrived…well, the marriage had been over before she was conceived. Yet, Renee had stayed. Drinking her failure away with her two solid friends, Jack Daniels and Jim Beam and the occasional visit by Captain Morgan on holidays.

So many bad choices. A lifetime, really. Was she poised at the precipice of yet another bad Renee Dolling decision? She just wanted her kids back so they could get back to their lives.

But then what? Her chest tightened with panic and uncertainty. She'd been so focused on finding the girls she didn't actually have a plan as to where they'd go from there. Renee's mother had always called her flighty. So far, she hadn't proven the woman wrong and the time was past to do so. Her mother had long since written her off as a daughter. So now she only had herself and her children to prove something to.

But it was enough. She wouldn't let the girls down. That was a promise. Friday couldn't come soon enough in her book.

John spent most of the morning working with a skittish mare that'd been brought the day before and he was thankful for the hard work. The moment he entered the arena, she shied away, stomping the ground with her front hooves as if daring him to get closer so she could stamp a nice U-shaped mark on his forehead. He let her settle down but didn't leave the arena. He let her know that he wasn't going anywhere but didn't try connecting the lead rope to her halter, either. The two eyed each other and John settled into a comfortable space inside his head. He could sense her distrust and knew this girl would take considerable work on his part to get her to the point where she didn't try to kill anyone who came near her.

As it was it took four men to unload her into the horse paddock and she'd shown her displeasure by kicking the shit out of the stable gate as she tried to get out of her stall. Her wild screams told him she didn't like enclosed spaces and he soon moved her to a bigger, much roomier stall that he usually reserved for foaling mares. Luckily, at the moment he didn't need the special sized stall. Once she didn't feel the walls closing in on her, she settled with an uneasy whinny but none of the ranch hands wanted to go near her. John didn't blame them. He instructed everyone to steer clear of the young mare appropriately named Vixen and so far they had. Today was the first day he'd had the chance to formerly introduce himself so to speak and by the murderous glint in her eye, the introduction wasn't going so well.

"You and I are going to get along just fine," he said low and soft as if the horse could understand every word. "I know you've had a hard time of it but no one is going to hurt you here. You have to behave, though, you hear me? No more kicking stable doors and scaring the life out of my ranch hands. I don't pay them enough for that shit."

Vixen tossed her head as if to say "that's your problem" and he chuckled softly. That it was. "We're going to get along just fine, aren't we?" he asked, a small grin lifting the corners of his mouth. There was nothing he enjoyed more than a challenge and judging by the proud and stubborn toss of the young mare's head, he'd found a damn good one.

Vixen reminded him of Alexis—all spit and fire— if only to draw attention away from the wound inside. He knew Alexis cried at night when she thought no one could hear her, when her sisters were fast asleep and she thought he was crashed out in front of the fire. But he heard her heartbroken sobs clear as if she were curled in his lap soaking his shoulder. And he'd be a liar if he didn't admit it hit him hard. But what did he know about consoling a little girl's broken heart? How was he supposed to help her heal? He was out of his league. You didn't ask a horseman to wrestle with alligators because it wasn't his specialty and he was likely to get his hand chomped off. That's how he felt. Caged with an alligator with nothing but a lead rope and a prayer. By his estimation, neither one was going to do much good.

So where did that leave him? The mare stared warily, watching and waiting for his next move, and the answer came to him with the slow cumbersome gearshift of the truly reluctant. The only way Alexis was going to heal was if she had her mama back in her life, which meant, and he really didn't like the sound of this, he was going to have to help Renee mend the fence.

And that meant playing nice with the woman.

Aww hell.

He didn't know how to do that, either.

He glanced back at Vixen, who nickered—or maybe it was a snicker—and said with a shake of his head and a promise in his eye, "Oh, don't look so smug. You're next, hot hooves. You're about the *only* thing I know how to handle around here. So, let's get to work, shall we?"

Renee glared at the sky and cursed the snow spiraling out of the dark, ominous clouds as she wrestled another box out of her car and struggled to keep her footing on the slippery ground.

"Here, let me take that before you land face-first in a snowdrift," John said gruffly, lifting the box from her arms before she could protest. "We could've waited until Monday, after the storm passed us by," he said over his shoulder as she hurried to catch up.

"No, I've waited long enough to be around my girls. I'm not letting some— Oh!" She slipped a little and nearly landed on her rear but somehow caught herself before doing so. John didn't slow nor did he glance back at her. Straightening, she took more care as she made her way toward the guesthouse. "I'm not going to let some storm get in my way. Besides, who's to say this storm would be over by then? No way. I'm settling in and getting comfortable as soon as possible."

He turned abruptly and she almost ran into him. "Oh! You should say something before you do that!" she admonished with a glare, her breath pluming in a misty curl between them. "The ground is hard enough to walk without you stopping for no good reason in the middle of the path. Have you ever considered putting in a nice sidewalk to the guesthouse?"

"No. That would encourage people to stay longer than they're welcome," he answered, shifting the box easily although Renee knew it was heavy. So there must be some muscles hidden beneath that flannel shirt, she noted with a private shrug. Big deal. She'd never been one to swoon over some hunky cowboy type. Wrangler butts don't drive *her* nuts. Good thing, too, because a cursory, almost defiant sweep of his butt revealed an ass that she couldn't help but admit was on the perfect side. He caught her unfortunate perusal and his eyebrow lifted only so slightly as he said, "Flattered but not interested. The house is the only thing available in this deal."

The nerve of this guy! As if she'd be interested in him. The idea bordered on ridiculous. Pulling the box from him and grunting only slightly from the effort, she said coolly, "I wasn't inquiring. I can handle the rest, thank you. What else did you have to say when you nearly made me run into you?"

She expected him to fight her over the box but he didn't. The jerk merely shrugged and pulled a key from his pocket, saying, "I was just going to mention that you can help yourself to the woodshed out back and I suggest you build a fire right away. It's the only source of heat in there. Here's the key." And then after pushing the key into the lock since her hands were full, he walked away, not slipping even once, although Renee was really hoping he would—it would serve him right—and disappeared in the direction of the barn.

Nerve, nerve, nerve! The man had it in spades. Oh, sure, he gave off that quiet, unassuming vibe but the man actually had an ego the size of…well, for lack of anything more witty or clever, *Texas!*

She managed to hold on to the box and open the door with a minimal amount of swearing and despite the bone-chilling cold was actually sweating from the exertion.

Dropping the box with less delicacy than she should've, she winced as she heard the muffled crack of something breaking and wondered which of her precious few possessions she'd just shattered. After huffing a short breath and vowing to open the box later to find out, she decided to wander the small house to see what she was looking at as far as living conditions go.

Well, it was better than her hotel room, she noted after a quick perusal of the small house. One bedroom, one bathroom, a kitchenette and a tiny living room. Not bad.

If only it weren't wallpapered with some kind of hideous rose wallpaper that looked like it was taken straight out of the pages of a Sears, Roebuck catalog, circa 1920. She grimaced. Thank God she wasn't planning on staying long. This wallpaper might make her lose her mind. She peered out the small front window. Nothing but more snow fluttered from the sky, threatening to bury the small house and the ranch itself if the storm didn't let up. Flicking the living room light on, she pushed the box out of the way of traffic and readied herself for another trip to the car. She didn't have much but at the moment, even one more trip outside wasn't a pleasant thought. Get on with it, she chided herself, wrapping her shawl more tightly around her neck. If she didn't want to sleep in her jeans tonight, she'd better get the rest of her stuff before the path from the driveway to the guesthouse became damn near impassable.

Trudging through the gathering snow, her toes freezing in her worn hiking boots, she couldn't help the quick glance toward the barn as she wondered what kind of woman—if any—would turn John Murphy's head.

Likely as not, that woman didn't exist. She scowled at her thoughts.

Yeah, well, who cares? It's not like she was hoping to be that woman, anyway. She just wanted her kids back. End of story.

Besides, no one in their right mind would want to live here, she thought with a surly temper as she sank to her knee in fresh powder and nearly toppled forward in a frontal snow angel dive. Pulling her foot free, she muttered with a fierce glower, "I hate snow. I really, really, *really* hate snow." *And I think I just might hate you, too, John Murphy.*

Eight

The storm didn't let up as John had thought and since there was little work he could do with the horses in the current weather, all he could do was wait it out. Normally, he'd just tinker around the house, doing odd jobs he'd put off, but he couldn't turn around without stumbling over a little girl underfoot since Alexis and Taylor had been given a snow day.

Peering toward the guesthouse, he was satisfied to see that the little chimney was pumping out smoke, which meant Renee, despite the odds he was betting to the contrary, knew how to build a fire. At least she wouldn't freeze. Not that he was worried.

He moved to the living room and thought about reading the local paper he'd missed from the previous week but as he entered the room it was hard to avoid the long, sullen faces of three little girls who were dying from boredom.

Earlier Renee had found an old puzzle and she and Taylor had spent an hour putting it together only to discover it was missing a piece. But Taylor had just giggled and Renee's expression of pure joy had been hard to walk by without taking notice. He could see the happiness shining from her eyes at her daughter's carefree laughter and it jerked his foundation a little. Alexis, of course, had had nothing to do with her mother or her invitation to join them. For a split second John regretted seeing the light dimming in Renee's eyes at her daughter's open rejection and it had bothered him that he cared. Later, Renee had returned to her cottage and the girls had slowly slipped into terminal boredom when Gladys had taken to her bed early.

It was one thing to be locked in a house of your own with your own things to keep you company, but it was completely something else when you're locked in a stranger's house with nothing familiar.

He remembered what he and Evan used to do when the snow piled high and their mom had had enough of their tussling in the house. She sent them outside in the snow with the order to stay out of trouble or else.

A speculative glance toward the girls had his mind moving. If memory served, there was still a toboggan in the attic gathering dust along with the rest of his childhood mementos. He'd be willing to bet Taylor would love a ride down the hill on that thing.

A few minutes later, he entered the living room with an announcement.

"Bundle up, we're going outside."

"It's snowing," Alexis said.

"Are you going to melt if a snowflake lands on you?"

She scowled. "No. But it's cold outside and Chloe's still sick."

"Fresh air never hurt anyone. Besides, her cough is getting better by the day. Discussion over. Go get dressed and help your sisters, please. We're going outside."

Alexis didn't argue further but the unhappy pout told him volumes about her disposition. He didn't let it get to him, though. He suspected her attitude had less to do with the snow and more to do with the fact he'd let her mama move into the guesthouse. He withheld a sigh. Despite some reservations, he supposed he had to find a way to get those two talking again. He glanced at the small guesthouse, and figured he might as well stop putting it off and start lending a hand. To that end, he made a decision that he hoped didn't blow up in his face.

"I'll be right back," he told the girls who were in the process of being bundled into new jackets and mittens that had been part of the back-to-school shopping spree that he'd instructed Gladys to make. He had to admit, Gladys had a better eye when it came to girly stuff than he did. His idea of high fashion was a clean flannel shirt but, shoot, the horses didn't care what he wore. "Make sure you zipper up good. The wind is blowing a bit," he instructed.

"Maybe we should stay in the house then," Alexis muttered but continued to help Taylor into her mittens.

Making his way to the guesthouse, he gave the door a short rap. A minute later Renee appeared wearing a pink fuzzy sweater that plunged at the neckline in an enticing V, practically plucking John's eyeballs from his head and nestling them between her ample breasts, until she crossed her arms at the immediate chill to ask, "Is everything okay?"

Uh. Shaking off the odd spell—had she been wearing that sweater earlier? Seemed funny that he just now noticed how much it flattered her figure—he focused

see through the bullshit. I wish I'd had that talent when I was young."

John wondered at that statement. He was slowly beginning to realize that Renee's past may well be a chaotic one. Shrugging, he said, "She'll come around."

"I know. But it hurts to be on the outside."

"Give it some time. She's still getting used to having you around again. But she misses her mama and that's the truth."

Renee looked at him sharply. "Really? Did she say something?"

"Not in words. It's a feeling. A hunch."

Her expression fell and she sniffed. "Forgive me if I don't put much store in hunches and feelings. My daughter hates me and goes out of her way to make sure I feel the sting of it every day. I would've been more hopeful if she'd actually admitted something to you."

"You don't always get what you want the way that you want it. Hasn't anyone ever told you that?" He cocked his head at her, while Chloe tried to catch snowflakes. Renee smiled at Chloe but gave him a hard look.

"Of course I know that. I'm just saying—"

"And so am I."

Silence stretched between them as they both processed what'd been said, and just as John was thinking he'd said too much and perhaps should've kept his opinion to himself, they arrived at the small hill John had had in mind.

"Are you sure it's safe?" Renee asked, peering anxiously down the gentle slope as John put Chloe on her feet near her sisters. "I mean, it looks a little steep for the girls."

John chuckled. "Chloe could go down this hill by herself. I'll set up the track and then we'll take turns taking the girls down. Okay? It's completely safe. I promise."

And then he gave her a wide—almost daring—grin. Why? He hadn't a clue but her reaction was worth the confusion.

Renee felt a subtle jump in her heartrate at the smile playing on John's lips and her imagination kicked into overdrive at the worst moment. Pulling her gaze away with obvious effort, she glanced back down the hill and then at her girls. "All right…I guess that'd be okay. How are you going to make the track?"

"That's part of the fun. I'll pave the way so that when we go down with the girls, we have something to stick to. Sort of like a road."

She didn't have a clue as to what he was talking about but she was willing to watch and see. "Be my guest, road master. Carry on. We'll sit back and watch as you crack your head open."

John's bark of laughter surprised her and she smiled in spite of herself. "Watch and learn, city girl," he said.

Were they—*good Lord*—almost flirting with each other?

Maybe a tad, a small voice answered, encouraging her to continue playing, which she obliged with little resistance.

"You say that like it's a bad thing," she retorted, her smile growing, then gestured. "We're waiting…"

"Right. Step aside, females. Watch the Toboggan King work his magic."

Renee laughed, enjoying seeing this different side of the man she swore she'd never like, and picked up Chloe. "I hope my cell phone works out here," she said to her youngest daughter in a conspiratorial tone. "Because I sure as hell can't carry him if he goes and breaks himself."

John looked back at her. "Ye of little faith…"

Chloe giggled and pointed as John positioned himself on the sled at the top of the hill and shoved off. Renee gasped as he skimmed the snow and left behind a sleek trail that looked smooth as ice before slowing to a stop at the bottom, safe and sound and grinning from ear to ear.

Oh, he shouldn't do that. Who knew there was a Colgate smile—blindingly white—hidden behind that stern scowl? It was as if she were seeing him for the first time and that was patently ridiculous but, hey, it was the truth and she was never much of a liar, anyway. Million watt. Straight, white teeth. What a killer smile. A lady killer, that is. She drew a shaky breath, fitted a tremulous smile to her own lips and tried to let the moment of insanity fade without drawing too much attention to the odd flutter and quiver she was feeling on the inside.

As he trudged back up the hill, he said, "I can't believe I'd forgotten how much fun that is. Evan and I used to spend whole days crafting these amazing trails for the sled, going so far as to make jumps, too. Okay, who's next? Alexis? How about you and me? We'll show these kids how it's done."

Alexis, interest piqued in spite of her earlier bad attitude, agreed readily and climbed in front of John as he wrapped his arms around her to tuck his feet. "Hold on, this train is moving fast," he called out as the toboggan started the slow descent and quickly picked up speed.

Renee laughed at the delighted shriek Alexis let out and John's accompanying deep-throated laughter. A warmth that had nothing to do with her wool coat filled her and Renee, for a second, lost herself in the idyllic scene before her. She wondered why John never married and had a family of his own. He seemed to be a natural with kids, though at first glance she'd never have guessed by his surly attitude. John was an enigma that Renee had to admit she was fairly curious in figuring out.

Alexis and John made their way back up the hill, cheeks a ruddy pink from the cold, and for the first time since she'd seen her daughter again, she wore a smile instead of a frown. It lit up her features from within and her daughter's natural beauty transformed her young face to one that would surely break hearts someday. Renee could only hope that her daughter wouldn't make the same mistakes as she'd made, falling in love with the wrong man, giving up her hopes and dreams, and lastly, giving up on herself. Shaking off the sad thoughts, she focused on the joy of the moment and soon her spirits lifted as she watched Taylor hopping up and down. "My turn! My turn!"

"I'll go down with you," Renee volunteered, even though she was a little leery of the whole idea of flying down the hill with nothing more than her feet for brakes.

Renee settled into the back and John placed Taylor in front. With a gentle push, they started the descent, which at first was pretty sedate but then it was like being on a Disneyland thrill ride without the benefit of being strapped in. Taylor squealed in delight and within seconds Renee was doing the same.

Who knew hurtling headlong down a monster hill could be so thrilling?

"Let's go again!" Taylor exclaimed, pulling impatiently on Renee's hand as she dragged the toboggan back up the hill.

"You bet!"

And so they spent the better half of the day slipping and sliding, laughing and giggling until they were winded and exhausted and barely able to drag their bodies back to the house for some much needed hot apple cider and hot chocolate.

And Renee couldn't remember when she'd had so much fun with such an unlikely partner. She slanted a short look at John as he walked beside her, pulling the toboggan with Chloe riding on his shoulders. Maybe there was more to John Murphy than immediately met the eye.

Just maybe, she might be in a mind to find out.

Nine

While John worked on the hot cider and chocolate, Renee helped the girls out of their wet and snow-caked clothing and into soft pajamas and slippers.

"These look warm," Renee observed casually of the girls' pajamas. "Did you pick these out?"

"Yep. On the 'net," Taylor said, wiggling with delight into her horse-patterned top. "Mr. John said there's no mall anywhere near here and he hates to deal with the people so Mr. John had Grammy buy our stuff on his computer."

"That was nice of him to buy you girls some pj's."

Alexis nodded but it was obvious she wasn't going to elaborate for Renee's benefit. Thankfully, Taylor wasn't exactly a locked box when it came to safeguarding information.

"We didn't have any clothes 'cept for the ones that we was wearing the night we came and Mr. John said they weren't fit to line a dog's bed. My jeans had holes in them," Taylor said. "But now, I got lots of jeans with no holes and I love my new shoes."

Renee made a mental note to talk to John about the purchases made thus far. It wasn't right for him to foot the bill. She'd have to find out how much he'd spent so she could make arrangements to pay him back.

But for the time being, the girls were running from the room toward the kitchen, squealing and laughing as they called out for their warm drinks.

Renee hung back a moment as she gazed about the room that her girls had taken over. It was much like the rest of the house, masculine in its decor, but somehow her girls had put their stamp on things with small accents. A Little Mermaid lamp here, a pink throw blanket tossed casually on the bed over there, and lots of clothes strewn about that were certainly the sign of little girl territory. It was the nicest place they'd ever lived and it hurt that Renee hadn't been the one to provide it for them.

Smoothing the wrinkles from the comforter, she wondered if John would let her buy some girly sheets for their bed. But as soon as the thought crossed her mind, she discarded it. There was no sense in buying sheets for a bed they were only going to be in temporarily. Swallowing a sigh at the fight she'd have on her hands the day the girls had to say goodbye to the ranch and to their Mr. John, Renee shelved the unhappy thoughts and pasted a bright smile on her lips for her daughters' benefit.

They weren't leaving today. Her aunt used to tell her, don't borrow trouble from tomorrow when there was happiness to be found in today.

Good advice, Renee realized, for she really didn't want to think about that day, either.

* * *

Later that night, after copious amounts of hot chocolate, cider, a dinner of steak and potatoes, games of Uno, and after the girls had been tucked into bed exhausted from the day's activities, John felt himself reluctant to say good-night to the one woman in the world he ought to steer clear of.

Funny how those things work.

"I guess I should turn in, too," Renee said, although she wasn't making a move toward the door just yet. He took that as a sign that she was hesitant for her own reasons and much to his shame, he jumped at it.

"Come sit a minute," he suggested, gesturing toward the crackling fire in the hearth. The dancing light threw soft shadows into the living room that offset the eerie glow from the snow-packed window. "There's no need to run off just because the girls aren't here. I don't bite."

She smiled. "Are you sure?"

"Am I sure that I don't bite or am I sure that I wouldn't mind some company?"

"Um, both."

He chuckled and followed her to the sofa. "I think the girls had a really good day and I want to thank you for making that effort for them. I get the feeling that playing in the snow isn't your idea of a good time on most days."

"It's not but I didn't realize it could be so much fun, not to mention one heck of a workout. I think muscles I never knew I had are going to be protesting tomorrow morning."

He smiled but his overactive imagination had already snagged the opportunity to be distracting and the effort was forced. Stop thinking about her curves, he instructed his brain, searching wildly for something else to fill the space in his head. Think of taxes, the fence that needs mending—*anything!* "Tell me a bit about yourself," he suggested and she faltered, the light fading quickly from her eyes. "You don't have to. I'm just a little curious about the woman—"

"Who left her kids behind?" she interrupted sharply, moving to leave but he stopped her with a firm hand.

"No, that's not what I was going to say. Are you always in a habit of jumping to conclusions?"

She bit her lip. "Lately. I guess. What were you going to say?"

"Just that I'm curious to know more about the woman who is nothing like I thought she was."

Renee settled back on the sofa as she said, "What do you mean?"

"Well, you're a bit of a wild card, if you know what I mean. Unpredictable. What I knew about you was that you left your girls behind for reasons I don't know but then you've shown your fierce determination to get them back. To win their love. Something tells me that there's more to Renee Dolling, deep down. Tell me about that woman."

She blushed, and in the soft light with her wind-chapped lips and burnished cheeks, she bloomed into an incomparable beauty right before his eyes. He resisted the pull, the urge to sample those lips, to nibble along her collarbone and taste the silken skin, but the effort cost him.

She cleared her throat and glanced away. "You give me too much credit. I'm just a mother who made a terrible mistake who's trying to fix it. Contrary to what it may look like, my girls mean everything to me. They're all I have. I married Jason right out of high school. We were big dreamers with even bigger plans. Unfortunately, neither one of us had the wherewithal to figure out how to make those dreams a reality. And then, I got pregnant."

"So Alexis wasn't planned I take it."

"None of the girls were planned," Renee said drily. "But they were the joy of my life. I was just too…" she drew a deep breath "…too drunk most of the time to realize it."

"Drunk?" An echo of her admission in court about rehab came back to him.

She met his stare. "Yeah. Drunk. I was…I mean, I am an alcoholic. That's why I left."

He digested her admission in silence, taking a moment to let it sink in. "What did your ex-husband think about you wanting to get sober?" he asked.

She smiled without humor. "What did he think? He tried to talk me out of it. Jason was constantly trying to get me to drink because when I drank I forgot how I wanted to get away from him. I'd been trying to leave him for almost a year when I got pregnant with Chloe."

"So you were still having sex with him even though you wanted to leave…"

"That's a little personal, don't you think?" Renee's mouth hardened.

"I'm just trying to understand, you know…connect the dots," he said by way of apology.

"If you figure out my twisted path from then to now, leave a breadcrumb trail. Sometimes I still don't know how I got here," she retorted with a trace of bitterness. Then she sighed and shook her head in answer to his bold question. "No. I wasn't."

Dawning came quickly. "Chloe isn't your husband's child."

A long moment passed before Renee slowly shook her head again.

"Yet he agreed to raise her as his own?"

"He thought it would make me stay and it did…for a

while. But the drinking and the fighting just got worse and worse…until the night I blacked out and woke up with a gash in my forehead and the girls crying in the backseat of my car. I'd tried to drive away with them and I was smashed."

"You're lucky you didn't kill someone."

"I know that. That's why I knew I had to leave in order to get sober. There was a rehab facility with an opening but I couldn't take the kids with me. I told Jason I had to get sober for our marriage. I lied. But it was the only way he'd agree to take care of the kids. I was in for two months and toward the end of my stay, I finally told Jason when he came for visitation that I wanted a divorce. I never expected him to split with the kids. I thought he might try to intimidate me into staying with him but when he didn't, I just assumed he agreed with me that it was over. I got out and realized they were gone. Up until that day I found them here, I'd been looking for them ever since."

"And Chloe's father?"

Shame burned in her cheeks as she answered, "Never knew him. It was a one-night stand that I barely remember."

John leaned back into the sofa and exhaled softly. It was a lot to take in. Renee admitted to her mistakes and didn't flinch from the truth even if she hated her part in it. He had to respect that even if he didn't understand.

"You should've told the judge all this," he said quietly. "It might've made a difference in the outcome."

Her mouth twisted in a sad, wry grin. "Don't you remember? I tried. He wasn't interested in hearing what I had to say. He took one look at me and wrote me off as a bad mother who abandoned her kids. Just like everyone else in this town who knows my situation, which seems like just about half the population."

Renee misconstrued his silence as condemnation and ice returned to her voice as she said, "I can't change who I was…only who I am now. If you can't deal with that, that's your problem." She rose stiffly and walked to the back door as if to leave but John wasn't ready to end the night on a sour note.

"Hold on now," he said, hurrying after her. She stopped and he could see the hurt in her eyes even though she was trying to hide it. He reached out and put his hand on the door to keep her from storming out. "There you go jumping to conclusions again. Bad habit," he murmured, distracted by the soft heave of her chest and the gentle parting of her lips as she stared up at him. He blinked away the fuzz in his brain but his thoughts were foggy from being so close to her. Damn, she smelled good— earthy and sweet, like fresh alfalfa hay on a summer day. Where was he going with that thought train? *Off track.* He paused to give himself a mental shake. "I didn't mean to rile you up," he said.

She ran the tip of her tongue along her bottom lip as if she were nervous and said, "Well, you did. Rile me up," she added with a fair amount of shake in her voice, making him wonder if she was struggling with the same odd assortment of inappropriate feelings, too. He hoped so. He'd hate to realize he was traveling a one-way street. She swallowed. "But I accept your apology," she said, lifting her chin.

Her lips were so close, her mouth so tempting…he jerked and took a step away. When he grinned, it almost hurt. "Good," he said. "It's better if we get along. For the kids."

"Where have I heard that before…" she said, but her voice was strained. "All right then. Good night."

He watched her cross to the guesthouse and waited until her door closed before he shut himself in his own bedroom, feeling oddly discontented. Jerking his shirt out from the waistband of his jeans he pulled it off and over his head to toss in the laundry basket. He'd wanted to kiss her. And yet, he knew that was a bad idea. Laying a lip-lock on the one woman who was so *not* available was pure lunacy and an exercise in futility. And he wasn't usually the kind of man who dabbled in stupid ventures.

When he was down to his boxers, he climbed into the bed and punched the pillows a few times in an attempt to fluff them more to his liking but it was really just a way to blow off steam. He wanted her. Wanted her in the worst way. He pushed at his hardened erection in annoyance. Down, boy. Nothing happening for you.

Think taxes, mending fence—yeah, that didn't work the first time around, and it didn't work now. He turned onto his stomach, grimacing at the discomfort from his groin and closed his eyes, determined to put the whole incident behind him and just go to sleep.

And it almost worked. But just as he hovered between asleep and awake, Renee floated into his mental theater and instead of wearing a look of uncertainty, she smiled suggestively over her shoulder and beckoned for him to come to her as her robe parted and slid to the floor in a discarded heap.

He drifted into slumber on a tortured groan.

Renee paced her small living room unable to sleep. She twisted her hands in agitation, not quite sure what she'd hoped would happen but definitely disappointed that nothing had.

Yet, the very fact that she'd looked into his eyes and felt a tingle zing from her stomach to her feminine parts made her extremely wary. She wasn't supposed to be attracted to John Murphy. The man had complicated her life in a way that should make him Public Enemy #1 in her eyes but she was slowly seeing him in a different light.

And that was not good. Better to keep the battle lines firmly drawn. They were not on the same side. They were simply being civil to one another for the sake of the kids. Kinda like being stuck in a loveless marriage…yeah… she knew what that felt like.

This year was not going to be Renee Dolling's year of living dangerously but rather the year of practical and sound decisions that do not encourage her to drink. Okay, so the thought wasn't something she could put on an inspirational button but it had to keep her on the straight and narrow. Thus far, it had. And that was saying something after all the stress and disappointment she'd endured while searching for her girls.

She sighed. Technically, she *could* date. She was past the prescribed time of no dating after making her commitment to sobriety but somehow keeping her distance seemed so much safer for everyone involved. No entanglements. No conflicts. No…sex.

That's where the pacing came in. Renee stopped and rubbed her palms down her jeans to wipe away the sudden clammy feeling. Sex. She missed it. Needed it. God, *craved* it.

But not with John Murphy.

Anyone but him. Why not, a voice whispered in her head and she nearly barked in laughter. Why? Because that man would likely brand her soul if he so much as touched her in a sexual manner. If they breached that intimate barrier there'd be nothing stopping her from falling headlong in love with him. Was that a bad thing? Yes! She didn't want to love John Murphy. She wanted to leave Emmett's Mill and put this whole awful chapter of her life behind her. She wanted to start a new life with the girls somewhere else. Was that so much to ask?

Her hormones seemed to think so because even as she berated herself for shooting periodic looks of intense longing toward John's house, she couldn't stop wondering what it might feel like to sample just one taste of that firm, sexy mouth.

Climbing into bed, she closed her eyes with an unhappy frown and tried to ignore the twisting tendril of achy tension that taunted her lady bits without mercy, reminding her that no matter how hard she may try, her curiosity was not fading but simply becoming stronger.

Well, she knew what curiosity did for the cat. She just needed to keep that reminder front and center in her mind when she started to feel her defenses drop around that man. That way her panties wouldn't drop, as well.

Ten

John awoke early and, before anyone else on the ranch was up and around, made a trip to town.

Gladys needed a few things from the grocery store and the girls needed a laundry list of school supplies. But really, as he drove, it wasn't his list that preoccupied his thoughts.

It was Renee. Sleep didn't come easy and when he finally did succumb to a fitful state of drowsing, Renee filled his dreamscape in a variety of different states of undress. Really, that was plain ridiculous. He hadn't been so preoccupied with a woman since…well, it was in high school, he knew that much.

Needing a change in scenery, he went straight to the sheriff station to talk with Sheriff Casey about something that was gnawing at him more so than Renee.

Pushing open the double doors, he greeted Nancy with a nod. "The sheriff in?"

"She is. May I ask who…oh, wait a minute, you're John Murphy, aren't you?"

John nodded. "Guilty."

"How are those girls you inherited?"

"Doing good as to be expected I suspect, given their circumstances. Ranch life seems to agree with them, Taylor especially. She loves the horses."

"Bless their hearts," Nancy exclaimed then shook her head with a tsking motion. "It's so good of you to take them in with their mother being a fruit loop and all. With a temper no less."

"Renee's not a bad person. You just didn't see her at her best."

"I'm not saying anything to the contrary, but she did seem a bit unstable if you ask me."

John resisted the urge to comment further realizing that the receptionist was an avid gossiper and just looking for fresh fodder. Well, she'd have to get it elsewhere.

Nancy seemed to recognize her well of information had just dried up and buzzed him through to the other side. He went straight to Sheriff Casey's office.

Pauline Casey, a friend of John's since high school, smiled when she saw it was him.

"I see you made it past Nancy. What brings you into town? I know you hate to leave that ranch of yours. Oh, by the way, you worked a miracle with Tabasco. We were afraid we were going to have to put him down until you got your hands on him. Now he's a wonderful horse. You've earned that reputation of yours."

John didn't roll his eyes but wanted to. Somehow he'd been dubbed the Horse Whisperer of Mariposa County and he was pretty sure Evan had something to do with it. "Glad to hear he's doing better. Can I talk to you about something?"

Suddenly all business, Pauline nodded. "Sure. What's wrong? Something with the girls?"

"In a way. I've been thinking about the father. What happens if he shows up wanting to take the girls away? Can he do that?"

Pauline's stare hardened. "No way in hell that's going to happen. We have an I&B out for his arrest on charges of child neglect, and cruelty to a minor."

"What about the arsenic? Can't you slap him with attempted murder?"

"Hard to prove. A defense attorney could just say that Chloe, being as young as she is, could've accidentally ingested the stuff when he wasn't around."

"We have the girls' testimony that he made Chloe eat eggs that he made for her special. Isn't that enough?"

"I wish it were. Damn, I wish it were. Trust me, I want to get this guy as much as you but we have to have something that will stick or it will hurt the case against him, which could land those girls back in his custody on a technicality."

John felt himself pale but he managed to grit out, "Not on my life. Those girls aren't going anywhere near that bastard. He tried to *kill* Chloe. You and I both know it."

Pauline nodded. "I hear you, John, and believe you, but we have to do things the right way or else it could backfire and screw everything up. But before you get yourself all worked up, it's likely the girls would end up in protective custody before they'd land back in his hands, at least at first. You know family reintegration is a top priority if the parent can be rehabilitated."

His mouth curled in disgust. "The only thing that would rehab that son of a bitch is a bullet to the brain."

"Careful now," Pauline warned. "Talking like that can get you in trouble. But don't worry, they're not going anywhere just yet so let's cross that bridge when we come to it."

He supposed she was right but it made his gut curdle at the thought of letting that man even a hundred yards within the girls and damn, if that didn't make his trigger finger itchy.

Pauline deftly changed the subject. "How are things going with the mother? She any trouble?"

Distracted, he waved away Pauline's question. "She's not a problem. Not yet, anyway," he grumbled, his thoughts still sour.

"I'm surprised I haven't had a call from you saying she's tried to up and steal them in the middle of the night. She seemed the type to grab and run."

Pauline's offhand comment startled him. He'd never thought of that. Suddenly, he felt uneasy. Would she do that? He didn't know her at all and Alexis clearly didn't trust her. Perhaps he'd been too quick to let her move in. And what if he'd kissed her? What a royal idiot he was. She could be playing him for all he knew. It wasn't like she was trustworthy. She was an addict for crying out loud. She was probably a pro at lying to get what she wanted. He realized Pauline was watching him closely and he gave her a short nod as if in thanks. "I'll keep an eye on her," he said. "Who knows what she's capable of."

"Smart thinking."

Pauline seemed ready to play the amiable devil's advocate as she added, "Then again, she got off to a bad start here but maybe, deep down, she's a good person and if she's given half a chance, she could be a good mother again. Who knows. Stranger things have happened. Remember that time Fudder found that two-headed snake down by Hatcher Creek? Creepy little thing. The snake, not Fudder," she said with a small chuckle. "Anyway, hopefully things will work out for everyone involved. This is an unusual case."

Yeah, you could say that again.

Pauline offered a wise smile and John realized there was a wealth of unsaid knowledge behind that subtle twist of the lips. "What?" he asked, eyeing her suspiciously.

"Nothing."

"Nothing my ass. What's with that look you just gave me?"

She leaned forward, her gaze intent. "Have you considered what it's going to be like when your chicks fly the roost? Their mom is going to regain custody eventually."

"I know," he admitted with a slight scowl. "That's good. My life can get back to normal."

"True. But what if normal to you now is what you want normal to be forever?"

He balked initially at Pauline's question but once it sank further into his brain he realized she might have a point. When the girls went on with their lives…he'd miss them. A lot. He drew a deep breath and shook his head.

"We all adjust, right? No matter what the situation. That's life."

"True again," Pauline agreed.

He cleared his throat and focused on the one thing he felt he could control. "I want a restraining order against Jason Dolling."

"For your protection?"

"No, for his."

"I don't follow."

John met Pauline's curious stare. "If he comes on my property, I'm going to shoot first and ask questions later. He's not getting near the girls. I made them a promise and I aim to keep it."

"Consider it done. But John—"

"Yeah?"

"Don't shoot him. Just call us and we'll take care of things."

He tilted his head at her and offered a slow, dangerous smile, saying, "I'll call, but no promises on what kind of condition he'll be in when you arrive. Drive fast. See you later, Pauline. Give Roy my best."

Renee finished putting the dishes into the dishwasher and caught a glimpse of Alexis lurking around the corner. Pretending not to notice, Renee began to hum a tune she used to sing when Alexis was small.

Taylor and Chloe were in the rec room, attempting to play a game of pool, though neither could actually handle the pool sticks very well so they were just rolling the pool balls into the corner pockets on their own. Chloe was too short to really see much above the table so Taylor had to help her. Renee could hear their giggles from the kitchen and it warmed her heart.

"How's school so far?" she asked casually as she wiped down the tiled counter. "Do you like your teacher?"

"He's okay." Alexis slid around the corner but stayed close to the hallway as if she wanted to remain near an exit. "He has really big ears. Like an elephant."

"All the better to hear you with, I suppose," Renee said, holding back a smile.

"That's what he says, too."

"Sounds like he has a pretty good sense of humor about them."

Alexis shrugged. "I guess." She slid a little closer.

"Well, I hope no one is mean to him just because he's a little different."

"No. Everyone likes him so they don't call him names."

Renee folded her dish towel and hung it to dry on the oven handle. "What do *you* think of him?"

Alexis's expression was quietly reflective as she answered. "He's very nice. He doesn't make me feel behind even though I am."

Renee wanted to kiss this man. Or at the very least shake his hand. "That's a wonderful trait in a teacher. What's his name?"

"Mr. Elliot."

"Nice name for a nice man. Taylor likes her teacher, too. Mrs. Higgenbotham. She calls her Mrs. H. for short."

"I would, too. That's a long name and it sounds made-up."

"I agree."

With the kitchen clean, there was little else busy work to do so she took a seat at the kitchen table and hoped Alexis would follow. She held her breath as Alexis seemed to consider the idea and then slowly slid into the chair opposite her.

"So, how long are you staying?" Alexis asked.

"I'm not going anywhere."

Alexis looked up sharply, her eyes lighting with wary hope. "You mean, you're going to stay here with us at the ranch…forever?"

Renee sucked in a breath and proceeded with caution. "Alexis…when the time comes and we get this court situation figured out, you, me and your sisters will leave the ranch and John can get back to his life."

Alexis stood up abruptly, her expression darkening. "I don't want to leave the ranch. Or Mr. John. If you want to leave, then go. But we're not going with you."

"Sweetheart, that's not possible," Renee said, trying to appeal to her sense of logic. "This is not our home—"

"It's not *your* home. Don't try to take us away from it."

"Alexis, wait…let's think this through a bit. What happens if—sometime in the future—Mr. John falls in love with someone? And he starts a family with this person? Where does that leave you girls? Just because we don't live with him any longer doesn't mean we can't be friends, though, right?"

Tears welled in Alexis's eyes but she didn't let them fall. Renee almost wished she would just so that Alexis would allow her to comfort her. But her daughter remained stoic and it really broke Renee's heart to watch.

"You should marry Mr. John then," Alexis announced as if that were the answer to everyone's problem.

"M-marry John?" Renee nearly choked on her own spit. She couldn't quite believe those words had tripped out of her daughter's mouth so easily. "That's not going to happen."

"Why not? You made a deal to take care of us and clean the house, what else does a wife do?"

Uh. "There's so much more involved, sweetheart. Things that a nine-year-old wouldn't understand."

"Like kissing?"

Renee nodded reluctantly and felt her cheeks redden. "Sort of. But kissing is definitely involved."

"Well, maybe you could work on the kissing part. And maybe you could get him to like you enough to marry you. Because we're not leaving."

And then Alexis turned on her heel and left the kitchen.

Marry John…good Lord. The thought was enough to curl her hair.

Eleven

Saturday, the crisp winter morning broke early and bright despite the forecasts of rain and snow, and John wasted little time in getting outside to get some things done.

His little shadow, Taylor, donned her alligator-green galoshes and her winter coat and promptly followed him out the door.

He glanced back at her. "Going somewhere?"

"We've got chores to do, right, Mr. John?"

He nodded. "Want to help me feed the horses today?"

"You betcha."

"You betcha? Where'd you learn that?"

"From Mrs. H. She's always saying it and I like the sound of it so I'm gonna say it, too."

"I see. Well, let's get to the stables. I can almost hear Vixen kicking the stall door wanting to know what's holding up the gravy train."

"Vixen is very big but not as big as Cisco," Taylor observed, falling into step with John. "Cisco is like a giant. But he doesn't scare me. He's sweet and he nibbles on my hand when I give him sugar cubes. I think it's sad that someone was mean to him. He's so pretty." She looked up at him, a wealth of trust and childish innocence shining in her hazel eyes, as she asked, "Why are people mean sometimes?"

He knew she was asking about more than cruelty to animals and he wished he knew the answer but, frankly, he didn't know why people did the things they did. "I don't know, honey. Sometimes people just aren't right in the head and they take out their frustrations on other people or their animals. They're bullies, plain and simple. But you know what? Bullies are really cowards because they only pick on those who they think won't or can't fight back."

After a long moment, Taylor nodded sagely. "I think my daddy was a bully. What do you think?"

"I think you're right."

She slipped her mittened hand into his and when she looked at him again, his heart contracted at the sadness and fear he read in her expression. "Mr. John, is it bad if I don't want to see my daddy again?"

"No."

"Good." Her relief was palpable. "Because I don't think I want to see him again ever. He was real mean to Chloe and he scared me. Sometimes when he looked at us, it's like he wished we were gone. You never look at us like that and I like it here. You're not ever gonna make us leave are you, Mr. John?"

"If it were within my power, honey, you could stay for as long as you want but your mama is here and she wants to rebuild your lives together. Don't you want that?"

Taylor nodded solemnly. "Yeah, but why can't we just all stay here? Renee has a nice little house in the back so she doesn't take up much room. Plus, she makes really good cookies, as good as Grammy Stemming, don't you think?"

"There's more to the situation at hand than good cookies," John said, wishing it were really that simple. If only all of the world's problems were easily solved by a warm batch of snickerdoodles. "But I'll tell you what, let's not worry about things we can't do anything about today and just enjoy the time we have together. How's that sound?"

"It sounds like a co-pro-mise."

"That's a big word and you're right again."

"Well, Mrs. H. is full of big words and she says that one a lot. She'll be happy to know I used it. She says our brain grows when we add a new word to our vo-cab-u-lary. Is that true?"

"If Mrs. H. says so, then it probably is." He chuckled and gave her hand a squeeze. "What say we get to our chores before Vixen tears down the entire barn?"

She grinned up at him, revealing the sweetest smile he'd ever seen, and he wondered how he was ever going to manage to say goodbye to three little girls who stole his heart the minute they showed up on his doorstep.

Gladys felt her age today and that was a hard thing to admit even if she was only admitting it in the privacy of her own thoughts. But this morning her bones felt as if they were grinding against one another and her arthritis finally kept her from working on her crochet project.

"You okay?"

Gladys startled at Renee's voice. For a moment, Gladys had forgotten she wasn't alone in the house. She stopped rubbing at her wrist and smothered the grimace for the younger woman's sake. If there was one thing Gladys hated, it was the pity of strangers. "Oh, just fine. Didn't hear you come in." She paused. "You're doing a good job, by the way," she added with a brief smile but the pain in her joints prevented a long-lasting effort.

"You come sit down," Renee instructed gently, yet the firm set of her mouth said she wouldn't take no for an answer. "There's nothing in the kitchen that needs to be done just this second."

Gladys waved her away with a slight frown. "Don't make a fuss. I've got a schedule to keep. It's Meatloaf Monday, you know, and if you start deviating from your schedule, the next thing you know you'll be eating spaghetti when you should be eating shepherd's pie. Puts your digestion in a tailspin. Plus, John loves Meatloaf Monday."

That last part was delivered in a wheeze that Gladys immediately found pitiful and if it hadn't rattled out of her and had come from someone else, Gladys would've told that person to stop being such a stubborn fool and take a load off. But Gladys was of the "Do as I say, not as I do" generation and she wasn't of a mind to change her ways at this juncture of her life.

"I doubt your precious John Murphy is going to keel over dead from a digestion—what did you call it—*tailspin?* just because he didn't get his Meatloaf Monday. Now sit your rear in that chair and relax before you crumble to dust right before my eyes and I have to clean up the mess."

Gladys stared but a low snicker popped out of her mouth, surprising them both. "I see where the girls get their spunk," she said and then in spite of her previous declaration shuffled to the wide, comfy chair directly in front of the fireplace and sank into it. She gestured at Renee impatiently. "So, come and keep me company then if you're going to make me sit here like the old lady that I am. There's no way in hell I'm going to sit on my duff while you do all the work around here. If I'm going to be lazy the least you can do is help me pass the time while I do it."

Renee smiled and after putting another log on the fire, sat on the sofa and tucked her legs up under her. "How long have you been making John meatloaf?"

"Since his mother died."

Her smile faded and Gladys was sad for that. She had a beautiful smile when she chose to show it. But Gladys appreciated her respect. Addie Murphy had been her best friend. Even after all these years, the pain of her passing hadn't completely faded. "When Addie died those boys were so lost, especially Evan, and John felt the pressure to keep everything together. This ranch was all they had, all Addie had after that dirty rat husband of hers turned tail and ran leaving them with a hill of debt and, well, meatloaf seemed the only comfort I could offer them."

Gladys happened to meet Renee's gaze at an opportune moment and caught a softening. It was probably not Renee's intention to allow that small slip and it caused Gladys to wonder. And because Gladys was known to dabble in business that was none of her concern, she decided to put her arthritis to good use.

"Maybe you're right. I don't think I'll be able to cook tonight. These old hands are cramping pretty bad. It's that darn storm that blew through here. Haven't been myself since. Rotten old bones." She leveled a finger at Renee and shook it at her playfully, saying, "Don't get old. It stinks. Can you believe this old body went white-water river rafting just a few years ago?"

Renee's eyes widened and Gladys chuckled, loving

the shock value of the statement. "Yep. Went down the Colorado. It was Evan's suggestion and damn if I didn't shock everyone and go and do it." Gladys leaned in to whisper, "I think everyone half expected me to land in the drink but no, I did quite well. Had the time of my life. You should try it sometime. Evan can probably get you a discount."

Renee shuddered. "No thanks. I'm afraid of water. Now, tell me more about this Meatloaf Monday business. Is it hard to make? Maybe I could use the recipe and make it for you?"

Gladys smothered the triumphant grin. Young people nowadays were just too easy to figure out. She sent a silent prayer to Addie if she was listening or watching and asked for a little help in making things turn out right. Lord only knew it was time for John to settle down and why waste a perfectly good opportunity when it was staring everyone right in the face?

Renee couldn't believe she was actually playing Betty Crocker but there was no denying that it was her mouth that had offered and it was her standing before a hot oven, worrying that John wouldn't like it or that she'd somehow messed up the recipe.

Well, it was meatloaf, she countered to the prattle in her head. How hard could it be? Mash up some meat, throw in some bread crumbs, a little egg and season. And then cook it to death. At least that was how she used to make meatloaf, but, come to think of it, she'd never won any awards for anything that came out of her oven.

So she was nervous. Understandably.

"Renee, that smells very good," Taylor said, taking a break from her coloring book to smile encouragingly at her mother. "It smells like Loafmeat Monday. How come Grammy Stemming didn't make it?"

"She wasn't feeling well," Renee answered, looking distractedly at Taylor, then added, "Honey, think you might want to call me Mom now?"

Taylor thought for a moment and then said, "I will take it under con-sid-err-ation. That's what Mrs. H. says when we ask for something in class."

"You're sure using lots of big words these days," Renee observed, smiling. "Imagine what you'll be saying after a full year of school. I might need a dictionary to keep up with you."

Taylor giggled and her eyes twinkled in a way that made Renee's heart sing. Suddenly Taylor looked quite serious, "So, Grammy Stemming makes smashed potatoes to go with the meat. Did she show you how to make those, too? 'Cuz we can't have the meat without the potatoes, that's what Mr. John says. He's a meat-and-potatoes kind of guy he says."

Taylor's statement dripped cute but the message Renee caught and processed in her brain just made her blush. John was all man, that was for sure. It was almost unfathomable that he was still single. Renee had to wonder what was wrong with him that some woman hadn't snatched him up long ago. She itched to know more about him but there was never a truly opportune way to nonchalantly dig for clues when the man rarely uttered more than a sentence or two. John Murphy wasn't what anyone could call verbose. She cleared her throat and smiled. "Of course. You can't have Meatloaf Monday without potatoes…that would be like cake without ice cream, or pizza without cheese."

Alexis piped in as she walked in from around the corner. "Or peanut butter without jelly."

Renee grinned, absurdly pleased that Alexis was playing along. "Right," she agreed. "So, the only question we need to answer is, red potato or russet?"

"Red, with the skins on," Alexis said. "I mean, that's how Grammy Stemming made them and they tasted pretty good."

"Sounds perfect."

Renee rummaged around for the potatoes and found them with a little help from Taylor, who seemed to know her way around quite well, and tried using the relatively mellow moment with her girls to start getting to know them again. The problem was, each time a question popped into her brain, she quickly discarded it for fear that it would come out wrong or Alexis might hightail it out of the room. She bit her lip. The silence grew and Renee started to feel the walls close in until Taylor began chirping as if she hadn't noticed the awkward moment.

"How come we don't have a grammy?"

"Excuse me?" Renee stammered, as the total off-hand delivery of the question caught her off guard. "What do you mean? You have a grandmother."

"Where?"

"Uh…" Renee stalled, suddenly wishing for a slice of that god-awful silence again, yet when she noted Alexis watching her keenly for a reaction, she cleared her throat and opted for a vague version of the truth. "Well, you've met your grandma Irene, uh, once I think, but you're probably too young to remember and as far as your dad's mother…oh, goodness, she died a while before you were born."

"Why isn't our grandma Irene around much? Doesn't she like us?"

Renee tried a disarming grin but her middle child's innocent question struck a sour chord and made Renee

flinch. "Of course she does." That's a lie. A big fat one
at that but she wasn't about to tell a child that her grandmother was as cold as a Michigan winter when it came
to her only daughter and any of her issue. Renee remembered the phone call she'd placed when Alexis was born
and how badly it had gone down. Just one more shitty
memory she'd tried to erase with plenty of booze. She
scrubbed her hands down the apron she'd found hanging
in the broom closet and forced a smile. "So who's going
to help me with these potatoes?"

Alexis's sharp gaze caught the fidgety movement
and Renee had to fight the urge to shove her hands in
her pockets to hide them. She smiled Alexis's way and
tried to communicate without words that she'd changed.
But the moment was lost. Alexis slid from the chair and
scooped Chloe along with her. Renee longed to chase
after her but Taylor was still beside her, chattering like
a magpie, totally oblivious to the emotional tide that had
just swept out, and Renee clung to her middle daughter's open nature as if her life depended on it because
in a way…it did.

John hadn't expected Renee to roll up her sleeves and
hit the kitchen but he wasn't about to complain. One
might think that after so many years of Meatloaf Monday a guy might get sick of it but he truly found comfort
in the constant and it wasn't lost on him that Renee had
tried to accommodate him.

The girls had cleared the dinner plates and Alexis
was running the bath for her sisters. It was just him and
Renee left in the room. He ought to say something nice.
He ought to…stop his eyes from sinking to the midlevel
of her fuzzy sweater and taking up residence. Glancing away, he absently tapped the table with his knuck-

les. Clearing his throat, he offered a gruff, "Dinner was good."

She looked up and gave a short smile. "Thanks." Then shrugged. "Taylor was a big help. She must love spending time with Gladys or something because that girl certainly knows her way around a kitchen. Not sure how I feel about that," she admitted with a slight frown.

"What's wrong with a girl being at home in the kitchen?"

"Because it gives men the wrong idea."

Wrong idea? His mother had been a whiz in the kitchen. That was a bad thing? "I'm not following you."

"Forget it."

"Tell me."

"I just don't want my girls to think all they're good for is to be stuck in the kitchen, you know? They're smart girls. They deserve better. I want them to go to college and make something of themselves."

"Did you go to college?"

"No." She looked away but not before John caught the stark look of regret in her stare. It pulled and poked at the soft side of his underbelly. He shifted in his chair as if to escape but there was no relief. She continued, "Which is why I want better for my girls than just being a housewife, stuck in the kitchen with a passel of kids hanging off them."

He startled at the bleak and insulting view she'd just shared of her opinion on what he'd considered the greatest gift a woman could give to her children and couldn't stop the stiff comment that followed. "My mother was a housewife."

Guilt flashed in her expression and she lifted her shoulder in apology. "I'm not putting down anyone who chooses that life. I just don't want that for my girls."

"And what if it makes them happy?"

"It wouldn't." Her answer was short and vehement. She recovered with a subtle smile but her shoulders were tense. If he wasn't so riled at her comment he might be tempted to ease the knots out of the soft flesh but as it was he wanted to tell her to get off her high horse. And while she was at it, why didn't she pull out the stick that was wedged up her rear.

"There's nothing wrong with a woman who wants to spend time raising her kids right. But if you're the kind of woman who would rather dump her kids off at day care and forget about them for a good eight or nine hours a day that's your own business, but don't go judging others on their choices because they're different than yours. And your girls should be free to make their own choices even if it doesn't cotton to what you want them to do with their lives."

Her smile was wintry. "How nice of you to go all parental when you've never had any children of your own. Perhaps you'd like to write a book on the subject? I'm sure it'll be a bestseller."

What a sassy mouth on this one. All piss and vinegar as Gladys would say. He leaned back in the chair and regarded her with shrewd objectivity. "Your mom a career-type?"

"She was an image-is-everything type," she answered, probably unaware that she had visibly tensed. "Why do you ask?"

He shrugged. "Just wondering. Seems you're pretty sensitive about certain things. You and your mom don't get along?"

She barked a short laugh as if the question wasn't worth answering because the answer had to be patently obvious but the sound was ragged and tattered around the edges to John's ears. "Must be my lucky day. First Taylor, now you. Is this some kind of conspiracy to get me to work through my feelings about my mom? Look, I'm over it. To answer your question, no, me and the mom don't get along so well. In fact, I'm pretty sure if I was on fire she wouldn't waste a drop of spit to put it out."

He whistled low and deep. That was pretty hard-core. John understood that kind of animosity. It was about the same way he felt about his own father. "What happened between you two?"

"It doesn't matter. It was so long ago I'm not even sure I remember."

"I think you remember just fine."

She shot him a dark look. "Maybe I do. Too bad for you, I don't feel like walking down memory lane."

"Fair enough."

"Really. Just like that. First you're grilling me and now you're fine with letting it go?"

He shrugged. "Sure. You don't want to talk about it. It doesn't interest me enough to coax it out of you."

"Aren't you a charmer," she said drily and he chuckled in spite of the vague insult she'd just thrown his way but he couldn't dispute it. He was no good at this talking shit. The woman didn't want to talk about why she was so sensitive about her mom, it was none of his business.

"That's me. Grade A Choice."

He got up, ready to leave the faintly aggressive tension between them behind, but she cocked her head to the side and regarded him as if he were suddenly someone who fascinated her.

"Why don't you wear a cowboy hat?"

He paused and returned the assessing stare as he countered, "Why don't you like housewives?"

"I asked you first."

He shrugged. "I'm not a cowboy. I just work with horses. There's a difference." He pinned her with a look. "Your turn."

She inhaled sharply and for a split second he was sure she was going to turn tail and run but she didn't. Instead she answered with an unwavering but undeniably sad stare.

"Because I never wanted to be one but somehow that's where I ended up."

Twelve

Renee slid into bed and winced as the cold blankets shocked her skin. She'd left a fire burning in her small woodstove but sometimes the heat didn't make it to the tiny bedroom and it felt like she was sleeping on a block of ice until her own body heat started to kick in.

What an odd man, she mused as scenes from dinner replayed in her head. He was an enigma. Just when she thought she knew what he was about, he went and turned her assumptions upside down, leaving her to gape in confusion. She sensed something between them. Something that ran hot one minute and cold the next. Wasn't that a bad thing? If she were made of glass such rapid change in temperature would surely cause her to shatter. Well, thank her lucky stars she wasn't made of glass, she thought wryly. One thing was for sure, he was frightfully good at reading people. Or maybe he was just good at reading her. Now *that* was a scary thought.

What had she been thinking? Meatloaf Monday. How ridiculous. She should've left him to fend for himself. Damn, if she hadn't always had a soft spot for the weak and vulnerable. Um, yeah. Who was she trying to call weak and vulnerable? Certainly not John Murphy. Cornbread farm boys with wicked smiles did not grow up to be weak or vulnerable. They grew up to be men who filled doorways, with thick roping muscles honed from years of working with their hands, and quick, sharp gazes that saw through piles of bullshit to the truth underneath.

Gazes that lingered and caressed the tingling flesh under your sweater until your nipples peaked and ached and all but poked out of your bra for need of someone to put their big strong hands all over them.

She shuddered and moaned as she gave her pillow a sound whack for even allowing her mind to wander into such dangerous pastures—uh, territory!—even her metaphors were going country. Good grief. Was it contagious?

Rolling to her stomach, she tried quieting her mind with deep-breathing exercises and for a while it worked. Slowly her mind emptied of everything involving John and his big, strong man-hands and what she wanted him to do with them, and she focused on the calm, serene landscape of her favorite place—a picture of a waterfall in Maui, a place she'd never been but the image always soothed her—and slowly drifted into peaceful slumber.

She wasn't sure why her eyelids fluttered open; the darkness told her sunrise was still hours away, but seconds later she caught the faint but undeniable sound of a child screaming inside the house.

Kicking herself free from the tangle of blankets, she ran shoeless and fumbling in the dark, toward the sound, mindless of the rocks that bruised her heels and the bitter cold that froze her exposed skin. All that mattered was getting to her children.

Alexis held Chloe close, rocking her in spite of her sister's frantic attempts to get away from the invisible hands that tried to hurt her. Alexis's heart felt ready to jump out of her chest as tears filled her eyes but she didn't let go. She just kept murmuring in a soft, soothing voice that everything was okay and that no one was going to get her.

Taylor huddled against the headboard, her thumb popped in her mouth like she always did when she was scared, scrambled from the bed and catapulted herself into John's arms the minute he appeared in the doorway, eyes bleary but searching for the cause of Chloe's fear.

Renee nearly crashed into him as she pounded down the hallway.

"What's going on?" she asked, breathless, moving toward the bed until Alexis shook her head vehemently. Hurt crossed her mother's features but she stopped. "What's wrong with Chloe?"

"She gets nightmares sometimes," Alexis answered, pulling Chloe closer even as the baby shook and shivered. "I can take care of her. You can go back to bed."

Taylor wrapped her arms around John's neck all the more tightly. Her voice watery and frightened. "It's Daddy's fault, Mr. John. It's all his fault Chloe is so scared at night."

Renee looked at Taylor, confusion and fear crossing her features. For a moment, Alexis was tempted to let Renee take over just so Renee could feel Chloe shake in her arms but instead her fingers tightened around her little sister and hoped they'd all just go away. "Just go back to bed. I'll handle it."

Renee turned to John and murmured something and he nodded reluctantly, taking Taylor with him. Renee approached the bed. Alexis scowled. "I said, you can go."

Renee shook her head and took a seat beside them. Alexis felt tears stinging her eyes and tightened her grip on Chloe. "I can do it," she insisted. "I've been the one here for her. Not you."

"I know," Renee acknowledged quietly. "What do we do to help Chloe?"

Surprised to be asked, Alexis answered haltingly, "She's not awake when she does this and if you try to wake her up too fast she just starts screaming and kicking. I just hold her real tight and tell her it's okay. She seems to like that."

Renee nodded, tears filling her eyes. "How long has this been happening?"

"Since Daddy started locking her in the closet with the spiders and the other bugs."

"Your daddy…he did that?" she asked, her voice breaking.

"That's not all," Alexis said. "He—"

"I understand," Renee cut in, her eyes filling again.

"No, you don't," Alexis whispered, anger seeping inside her, hot and mean. Chloe whimpered and she loosened her hold until Chloe's breathing returned to normal. "Because if you did…you never would've left us behind. Especially Chloe."

And then the tears she swore she'd never let her mother see, started to pour out of her eyes in a way she couldn't control and it made her all the more angry. "Please get out. We don't need you."

"Alexis—"

"Get *out*," she cried and her mother drew back. The

hurt in her expression giving Alexis no joy even though she'd thought it would. She choked on her next words. "Just leave. *Please*."

Renee forced her feet to move. This was not the time to press the issue although she yearned to take her baby in her arms and cuddle her as she should. She paused at the doorway and saw Alexis settle into the bed with Chloe lying against her small chest, her fingers clutching Alexis's forearm.

Swallowing a toxic mixture of grief, fear and guilt that had congealed in her throat, she started to return to the guesthouse when she saw John talking with Taylor in a low voice in the living room. Not wanting to be seen, Renee pulled into the shadows and listened intently.

"My daddy is a bad man, isn't he?" Taylor asked, the sadness in her tone cracking Renee's heart for the sorrow in it. "Why was he so mean? Are we bad girls?"

"Of course not," John answered softly. "Why would you say that?"

Taylor hiccupped. "Because maybe if we were better, Daddy wouldn't have been so mad and Renee wouldn't have left. And then, maybe Daddy wouldn't have been so mean to Chloe. Chloe's not a bad girl, even if Daddy said she was. I don't believe him and neither does Alexis. Do you think Renee thinks Chloe is bad? Sometimes she pees the bed but she doesn't mean to. She just forgets and has an accident. You would never spank Chloe for having an accident, would you?"

"No, I wouldn't and I don't think your mom would, either."

"You don't?"

There was a long pause and then he answered solemnly, "No, I don't."

His answer pierced Renee's chest in an unexpected manner. She wasn't accustomed to others being in her corner, much less a man who made it no secret of how he'd felt about her from the very beginning.

Renee melted against the shadows, wishing she could dissolve into a spray of mist and just disappear so that she could escape the awful feeling crushing her. Tears stung her eyes. What the hell did you do to our babies, Jason? He only hurt *your* baby, a voice whispered. Chloe was no blood relation to him but he'd been raising her as his own. For all intents and purposes, Chloe looked at Jason as her daddy. And yet, he'd done unspeakable things to her. In essence, she'd left her baby in the hands of a monster. Biting her lip hard to keep it from trembling, she slipped out the back door unnoticed.

The next morning, John rose and went about his chores with Taylor beside him. Last night's excitement all but forgotten, she chattered amiably to the horses as she gave them each a good scoopful of oats while he busied himself with throwing out the hay and filling the giant buckets with fresh water for the day. While Taylor may have been fresh-eyed, John's mind was haunted by the stricken expression frozen on Renee's face after Alexis had tossed her out of the room. He'd been tempted to help smooth things over but his hands had been full with Taylor and he figured Alexis and Renee had to start working things out on their own. To his mind, that wasn't going too well. For too long Alexis had been acting like a surrogate mom and didn't know how to let go of the reins, so to speak, and Renee, too riddled with guilt and whatnot, couldn't just pull forward and assert her authority.

It was a pickle—one he shouldn't give a whole hill

of beans about, either, but damn if he wasn't getting a headache over the predicament.

"You about done over there, half pint?" he called out to Taylor and she nodded, running over to return the oat pail to its peg on the wall before skipping to his side. "Did you double check the gate latches?" he asked.

"Yep. Have you figured out how you're gonna get Vixen to stop stomping on your helpers?" she asked, an excited gleam in her eye. "Yesterday, I thought she was going to stomp Mr. Tony to death! She was so mad that he was trying to come into her stall."

"Yes, she was. And, no, I haven't figured that one out yet. She's the toughest horse I've ever worked with."

"Someone was mean to her, huh?" Taylor asked, her eyes solemn. "That's why she don't like no one. What happens if she *never* likes no one? Will you keep her forever here at the ranch?"

He shook his head. "She doesn't actually belong to me, half pint," John said, his mouth twisting sadly. "Her owner is paying me to gentle her so that he can ride her."

"I don't think Vixen would like that very much," Taylor said, shaking her head like a miniature version of himself. He would've laughed except the subject matter was rather serious. Vixen's fate was dire if he couldn't get her on the right track. Her owner wasn't known for his compassion. He'd bought Vixen because she was beautiful with solid lines and a proud disposition but he hadn't listened when the seller had tried to tell him that she wasn't no kiddie pony. Now, she was so riled and cantankerous, if John couldn't get her under control, she was bound for the glue factory. And that was a crying shame, one that he tried not to think about. Returning his attention to Taylor he ruffled her blond mop, chuckling as he said, "Is that so? Well, we'll do our best with

Vixen. Until then, it's school for you. Run on and go see if your sister is awake yet."

"Yessir, Mr. John!" Taylor saluted John with a lop-sided grin and took off running for the house, her blond hair fluttering behind her like a kite tail, tugging a grin from his lips before he could stop it. If he'd ever seen fit to settle down and raise a family he knew he would've wanted a daughter just like that kid. He couldn't imagine walking away from his kids, not even if his life depended on it.

Renee peeked in on Gladys, anxious for something to do, and was surprised when she saw the old gal up and moving around.

"Aren't you supposed to be in bed?" she asked, a frown creasing her forehead. "You look pale."

"Takes more than a fever and some sore bones to keep me down. Besides, I promised Chloe chocolate chip cookies and there's no sense in lying down when there's stuff to be done. Right?"

"I suppose," Renee said, feeling worlds from this stout old lady. Back when she and Jason were still married they used to spend whole days doing nothing except making beer runs. The house had been a pigsty, beer cans overflowing the small plastic garbage can, and pizza boxes littering the kitchen because neither one of them could do much more than speed dial with any efficiency. Out of nowhere her cheeks started to burn for her own laziness. She'd been raised differently and so had Jason for that matter, but it hadn't mattered. They'd both acted slovenly.

"Something on your mind?" Gladys inquired when she noted Renee had stopped folding the blanket in her hand and it was hanging limp from her fingertips. Gladys gestured and Renee snapped to attention with a flustered apology but Gladys waved it away. "No need. You know, I think we ought to get to know each other better. Seems you're not the person I might've thought you were."

Renee startled. "What do you mean?"

Gladys shrugged, making no excuses. "My opinion of you was pretty low until recently. I know it's not right but the first time I met you I thought to myself, 'Now there's a flighty, snooty slip of a girl' and then of course, if you were shacking up with Jason you couldn't be worth all that much because frankly, that boy was never going to amount to much, bless my sister's heart for never giving up on him." Renee stared, unsure if she should be offended or not but Gladys didn't seem to mind and kept talking. "I suspect you two have been living off the inheritance my sister left for you when she died?"

There was no sense in denying it. The money—not that thirty-five thousand dollars was a lot in the big scheme of things—had allowed them to party unchecked, unhindered by jobs or other inconsequential things, and gloss over the major problems in their marriage. The burn in her cheeks flared bright as she nodded and her throat seemed to choke off her voice. "We were going to buy a house," she said. "But it never worked out."

Gladys continued to tidy the room but the ensuing silence made Renee wish she'd bypassed the old woman's room. "We made a lot of mistakes," she admitted after a long moment. Gladys glanced up and seemed to nod in agreement. "But I'm trying not to live in the past. If I keep looking backward I'll go crazy. It's bad enough that I can hardly get near Chloe because Alexis blames me for everything that happened after I left, and the guilt and shame is enough to kill me already. I don't need to overload myself with the stupid mistakes Jason and I made with his inheritance. I feel bad enough."

"You know...I believe you."

Renee met Gladys's steady gaze and felt tears well in her eyes but she wasn't willing to trust so simple a declaration. How could Gladys feel anything but disgust for her when she'd clearly been a terrible mother to her three children, abandoning them with a man who was not fit to raise a dog? "Is that so?" she said, unable to keep the mocking tone from her voice. "And why is that? I seem to recall you saying that you didn't think much of me when we first met."

"True enough. But I've seen the heartbreak in your eyes over what your girls have been through and I don't believe you ever meant to hurt them or put them in harm's way. I know Jason didn't start out a good-for-nothing. It was a process of evolution. I blame the drugs."

"Oh..." Renee whispered, cringing that Gladys knew. "How'd you..."

"A person doesn't blow through the kind of money you two were blowing without a little help. He called me a few times looking for money. I turned him down. I knew it wasn't going to help things. I told him to get a job and earn an honest wage. He hung up on me. That was the last time I heard from him until the night he dropped off the girls. I hardly recognized him. He'd always been on the thin side but he looked no more than skin and bones. A ghost in ripped and faded jeans with hollowed out eyes. You don't get like that unless you're doing something terrible to your body." Then Gladys pinned her with a hard look. "The question is...were you doing drugs, too, Renee?"

It was an honest question and Renee tried hard not to bristle but it was difficult to allow another person to poke around in your personal business without getting at least a little defensive. She swallowed hard before answering.

"No. I never did that…but I am…an alcoholic, which is no better…no worse."

"You go to meetings?" Gladys asked.

"Yes. Every Tuesday evening, even when I was on the road. I'd grab a local newspaper, the listings are usually in the community events section. Although, to be honest, I don't attend the Emmett's Mill meetings. I've been going to Coldwater."

"Afraid people are going to judge you." It was a statement, not a question. "Smart. It's hard to make a fresh start with everyone knowing when you've fallen and skinned your knee."

Renee nodded, grateful for the woman's understanding, though why she cared, she hadn't a clue. She suspected it had something to do with her ragged emotional state but it was a relief not to have to be on guard for the moment. "I do want a fresh start," Renee said, unshed tears filling her eyes. "I just don't know how to go about it."

Gladys chuckled and patted her arm. "Well, I believe I can help in that department. But first, we bake. Chloe is getting her chocolate chip cookies today because a promise is a promise. Don't you agree?"

Renee thought of the string of broken promises she'd left behind in a trail of failures throughout her life but in her mind she heard Chloe's terrified shrieks and it gave her strength. She gave a resolute nod. "Yes," she said, making the answer a solemn vow inside her heart. *No more broken promises…*

Later that day, as John was picking up Alexis from school, he was thankful Taylor was released at noon rather than at the same time as Alexis. He needed to have a private talk with Alexis, but he wasn't quite sure

how to broach a certain subject. He ought to just leave
well enough alone and let Renee sort out her own mess
with her daughter but the fact was, he wasn't doing it
for Renee.

Alexis was hurting, even if she didn't want anyone
to know. Clearing his throat, he rested his hand atop the
steering wheel and drove at a slow clip as if he had all
the time in the world when in fact he had more to do at
the ranch than he possibly knew how to accommodate
within a twenty-four-hour period. Mentally assigning
a few extra jobs to the "helpers" as Taylor liked to call
them, he drew a deep breath to begin but Alexis must've
sensed something for she launched enthusiastically into
her day. John wasn't fooled. Alexis was never this chatty.

"And so this girl, I don't really know her name, she
likes this guy, I don't really know his name, either, and
they kept passing notes back and forth all day and it was
so *annoying.* Now that I'm back in school, I can't really
remember why I wanted to return. I mean, all the kids
care about are stupid things like iPods and cell phones
and who has the coolest clothes…it's all so dumb and
juvenile."

"Juvenile?" He couldn't stop the chuckle that followed.
"That's a pretty sophisticated word for a nine-year-old."

She leveled a stern look his way that nearly broke
his heart for its misplaced maturity and said, "Please.
Now *you're* just being dumb. I may be nine but I can't
remember the last time I worried about anything so…"
She searched for the right words and came up frustrated.
Seems as much as she might like it otherwise, her vocab-
ulary was still on the limited side. "Well, I don't know…
stupid."

He sighed. Alexis turned to glower out the window
and watch the scenery pass them by. He was tempted to

just let the silence continue but he knew that wasn't the prudent thing to do, especially when they were dealing with such a sensitive subject. "I need your help, Alexis," he started, risking a quick glance her way to gauge her reaction. He wasn't disappointed, her head tilted subtly indicating she was listening. "I think Chloe and Taylor could benefit from talking to someone—you know, like a counselor who specializes in traumatized children— after everything they've been through. What do you think about that?"

At the mention of her sisters she went into protective mode. It took a long moment before she answered. "I don't know…maybe it might be good. Especially for Chloe," she admitted.

"That's what I was thinking. But you know it might be good for you, too."

She looked at him sharply, her fine-boned features narrowing in suspicion. "Why me? There's nothing wrong with me. I don't need to talk to anyone."

"That's where our opinions differ. You're pretty mad at your mom. I think it might help to talk to someone about it."

She snorted. "How's that supposed to help? Is this her idea? Did she put you up to this?"

He shook his head solemnly. "No. The blame falls squarely on my shoulders."

Alexis turned away, her gaze finding the scenery again. "Well, I don't want to. Taylor and Chloe can go. I don't need it. Just send Renee away and everything will be fine. I can take care of my sisters and you. We don't need her, anyway. I can't believe I actually told her she should marry you." She laughed, but that sound coming out of her small mouth was harsh and unforgiving, and John had his answer even if it wasn't something she was going to agree with. "She should just leave. Everyone would be happier."

"You think so?" he asked, though he knew the opposite to be true simply by the sad quiver in her stiff upper lip. "Well, we'll have to see what happens. In the meantime, I think you ought to consider what I said."

She shot him a dark glare but remained quiet. Something told him her silence wasn't voluntary. He had a feeling if she'd tried to say anything the tremble in her voice would reveal far more than she was comfortable sharing.

He knew that anger, how it mixed with fear and longing to jumble a young mind. As often as he'd gone to bed every night hating his father for leaving like the coward he was, there were times when he was ashamed to admit he would've done anything to be relieved of the burden he carried for his mom and brother. He rubbed his chin absently. He'd been a teenager when their dad flew the coop. It was a lifetime ago but he remembered the anger...the same anger he felt radiating from the little girl across the seat from him. But there was something else he remembered and this part was probably the same thing that was tripping Alexis up, too—as much as he'd hated his father, a part of him had still loved him. Just like Alexis loved her mother. No matter how hard she tried not to.

Renee went very still. "You think my girls need... professional help?" *Badmotherbadmotherbadmother*— the damning words were all she heard in her head no matter how she tried to remain calm and rational. Her shoulders tensed but she tried a disarming smile as she continued to clean the kitchen after that night's dinner. "Well, maybe when we get settled somewhere else I'll look into it," she offered with a shrug. "But for now...I think we all have our hands full with just getting through this weird custody…uh, situation."

"You won't." His knowing comment almost made her drop the bowl in her hand. Carefully placing it on the counter, she turned to face him. His tanned face, creased at the corners of his eyes from too much time spent in the sun, scanned her own and she felt ridiculously exposed. The man saw too much and that was dangerous.

He continued softly, "You're just saying what you think I want to hear."

"So? What difference does it make? My girls are not your concern. I appreciate your suggestion but I don't agree with you. All my girls need is to get out of here and back to a normal life."

He stood abruptly. "A normal life? Is that what they had with you?"

God, no, but she wasn't going to admit to that. It was going to be different this time around. She lifted her chin. "I'm their family. Not you. I decide what they need. And what they need is something less…uncertain."

He expelled a short, annoyed breath. "All you know is uncertainty. If you don't know what it's like to be stable how are you supposed to give it to the girls? What's your plan if you get custody back? What then? Just pack them in the car, close your eyes and let your finger drop on a map?"

"And what if I did?" She shot back, hating that he'd struck a raw, very tender nerve. She didn't know where they would go but at least they'd be together and that's what counted, right? She threw the dish towel to the counter and closed the distance between them. "And what do you mean *if* I get custody back? It's a matter of time before the judge comes to his senses and I get my girls."

"You're not going to drag those girls around while you

try to figure out what to be when you grow up. They have stability here. And you're ignoring a very serious issue because of your own damn insecurities."

She gasped and took a faltering step backward, her eyes stinging as surely as if he'd backhanded her. "How dare—"

With the quick movement of a rattler striking, he jerked her to him, his grasp rough, but his eyes held a tender caress that stopped the breath in her chest. "Woman, stop thinking of only yourself. Those girls need you to be their mama…not their friend or buddy. And they *need* professional help." He held her tightly, his mouth compressed to a hard line but her stomach twisted in confusion when her own lips parted as if in invitation. He pulled away slowly. "They need their mama to do what's right for them. Even if it doesn't feel good and damn near breaks your heart to do it."

The tears that sprang to her eyes a second ago slipped down her cheeks and she swallowed convulsively. "What if the counselor makes them hate me even more? I left them. What kind of mother am I?" Self-loathing curdled in her stomach and her mouth suddenly hungered for the smooth, liquid anesthetic of a shot of Jack Daniel's. For a split second, she could nearly taste it at the back of her throat. Horrified, she sprang from John's arms and immediately put a good distance between them. "I can't."

"Can't what?"

Can't feel anything for you. Can't let anyone else into my girls' heads. Can't forgive myself for leaving them in that situation. Oh, God…can't *deal*…

"Renee?" John's soft voice pierced her heart clean through and she took a step back as he took one forward. "Wait…"

She put her hands up, stopping him with a whisper.

"No." Shaking her head, she backed away. She had to get away from him, from the feeling in her chest, from the ache in her heart. It was too much.

Thirteen

Over the next few days John and Renee kept their distance from one another, both preferring to keep what had happened between them locked in the privacy of their memories. They made polite, stilted conversation for the girls' sake until John felt ready to jump out of his skin.

Sitting across from her at the dinner table, Gladys seated to his left while the girls filled the rest of the empty seats around them, John wondered if this was what hell felt like.

Gladys tucked into her lasagna with gusto, proving that something as small as surgery couldn't put a damper on her appetite, and John pretended not to notice the furtive glances Renee sent his way when she thought he wasn't paying attention. What a right mess he'd made of things, he groused silently, shoveling a large bite into his mouth before he was tempted to let the words percolating in his brain fly. He didn't know much about recovery or the process or even what it entailed aside from avoiding whatever it was that put you in that situation in the first place, but he did know that Renee was acting like a fool about this counselor business. Now was no time to start acting selfish but that's exactly what she was doing.

"John? Did you hear me?" Gladys broke into his turbulent thoughts. She frowned. "You're as friendly as a winter bear right now. What's got you all twisted up tonight?"

He shot an accusatory glare Renee's way but his gaze slid away before Gladys could call him on it. He shook his head and stuffed another bite in his mouth, speaking around the cheese burning his tongue, "Nothing. Just hungry."

Gladys eyed him speculatively but let it go, for Taylor, as usual, filled the silence with her chatter until she'd exhausted all her pent-up news for the day. Chloe giggled as Taylor slumped against her chair with a melodramatic sigh and declared, "Yep. Mrs. H. says learnin' is hard work and it must be true 'cuz I'm ex-haus-ted. May I be excused, Mr. John?" She let loose a yawn and rubbed her bleary eyes. "I think I better hit the haysack."

"It's hit the hay, dumb-dumb," Alexis muttered, earning a frown from Renee that she completely ignored as John nodded. "C'mon, I'll get your bath ready."

Chloe and Taylor slid from their chairs ready to follow their sister when Renee stood and intervened. "I'll get their baths ready, Alexis. You go ahead and finish your homework."

"I'll do it after their baths."

Renee placed her napkin down with a gentle, restrained movement that mirrored the subtle pull of her lips as she tried asserting her authority again. "No. I want to help the girls. Go on. Please don't argue with me."

Alexis looked to John or Gladys for help and when

neither seemed ready to back her up, she lifted her chin and threw a "whatever" over her shoulder before disappearing from the room in an angry huff.

"Preteens," Gladys quipped as if teenage hormones were to blame for Alexis's attitude. She helped herself to another garlic bread as she said cheerfully, "Well, look at the bright side, you only have seven more years before she returns to normal. Not so bad if you ask me. Although I never had kids of my own so who am I to judge?"

Gladys chuckled at her statement and took a big bite.

"Maybe you ought to go easy on the bread and butter, Gladys," John said, more than a little alarmed at the way Gladys was eating without regard to her doctor's orders. "You trying to clog another artery?"

"You hush. I don't tell you how to eat, now do I?"

"I didn't have a triple bypass," he commented wryly, watching as Renee put her plate away and walked from the room with the little girls' hands tucked into her own. She wore a smile but John sensed the pain it was hiding. The situation with Alexis was killing her but she was too damn stubborn to ask for help. Even from a professional.

As soon as Renee was out of earshot Gladys dropped the innocent chatter and pinned John with a look that made him squirm in spite of the fact that he was a grown adult.

"What's going on with you two?"

"Nothing."

"That's a line of bullshit if I ever heard one. I may be old but I'm not blind. There's definitely something going on and I want to know what it is."

He stood and took his and Gladys's plate to the sink even as she protested that she wasn't finished. He arched one brow at her. "I'm not going to watch you put yourself into an early grave with a second helping of lasagna."

"Fine. But you're not going to stop me from having a cookie. Bring me one, if you please."

He sighed and selected the smallest on the plate. Handing it to her, he leaned against the counter. "I think Renee and the girls should see a counselor," he admitted slowly, looking up to catch Gladys's reaction. Hell, maybe Renee was right and he ought to leave well enough alone between them but as Gladys, a woman he trusted above all others, nodded her head in understanding, he felt a weight drop from his shoulders. "What happened to them…it's left its mark. I think it's more than Renee can handle."

"Perhaps."

Wait a minute… "What do you mean *perhaps?* I thought you agreed with me."

"Johnny-boy, you always were a smart one but you have a lot to learn about how a woman thinks, especially a mother."

"What makes you say that?" He tried not to be offended but his ego felt a little tweaked.

Gladys smoothed the crumbs from the surface of the oak table into her palm and rose to deposit them into the trash. "You can't possibly imagine the guilt that woman is feeling about what her girls went through. From the outside looking in it's easy to assume that she's being selfish for not wanting to send her girls to a shrink. But think of things from her side of the door. Would you want someone to know your private hurts and humiliations and be judged for them?"

"It's not about her." He wanted to snap but somehow kept his voice calm. "It's about the girls. They need help."

"I don't disagree with you. But she's not ready to take that step with them and it'll have to be together or they'll just get in each other's way. She needs to believe that she's a good mother before she can let someone else come in and start poking the tender spots. You understand?"

"Sort of," he admitted. "So what should I do? I can't just sit by and watch as Chloe continues to scream at night and Taylor is terrified that her daddy is going to show up and take them away, and Alexis…she's so angry. I don't want her to grow up with that inside her. It can warp your mind."

Gladys's warm gaze told him she understood that he spoke of something he knew well and she loved him for his sacrifice. "I don't want that for her," he finished quietly.

"I know. But you can't make Renee be the person you want her to be unless she's ready to go there herself. Give her time. She's scared and trying desperately to make things right. Just help her get there."

He didn't know how to do something halfway. Either he was in or he was out. And he knew there was no kidding himself that he was starting to think of Renee in more ways than just the mother of Gladys's wards. He was starting to think of the girls as more than just temporary roommates. And a part of him hated it. His life had been turned upside and inside out that rainy night and he didn't know how to make it right again. A sinking feeling in his gut told him that making it right had nothing to do with emptying his house of his guests.

And he was man enough to admit that scared the shit out of him. He was a bachelor for a reason. He was surly, cantankerous, a plain grouch on the best of days. Animals were the only ones who didn't seem to hold any of those traits against him.

Yeah, but let's be honest, when was the last time you felt satisfied with just a one-way conversation held in the barn with a horse's hoof between your palms?

It's been awhile, he admitted to himself and bit back the sigh that wanted to follow. That put him in a bit of a predicament that he didn't know the answer to but he knew it had *Renee* written all over it.

Renee tucked her youngest daughters into bed, trying not to let Alexis's attitude douse the joy that giving the girls their bath had created. Such a simple thing but God, she'd missed it. Singing "Oh, I wish I were a little bar of soap" with the girls as they giggled and splashed, washing their beautiful blond hair and then gently combing out the snarls gave her a peace she hadn't felt in a long time. Except for the fact that Alexis refused to look at her and when she did spear a glance her way, it was black with open resentment. Renee couldn't help but shrink away from that stark emotion, hating the echo of John's words in her memory.

She needs a counselor. So do you.

He was wrong. Her girls didn't need a head doctor. Just time to see that she'd changed. She risked a warm smile Alexis's way and was instantly rebuffed as Alexis turned, giving Renee her back.

"Alexis…" she whispered. "I love you."

In return, Renee received silence. She swallowed and vowed not to give up.

Alexis sat across from the woman at the table and nerves made her tummy ache. The woman was from social services. She smiled a lot and scribbled notes on her little pad but Alexis knew things were not going well. At least not by Alexis's way of thinking. Renee was winning. At this rate, she'd have them packed up and gone within the hour if this kept up and Alexis was not going anywhere with her mother.

"Alexis, how are you enjoying your new school?" she asked.

"I love it," she answered eagerly, putting as much emphasis on the words as possible. Shooting Renee a dark look she added, "It's a better school than any of the schools I've ever been to."

"Oh? Have you been in a lot of schools?" she asked.

Alexis nodded. "Oh, yes. My parents didn't like to stick around one place too long. I guess right about when the bill collectors started calling is when we'd split. Isn't that right, Renee?" She looked innocently at her mother who was gaping at her in shock. Take that and choke on it, she thought smugly.

Renee colored and took a moment to clear her throat before defending herself. "We made a few mistakes here and there but I'm so glad Alexis has finally found a school she enjoys. That's all that matters."

Ms. Thin As A Pencil scribbled something down and Alexis desperately wanted to read what she'd written. Hopefully, it was something along the lines of "Terrible mother. Give permanent custody to John Murphy." But Alexis was pretty sure that wasn't going to happen without a little nudging, which she was plenty happy to provide.

"Do you always call your mother by her name?"

Renee jumped in before Alexis could answer. "Only recently. Things have been a little bumpy between us but we're working on it, aren't we, sweetheart? Before all this happened we were very close, Lexie and I. She was my little helper."

Alexis ignored Renee and gave Ms. Social Services a sad nod. "Well, someone had to pick up the booze bottles in the morning and get the babies breakfast 'cuz she and Daddy sure as heck weren't going to do it. Remember that time you slept all day and Chloe got a really bad diaper rash 'cuz you let her sit in a poopy diaper all day? I would've changed her but we were out of diapers."

Renee paled and her mouth compressed to a fine, tight line, so much so that Alexis wasn't quite sure if she was going to be able to get the words out but she did. Barely.

"Alexis, that's enough. Ms. Nagle doesn't want to hear about things that happened in the past. She wants to hear about how well we're all doing *now*."

"You're right. Things are so much better now that Daddy is gone and you're no longer our mother." She turned to Ms. Nagle who was watching the scene unfold with alarm and pleaded with the woman. "Don't give us back to her. She doesn't want us. She just doesn't want Mr. John to have us because she's jealous that we're finally happy and she's not. I hate her and if you send us back I will run away and no one will never find me! I promise!"

Alexis spun on her heel and ran from the room, her heart slamming against her chest like something out of a cartoon as she burst from the house and headed for the open field behind the house. She ran until her leg muscles burned and her lungs felt ready to cave in. It wasn't until she'd collapsed in a heap on the cold ground that she realized it wasn't the wind stinging her cheeks but her tears. Folding in on herself, she cried until she had nothing left and her heart hurt and her guts felt sick.

She didn't want to leave.

Renee stared at the paperwork that had come in the mail and tried to comprehend what she was reading. She looked up and thrust the paper in John's hands. "Did you have something to do with this?" she demanded, although a part of her knew he didn't but she needed someone to blame. He shook his head and for what it was worth, he seemed apologetic.

"No, I didn't but—"

"But of course you agree because it was your original idea in the first place," she said bitterly. "You win. Court ordered therapy for Alexis and myself to deal with—" she snatched the paper from John's hands "—Alexis's issues with her mother. It is my recommendation that the Dolling children remain in temporary custody of Gladys Stemming until the successful completion of six weeks of therapy. Further evaluation to follow." She slapped the paper against her thigh. "Six weeks!"

"First of all, calm down," John instructed, but Renee wasn't in the mood to listen to anyone, least of all him. "You're making a mountain—"

"Don't say it," Renee warned, her voice ending in an unattractive hiss. "Just don't. This is my life they're playing with. Not yours. No one is suggesting they root around in your head now are they?"

"What are you so afraid of?"

"Afraid?" she scoffed, yet her insides quivered. Everything! *I'm afraid that they'll find that Alexis is right. That I'm a terrible mother who doesn't deserve three beautiful girls.* She sniffed back a sudden wash of tears and swallowed the wail that was building on a wall of hysteria. "I'm not afraid of *anything.*"

"Good. Then you have nothing to lose by complying with the court's recommendation." He crossed his arms over his powerful chest and for a heartbeat Renee wished she could just fold herself into that solid warmth but she was fairly spitting at him in her misplaced anger and she doubted he'd welcome the attempt. Which, she realized, was better for the both of them.

"Glad to see you've come to your senses," he said,

though they both knew he was mocking her because she was being irrational.

"Shut up," she said.

"Grow up."

Renee skewered him with a glower, which he matched. And then they both stalked from the room. In opposite directions.

Fourteen

Renee perched gingerly on the edge of the soft sofa designed to make her feel comfortable and fought the very real urge to bolt. Everything about the room made her uneasy, from the bucolic Thomas Kinkade prints on the neutral, taupe-colored walls to the annoyingly distracting gurgle of the large water fountain in the corner. It was like having Niagara Falls in the corner of the room. Renee had never understood someone's desire to have fountains large enough to—

"You don't want to be here."

Renee cut her a short look. Brilliant observation, Doc. What tipped you off? Renee forced a short smile. "I'm fine. I just didn't realize I should've brought a life vest," she muttered.

The doc gestured toward the fountain. "Does it bother you? I can turn it off. Most of my clients find it soothing."

"It's loud."

The woman chuckled and clicked a remote control sitting on the delicate, antique table beside her. Silence filled the room. "Better?"

Not really. *Better would be listening to Bob Seger on the CD player as I blast out of this place.* Renee shrugged. "Fine. Let's get this party started."

The slender woman sitting across from her in a sumptuous leather chair that probably cost more than Renee's entire wardrobe sighed softly as she shifted position and smiled warmly. "All right then. You're here because the court believes you and your daughter could benefit from having someone to talk to."

Renee bit her tongue to refrain from saying something caustic and instead nodded her head.

"Well, first, I'd like to say I am not your enemy. I'm here to help. Your body language says you're holding in a lot of anger. Let's see if we can't identify the source and help to dispel it so you don't have to drag it around anymore." The brunette doctor gestured, adding with another smile, "So settle in and get comfortable. You're here for an hour. Might as well get the county's money's worth."

Renee sat back but the tension in her shoulders remained. The only kind of sharing she did was at her AA meetings and only because everyone there was going through the same issues. There was no judgment. Here—her gaze raked the professional woman seated across from her, watching from behind delicate yet devastatingly stylish designer rims—the doctor would certainly judge her once she heard the facts. And frankly, Renee wasn't interested in listening to one more know-it-all tell her what a bad person she was. She already knew. "Listen, Dr...." she took a quick look at the nameplate on the desk to the right "...Phillips—"

"Please call me Lauren," she broke in with another

soft, doe-eyed expression that immediately set Renee's teeth on edge for its sweetness. The last thing Renee needed was to feel some kind of false security with this woman.

"Dr. Phillips," Renee repeated with a little frost just to get her point across. "Let's cut the crap. As far as I'm concerned you *are* the enemy. Maybe that's not fair but frankly, I don't care. Because of some dingbat woman who clearly could not tell that my daughter was playing a manipulative little game to get her way, I'm another six weeks away from getting my kids and getting the hell out of this place. And by *place* I mean both your professionally decorated office and this stupid, little town where they make up the rules as they go along, and people pay for legal services with a barter system, and it snows like a mother, and you have to keep a fire going 24-7 if you don't want to wake up with frostbite!"

Dr. Phillips, smile fixed to her lips as if it came with her outfit, scribbled some notes, prompting Renee to ask, "What'd you just write?"

The woman just chuckled and despite the soft nature of the sound, Renee got the distinct impression she'd just screwed herself again. When Dr. Phillips answered with a sigh, "I think we're going to need more than six weeks," Renee let loose with a juicy curse word that she rarely used but damn, it felt good to say it.

"All right then. Let's begin, shall we? Tell me about your childhood…"

Oh, goody. A trip down memory lane. My favorite.

Renee closed her eyes and wished the earth would swallow her whole.

John didn't hide his opinion of the man standing before him, but he did bite back the names he wanted to call him since he knew Taylor was watching the whole scene from the stables.

"You've had her for nigh three weeks. What's the holdup? Aren't you supposed to be the best? That seems plenty time to break one stubborn horse."

John shifted his position just in time to avoid the disgusting splatter from Cutter Buford as he let loose a dirty stream of chewing tobacco juice.

"I told you, that isn't an ordinary horse. She's high-spirited and smarter than you. You knew that when you bought her. I'm making progress but I can't make any promises that she's going to be the horse you want her to be just because you're paying me to gentle her. The fact is, she might always be squirrely." John refrained from adding that Cutter's own mishandling of the horse had created a whole slew of new problems. Because of Cutter, Vixen didn't trust or *like* anyone. He'd only just gotten to the point where she didn't try and stomp him to death when he entered the arena with her.

"Shit," Cutter muttered, kicking at the hard, frozen dirt with the heel of his expensive, shiny boots. John held back a snort. Cutter was the worst kind of owner. Plenty of money to waste but not a lick of sense in his fool head to go with it. Cutter—if that was even his name. Rumor had it his real name was Ralph—was new to the area but was trying to build a reputation as a horseman. He *thought* he knew horses. Sort of like the city boys who came to the country to buy a ranchette and considered themselves cowboys because they owned a spotted cattle dog, a horse and a few head of steer. You can buy a tractor but it don't mean you know how to drive it just because you hold the keys in your hand.

Cutter cleaned the wad from his cheek with the stub of his finger and flicked it to the ground. When he spoke again, there were black flecks stuck in the crevices of his teeth that made John want to puke. "I'll give you two more weeks. Then, I'm taking my horse."

John nodded, but he wanted to stick his foot so far up Cutter's ass he could see the tops of his well-worn boots tickling the man's tonsils, so he didn't trust opening his mouth. Thankfully, Cutter didn't seem to notice or care that John was a man of little words. He was already returning to his monster diesel truck, pausing only a minute to curse at the splash of mud dirtying the shiny chrome on the wheel well. John smirked. That ain't no working truck. Just as Cutter wasn't no horseman.

He felt a small hand curl into his own. He looked down and saw Taylor watching Cutter leave with the same look of contempt on her young face as he felt in his heart and it warmed him to the bone in spite of the cold. "I don't like him," she stated firmly.

"Me neither."

"Why can't we just keep Vixen?"

John glanced down at Taylor and his heart contracted at the simple question. Funny, it's about the same as he was starting to feel about the girls. Why couldn't he just keep them? All of them? A voice whispered, knowing he was thinking about Renee. He was attracted to her, that was for certain. Each night he went to bed with an ache in his groin and his mind full of things that shouldn't be there but the woman was enough to age him prematurely. Stubborn, mean-tempered, beautiful and dangerous. Hell…Vixen and Renee…sounded about the same right about now. And, yeah, he wanted to keep them both.

Too bad neither belonged to him.

Renee returned from her therapy session and from running errands to find the girls and Gladys gone. She wandered the house and still finding no one, she reluctantly sought out John to learn where the girls were. She found him brushing down that monster horse of his, talking low and soft as he did the job.

He was a handsome man, she'd give him that. Usually, cowboy types didn't do much for her, even though John said he wasn't one. To her untrained eye he looked the part, especially when he was handling that horse with such loving care. His hands, large and callused, made slow and easy progress down the horse's flank. She imagined when he put his mind to something he didn't rest until he did it well. Her imagination obligingly provided a scenario of his hands touching her in such a reverent manner and the tension from the day lessened, though she would've thought being in such close proximity would've been less than soothing. But even as she watched him, a part of her began to fill with languid warmth as tendrils of longing curled around her senses and tightened uncomfortably. Of all the men in the world…why him?

He finished and with a final pat on the horse's neck, he exited the roomy stall and startled at seeing her standing in the doorway. "How long you been there?"

"Not long," she lied. "Where is everyone?"

"Gladys took the girls over to her place for a spell after school. Said she needed to make sure her plants weren't all dead. They'll be back before supper."

"Oh. Okay." Alone in the house. Ridiculous temptation started to jabber indecent suggestions in her head that frankly, made her wonder if she were suddenly channeling a nymphomaniac.

"How'd your first therapy session go?" he asked, effectively dousing the fire licking her insides as easily as a bucket of water killed a campfire. Noting her sudden scowl, he chuckled. "That good, huh? Why am I not surprised?"

A grudging smile found its way to her lips in spite of her decision to return to the house and she said, "Her name's Lauren Phillips. Know her?"

"Nope. Contrary to what you may think, I don't know everyone in Emmett's Mill."

"Just the important people. Like the sheriff. And the judge. And nearly everyone else I've come into contact with since landing in this place."

"True enough. So, what did you think of her?"

"I think she's an impeccable dresser with questionable interior design tastes," Renee quipped.

"I mean what did you think of her as a therapist?" John asked with only a hint of exasperation. "Do you think you'll feel comfortable talking with her?"

Renee leveled her gaze at him. "I don't think I'd be comfortable talking with *anyone* about my past. She could be Mother Teresa and I'd still want to run for the hills. Scratch that. I'm already in the hills. Stuck in the hills is more like it, actually," she muttered darkly.

"You don't like it here, do you?"

"What's not to like?" she shot back sarcastically. When he didn't retort, she softened only a little, saying with a shrug, "Well, it's not my first choice. I prefer places with a little less—" small-town prejudice, nosy neighbors "—snow."

"You like to live where it's hot all the time?"

"Remember? I came from Arizona. That should answer your question."

"Originally?" he asked, curiosity lighting his eyes in an inviting manner that she tried to ignore.

"Uh, why do you want to know?"

He shrugged. "No reason."

She supposed there was no harm in sharing that bit of information. "Yeah. Born and raised near Tucson."

"So you do like it hot."

She laughed. "I guess so."

"Well, if you stick around you'll see it can get pretty hot around here, too, come summer. And it's a dry heat, like your Arizona." He winked at her and she startled at the playful gesture. John wasn't the type to wink. But, as her smile grew, she realized she kind of liked the lighter side of John Murphy. Made her wonder just how many facets this man hid behind that tough exterior.

Also made her wonder if she had the guts to find out.

His cell phone rang at his hip and he answered it on the first ring. Listening for a moment, he pulled the phone away from his ear to ask, "You mind if Gladys and the girls go for ice cream?"

Renee shivered. "It's not quite cold enough already for them?" He shrugged as if he didn't know if that was a rhetorical question and she sighed before answering. "I guess that's fine. So much for dinner if they're eating ice cream so late in the day."

John returned to the phone. "That's fine, just be careful out there, once the sun goes down the roads are going to slick up. A storm's coming." A moment later he disconnected and returned the phone to his hip.

Renee's ears pricked up as she glanced fearfully at the sky. "What kind of storm? A big one?"

"Sounds like a pretty good one. But don't worry, they'll be back before it starts."

Renee hated the idea of waiting out another storm all alone in that little cottage while everyone else was warm and snuggled together in the main house. "I wish Gladys would've told me she was in the mood for ice cream. I could've just picked up a quart of something while I was in town," she said, worried about Gladys and the girls on the road when the weather was about to get ugly. "I mean, honestly, for an older woman, she's not very bright. What if she gets into an accident with the girls?"

John chuckled and she jerked around to stare frostily at him. "You find this funny?"

"A little. Everything will be fine. You get yourself worked up about the oddest things."

"Is that so?"

"Yes."

"Well, I'm glad to hear you find me amusing."

The smile left his lips but an intensity returned to his eyes that immediately set her previous fire to smoldering again. She inhaled sharply, mildly alarmed at how quickly he could kindle desire with only a look her way.

"We should get back to the house," she said, licking her lips unintentionally yet her toes curled inside her boots as his gaze tracked the movement of her tongue. Blatant hunger shone in his eyes and caused her lungs to constrict in the most annoyingly female way that was at once delicious and telling. She wanted him, too.

He slowly stalked toward her and she backed away until her backside met the smooth wood of the stable wall and she could go no farther. "Wh-what are you doing?" she asked, trying for calm when in fact she felt ready to jump out of her skin.

John leaned in, one hand bracing himself near her left ear and he shocked her by taking a deep whiff near the soft, exposed skin of her neck. "You smell good," he said softly, his breath tickling her ear. "You know that?"

"Thanks," she whispered, unable to say much more without betraying the tremble in her voice. "You smell like horses," she managed to add, eliciting a low, throaty chuckle on his part. What she didn't say was that she didn't mind.

She risked a smile and looked into his eyes. Such soulful, deep and arresting eyes, she noted as she allowed her gaze to travel the lines of his face. "Why didn't some woman snatch you up a long time ago?" she wondered, realizing a half second too late she'd said it out loud.

"Never found the right one," John answered without hesitation. "I guess you could say I'm particular."

She uttered a short, soft laugh. "Then what are you doing here pressed up against me?"

"The one thing I swore I wouldn't do," he answered with a faint grimace but before she could react he took her mouth with his own, the offended retort dying on her tongue as she was suddenly busy with other things.

John pulled Renee into his arms, his senses alive with the solid feel of her body against his, and gave in to the tremendous wave of pleasure that came from the seductive dance of their tongues twining and retreating. It was a slow and steady assault on his defenses and it was a battle he didn't mind losing in the least. His groin tightened until his jeans bit uncomfortably into his taut skin and he wanted nothing more than to lay Renee down in the hay and warm every inch of that beautiful skin of hers. But even as desire attempted to blot out every useful thought in his head, there was a voice—faint as it were—demanding that he stop. For one, he doubted Renee would much enjoy a quick roll in the barn. She made it abundantly clear she was no country girl. And two, well, this just smacked of a bad idea on multiple levels.

But damn...for something so wrong, it felt pretty right.

Biting back a sigh of frustration, he pulled slowly away. Her lips, swollen and reddened, called to him and he had to catch himself before he leaned in for another taste. "I'm sorry…" he started, but then stopped. "I take that back. I'm not sorry. I've been wanting to do that for a while now and well…you looked so beautiful standing there that I didn't want to hold back. I am sorry if it complicates things more than they already are."

It was a moment before she spoke and the silence had started to make John sweat. Finally, she nodded. "I'm not going to lie. I'm attracted to you in the worst way. I want you so bad my teeth ache. But…what happens afterward? We may be playing house for the moment but eventually I'm leaving and I'm taking my girls with me. And then what? Broken hearts all around? No. It's bad enough that my girls are going to bawl their eyes out when we have to leave. Someone has to stay strong for their sakes."

"You're right," he murmured, regretfully putting more space between them. "It's a good thing one of us is thinking clearly. Because right about now I've got some crazy thoughts running through my head and I can't say they're not motivated by the wrong things."

She blushed a pretty shade of pink and he grinned. "Damn, you're beautiful," he said.

"Stop that," she said, trying to be serious, though her eyes had warmed with a sweet light. "How am I supposed to stay strong when you're handing out compliments like candy? I'm just as vulnerable as the next girl when it comes to sweet-talking men."

"Somehow I doubt that," he said. Moving toward the barn entrance, he jerked his head, saying, "Let's get out of this cold barn before we freeze, and see what we can throw together to eat. If I can't feed one appetite, I can certainly feed the other, right?"

"Lucky for you, Gladys left a potato casserole in the oven. That woman spoils you rotten."

"It's true," John acknowledged with only a hint of cheeky laughter in his voice. "But if Evan were around she'd do the same for him. She's always been our surrogate mom since our own mom died," he said.

"I know. She told me. That woman thinks a lot of you two. You're really lucky."

He grinned again. "I know that, too. Why do you think she pretty much has the run of anything I own? It's because I know I could never repay her for what she's given to Evan and me. You can't put a price on that."

"No. You can't," she agreed softly and the wistful expression on her face made him wonder what her childhood had been like. Something told him it wasn't full of hugs and kisses and cozy Christmas mornings. His mother may not have had much in the way of money, but she always had an abundance of love and when she died, Gladys stepped in without a beat. A long, pregnant silence passed between them until John, not interested in ending the moment in melancholy, reached out and tugged gently on her hand.

"C'mon, I'm starved and it's not getting any warmer in this barn."

She returned his smile and he pretended not to notice the subtle sad pull at the corners of her lips as she allowed her hand to rest in his as they trudged back to the house. He let go first because he sensed it was coming. He tried to push from his head the urge to ask what was behind that enigmatic expression because he knew that was a boundary she hadn't invited him to cross. Hell, she'd pretty much just drawn the line in the sand and it was up to him to respect it. And he did. Fully. Even if knowing that he couldn't touch her in the way he desired was tying him up in knots.

But worse still than the knowledge that he couldn't

bury himself in that soft and yielding body was the fact that no matter what happened between them, Renee couldn't get out of this place fast enough.

And that killed him.

He wanted her to stay. *Damn it*. He wanted her to stay.

Rubbing his chin at the realization, a dry chuckle followed. Well, if that didn't wedge him in a difficult spot he didn't know what did. But something told him he was about to get a helluvan education with Renee around.

Fifteen

Renee stared in dismay at the fat flakes spiraling down from the slate-colored skies to land silently on the ground, and offered a nice, mean curse to Mother Nature for her winter bounty.

No fair, she wanted to grouse. It had snowed last weekend, too. Not a lot and not as much as the weatherman had predicted but it had prevented her from taking the girls on an outing. She'd shelved her plans for the following weekend, yet here she sat, muttering at the sky for ruining her plans—again.

"I hate the country," she said under her breath as she shoved another log inside the woodstove. "When I get out of here, I'm never going to live in another place where there's even a chance of snow. It's cold and you have to stay bundled up all the time and...and..." She searched for another reason to hate winter in the country but she was suddenly distracted by the undeniably sweet sound of her daughters' laughter out in the yard.

Dusting the bits of bark from her palms, she rose and peered out her small window to see Alexis, Taylor and Chloe twirling in the snow to catch flakes on their tiny, outstretched tongues. Chloe, unsteady on her feet, was the first to tumble to the soft snow. Taylor's unabashed joy shone in her young face as she fell backward without fear into a thick snowdrift. But even as her younger daughters made her smile with their giggles, it was Alexis with John that made her breath stop. She and John were building a snowman. It was lumpy and odd-looking but the smile wreathing Alexis's face brought tears to Renee's eyes just for the lost beauty of it. How long had it been since Alexis smiled at her like that? The lump in Renee's throat was answer enough. Her first impulse was to rush out there to be a part of their fun. But the fact that she hadn't been invited stung more than her pride. And so she didn't follow her instinct. Instead, she contented herself with leaning against the window and watching silently.

As she stood there, chuckling softly at their antics as snowman building turned into snowball wars, she realized how much her daughters had missed in their previous life. Jason had never spent so much time with their girls. For that matter, she hadn't, either. Her own mother hadn't been much for setting a motherly example, not that Renee was trying to use that as an excuse but it was true. Had her life with Jason always been an exercise in bad parenting? Every moment of it? She searched her memory, desperately seeking for something that wasn't coated in a haze of alcohol, but came up empty. Her gaze returned to John and a sigh escaped her. She'd give anything to see Alexis turn that beaming smile her way. A tear surprised her as it snaked its way down her cheek. As she wiped it away she knew she'd do anything to deserve her daughter's love.

Pulling away, Renee let the lacy curtain fall from her fingertips, but was surprised by a soft knock at the door.

Opening it, her heart leapt as Taylor stood there.

"What is it, honey?" she asked, afraid to hope.

Taylor pushed her hair from her eyes and said breathlessly, "Grammy Stemmy and us are gonna make snow-cream. You wanna come help us?"

Snow-cream? She didn't have a clue what that entailed but since she was being invited, Renee didn't much care and her smile reflected as much. "Absolutely," Renee answered enthusiastically, wasting little time in grabbing her jacket and following Taylor into the yard where Gladys was instructing the girls in how to collect the snow.

Renee stopped. "You mean, you use the snow? The *actual* snow that's falling out of the sky? Is that safe? I mean, healthy?"

Gladys and John shared a look that plainly said "city girl" and Renee set her jaw in annoyance. "What?"

Once everyone had their large bowls full with fresh powder, they tromped back to the house, the girls' chatter filling the silent, white landscape as surely as it filled Renee's heart and for a small window in time she actually didn't hate snow any longer.

Fire crackling in the fireplace, it was warm where Renee was sitting but she wasn't sure if the heat came from the cozy fire or the hormones percolating her blood.

"Girls asleep?" she asked unnecessarily when John returned from one last tour of the house, knowing that he would've checked on the girls and Gladys along the way. He gave a short nod and then settled on the floor beside her. "Nothing wears them out faster than a day spent outside in this kind of weather," she noted, trying to keep calm and detached even though her heart had started to race.

"You've never had snow-cream before, have you." It was a rhetorical question. Her baffled expression had surely said it all as Gladys had poured an odd assortment of stuff in a giant bowl then whipped it together to create something that—bless her heart—was damn good.

"Not a lot of snow where I come from, remember?" she murmured, glancing at him from beneath her lashes. A small smile followed when he chuckled.

"You don't know what you've been missing," he joked.

"Apparently."

He nudged her gently. "C'mon, admit it. You thought it was pretty good."

"Yeah. It was. Although, I'm still not sure it's healthy to eat what's falling out of the sky."

"It's fine," he assured her and his easy smile was infectious. He lifted a stray strand of hair away from her cheekbone and tucked it behind her ear. The action was enough to steal her breath. For what it was worth, it seemed she wasn't the only one affected. "I'm going to have to kiss you," he said softly.

"Oh?" She tried to seem disinterested but it was a losing battle that she gave up on real quick. Her tongue darted out to lick her lips and she knew it would seem like an invitation. He wouldn't be wrong. He leaned in and sampled her lips, moving slowly and sensuously across the surface of her mouth, tongues touching, exploring and stroking in such a way that Renee lost her ability to recall why she'd put a stop to this type of behavior in the first place. At that particular moment Renee would've pointed a gun at anyone who caused him to stop.

They kissed as if there was no rush. The moment was all about exploration and John used the same single-minded attention he used with his work on her body. His hands searched and roamed every hill and valley until Renee felt as if he'd memorized every inch and it made her feel valued and cherished in a way she'd never imagined possible. She hardly noticed when her clothes fell away, but the moment he peeled his own clothes off, she sucked in a wild breath as her gaze traveled the hard, toned and muscular body of a man accustomed to making a living by the sweat of his brow. His hands were rough and calloused and they excited her in a way she'd never known. Jason's touch had been soft and impatient as he grabbed and pinched for his own pleasure, regardless of what she liked or wanted, but she'd stopped trying to get him to be more considerate long ago. She sucked back a gasp as John kneaded the firm flesh of her breast, teasing the nipple through the fabric of her bra and any residual memory of Jason or any other lover faded from her mind.

They might've remained there if not for an errant sound outside that reminded them they were in danger of being discovered by any one of the houseguests and neither relished the idea of being caught in an indecent position. So with her hand tucked into his, Renee grabbed her clothes and followed John into his bedroom and closed the door softly but firmly behind them.

Moonlight reflecting off the white landscape outside dusted the room with pale light and danced on Renee's naked skin, giving it a luminance that seemed unworldly. John's heart beat an erratic rhythm that labored his breathing as if he'd just spent the afternoon splitting wood with a dull-bladed axe. He'd never seen a woman so beautiful. Her eyes shone with vulnerability mixed with desire and it made his vision swim with the power of it. Bracing himself above her, one heavy thigh trapped between the soft, silken skin of her legs, he leaned down and kissed her deeply, pausing only long enough to make sure she wanted this as much as he did.

"I wouldn't be here if I didn't," she assured him in a husky whisper. "I want this. I want you."

Her words thrilled him unlike any other and he claimed her lips again but he was hungry for the rest of her and his appetite was no longer whetted by just the taste of her lips. Pressing an ardent trail of kisses down the column of her soft neck, her sharp intake of breath encouraged him to go farther, until he reached her full breasts. Lavishing each one in turn with his mouth, he didn't rest until she was twisting and writhing beneath him, clutching at his shoulders and begging him for more.

Sliding down farther and ignoring the near painful ache in his groin as his hard length demanded to know her fully, he took her into his mouth with slow and measured strokes taking quick note of which strokes elicited the best response and as her thighs started to shake with gathering need and she began grabbing the bedsheets in her clenched hands, he brought her home with loving attention.

Renee exploded, gasping as she climaxed harder than she ever thought her body capable. *Heaven help her, the man had talent!* Head lolling to the side, trying to draw breath into her lungs, she barely had time to form a coherent thought before John was drawing her pliant and sated body to his. His tongue swept her mouth, the smell of her own musk igniting the fire once again, kindling the banked desire as if it had not been just satisfied.

His eyes gleamed with a dark and sexy light that told her he was not nearly finished with her and she wasn't wrong.

Flipping her to her stomach, he rained kisses down her back, hitting erogenous spots she hadn't been aware existed, and as he drew her to her knees her arousal hit a plateau that made her wild with need. She'd never been fond of this position, always too conscious of how her behind might look, but at this moment she felt incredibly sexy and wanton and when John seated himself to the hilt the last thing on her mind was if he was thinking she could stand to lose a few pounds.

His strokes took on a tell-tale urgency and his labored breathing gave Renee a dark, powerful thrill knowing that he was nearing his release. That coupled with the hard glide into her body, hitting the deepest most elusive spot inside her, sent her hurtling toward her own release that shocked and delighted her, as she'd never been able to reach the Big O from sex alone. She tensed as he did and they tipped over the edge together, collapsing to the bed, panting with the force of what they'd achieved with near perfect synchronicity.

It was several moments before either spoke but as the sweat dried on their bodies, Renee was relieved to see that a condom wrapper was on the floor. She hadn't realized he'd even put one on but she was ridiculously grateful that at least one of them had been thinking clearly enough to use one.

Renee turned away so that John could discreetly dispose of the used condom but in doing so, the moment seemed to turn awkward. She got up to retrieve her clothing but John's hand gently pulling her back to the bed stopped her.

"I should get back to my...um, house, cottage-thing," she whispered, not quite sure what to call the small guesthouse. "I don't want the girls to see me come out of your room in the morning."

"It's a long ways before morning," he reminded her and her gaze sought the alarm clock beside the bed. It was several hours before dawn. The entire house was still sleeping soundly. Was he interested in Round Two? His lips lifted in a smile but there was nothing suggestive about it. "Stay a bit longer," he said, drawing her into the shelter of his arms without waiting for her response. As John nuzzled her neck she tried not to think how wonderful it felt to be snuggled against him but her body betrayed her.

"I can't stay long," she finally said, settling against him, telling herself it was only for a few more minutes longer. "The girls…"

"I know," he said, the faint hint of resignation in his voice telling her he understood but his arms tightened around her just the same. Her eyelids drooped against her will. It was too comforting, too inviting to remain there in his arms. For something that smacked of a terrible idea, it sure felt good.

Was it the phenomenal sex? she wondered silently. It had to be. Who knew John Murphy was a love guru? She tried to look past what had happened between them because it was too real, too big to acknowledge, but it stared at her with the unwavering gaze of a predator stalking its prey. It was just her style to fall in love with a man whom she had no business fooling around with. It was *so* her style. Self-destructive, stupid and selfish. Yep. That was her style all right. So much for changing patterns.

"Stop."

She startled, all traces of sleep gone from his voice. She turned to face him, his expression, illuminated by the silvery light streaming from the frosted windowpane, was troubled and knowing. It was the knowing part that made her want to run. "Stop what?" she asked.

"Stop thinking whatever's running through your head," he said.

"What makes you think I'm thinking about anything?" she tried bluffing but he saw through her and that made him dangerous.

"You've got that look on your face," he said, smoothing her forehead. "A subtle frown that says you're upset about something."

"What's to be upset about? We're two consenting adults. We didn't do anything wrong. Everyone needs release every now and again." She watched him from beneath her lashes, holding her breath against the reaction she knew her words would cause.

"Release. I see," he said, moving away from her. "That's all it was to you?"

"Wasn't it for you?"

"Yeah. Sure." His answer was flippant but his sharp movements as he jerked his boxers back on told a different story. She winced inwardly because deep down she knew she was hurting him even if he was too prideful to let it show. But, really, who were they kidding? It wasn't as if she was going to move in and be his little country wife and he was going to adopt three kids that weren't even his. In what kind of world does that happen? She lived in the real world even when it sucked.

She made quick work of finding her clothes and putting them back on, all the while avoiding any eye contact with John. She didn't want to see the pain that would be there. Didn't want to acknowledge the odd ache in her own chest that rightly shouldn't be there. Get real, Renee! You don't fall in love with a man after only two months of knowing him. She paused at the door and met his gaze briefly. "Let's keep this between us, okay? I don't want the girls to know," she said, not expecting the cold look he sent her way.

"I've already forgotten about it," he answered and her knees threatened to buckle from the wave of hurt that followed but she'd be damned before she let him see it.

She stiffened. "Great. So have I."

Taking care not to slam the door behind her when in fact she wanted to bring the house down with the force of her pain, she gritted her teeth against the cold and made the short, slippery walk back to her little cottage. Each step affirming her decision that playing house with John Murphy had been the stupidest idea on the planet.

Sixteen

Renee stared morosely at the expensive off-white Berber carpet covering the expanse of her therapist's office and wished she had control over the passage of time. If she did she'd zip past her mandatory meetings with Dr. Perfectly Put-Together and move straight to the part where she received the all clear to get the hell out of this place.

"Tell me what's bothering you today," Dr. Phillips suggested, her unwavering gaze soft and knowing at the same time, and Renee shifted in her chair. "The last few sessions have gone so well, yet today it seems... you've had a setback. What happened?"

I think I fell in love with a man who's totally inappropriate for my life. As usual. Obviously, this therapy stuff wasn't working. She speared the doc with an annoyed glare. "Can't we just skip to the part where you tell social services that everything is fine and I deserve to get my girls back?"

Kids on the Doorstep

Dr. Phillips smiled her answer, which clearly said Renee was asking for the moon, and merely waited for Renee to open up. Surprisingly, and almost against her own will, Renee started talking, or rather, her mouth just started blurting out things that under ordinary circumstances she would never share. Either way, the cat was out of the bag.

"I slept with John Murphy. And it was good. No, it was better than good. It was mind-blowing and frankly, I didn't even believe that sex could reach that kind of level but it did and it's messing with my mind. I mean, *really* messing with my mind because now I've been wanting things that are impossible and ridiculous—"

"Such as?"

Renee scowled at the doctor. "Such as things that are completely out of my reach."

Dr. Phillips smiled again and in Renee's present state of agitation it was like gasoline on a fire. "Please stop smiling at me like that. Like you know something I don't. Don't you understand? I'm bad news. And John doesn't need or want the kind of complications I bring to the table. I'm talking major baggage. The kind you should have to declare before you board the relationship airplane."

"And you think he doesn't realize this?"

"Of course he doesn't," Renee snapped. "If he did he'd run far and fast."

"And he's not."

"No." Was that her voice that sounded just a bit mournful? Renee bit her lip to fight the inexplicable tears that filled her eyes. "No, he's not."

"Maybe he sees something in you that he likes and that makes him willing to shoulder your 'baggage' as you call it."

Renee snorted. "Like what? A recovering alcoholic with a loser ex-husband who could show up at any moment, and three little girls, one of whom can't seem to stand me, and barely tolerates anyone else. Oh, yes. I'm a prime package. Who wouldn't want to take me on?"

"Renee," Dr. Phillips leaned forward. "Anyone can change the course of their life. Just as you did when you chose sobriety. When you chose to find your girls no matter what. When you chose to stick it through even though Alexis is not making it easy. You don't give yourself enough credit. John is an adult. He doesn't need you to protect him from whatever he might choose to take on."

Renee hated the logic of that statement. It stripped away her carefully constructed excuses as if they were made from thin strips of gauze and Renee was left with nothing but the ruin of it in her hands. Silence filled the room.

"It was more than sex," Renee admitted quietly. "I'm pretty sure I fell in love with him." Even before the sex happened. Possibly the moment she realized he'd protect her girls from everyone...including herself.

"You aren't sure?"

Renee twisted the strap on her purse and refused to meet the doctor's gaze. The inquiry in her voice was enough to make her cheeks burn. Of course she knew. It was just so mortifying to admit. Who falls in love within such a short time under these kinds of conditions? It practically screamed *dysfunction* and Renee was doing her best to avoid that kind of—

"Has he fallen in love with you?" The doctor broke into Renee's thoughts.

She swallowed. "I don't know."

"And if he has?"

Her heart stuttered painfully and while the possibility filled her soul with ridiculous misplaced hope that a future with John might be in her grasp, the cold hand of reality slapped her hard and fast and she forced the next words out of her mouth.

"Then he's not as smart as I gave him credit for. There's absolutely no future between John and me. I hate it here and I'm leaving as soon as I get the green light. How's that for the possibility of happily ever after?"

"Renee—"

Tears blinded her and she ran out of the office before Dr. Phillips could call her bluff and see the very thing Renee wanted to hide from everyone—including herself—and that was the fact that she'd fallen hard for the very man that she should've kept her distance from.

Renee wasn't thinking clearly. She drove like a madwoman to the house, one thing on her mind. Get out. Leave. Run.

Bursting into the house, she started calling for the girls, startling Gladys in the process.

"Goodness gracious, what's all the fuss for?" Gladys asked, trailing Renee with a worried frown. "You look like you've seen a ghost or something. Therapy not go well today?"

Renee ignored Gladys's question, intent on finding her girls. She found them in their bedroom with Alexis at the small desk doing homework and Taylor looking at a horse picture book with Chloe.

Wiping at the tears flowing down her cheeks, Renee went to the closet and started pulling clothes from the racks.

Gladys, hands on her hips, exclaimed, "Child, have you done lost your mind? What are you doing?"

"Leaving."

Alexis jumped up from her chair and fairly screeched at the top of her lungs, "No, we're not! And you can't make us! The court says—"

"I'm your mother! And I say we're leaving!"

Gladys paled and disappeared. Renee knew where she was going and panic fueled her thoughts. Kneeling before Alexis, she implored her oldest child. "Please, sweetheart. This isn't the place for us. This isn't real! The longer we stay the harder it will be to leave. Don't you realize that? We don't belong here. It's not our house. Not our family. We're all we have and we have to stick together. Please…please…" Her plea ended in a pained whisper and Chloe began to wail.

"Don't wanna go," she sniffed as Taylor hugged her close with wide, fearful eyes. "Don't wanna g-go."

Renee felt her heart crack as she looked at her children, their frightened faces searing into her brain, just as John skidded around the corner with Gladys on his tail. Brokenhearted and defeated, Renee dropped her face into her hands and started to sob.

The next thing Renee knew, she was in John's arms.

John held Renee as she cried what seemed like an endless stream of tears. When Gladys had come running to him in a panic, he'd simply reacted. But then as Renee had folded in on herself, he couldn't stop himself from going to her.

Leaving Gladys to calm the girls, he took Renee to the bedroom and closed the door for privacy.

After a long while, her sobs turned to watery hiccups and John felt her take a deep, shuddering breath.

"You probably think I'm insane," she said against his chest.

"The thought did occur to me," he said mildly.

"You wouldn't be far off," she said, pulling away and wiping at her face with the flat of her palm. "I feel like I'm being torn in two."

"How so?"

She sighed. "Because."

"Because why?"

She looked him square in the eye. "What's going on between us?"

The tender and protective feelings he'd felt moments earlier faded to wariness. "You said it yourself. Release."

She swallowed. "What if I was wrong?" She whispered the words as if afraid of saying them aloud.

It's the same damn question he'd been asking himself since that night. He'd always considered himself a simple man but since meeting Renee, his life had been turned upside down and everything he'd thought was black and white were really shades of gray. He shared the same insecurities as she did, it's just that he didn't wear his feelings on his sleeve for everyone to see.

"Do you…have feelings for me?" she asked.

The simple answer? Yes. But it wasn't as simple as that and he wasn't fool enough to believe that. Instead of answering, he pointed out, "You hate it here. So what difference does it make if I do have feelings for you? My life is here. I'm not going anywhere."

"I know."

"So…"

She hung her head, the corners of her mouth pulling down. "So, the very thing that I didn't want to happen, has happened and I don't know what to do about it."

John thought about what she was implying but he didn't have the courage to ask her to clarify. Did he want to know? He sensed she was talking about more than the physical act they shared. She wasn't the only one dealing with a barrage of inappropriate feelings. She was the last person he wanted to have feelings for. Renee was like a stick of dynamite, dangerous and ready to explode at any minute. John liked routine whereas Renee seemed to balk at anything smacking of customary. He'd been a bachelor for so long…he just didn't know if he was capable of becoming a husband and a father in one fell swoop, but the thought of watching the girls and Renee walk away and never come back took a chunk out of his heart.

"Wow. This sucks," Renee said wryly, her voice nasal from the crying jag. He chuckled but it sounded as hollow as he felt. She drew a deep breath and apologized for her earlier behavior. "I don't know what came over me. Tough day at therapy I guess."

He nodded but felt it safer to remain silent. There was too much going on in his head to trust what might come out of his mouth. He couldn't help but wonder what chink in Renee's armor had allowed such a breakdown. Something had obviously hit a nerve. A part of him needed to know. The other part shied away from the knowledge. She stood and he didn't try to stop her.

"I'd like to say that I'm never this irrational but the truth of the matter is…I have days where I don't do anything that makes sense. That's what scares me. I'm trying to change that part of myself and you seem to bring out that particular trait in me. I have to steer clear of any self-destructive patterns. Not just for my girls…but for myself. You understand, right?"

He did. Everything she said made perfect sense and he should've just nodded and agreed because essentially they were on the same page, but his heart was singing a different tune and the sound of it was drowning out the melody of reason.

* * *

It'd been several days since The Day Renee Lost Her Mind as Alexis liked to call it, and although Renee wished she wouldn't say that, she had to admire her daughter's wry sense of humor about the whole humiliating episode.

Renee was sitting outside on the porch swing watching John in the arena as he worked with Vixen when Gladys came out to join her with a hot mug of cider.

"He's something else with that horse," Gladys remarked mildly and Renee agreed, somewhat in awe of John in his environment. Something akin to wonder and pride swelled her heart even though she shouldn't indulge in such fanciful emotions. Gladys shook her head. "But then he's always been something of a miracle worker when it comes to animals. When he was a boy he used to give his mama fits for all the critters he'd bring home and stash in his room. Lizards, birds, squirrels…anything that needed his help. It was just his way."

The older woman handed Renee the mug and sat in the old wicker chair and sipped her hot drink in silence. Renee felt terrible for scaring Gladys that day. In the short time she'd gotten to know Gladys, she felt closer to the older woman than she had to her own mother.

"I'm sorry."

"I know you are."

Renee smiled above her mug. "Were you always this wise or did it come with age?"

"I've always been smarter than the average bear," Gladys answered cheekily, eliciting a chuckle from Renee. They settled into a companionable silence until Gladys brought up the one subject Renee wanted to stay away from. "I know you're in love with John." Renee started to protest but Gladys motioned for her to be quiet and listen. "John is a good man. Better than most I'd say. You're never going to find a man as solid and dependable and loving as that man right there. What more are you looking for, child?"

"What makes you think I'm looking at all?"

"It's in your eyes. You yearn for happiness and stability and that's not a bad thing. Why else would you have stayed with that good-for-nothing nephew of mine? You were trying to make a go of it even when you knew it was falling apart at the seams. A woman doesn't do that when she's hoping and wishing to be footloose and fancy-free."

"Gladys, I wish I could say that was the case but it wasn't. I stayed because I was a drunk and a failure. Where else was I supposed to go?"

"Stop that." Gladys's normal tone sharpened with her annoyance. "Everyone makes mistakes. It's how you deal with those mistakes that make up the strength of your backbone. You didn't run away from your girls. You went to get help for yourself first so you could take care of them properly. You couldn't have known that Jason was going to fly the coop or do something to Chloe. If you had, I know you wouldn't have left them behind. Stop beating yourself up, child."

If only it were that simple. "Alexis…she's never going to forgive me."

"She will. But it'll take time. She loves you something fierce. Trust me in this if nothing else."

Tears stung Renee's eyes. "I miss her." *Desperately.* Renee hadn't realized how much she depended on her oldest daughter until she fell into the void left by her absence. It also made her realize that she'd put entirely too much pressure on the child and somewhere along the way Alexis had lost her childhood. How could Renee give it back to her?

"And she misses you. Don't give up. She'll come around when she senses she can trust you. But you know, the problem isn't with Alexis or John."

"Oh?" Renee wiped at her eyes. "What is the problem then?"

Gladys pointed and tapped Renee gently in the chest where her heart beat painfully. "It's here."

"What do you mean?" Renee asked, though to be truthful she was afraid of what Gladys was going to say. Part of her already knew.

"Honey, you're afraid of opening up and letting go of that part of yourself that keeps you believing that you're not worthy of a good life."

"Why wouldn't I want to let go of that?" Renee asked, half joking, despite the look in Gladys's eyes that was anything but full of laughter.

"That's something you have to ask yourself, child. When you find that answer, everything else will fall into place."

Seventeen

John was on a short fuse the day Cutter Buford returned to collect his horse and Cutter's attitude didn't improve matters.

It had taken weeks to get Vixen to the point where she would tolerate John—and no one else—but Cutter wasn't pleased that his expensive horseflesh clearly seemed to hate him. Her nostrils flared and she neighed sharply as she punched the ground with her front hooves.

"What's this shit?" Cutter yelled, jumping away from Vixen and out of the arena as John followed. "I paid you good money to tame this horse! She doesn't look any different than when I brought her to you."

"She doesn't like you," John said, unwilling to sugar-coat anything for this dumb-ass abusive man. "I can't change that. For what it's worth, she doesn't act up around me."

"Well that doesn't do me any good, now does it?" he

sneered, sucking back a wad of spit before letting it fly at John's feet. "I paid you good money and all I get for it is 'she don't like you'? I want my money and my horse back you son of a bitch. Now."

John wasn't impressed or intimidated by Cutter's bluster but he was interested in one thing. "Let me buy her off you," he suggested.

"Excuse me?"

"You said it yourself, she's no good to you if you can't ride her. She's not likely to ever take a shine to you seeing as you abused her." Cutter's face turned florid at the accusation but John wasn't finished. "That's right. Abused. You're out of your mind if you think I can't recognize the signs."

"Watch what you're saying," Cutter warned. "I don't take kindly to being accused of beating my horses."

"And I don't take kindly to someone bringing me a horse they've mistreated and then threatening to put me out of business because I couldn't fix what you broke."

Cutter's jaw clenched and then ordered his horse loaded.

"What are you going to do with her?" John asked.

Cutter threw a dark look his way. "I'd say that's none of your business."

"Perhaps. But let me tell you one more thing. I filed a report with the Sheriff's Department about my suspicions and took pictures of the odd wounds that were on her flank when she arrived. Don't be surprised if you get a call. Who knows, they might find cause to poke around your stables and make sure the rest of your horses aren't suffering from the same type of *treatment*."

John was mildly concerned that Cutter was going to drop dead from a heart attack as the man's face went three different shades of red during the course of their short conversation but the truth was, John knew if he didn't persuade Cutter to cut Vixen loose, Cutter was going to more than likely put a bullet between her eyes. He was a cruel son of a bitch and John had grown fond of the cantankerous horse.

"Sell her to me and we'll conclude our business together," John said, a thread of steel in his tone.

Cutter paused, clearly torn between wanting to storm out of there in a cloud of dust and taking the money for a horse he would never be able to ride. In the end, greed won out and for that John was grateful for the man's baser instincts.

Biting out an exorbitant sum, John countered with a more acceptable one and Cutter, knowing he was still coming out on the plus side, accepted.

Cutter sent one last ugly look at Vixen and said, "You two deserve each other. I hope she breaks your neck."

John laughed at that and flipped Cutter off as he drove away. As Gladys would say, "Good riddance to bad rubbish." And damn if that wasn't the truth.

Out of nowhere, Taylor jumped into his arms like a monkey and rained kisses on his wind-chapped cheeks. "I knew you wouldn't let Vixen go to that bad man! I just knew it!"

His heart warmed at Taylor's unabashed adoration and he hugged her tight. He turned to walk to the house and caught Renee watching him and Taylor with a soft look in her eyes. If Taylor's belief in him warmed him, Renee's look started a fire deep inside. A man could spend a lifetime basking in the heat of that stare, he realized.

Shaken, he offered a lopsided smile as he approached.

"Renee, Mr. John bought Vixen so she never has to leave the ranch." She cocked her head. "Do you think Mr. John could buy us so we could stay, too?"

Renee laughed and the sound was something he
wished he could bottle up and savor. He was losing his
damn mind over a woman, but the funny thing?—he
didn't care as much as he thought he would.

"I'm thinking of inviting my brother and his family
over for dinner. How do you feel about that?" John asked
casually the following evening. Renee looked up from
her crossword with a startled expression.

"Oh, sure. Do you want me and the girls to cut out for
the evening? We could go for pizza or something I guess."

"No." He shook his head. "I'd like you and the girls
to stay."

She looked uncertain and he knew how she felt. He felt
the same but he wanted Evan to meet her. His younger
brother was the only person's opinion he trusted more
than Gladys's, and right now he could use all the help
he could get in sorting out the mess that was going on
in his head.

Renee was a nervous wreck. Why did she agree to
this? She should've flat out refused. She had no business
meeting his family. That just tangled an already confusing situation. But she'd be a liar if she wasn't touched by
his desire to open up to her like that. From what she'd
learned of John he was an intensely private person and
he rarely invited any woman into the inner sanctum of
his life. So what did it mean that he was inviting her and
the girls? Well, it wasn't so much about the girls. She already knew he'd fallen in love with them. Not that that
was hard. Her daughters were pretty awesome but what
did that say about her? Was he falling for her? He'd never
actually said the words to her and she wasn't about to put
money on a feeling or a hunch.

Voices carried from the living room and Renee knew she couldn't hide in the bathroom forever. Smoothing her western-style skirt she'd purchased in town, she gave one final look at her hair in the mirror and noted in despair that it was springing free from the fashion clip she'd tried to use, and with an exasperated sigh she pulled it free. Ruffing her hair for some lift, she just hoped for the best and left the bathroom.

She rounded the corner from the hallway to see a very blond family getting out of their overcoats. Evan and his wife shared nearly the same shade of blond as one another and there were two young boys with only slightly different shades of blond bounding around the room. Taylor was squealing with delight at their antics.

"You must be Renee." The blond woman came toward Renee with a warm, inviting smile that immediately put Renee at ease as she accepted a handshake in welcome. "I'm Natalie. That man over there is my husband, Evan, and those little monsters tearing up the living room are our sons, Colton and Justin. Your girls are beautiful. But it's no wonder, just look at their mother."

Renee blushed but loved the compliment for her daughters' sake. She took pride in her daughters and knew they were all quite pretty. "Thank you. Your sons aren't hard on the eyes, either," Renee said in return.

Natalie smiled and then the boys, who looked roughly two years apart, with the younger looking to be close to the same age as Chloe, took off for the rec room. Moments later the sounds of cue balls smacking into one another were heard followed by laughter.

"Seems they've hit it off," Natalie observed, then gestured toward the kitchen. "Let's go see if Gladys needs any help. Did she ever tell you she's the reason I met Evan in the first place?"

"Um, no, I don't think so." Renee followed, intrigued by this personal history. "But I'd love to hear that story."

"Well, I got duped into going white-water rafting and Gladys was the first person I met on the trip, aside from Evan, who was the river guide. Long story short, we met and now that I look back, I realize it was love at first sight. Oh, and then I got pregnant."

That shocked a laugh out of Renee. "Love at first sight, huh? You sure it wasn't just baby hormones?"

"Oh, I tried to tell myself that at first because I wasn't planning to be a mom or a wife at the time but things happened as they should have and I'm so glad."

They reached the kitchen and after a lot of exclaiming and hugging between the two women, Gladys enlisted the help of both Renee and Natalie to put the finishing touches on dinner.

Renee silently marveled at the easy camaraderie between the two women as well as the obvious love and she couldn't help but compare the relationships she'd had in her life even though it was like comparing apples to oranges. She'd never known female companionship such as this. Not with friends, certainly not with her mother. The closest she'd ever come to something like this was the brief relationship she'd shared with her elderly aunt Katherine. Aunt Kat, as she'd liked to be called. Melancholy followed the precious few memories she had of Aunt Kat, which was why Renee rarely called them up.

Then her thoughts wandered to her girls and what kind of relationships they'd had in their lives. Alexis had been right when she'd said they'd moved around a lot. Sustaining ties wasn't something the Dolling family had excelled at. Jason had a tendency to get itchy like a caged animal if they stayed in one place for too long. Plus, it was true, just about the time Jason was ready to get out of Dodge, was about the same time their luck had run out with local creditors. Renee came out of the morass of her own thoughts when she realized Natalie was asking her a question.

"I'm sorry...what did you say?" Renee asked, embarrassed to be caught in her own head like that. "I didn't catch what you said."

"Oh, it was nothing. Gladys and I got to talking about my sisters and what they've been up to and I asked if you had any sisters or brothers."

"No. Single child. I wish I'd had siblings, though," Renee said, which was true. She'd always hoped for a sibling, if only to take the pressure from herself. Bearing the weight of her parents' hopes and dreams all by herself had been a little daunting. "But it was just me."

"I can vouch for having sisters. I'd be lost without them," Natalie said and Gladys chuckled knowingly. "Oh, don't get me wrong. They drive me crazy but it's nice to always have someone in your corner."

"I bet," Renee murmured, thinking of her daughters and how close they were. She smiled in spite of the lingering pain that ghosted her heart when she thought of her girls and what they'd been through. "I'm glad my girls have each other."

Natalie nodded, then as she brought the salad bowl to the table, her eyes took on an interested sparkle as she asked the one thing Renee didn't know how to answer without ruining the whole evening. "So, I'm a little unclear...how did you and John meet?"

Renee thought hard on how to answer. She didn't want to destroy the nice impression Natalie had of her but then again, she didn't want to lie, either. She glanced at Gladys as if looking for guidance and she received an encouraging smile. Taking a deep breath, Renee said, "I lost custody of my girls, and Gladys and John are taking care of them for me until I can get them back. That's all."

"Oh." Natalie looked nonplussed. "But I thought you and John were...dating."

"No. He's just being a Good Samaritan."

"Well, he's definitely good at that. Hmm, well, it's nice to meet you just the same. I'd hoped for something a little more, to be truthful. From what I know of John, he's never let a stranger move into his space without a good reason and the only reason I could imagine was that he'd finally fallen in love." Natalie huffed a disappointed sigh. "Well, I guess it's true. I'm such a hopeless romantic."

Renee smiled and secretly wished Natalie had been right. She wanted John to want her—not just the girls— in his life. And the knowledge that she still yearned for something so foreign and quite possibly out of reach was disturbing.

John took Evan out to the barn to see his newly acquired horse after sharing the circumstances as to how the mare came into his possession. Then the brothers chitchatted about nothing for a while until John got around to broaching the subject he needed his brother's opinion on.

"She seems like a passionate woman," Evan remarked to John's surprise.

"What makes you say that?"

"I can see it in her eyes. She was holding back at dinner. Am I wrong?"

John thought of Renee throughout dinner and how reserved she seemed and he had to agree. "No. You're right. Something was weighing on her mind tonight. No doubt she was nervous about meeting you and Natalie. She's been judged pretty harshly by people recently. I think maybe she was afraid you guys might judge her, too."

"I hope she knows after tonight that we're not like that," Evan said seriously.

"I think she does."

"Good. I like her," Evan announced.

John looked at his brother. "You do? No reservation? Even after what I told you? With the kids and the ex and all that?"

"People make mistakes. She seems to be a good person. You could do a lot worse."

"What makes you think I'm interested in her in that way?" John bluffed, silently chafing that Evan could read him so easily. He was the older brother, for crying out loud, yet Evan seemed the wiser at the moment. Had to be Natalie's influence, thought John peevishly, but then in all fairness to Evan he had to admit that fatherhood had treated Evan well, rounding out the rough edges until he was a man to be proud of. "She's a handful," John admitted.

"The best ones usually are."

"What if I'm not ready to be a father and a husband?"

Evan chuckled. "Seems to me like you're already playing the part, minus a few details here and there."

"I've been a bachelor for a long time," he reminded Evan. "I might not be able to change to accommodate an instant family."

At that Evan laughed aloud. "Brother, you're kidding yourself. You've already changed. Those girls have you wrapped around their finger. Face it…you're in love."

John grunted. There was no sense in denying it. He did love those girls. But what about Renee? He knew the answer to that, too, but couldn't seem to admit it just yet.

"She's leaving as soon as the court awards custody," he said, his heart contracting at the very thought. "She's pretty vocal about that. Can't stand living in the country.

She's going to go back to where it doesn't snow and it's one hundred degrees in the shade."

"How much more time before the court awards custody?"

John's mouth pulled at the corners. "Not long. Two weeks, I suppose. We have another court hearing coming up."

Evan surprised him with a hearty thump on the back. "Then I suggest if you don't want to lose all of them you better get to work finding a way to make this place somewhere Renee would happily call home."

"And how do you suppose I do that?" John asked dourly. "Offer to paint? New wallpaper?"

Evan laughed. "That would be your problem. I can't do everything for you. Isn't that what you used to tell me when I'd get myself into a scrap? Damn, it feels good to finally be able to say that to you."

He gave John a wide grin and John couldn't help but return it before muttering, "If that's the extent of your wisdom let's get back to the house before we freeze our asses off."

Eighteen

Alexis sat as far away from Renee as she could, on the farthest edge of the sofa, but at least she wasn't glaring at her, thought Renee, trying to cling to any semblance of progress with her daughter.

It was the second integration therapy between her and Alexis and the first one had been a disaster, not that Renee had expected much else. But Renee was willing to do anything to bridge the gap between them, even if that meant more sessions with Dr. Phillips, which frankly set her teeth on edge.

"Alexis…did you bring your letter?" Dr. Phillips inquired gently. Alexis gave a faint nod. Renee nearly let out a whoosh of breath she'd been holding. Dr. Phillips looked to Renee. "Renee…did you bring yours?"

Renee nodded and pulled a folded up piece of paper from her purse.

"Excellent. Now this is how it will work. Last week

I gave you both an assignment. You were to write a letter to the person you are most hurt by and tell them all the things you are sorry for and all the things that you feel the other person should apologize for." She held up a finger to silence Alexis before she could interject something caustic and continued in her soft voice. "This is a safe place. When you are reading your letter there will be no interruptions from the other party. This is about healing and listening."

Renee's palms felt sweaty but she waited for Dr. Phillips.

Alexis shot Renee an uncertain look before turning to Dr. Phillips. "Do I have to go first?" she asked in a small, hard voice.

"Only if you want to."

"I don't."

Dr. Phillips nodded and turned to Renee. "Then Renee shall go first. You don't mind, do you?"

Renee shook her head and lifted her letter so she could read it, although tears were already clogging her throat as she cleared it. She started, only to stop and have to start again before she could get her mouth to cooperate.

"My darling, sweet Alexis. I am deeply sorry that I put you in a position where you had to be the parent because I couldn't be. Your father and I took your childhood away from you with our selfish behavior and I can't change the past but I can give you a better future if you'll let me. I am so sorry for the missed birthday parties, the constant moving around and the burden we placed on you at such a young age. Even though I thought I was doing the right thing, I never should've left you and the babies behind with your father. I should've realized he was unstable. His drug use had gotten out of control but I was panicked. I couldn't stay there a minute longer without doing something crazy and in a moment of pure desperation I put myself before my children. I'll spend the rest of my life regretting that choice. Every night Chloe screams in her sleep it rips my heart out. Every time I see that frightened look in Taylor's eyes I want to cry, but worse…every time I see that cold, hateful expression in your eyes when you look at me, I cringe because I know I deserve it."

Renee paused a minute to gauge Alexis's reaction and was bolstered by the silent yet wide-eyed look as her oldest daughter listened. She continued.

"Alexis…my golden girl. My soldier. Child of my heart. I can never explain the depth of my love for you. It's bottomless. I can only hope that someday when you're holding your own child in your arms you'll understand the depth of what I feel for you. Until then, I just want the privilege of being your mother. If you'll just let me in, I promise I'll never let you down again."

Renee wiped her eyes and slowly folded her letter. Dr. Phillips gestured to Alexis, encouraging her gently. "It's your turn, sweetheart. Say what you need to say to your mom."

Alexis turned her blue eyes to Dr. Phillips as if pleading with her but when the doctor simply offered a smile of encouragement, Alexis pulled a crumpled piece of paper from her pocket and smoothed it out so she could read it. Swallowing hard, she began in a small voice.

"I'm mad at you for running away and not taking us with you and leaving us with Daddy. I'm mad because I tried to be the best daughter but you left anyway. You left us all behind and then you didn't find us in time before Daddy hurt Chloe. I'm mad because I couldn't stop him from putting her outside in the rain. I'm mad because you didn't love us more than you loved your drinks. I'm mad because—"

Alexis stopped long enough to suck back a watery hiccup,

"—you said you'd never leave us and you did. You left us behind. Why?"

That last part came out a pained whisper and Renee felt her heart splinter in a million pieces.

"I do love you," she whispered back. "I do. So much."

Alexis wiped a sleeve across her running nose and her eyes were red-rimmed and glassy. "I don't believe you."

"I know. But I will gladly spend the rest of my life showing you how much I've changed if you'd just let me try."

"What if you leave again?"

"I won't." Renee made that a solemn promise.

"What if you start drinking again?"

Renee took a deep breath. She wouldn't lie to her daughter. "Every day is a struggle not to drink but I am committed to sobriety. I haven't slipped yet and every day that I don't drink is a victory that I celebrate. It's one day at a time, sweetheart. That's the only promise I can make."

"Alexis…do you miss your mom?"

Her small bottom lip quivered, giving away the answer even though Alexis remained silent. Then, Alexis looked to Dr. Phillips and nodded.

"Then tell her."

Alexis slowly met Renee's gaze and time seemed to stop for Renee as her daughter struggled to get out the words that seemed trapped in her small chest. But finally Renee heard the words that she so longed to hear and nearly collapsed from the weight of it.

"I miss you…Mom."

Renee didn't wait and scooped her daughter into her arms, clutching her young body to her own as if it were a lifeline to heaven and her own sobs mingled with Alexis's. She whispered into her hair, inhaling deep the sweet scent of her child as she clung to her, "I will never let you down again. Ever."

And that was a promise she'd never break.

John noticed the difference in Alexis the moment she and Renee returned from their therapy session. There was a tentative peacefulness that hadn't been there previously. A weight fell from his shoulders as he realized they must've turned a corner together. He was glad. It hurt him to see Alexis so twisted up inside over this thing with her mother.

But even as he was happy for Renee, his mind was turning in circles over what was soon to come. Their court date was fast approaching, which meant it was likely the judge was going to rule in Renee's favor. And he should. She was a good mother and she deserved her children back. If only it didn't hurt like hell to think of how empty his house and his life would be with their absence.

He was accustomed to his little shadow out in the

barn as Taylor never missed a morning to get up and help him before she went off to school, no matter how early or cold. She was an endless source of entertainment with her playful antics and unique slant on things. She was more like him than he would've ever deemed possible even though they shared no blood. Alexis was a beauty he knew would need someone to watch out for her when the boys started to realize just how pretty she was. He wanted to be around to make sure that she was treated right by any boy who happened to catch her eye and heaven help any kid who made her cry. And Chloe... a perpetually soft spot was held for that sunny kid. The other day she'd called him Daddy. He'd kept it to himself but it had affected him in a powerful way. He didn't correct her though he knew he should've.

Of course, it all came down to Renee, though. She dominated his thoughts morning and night. His hungry gaze sought her out and feasted whenever he found her. Her fair beauty, wonderful curves and hearty laughter made him grin like a silly boy.

For the first time in his life, he knew what it was like to pine for someone who was out of his reach. Before he realized it, he'd left the arena and had wandered to Renee's cottage. He meant to stop and turn around once he realized where he was headed but his feet weren't listening any more than his heart was and soon he was knocking on her door.

She opened it and offered him an unsure smile. "The girls okay?"

"They're fine. Doing homework and eating cookies. Can I come in for a minute?"

"Sure." She held the door open wider and he moved past her, their bodies touching briefly and electrifying the space between them.

"Things go well at therapy?"

She smiled. "Actually, I can't believe I'm going to say this but yes, it did go well. I think Alexis and I are going to be okay."

"I'm glad."

"Any problems with that Cutter guy since buying Vixen?" she asked.

He shook his head. "He's a puss. Sheriff Casey paid him a visit a few days ago and a little bird told me that he might be leaving town. Just doesn't fit in, I guess."

"It's hard to fit in with a small town," Renee murmured. "Outsiders...they aren't exactly welcomed with open arms around here."

"For people like Cutter Buford, you're right. But if you're talking about yourself, you're wrong. This town would embrace you if you let them."

She looked at him and he read a wealth of insecurity there. Finally, she shook her head sadly. "I'm not small-town girl material. Even if I wish I were."

That last part came out a soft whisper that twisted his heart in wicked knots.

"You could be," he said.

"What would I do here? I can't continue to be your housekeeper. What would happen to me and my girls when you meet someone you want to settle down with? I'm tired of having a throwaway future."

He wanted to tell her that he'd found the person he wanted to settle down with but his damn mouth wouldn't cooperate. She was set on leaving. Who was he to try and convince her otherwise? Seemed an exercise doomed to fail in his book. He gave a curt nod as if he understood and perhaps even agreed when in fact he was just afraid of being rejected. He really didn't have all that much practice with putting his heart on the line. He didn't know what to say or do to make it right for the both of them.

Instead he changed subjects. "Are you nervous about court?" he asked.

She risked a small smile but it looked ragged on the edges as she admitted, "Yes. Very."

"Don't be," he assured her roughly. "You've done all the right things. You deserve to get your girls back."

Her eyes warmed with gratitude and it nearly knocked him over. She grasped his hand tightly. "Thank you. For everything you've done for my girls…and for me. I can never repay you."

He wanted to shuck off her gratitude knowing that he selfishly wanted to do anything to hold on to them, but he merely accepted her thanks with another short nod before grasping the door handle to leave.

"John…"

He turned. "Yeah?"

Her eyes shone with a soft light that he'd happily go blind from and it seemed she yearned for him to say something to fill the space between them, but the odd ache in his chest was making it difficult to think clearly. Crossing to him, she wrapped her arms around him and he automatically reciprocated, sheltering her within his arms as her lips found his in a tender, soul-searing kiss that rocked him to his toes.

He gripped her tightly, afraid to let go, afraid to continue. Slanting his mouth greedily over hers, he was tempted to devour her for the need fueling his blood. He'd never get enough. In a million years he'd never have his fill of this woman. Her body molded to his in perfect symmetry like two pieces of a puzzle locking together and he wondered how he'd ever thought he'd been in love before this moment. He knew this was love because he'd watch her walk away if he knew that would make her happy.

Pulling away slowly, he memorized the features of her face. Then with a final crack of his heart, he made his voice take on a light tone as if what had just happened between them hadn't just laid bare every emotion he was capable of feeling, and he said, "A simple thank you would've been fine."

Her expression dimmed and she looked at him with open hurt for his flippant comment. "Why do you have to do that?"

He sighed and tugged at his baseball cap. "Renee... we always knew this day would come. I've never been one for long goodbyes and obviously I'm no good at this stuff."

"You don't have to make it worse," she said coldly.

"You're right. I'm sorry."

That seemed to mollify her slightly and she nodded. Without much else to say that wouldn't inadvertently make things worse between them, John let himself out.

Tomorrow was her court date and she was all packed and ready to go. She knew there was a slim possibility that the judge might not rule in her favor but she'd been in contact with her social worker and since Alexis's turn-around in therapy, she had reason to hope for a good resolution. By tomorrow, she and her girls could leave this place behind and everything it entailed.

So why did her heart feel like lead in her chest? Sinking her head into her hands as she plopped down on the edge of the bed, she exhaled loudly and wanted to groan.

She just needed space to think. Once she and the girls were settled somewhere else without John around to cloud their judgment things would clear up. She avoided thinking about how upset the girls would be when she told them they were leaving. Alexis knew the court date was coming yet she had remained silent, knowing as well that the little girls wouldn't understand why they couldn't stay. Renee wasn't sure if Alexis understood, either, but she was placing her trust in Renee to do what was right for them.

That was it, though. Right now, Renee didn't know what was right. If she listened to her traitorous heart the right thing was to stay here with John and build a life in the sticks even though that went against everything she thought she wanted. If she listened to her head and consequently her pride, the right thing was to get in the car and drive far, far away and try to blot out the memory of ever being here. The girls would adapt and everything would be fine.

Easier said than done. Her heart already wailed at the thought of walking out that door and never coming back. She'd miss John in a way that was palpable. How'd that happen? Sneaky man with his handsome face and rough disposition, she groused. Slapping the bedspread and causing dust motes to float lazily into the stream of sunlight coming through the window, she was nowhere closer to finding the truth of her feelings than she was when she started asking questions.

Here's what it came down to: Did she love John Murphy? The kind of love that was gritty and messy and strong and wonderful? Or was this a fleeting infatuation that would eventually weaken under the strain of everyday living?

She thought of John with her girls and her heart filled with love for his willing sacrifice. She thought of John with Gladys and his deep feelings for an older woman who wasn't his blood and respect blossomed. And lastly, she thought of John the night they made love and she had her answer.

So why did that make her want to cry?

Nineteen

The day of court broke with bright rays of yellow sunshine and birds chirping as if it weren't the worst day of John's life.

Showering quickly, he told himself it was better to get this over with than drag it out. He knew Renee hadn't told the girls that today was the day they might leave and he knew why she was reluctant. The news wasn't likely to go over very well. He didn't begrudge her wanting to put off that moment for as long as she could. Besides, there was always a slim chance the judge might want a little more time to decide. The flicker of hope he felt at that possibility filled him with guilt. It was plain selfish to think that way and he was instantly ashamed for even considering it. Renee deserved her children and he wouldn't say or do a thing to keep them from her.

She'd come a long way from the woman he'd first seen that cold winter day. He didn't even recognize her

as the same person. There was no way he could've seen
the true woman hiding behind that angry facade that
first day. He wondered how things might've been different if he had…shaking off the useless direction of his
thoughts he trained his focus on his breakfast, not trust-
ing his own mouth to remain buttoned without something to keep it busy.

In spite of the sunny day the morning was promis-
ing to turn into, the house had a pall over it that only the
adults seemed to notice. The girls got ready for school
just as they always did. Chloe sat at the breakfast table
eating her cereal while Gladys and Renee made lunches
for the two older girls.

"Bye, Mom!" Alexis and Taylor said in unison as they
grabbed their lunch sacks and ran for the door as the
sound of the school bus rumbled down the road. It was
all so damn normal and appealing that John had to blink
back an odd moisture in his eyes.

"What time is court?" Gladys asked once the older
girls were gone and Chloe had scampered off to watch
her favorite early morning cartoons.

"Eight-thirty," Renee answered, shooting a vulnerable look John's way.

"Then you'd better get going, I suppose," Gladys said,
her voice tinged with sadness. She hugged Renee tightly
and offered good luck. To John she said, "You driving?"

He looked at Renee and she shrugged. "Sure," he answered, though his chest felt tight.

They drove in silence until John couldn't take it any
longer. Desperation had started to set in and all he could
think of was that he was about to lose the people in his
life that had come to mean the most.

"Renee—"

Suddenly Renee twisted to stare out the window to

the vehicle that had just barreled past them and she cut
him off with a shriek. "Oh my God! That was Jason!"

Everything else forgotten, he looked at Renee sharply.
"Are you sure?"

"I'm positive. He's headed for Gladys's house and
Gladys mentioned that she and Chloe were going to go
and water her plants this morning. Turn around, turn
around!"

Wrenching the wheel, John chewed up the gravel on
the shoulder and punched the gas to head back where
they'd come from.

"Why is he coming back? What does he want?" she
asked, clearly talking to herself. The panic in her voice
mirroring the growing rage that was building inside him
if that man so much as touched a hair on Chloe's head.
"Thank God the older girls are at school," she said to
John and he agreed. The less they witnessed the better
off they'd be. John had a feeling things were about to get
ugly. She turned to him, clutching at his shirtsleeve with
wide, frightened eyes. "What if he tries to take Chloe to
get back at me or he forces Gladys to tell him where his
girls go to school? Oh, God…why is he doing this? Why
couldn't he just stay gone!"

"There's a restraining order filed against him, bar-
ring him from contact with the girls or coming onto the
ranch and there's a warrant out for his arrest. He's not
going anywhere."

"Pieces of paper aren't going to stop Jason if he wants
to take them," Renee said. "He's never had any respect
for the law, he's not about to start now."

"We'll see about that." Flipping open his cell phone,
he dialed Sheriff Casey's cell phone. "John here. That
SOB is back and he's headed for Gladys's place. Send a
deputy if you want things handled your way. We were on

our way to court when we passed him on the highway. He's driving a beat-up silver Nissan with Arizona plates."

"Jason is unstable," Renee told John in a thready voice tinged with true fear. "He was always a bit of a wild card…it's part of what attracted me the most," she added in a shameful whisper. He couldn't help but wonder if that sort of thing was still what turned her clock but his question must've planted itself in his expression because she shook her head decisively. "Not now. Back when I was a stupid, rebellious kid. I've had enough of that kind of excitement. But right now…I want to plant my fist in Jason's face."

"You and me both," John muttered darkly. God help the man if they got there before the deputies. The way John figured it, he and good ol' Jason had a few things to settle.

"He might take Chloe for leverage," Renee said suddenly, the furrow in her brow deepening with pain. "He's used the kids against me before. He'd do it again. Oh, God, John, please don't let him hurt my baby again."

"He won't touch her." That was a promise.

Gladys was in the process of watering her spider plant and singing "You Are My Sunshine" with Chloe when Jason walked into the kitchen.

Chloe saw Jason first. Gladys didn't realize someone was in the house with them until Chloe started crying.

"What's wrong, sugar?" she asked, nearly dropping the watering can in her hand when she saw Jason standing there looking like a man on death row. "Jason? What are you doing here?"

Gladys kept Chloe behind her and glared at Jason, though in truth the look in his eyes made her knees quake. He looked like death warmed over in his filthy clothes and oily hair, but it was the emptiness of his eyes that made Gladys want to take the baby and run in the opposite direction.

"No hello? Nice to see you? How've you been? Well, thanks for asking. Things have been a little rough to tell the truth." His voice cracked as if he'd been shouting at the top of his lungs at a rock concert before he arrived. He came toward her and she took a few steps back, weighing her exit strategy. Jason shook his head at her as if disappointed. "Aunt Gladys, you're hurting my feelings. That's plenty far." His voice hardened. "If you know what's good for you you'll stop."

Jason pulled a gun from the back of his grimy jeans' waistband and Gladys couldn't help the gasp that followed.

"Have you lost your mind, boy? You can't come in here and start waving a gun. You're frightening Chloe."

"Poor Chloe," he crooned and the sound sent a chill down Gladys's back. "Poor little daddy-less Chloe. The baby no one wants."

"Shut your mouth," Gladys said, anger vibrating through her stout body in spite of the danger that radiated from Jason's wasted body. "You hear me? Shut your filthy mouth before I slap you into next week. You've got no call to come in here and be nasty to this little girl."

"All right, all right," Jason snapped, waving Gladys down as if the sound of her voice grated on his strung-out nerves. "God, can't you take a joke? I was just kidding around."

"What do you want? Money? Fine. I'll get my purse, write you a check and you can get the hell out of my sight and never come back."

He shook his head and wiped at the thin rivulet of snot that trickled from his reddened nose and sucked back the rest. "Now you're really hurting my feelings, Auntie. I want my girls," he said. "Don't they miss me? Where are they?"

"Not here."

"Then where?"

Gladys switched tactics, delaying for time, although she didn't know how she was going to get to the phone without him noticing. Somehow she didn't think he'd let her just walk to the phone and ring the sheriff.

"You look like hell. Let me guess, drugs?"

Jason scowled. "Shut up. Where's your purse?"

Petty little thief, she wanted to mutter but instead moved past him to grab her purse on the table. Chloe's cries had turned to soft whimpers that pulled at Gladys's heart. She narrowed her gaze at Jason. "How much is it going to take to get you out of my life?"

His gaze turned shrewd. "How much you got?"

Gladys thought of her nest egg and narrowed her stare. "Enough. What's it going to take, Jason?"

"My girls…are they doing okay?" he asked. A disconsolate expression pulled his mouth into a grim line and he rubbed at his red-rimmed eyes with the flat of his palm while still gripping the gun. "I mean…do they ask about me?"

"No, they don't." Gladys stared at him coldly. "In fact, they're fine. Better since they've seen the last of you."

He looked at her. "What the hell are you talking about, old woman?"

"You've lost custody. There are consequences for neglect and abuse, Jason."

His stare hardened. "You old bitch."

"Foul-mouthed hooligan." She lifted her chin.

Jason lunged at Gladys but spooked Chloe instead and the toddler tried to bolt, attracting his attention. Gladys couldn't catch her fast enough but Jason could, the rage in his eyes scaring the life out of Gladys for Chloe's safety, not her own. "Chloe, no!" she screamed but Jason already had the baby in his grip.

Grabbing the toddler, he hoisted her in the air, the gun still in one hand, tipping her upside down until she screamed and Gladys squeezed tears from her eyes. "Put her down," she ordered, trying for some semblance of authority but Jason merely laughed.

"Shut up, you old bag, and start writing that check. Besides—" he gave Chloe a shake "—I'm just playing. We used to do this all the time, didn't we, Chloe-baby? She loves it."

Gladys felt on the verge of begging, terrified for Chloe and of what Jason was capable of doing in his current mental state.

"I'm going to give you two seconds to put down that baby before I tear your head off."

The air rushed out of Gladys's lungs in undisguised relief as John and Renee came around the corner. There was murder in John's eyes and Gladys didn't feel sorry for Jason one bit for the beat-down that was coming his way.

Renee wanted to rush Jason and rip Chloe out of his grasp but she was afraid he might drop the baby straight on her head out of spite. Fear kept her rooted but hatred flowed through her veins, thick and hot.

"Hey Rae…long time no see. Who's he?"

"Put. The. Baby. Down."

Jason slowly lowered Chloe but then dropped her the remaining distance and she fell. Gladys, closest to her, pulled the crying baby to her and put distance between them.

John stalked toward Jason until he raised the gun. "Ah,

ah, ah. Remember who's holding the gun. That would be me, jackass, so before you go all John McClane on me just remember I could shoot your nuts off."

"Jason, what's gotten into you?" Renee gasped. "Look at what you're doing. Why would you be so cruel? You didn't used to be like this."

Jason looked bleak. "Things change. Wives leave. Life sucks. Whatever, right?"

"You need help. How many nights have you been up?"

"Drug addict," John sneered under his breath and Renee swallowed hard, knowing that at this point Jason was capable of anything. This was not the man she'd known.

"You need help," Renee tried appealing to Jason's long-buried sense of self, hoping to touch that part she'd fallen in love with so long ago but the bile in her throat kept choking her. "Jason, you're in no shape to be around the girls…you have to know that. Do you want them to remember you like this?"

"My girls are gone. You've poisoned them against me," he said. A shadow passed over Jason's eyes and he wavered on his feet but the gun never changed position.

Renee shook her head. "You did that all on your own, Jason. I left the girls in your care and you neglected and abused them. And what you did to Chloe…"

"You're the one who left," Jason raged, spittle flying from his mouth. "Don't you dare go all righteous on me. You're no better, you lying drunk whore!"

Renee felt John tense beside her and she knew time was running out for any kind of peaceful resolution. A part of her didn't care. She hungered for violence for what he'd done to her girls but she was trying to find an ounce of mercy in her heart for the pathetic excuse of a man standing in front of her. Renee tried not to grit her teeth and dialed back the growl in her throat, knowing she needed to keep him talking somehow. "Why, Jason? Why would you try to hurt a baby?"

For a second Renee didn't think he'd answer. Finally, he rubbed at his eye and Renee almost thought she saw moisture but she couldn't be sure, as strung out as he was. "I stopped, okay? I felt like shit but you left me stuck with the kids and one of them wasn't even mine. I lost it. But she's fine, see? No harm no foul." At that, he chuckled as if he'd actually said something worth laughing about. It took great strength of will to keep her hands loose and not clenched in tight fists but she managed it until Chloe, reacting to the tension in the room, let loose with a high-pitched wail.

The ear-splitting decibel distracted Jason long enough for John, who was just waiting for the right moment, to make his move.

"Shut up!" Jason roared but as he turned back around he was met with five knuckles smashing into his nose. Blood splattered everywhere and Jason stumbled back screaming in pain. He tripped on his own feet and went down. John reared back and sent his booted foot right into his ribs. As Jason writhed in pain, Renee tried to drum up some sympathy for the man who was probably suffering from a broken nose and several cracked ribs, but she felt nothing.

Her gaze traveled to John, breathing hard, big fists still clenched, and smiled. Holy hell. Suddenly amidst the bloody mayhem and the overall horrific nature of the last couple minutes…everything became blindingly clear. And for that she had Jason to thank. She let out a shaky breath as the adrenaline left her body in a rush and was replaced with something far more comforting.

Renee opened her mouth and…laughed.

* * *

"In light of the extenuating circumstances and the fact that your ex is in custody, I will forgive your missed court appearance."

Renee smiled. "Thank you, Your Honor."

Judge Lawrence Prescott II drew his paperwork together and then set it back down again, steepling his fingers in front of him. "From what I've read you've come a long way from the first day you stood before me. The children seem well-adjusted and ready to resume a relationship with you and you aren't carrying a chip on your shoulder any longer. I'm curious…what changed?"

Renee thought long and hard about that question. She let her gaze drift to John and his steady stare filled her with peace and happiness. Somehow she'd found a man who could love and protect three children who weren't his by blood, with everything in his power. She found a man who saw past her flaws and her issues and stood by her without enabling her to cling to bad patterns. What changed? For the first time in her life she fell in love with an honest-to-God good man. And you know what? She was going to marry that man. Not today. Maybe not even tomorrow. But someday. And she was going to learn to love the country.

And snow.

Epilogue

Renee looked stunning. John licked suddenly dry lips but couldn't pull his gaze from the vision standing before him. She was in a white halter dress that showed off creamy shoulders he longed to kiss and a nipped waist his hands itched to span.

His collar squeezed his neck but he didn't dare try to adjust it for he knew Evan would tease him mercilessly at the reception, or worse, knowing Evan, during the toast.

All three girls, miniature versions of their mother, stood to Renee's right while Evan's boys stood beside Evan to his left. Hot damn. John Murphy was finally getting married.

How'd he get so lucky? For as long as he lived, he'd remember the moment Renee walked up to him and said, "I'm in love with you, John Murphy, and if you have a problem with that you're just going to have to deal with it because I know you're in love with me, too." That was the best day of his life.

Then she'd grabbed him and laid a lip-lock on him that made bells go off in his head and his pants a bit tighter.

And that's what he loved about her. Well, one of the many things.

"Do you take this woman to be your lawfully wedded wife? To have and to hold till death do you part?" the minister asked, a smile wreathing his face as he regarded them kindly.

Renee gazed at him, her blue eyes shining like the ocean on a clear summer day, with a tremulous smile playing on her lips, and John knew there was nothing more he wanted in this life.

"I do," he answered solemnly.

Two words had never sounded so sweet.

* * * * *

"We'll have to kiss," she heard Luc say, and it took her brain a second to catch up with her ears.

"Kiss?"

"During the wedding ceremony," he said.

"Oh, right." Julie hadn't considered that. She thought about kissing Luc, and a peculiar little shiver cascaded down the length of her spine. Back when she'd first met him, she used to think about the two of them doing a lot more than just kissing, but he had been too hung up on Amelia and their recently broken engagement to even think about another woman. So hung up that he'd left his life in Royal behind and traveled halfway around the world with Doctors Without Borders.

A recent dumpee herself, Julie had been just as confused and vulnerable at the time, and she'd known there would be nothing worse for her ego than a rebound relationship. She and Luc were, and always would be, better off as friends.

"Is that a problem?" Luc asked.

She blinked. "Problem?"

"Us kissing. You got an odd look on your face."

Had she? "It's no problem at all," she assured him.

"We'll have to start acting like a married couple," he said. "You'll have to move in with me. But nothing in our relationship will change. We only have to make it look as if it has."

But by pretending, by making it look real to everyone else, wasn't that in itself a change to their relationship?

Ugh. She'd never realized how complicated this would be.

"Look," he said, frowning. "I want you to stay in the US, but if it's going to cause a rift in our friendship... Do you think it's worth it?"

"It is worth it. And I don't want you to think that I'm not grateful. I am."

"I know you are." He smiled and laid a hand on her forearm, and the feel of his skin against hers gave her that little shiver again.

What the heck was going on between them?

Don't miss
MORE THAN A CONVENIENT BRIDE
by Michelle Celmer, available March 2015 wherever
Harlequin® Desire books and ebooks are sold.

www.Harlequin.com

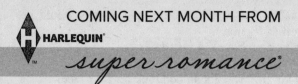
#1976 THE COMEBACK OF ROY WALKER
The Bakers of Baseball
by Stephanie Doyle
When Roy Walker left his professional pitching career, he was on top...and had the ego to prove it. Now, with a much smaller ego, he needs to make a comeback—something he can't do without the help of physiotherapist Lane Baker. But first, he must make amends for their past!

#1977 FALLING FOR THE NEW GUY
by Nicole Helm
Strong and silent Marc Santino is new to the Bluff City Police Department. His field training officer, Tess Camden, is much too chatty—and sexy—for comfort. When they give in to the building attraction, the arrangement is just what they need. But, for the sake of their careers, can they let it turn into something more?

#1978 A RECIPE FOR REUNION
by Vicki Essex
Stephanie Stephens is tired of people not believing in her. So when Aaron Caruthers comes back to town telling her how to run his grandmother's bakery, she's determined to prove herself. Unfortunately, he's a lot cuter than she remembers him being...and she definitely doesn't need her heart distracting her now!

#1979 MOTHER BY FATE
Where Secrets are Safe
by Tara Taylor Quinn
When a client disappears from her shelter, Sara Havens teams up with Michael Eddison to find the missing woman. The strong attraction between them complicates things. Michael's strength is appealing, but his young daughter makes Sara vulnerable in a way she swore she'd never be again.

HSRLPCNM0215

HARLEQUIN®

A *Romance* FOR EVERY MOOD™

Love the Harlequin book
you just read?

Your opinion matters.

Review this book on your favorite
book site, review site, blog or your own
social media properties and share
your opinion with other readers!

Be sure to connect with us at:
Harlequin.com/Newsletters
Facebook.com/HarlequinBooks
Twitter.com/HarlequinBooks

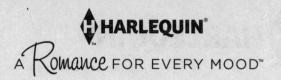

JUST CAN'T GET ENOUGH?

Join our social communities
and talk to us online.

You will have access to the latest
news on upcoming titles and special
promotions, but most importantly,
you can talk to other fans about your
favorite Harlequin reads.

Harlequin.com/Community

Facebook.com/HarlequinBooks

Twitter.com/HarlequinBooks

Pinterest.com/HarlequinBooks